Judgment

Also by Joseph Finder

FICTION

The Moscow Club

Extraordinary Powers

The Zero Hour

High Crimes

Paranoia

Company Man

Killer Instinct

Power Play

Suspicion

The Fixer

The Switch

NICK HELLER SERIES

Vanished

Buried Secrets

Guilty Minds

NONFICTION

Red Carpet: The Connection Between the Kremlin and America's Most Powerful Businessmen

Judgment

A NOVEL

JOSEPH FINDER

DUTTON
An imprint of Penguin Random House LLC
penguinrandomhouse.com

LIBRARY OF CONGRESS CATALOGING-IN-PUBLICATION DATA
Names: Finder, Joseph, author.
Title: Judgment : a novel / Joseph Finder.
Description: New York : Dutton, 2019.
Identifiers: LCCN 2018026165 | ISBN 9781101985816 (hardback) |
ISBN 9781101985823 (ebook)
Subjects: | BISAC: FICTION / Suspense. | FICTION / Thrillers. |
GSAFD: Suspense fiction.
Classification: LCC PS3556.I458 J83 2019 | DDC 813/.54—dc23
LC record available at https://lccn.loc.gov/2018026165

Printed in the United States of America
1 3 5 7 9 10 8 6 4 2

BOOK DESIGN BY GEORGE TOWNE

Judgment

You cannot judge a criminal
until you have come to recognize
that you are just as much a criminal
as the one standing before you.

—Fyodor Dostoyevsky, *The Brothers Karamazov*

1

A perfect May night in Chicago, warm but not quite balmy. A soft breeze coming in off the lake, carrying with it the faint murmurings of traffic from Michigan Avenue twenty floors below. Juliana was sitting alone on one end of a couch on the Peninsula's rooftop terrace, still wearing her conference lanyard, still wired from the speech she had given two hours earlier. She'd delivered a talk on the rules of evidence in front of five hundred people, and it had gone really well. She tended to be self-critical, but she also knew when she'd hit a home run. "Rules of evidence" wasn't exactly a sexy topic, but she had her own take on it, and people seemed to respond.

She'd just had a drink with six fellow attendees, all judges from Indiana, and she was talked out. Mostly she'd been the center of attention, which was flattering for a while, and then exhausting. For now, she wanted to sit by herself—not in her room, with CNN keeping her company, but out here on the terrace in the refreshing breeze off Lake Michigan. Be in her own head. She dropped her lanyard on the glass-topped coffee table and scanned an array of magazines fanned out in front of her. One caught her eye—a travel magazine with a cover story about Spain—and she started leafing through it, keeping one eye out for a server.

But she was still wired. Another drink? She almost never did that. One drink, that was her limit.

Her mother, Rosalind, had been a drinker. Rosalind never drank at work, but at night and particularly on the weekends she drank too much. When Juliana was twelve, Rosalind had taught her how to make a "pitcher of martinis," she called it, as if martinis were discrete entities with a shape and form, like eggs, and you could count how many were in the pitcher if you looked really hard.

So Juliana generally did what her mother couldn't: stopped at just one drink. But tonight she was keyed up and thought: *What the hell.* She waved over a server and was about to order another Sancerre when she changed her mind once again and ordered a Pellegrino and lime. She went back to her magazine—"The Unknown Mallorca," the piece promised. She felt someone's eyes on her, and she glanced up; when she saw nobody looking her way, she felt a little silly. *Too much time in the spotlight,* she told herself with a laugh. *Having delusions of grandeur. Black Robe disease.*

Juliana Brody was in her early forties, but as her mother liked to say immodestly, she had good genes. She looked younger. Rosalind had been beautiful. Juliana had long ago accepted the fact that she hadn't inherited her mother's looks, but she had her cheekbones and jawline, and the gray-blue eyes. And the russet hair—actually, L'Oréal called it "red brown." And then there was all the time Rosalind used to spend tending to her appearance, while Juliana couldn't be bothered.

Again she felt that strange sensation of being watched. She noticed a man in a charcoal suit making his way in her direction. He was tall, early thirties, with an olive complexion and wavy dark-blond hair that fell below his collar. She didn't recognize him. Maybe he was attending the legal conference too.

"Is this seat taken?" he asked. "Or am I interrupting?"

She gestured noncommittally to the chair by the couch. Her gaze could sometimes be stern and intimidating. "I'm not here for much longer, but help yourself."

Something about him gave off a slightly melancholy air, but he was a good-looking guy.

"Long day?" he asked.

She nodded. "And for you? Are you here with the law conference?"

"Venture capital. I think there are three conferences going on here this weekend." He paused, took in the magazine. "Planning a visit to Spain?"

"Looking at rentals in Costa Brava. In my dreams, mostly." She drained the last few drops of her seltzer.

"You should go for real."

"Oh, Spain is my favorite place on earth."

"I just got back from Mallorca a couple days ago."

She tipped her head. "Nice vacation."

"On business, but still nice."

She put down the magazine. "Never been to Mallorca. I hear it's beautiful but overrun by tourists like me."

"Not if you know where to go."

She put out her hand. "Juliana Brody."

He shook it firmly. His hand was dry and smooth, his nails neatly trimmed. "Matías Sanchez." Just the faintest accent.

"You're Spanish?"

"Argentine. Spanish and Argentinians, we're like cousins." He shrugged.

"But you know Mallorca."

"Quite well. I travel a lot."

"So where do I have to go in Mallorca to escape the crowds?"

He paused briefly. "The most spectacular sunset you'll ever see happens at Cap de Formentor. You've got to drive up a terrifying little winding road, but by the time you get there it's worth it."

"Yeah?"

"Oh, and there's this great little restaurant in the old town called La Bóveda, nothing fancy, but their tapas are to die for. And you can have a drink nearby at Abaco, this fourteenth-century house filled with flowers and baskets of fruit. You tell them Matías Sanchez sent you, they'll take care of you right."

"Okay, I'm sold." She laughed lightly. "When it comes to Spain." She flushed. Then, to cover her embarrassment, she gestured for the server again, who'd miraculously appeared. She held up her glass of ice and mineral water. "Another one of these?"

He ordered an Ardbeg, ten years old, on the rocks.

"You know what?" she said. "I think I'd like another Sancerre after all."

The waitress gave a quick double head nod, like a shore bird swallowing a bread crust, and strode off.

"I'm afraid I was staring at you before," Matías said. "It's just that you remind me of someone I used to know." He smiled again, a nice, frank smile. He had a sexy gap between his front teeth.

"It happens with me a lot," Juliana said. She used to remind some people of the movie actress Amy Adams. *"Used to" being the operative phrase,* she thought.

And then: *Is this guy actually hitting on me?* It had been a while since she'd felt that particular buzz. This fellow—Matías—was easily ten years younger. And unnervingly handsome, she had to admit.

This is exactly the kind of thing I don't do, she thought. Would never do. She wanted to say to the guy: *You've got me all wrong.* She'd say, *If you knew anything about me, you'd know I'm not your "live in the moment" kinda gal. You are wasting your time, buddy.*

He tilted his head as if assessing her anew. "Know what's weird? Up close you don't look anything like her. It's just— I can't put my finger on it, it's something in the way you hold yourself. A kind of self-confidence, or maybe it's elegance, or both."

She felt herself blush, asked a question to cover her embarrassment. "So who do I almost look like?"

"The woman I used to be married to."

"Oh, I see. Nothing quite like being compared to a person's ex."

The server put down their drinks. Matías averted his gaze. "It's not like that. . . ."

"I was only teasing. And anyway I'm sure you have a girl in your life already."

"I do. An amazing, beautiful girl. She's everything to me."

He pulled out his phone and swiped at it. She leaned in close to him and looked. An actual *girl*, a cute little blonde, maybe seven or eight, a gap-toothed smile, sitting in a rowboat. A red-and-white-striped T-shirt. Not what she expected.

She caught him watching her and smiled.

"She's a darling. Is she with her mother?"

"Her mother . . ." He looked away, put the phone back in his jacket's breast pocket. She noticed tears in his eyes.

"Hey," she said, touching his wrist. "I didn't mean to . . ."

"No, it's . . . We were swimming in Costa Rica, a place called Playa Hermosa, and she . . ." He compressed his lips. "She was a terrific swimmer, but the riptide was too strong, and by the time . . ." His face seemed briefly to crumple in on itself; then, just as quickly, he recovered.

"I'm sorry," he said. "I thought this part of it was behind me." He got up, bowing his head in apology. Juliana reached out a hand, caught his forearm, beseeching him to stay.

"Sit, please," she said. "How long . . . ?"

He picked up his drink, sipped, put it down. "Two years." He slowly sank into his chair. "I still can't really talk about it. I shouldn't have tried. I— I never do this. This isn't me."

"It's quite all right—Matías, is that right?"

"Yes. And—Juliana?" She nodded.

"I don't know you," he continued. "But I feel as if I do, that's the weird thing. Just something I saw when I looked at you. Don't ask me to explain."

"Okay, now you're going to have to explain."

"Well, I can try. You're beautiful, of course. But so many beautiful women have this icy reserve—they have to, it's how they protect themselves, keep guys out of their swim lane. But you—this is going to sound crazy. I saw a sense of a light inside you."

She blushed again, hoped it wasn't visible. "LED, I'm sure."

"You're making fun of me, and you should," he said, tipping his glass of Scotch toward her and taking a sip.

"No, I'm sorry, go on. What else did you see?"

"Honestly?"

Juliana reached for her wineglass, took a steadying sip. "Sure, why not?"

"I see a kind of . . . loneliness. Not by-yourself lonely. But lonely. Maybe because . . . well, didn't you say you're with the law conference? You are a lawyer? A judge?"

Juliana was momentarily speechless.

"I am so sorry," Matías said. "I swear I'm not normally like this. Let's blame the Ardbeg." He put his hand on hers briefly, and she felt the heat. "Four hours ago I killed a deal that looked great on paper until I met the management team. And I knew within two minutes these guys couldn't execute the plan. These were not the guys. Now, *that's* where my instincts are good."

She gave him a long look. "Maybe not just there," she said, and she took a good swig of the Sancerre.

They kissed leaning against the door to his suite. She could taste the single malt. She pulled back, took a breath. He smelled of wood smoke and leather. He found a tendril of her hair and ran his fingers under it, along her cheek. His eyes met hers for a moment. "I wonder if you know how beautiful you are."

She could feel the heat radiating off his body. "Tomorrow I'm flying off. Back to my life. This . . . this can't mean anything."

Something was happening inside her. Like a wave that suddenly, startlingly forms in a usually placid lake. A wave formed by that surprisingly good French Sancerre and some kind of reservoir of resentment at how goddamned predictable she'd become. Everybody knew she'd never do this. But shouldn't there be more to her than what everybody knew?

For just one night, she'd pretend to be that woman she's not. For just one night, she'd do what she never does. For just one night, she'd live a life that wasn't the one she'd so carefully mapped out.

Just one night.

He found his key card and the lock beeped open and he held the door.

2

The next afternoon, waiting for an Uber home from Logan Airport in Boston, she found herself in a reverie, replaying moments in her mind from the night before. She couldn't remember when she'd last been touched like that, by Duncan or by anyone else. It was as if he'd found her reset button; even now, her body hummed. At one point she had seen tears in his eyes, and she had wondered whether he was thinking of his late wife, making up for lost time.

Sitting on a corner of the king-size bed, she'd said, "I have a family."

"I understand," he'd replied, his voice gentle. "It can't happen again."

They were agreed.

She briefly wondered whether Duncan's "dalliance," as she thought of it, three years earlier, had played a role in her decision to go to Matías's hotel room. She didn't think so; she'd come to accept what had happened with him, and she wasn't a petty person. She didn't believe there was a balance sheet in a marriage, a ledger of rights and wrongs. In any case, the problems in their marriage, if she were being honest, were bigger than that one incident.

No, she had done something she'd never done before. She had taken a risk. She'd had a second drink. That wasn't her at all, that woman in the bar at the Peninsula. She was the A student, the obeyer of rules.

Judge Juliana Brody: sensible, prudent, and cautious. Unlike her mother (and because of her mother, who lived in her own dream world), she had always been a planner, always been careful to put her foot right, choose the next step thoughtfully.

And then she had gone and done one single incautious, impetuous thing.

And was it so bad? It had been a lovely evening, actually. Maybe she needed to let go more often.

Now, an e-mail flashed her phone alive, and she glanced at it despite herself. The reality of daily life was beckoning, haranguing. Her Uber was arriving. She had a couple of texts too, a voice mail, and a shit-ton of e-mails to sort through.

An ordinary, prudent life to get back to. She greeted that prospect with some relief.

3

One of the things Juliana liked most about being a judge was the routine, the predictability. Everything happened on schedule. She had something like 250 pending cases on her docket, but only one trial at a time. Every morning she arrived at her office before eight thirty, went through whatever writing she had to do—discovery disputes, motions, jury instructions—and then began presiding over a trial at 9:00 A.M. sharp. (These days she had a med-mal case—medical malpractice, a wrongful death.) The trial ended at 1:00 P.M. Then came lunch from 1:00 P.M. to 2:00 P.M., usually spent at her computer catching up on paperwork. In the afternoon, from 2:00 P.M. to 4:00 P.M., were often motion sessions. Which basically meant a bunch of arguments, made orally and on paper, on which she had to make decisions. These were cases that might go to trial but usually didn't. For the last few months she'd been dealing with *Rachel Meyers v. Wheelz*, a sex-discrimination case that seemed as though it would never end.

True, there were little things that popped up fairly often. People walked in with requests for ex parte relief, motions to attach property, and so on. Appeals from sex offenders. Condo disputes. A motion ordering a hospital to release a guy's medical records. Loads of paperwork. The Superior Court didn't yet do electronic filing, so her office was heaped with piles of paper, with more coming in every day. The workload could be punishing. It was unyielding, an unending cascade. There was always a load of homework. Reading and writing. It was like being back in school. It truly never stopped. And—in fact—she loved it.

No one said judging was easy. You had to be really committed to it. You didn't do it for the money. You didn't make any friends in this job. In a courtroom, Juliana once realized, half the room thinks you're just barely smart enough to get it. The other half just thinks you're stupid. Lawyers liked to tell a joke: What do you call a lawyer with an IQ of eighty? "Your Honor."

But the psychic income was high. You were making a difference in people's lives. That was worth something. Unfortunately, judges were also susceptible to the dreaded Black Robe disease, in which they come to believe the black robe lets them walk on water and that all their jokes are funny.

For almost a week after Chicago, she'd been able to lose herself in the routine. Which was not to say she didn't think about what she'd done at the hotel. She thought about it constantly, and the feeling that seemed to have settled over her was guilt. She was susceptible to feelings of guilt anyway. There'd been moments in her life she couldn't forget, moments when she'd let herself down, moments she still didn't like to think about. That time in tenth grade, when she was on the high school yearbook staff and she'd quietly removed an unflattering photo of herself, at the expense of another girl in the picture, glamorously captured spiking the ball. Or that time at the end of junior year in college, just back from France, when she'd promised her friend Sandy they could room together senior year—until Alyssa, to her surprise, asked her to join the quad she was creating, and Juliana had quickly accepted. Sandy had been crushed. *I'm not a good person*, Juliana had thought at the time.

That was how she felt about Chicago: it had been a rare error in judgment.

Fortunately, work was there to distract her. There was always another decision to write, another dispute to decide. She found herself conveniently distracted. She had piles of work to lose herself in.

She had her run too. Every morning she got up at six and did three miles. Running was important to her. It gave her calm for the entire day, reduced stress, helped maintain her sanity. She had her earbuds in, listened to some Sara Evans or Chris Stapleton. She thought a lot about cortisol, the hormone naturally released in your body by stress. It could make you superproductive. In some ways she was attracted to stress, to danger. But cortisol was bad for women's hearts. If you lived in a constant state of high stress, your levels of cortisol elevated and you were far more likely to have a heart attack.

After her run, she allowed herself precisely forty-five minutes to shower, dress, and do her hair and makeup. She had all her makeup ready to go, like an assembly line. Perfectly choreographed. She didn't have to worry too much about what she wore, since she covered it all in a black sack anyway.

Once, a defendant's girlfriend had erupted in the courtroom, yelling at Juliana. "You've destroyed my family—I'm going to destroy yours!" the young woman screamed. "And you need a makeover!"

That was truly the dagger in her heart, that bit about a makeover. Also not true, she thought.

On this morning's run, she admired, as she always did, the beautiful houses on her street in Newton, graceful houses of stone and wood on ample lots, some of them designed by famous nineteenth-century architects. Their house was by far the most modest on the block, a brick-and-stone Tudor, built in the 1920s, on a quiet dead-end street. She'd loved it on sight, which was why, when they first went to look for a house, she'd immediately urged Duncan to go for it—even though it was more house than they could afford at the time. She'd been an assistant US Attorney and he was a law school professor, neither making much money. Eventually she went into private practice and the money got better. When she became a judge, her pay dropped again. No one ever became a judge for the money. But they were getting by. They could even afford to rent a beach house in Wellfleet, on Cape Cod, for a month each summer.

When she came downstairs after her postrun shower, she could smell the bacon. Duncan was making breakfast, which was a nice surprise. Then she remembered: Jake had a big math test this morning, and Duncan's ritual was to make a serious breakfast on Jake's test days. Bacon, eggs, toasted English muffins. The menu never varied.

"Mm," she said, giving Duncan a kiss. "Smells great."

"Hey," he said. "Coffee?"

"Thanks." He turned from the stove to the coffeemaker, poured her a mug.

"Where's Jake?" she asked.

"Can you yell up to him?"

"Sure."

She felt a pang of guilt. Duncan was a wonderful father and a good person. *I don't even deserve the guy,* she thought.

Her first serious boyfriend, in college, had been Richard, the lockjawed Hotchkiss grad with the Nantucket red pants and the Bean boots, the vexing early bald spot and the perfect table manners. They were totally compatible, both prudent, rules-following, list-checking people. Whereas Duncan was a scruffy, bearded kid, an idealist, a pleasure-seeker, who for too long a time didn't want to get married.

He was a good-looking man. He still had a great head of curly hair, though it was more gray than brown now. A closely trimmed beard, killer smile. Maybe twenty pounds overweight, but he wore it well.

He was still, in fundamental ways, her polar opposite. That was what had really attracted her to him. He was impulsive and risk-taking, a terrible planner, but really smart. He loved adventure. He was a devoted scuba diver and skier and surfer. He didn't do extreme stuff like bull riding or motorcycle racing or bungee jumping, but he liked to have fun. His ideal vacation might be trekking on foot through the Cardamom Mountains in Cambodia. Hers might involve breakfast at the Brasserie Lipp in Paris. He once dragged her to some eco-resort in Costa Rica, where the howler monkeys lived up to their name. Her revenge involved dragging him to Paris, and a fancy part of it too.

As she walked over to the foot of the stairs, she thought: *I'm home. This is home.* The coffee, the sizzling bacon, Duncan, even the recalcitrant teenager upstairs. *This is something valuable and meaningful, something I don't want to break. This is good.* She felt a deep sense of gratitude.

She called out, "Jacob, come on." She didn't hear the shower running. So he was still in his bedroom. The kid was sixteen but acted like a child sometimes. He regularly slept through his alarms. She started up the stairs to get him and then heard his door open.

"I heard you," Jake said.

"I want us to call Ashley."

"I don't have time."

"Well, we're Skyping in five minutes, so let's get moving."

Ashley, who was eighteen, was spending a gap year, between high school and college, in Namibia, volunteering at a village outside Windhoek that took care of women with AIDS. Internet service there was intermittent. Juliana imagined a shack made from corrugated steel, with a 1998-model modem and a long extension cord.

Jake came into the kitchen, in jeans and a black T-shirt with a couple of cartoon characters with bulging eyes on it and the words RICK AND MORTY. Some TV show he liked. He had his father's brown eyes and curly brown hair, in need of a haircut. He was a good-looking kid, in a gawky, awkward teenage way, and she was pretty sure he'd grow up to be a handsome man like his father. But his eyes were bloodshot and glassy. He looked feverish.

"Hey, sweetie, you okay?"

"I'm fine, what do you mean?"

"Were you up really late last night?"

"No," Jake said too quickly. Which meant yes. She had no idea what he did in his room so late at night. Video games? Lights were supposed to be out by ten, but neither she nor Duncan regularly enforced that. She spent the day being a judge, being the arbiter, making sure the rules were followed. She didn't want to do it at home too.

"All set for the big math test?" she asked.

"What? Oh, I don't know." He shrugged. "I don't particularly care."

"Dude," said Duncan, turning around.

"You'd *better* care," Juliana said. She worried about the kid. He didn't seem to give a damn about anything. There was something self-protective about that, she figured. If you lower your ambitions, you won't get disappointed. You won't get slapped down by the Splintered Ruler of Life. But the way he was going, he could end up circling the drain, like her screw-up brother, Calvin.

"You look like you could use some coffee," Duncan said.

"What about Mom's rule?" Jake said.

"That's your *parents*' rule, Jake," she said. Jake wasn't allowed to have coffee until he was a senior in high school. A totally arbitrary policy, she had to admit. But it had been her father's. Then she added, "But you know what? Rules are meant to be broken. Go ahead and have coffee."

"Why not?" Duncan said, after throwing a surprised glance at Juliana. He took a mug out from the cabinet and poured some coffee. "You'll probably want a lot of cream and sugar."

"I'll take it black," Jake said.

"Really?" Duncan said.

Jake took a sip and grimaced. "Yeah, I like it black now," he said.

"Jake, can you sign me into Skype?" Juliana said. "I think you changed the password."

"No, I didn't," Jake said.

"Sign me in, okay?"

"Anyway, I don't have time to talk to her. I'll miss the bus."

"Talk to your sister," Duncan said. "I'll drive you to school. And sign your mom into Skype."

Duncan, a professor at New England Law, had an easier schedule than hers. His first class didn't start until ten. She had to be at the courthouse no later than eight thirty.

Duncan put *The Boston Globe* down on the table in front of her, folded to a story about Wheelz in the Boston market, about all the competition in ride-hailing apps and how the ordinary cabdriver was getting screwed big time. She saw a big picture of the extremely rich founder of Wheelz, Devin Allerdyce, a pointy-faced man of thirty-five with scraggly brown hair and a pinched face that reminded her of a mouse.

"That rat-faced scumbag," Duncan said. "Hope you drop an anvil on his ass."

She smiled, shook her head. "Dispassionate judgment. Procedure. Rule of law. You know, all the stuff you tell your impressionable law-student groupies is just a mask for the workings of power and hegemony? Call me old-fashioned, but that's still how I roll. We are *not* having this conversation."

He smiled, and then she admitted, "He does kinda look like a rodent."

This morning she found herself looking around the kitchen, watching Duncan slide a couple of sunny-side-up eggs onto Jake's plate, and suddenly her throat got tight and tears came to her eyes. This happened to her, every once in a while: her heart would swell. She never knew when it would come on.

"You okay?" Duncan said, putting two crisp pieces of bacon on her plate.

"An eyelash," she said. "I'm fine."

The Skype ringtone sounded, and she pulled the laptop close to answer. "Ash, baby," she said. "I miss you."

4

That afternoon, Juliana returned to the courtroom to hear oral arguments in the case of *Rachel Meyers v. Wheelz*, in which a young woman was suing a hot, new ride-hailing start-up in Boston for sex discrimination. The case had been going on for months, and it showed no signs of slowing its march to trial. Juliana sometimes thought of it as *Jarndyce v. Jarndyce*, the unending court case from Dickens's novel *Bleak House*.

"All rise," the court officer called out. She entered, and everyone stood. Long ago she'd figured out that they weren't standing for her. They were standing out of respect for the system of justice, respect for what they were all undertaking. You had to show respect. That was why she didn't let witnesses chew gum, wouldn't let people read newspapers or talk on their phones in her courtroom. She sat, and everyone in the courtroom sat.

At the plaintiff's table sat the lead attorney, Glenda Craft, a fit, slender woman in her late fifties who either wore false eyelashes or used a lot of mascara. She talked loud, walked quickly, and thought faster on her feet than any other lawyer Juliana had ever met. There were rumors that she had never lost a case, and others about the legions of opposing lawyers who were heard throwing up in the courthouse bathrooms before going up against her each day at trial.

She was wearing a St. John suit. You could tell from the knit. It was forest green with brass buttons, and it draped beautifully without clinging. Her necklace was three strands of oversize pearls, feminine but strong, a perfect balance. The outfit said *I've arrived.*

The attorney for Wheelz, Harlan Madden from the law firm of Batten Schechter, was his own kind of killer. He was a deceptively affable man of around sixty with a large potbelly, a Yalie who'd gone to Andover, whose father and grandfather had likewise gone to Yale and Andover, who'd been the captain of the tennis team in college and was said to have been ferociously competitive, back in the day. He was wearing a perfectly tailored charcoal suit.

When Juliana finished law school, trial law was still a boys' club, an occupation dominated by alpha males who were big and tall and had loud voices. She had no interest in imitating them. So she joined the US Attorney's office, where she learned to be twice the trial lawyer any of the guys in private practice were. In cross examinations, instead of intimidating witnesses like male trial attorneys did, she'd win over witnesses and then suddenly turn on them, catch them off-guard in a contradiction. Her male colleagues used to call her "the pit bull" because she never let go. Witnesses on the stand would wilt under her politely relentless questioning.

Both Craft and Madden had their assistants, associates who did the grunt work, and there was a lot of grunt work. Reams of documents to go through, hundreds of linear feet. In the courtroom behind the bar sat the plaintiff, Rachel Meyers, a fragile-looking blond woman in her mid-thirties. She wore a blue blazer over a white button-down shirt. Seated nearby was a sprinkling of lawyers there for the defense.

Or maybe there to intimidate. Wheelz was a competitor to Uber and

Lyft, nowhere near as big as either one, but growing fast. They had a self-driving-car unit that they believed was the future of the ride-hailing business, the near future. They had a lot of cash and could afford an expensive Big Law defense. They'd offered Rachel Meyers a generous settlement a few months back, but Rachel wanted to be heard. She wanted a trial. She didn't want to settle.

Juliana looked over her courtroom. Everything the way it was supposed to be. The court officers in their uniform, the white shirt and black tie, the American flag patch on one shoulder. The court reporter with her gray stenomask, the oxygen-mask-looking thing with foam rubber around the mouthpiece.

She took a breath and began. "Good afternoon, Counsel. We're here on the defendant's motion for a protective order. I've read the papers. I understand there's a dispute over whether certain documents should be produced or are entitled to a protective order. Mr. Madden, it's your motion; why don't you start?"

Harlan Madden stood. The lawyers always stood when addressing her. "Your Honor," he said, "as you know, this is a gender-discrimination case. The plaintiff alleges she was terminated due to sex discrimination. Whereas the evidence shows she was clearly terminated due to ongoing performance issues. It's as simple as that. But now they're asking for the records of hundreds, if not thousands, of private electronic company chats, which the plaintiff knows is how employees at Wheelz conduct company business, much of it proprietary and confidential—"

Juliana cut him off. "Why can't you simply redact them, remove the proprietary information?"

"I was getting to that, Your Honor," Madden said, and he smiled. "The plaintiff is quite aware that these chats contain proprietary company information intertwined throughout. It's impossible to separate the personal from the official. Now, under Mass. Rule of Civil Procedure 26, you have the authority to issue a protective order and rule that this discovery may not be had, that the plaintiff is not entitled to this information."

Juliana had heard enough. She put up her hand and turned to Glenda Craft. "Counselor, why do you need this? What do these chats have to do with your claim of gender discrimination?"

Craft rose to her feet. "The company chat platform, Slack, wasn't just used for work, Your Honor," she said in her smoke-raspy voice. "The chats between my client and Devin Allerdyce, the CEO of the company, were full of inappropriate communications."

Juliana had seen Allerdyce only once, on the first day of the pretrial motions, and had taken an immediate dislike to him, though of course she'd never reveal it. Allerdyce was rich and entitled, a sudden megamillionaire at an age when most people are just starting their careers. He didn't exactly dress up for court. He wore jeans and the obligatory hoodie, like so many Silicon Valley brats seemed to wear. Silicon Valley was replicating itself around the country, including in Boston.

Rachel Meyers, a hotshot young lawyer who'd made partner at WilmerHale six years out of Harvard Law, had been hired by Wheelz with a generous compensation package. If she'd stayed at least two years, and past the IPO, she would have made as much as $25 million. But that wasn't to be. What she encountered at Wheelz, she claimed, was a frat house, hard-partying and mostly male. She was often the only woman in a room of twenty men. She was subjected to demeaning comments and unwanted sexual advances. She was hit on by the CEO, whose advances she rebuffed. Before a year was up, she was fired. She got nothing.

On the face of it, it seemed clear to Juliana that the young woman had gotten a raw deal. That she'd been fired for objecting to an atmosphere of pervasive sexual harassment.

But cases were rarely simple, and the law was the law, and Juliana Brody was beginning to garner recognition as a fair and dispassionate jurist. This case, like every case, had to proceed step by step, motion by motion, argument by argument. Decision by decision. That's what she was here for. To play referee.

Harlan Madden had remained standing, ready for a back-and-forth, and swiveled as if he were back on the tennis court, preparing to return serve. "These chats were used primarily for business, Your Honor, and they include discussions of the most sensitive nature."

"And sometimes they were used socially," Craft said, "for non-business purposes—and I have proof of that, Judge." She grabbed a folder from the table and removed a few sheets of paper from it. "May I approach?"

"You may."

She handed Juliana a piece of paper, then gave one to Madden.

A moment later, as Juliana began scanning the page, Madden erupted, "This is—outrageous!"

It appeared to be a printout of a computer chat exchange. "This is a screenshot of the December 6 chat between my client and Mr. Allerdyce," Craft said.

Juliana looked over the page. It seemed to start in the middle of a chat.

RACHEL MEYERS: let me check my calendar

DEVIN ALLERDYCE: lmk. In other news, I'm in an open relationship.

DEVIN ALLERDYCE: U there?

RACHEL MEYERS: Haha okay.

DEVIN ALLERDYCE: You're single though right?

RACHEL MEYERS: Haha can't tell if you're serious.

DEVIN ALLERDYCE: As cancer. ;-)

DEVIN ALLERDYCE: So are you? Single?

RACHEL MEYERS: I mean

DEVIN ALLERDYCE: Yeah?

Allerdyce, the CEO, was hitting on his new general counsel, albeit in a clumsy and oily way.

Juliana looked up. "Why am I seeing this for the first time?" she said.

"Exactly," said Madden, indignant. "Why was this not produced earlier? Also, Your Honor, we have no idea where this came from. There's no date on it. No way, even, to substantiate its provenance. This should simply be stricken from the record."

"Ms. Craft? Where did this come from? And why didn't you produce this months ago, if you had it?"

"My client just gave it to me," Craft said. She spoke quickly, defensive-sounding. "She just got it. It was mailed to her anonymously over the weekend. So it wasn't in her possession until Saturday."

"Mailed anonymously?" said Madden. "Your Honor, she's gotta be kidding."

"Obviously someone within the company—perhaps someone repelled by a culture that appears to be hostile toward women—"

Juliana reacted even before Madden could. "Ms. Craft, table the editorializing."

"Printed it out and sent it to her, knowing she was suing the company."

Juliana turned to the defense. "Mr. Madden, you need to explain to me what there is about this clearly inappropriate exchange that qualifies as confidential and proprietary information." She gave him a cold, level look. Her "objection overruled" stare.

For just a moment, Madden was silent. He was a very smart guy, but this turn of events forced him to take a beat and compose himself. "The remainder of that conversation, I'm sure, dealt with company business of a highly confidential—"

"As you can see, this can easily be redacted, Counselor," Juliana said. She almost added, "Right?" Even after three years on the bench, she had to edit herself, modulate her natural conversational style. In court, she was the judge, and it was vital to be more firm, more . . . judicious. "All right," she said. She heard the door to the courtroom open, and she glanced up to see someone entering. "I want to see all chats between the plaintiff and Mr. Allerdyce, as well as any that mention the plaintiff—"

She glanced toward the back of the courtroom and saw a man with dark blond hair walk down the center aisle. She felt her face get hot. The man's walk was familiar.

She couldn't help but stare.

One of the spectators coughed. Someone snapped a binder closed.

It couldn't be.

It wasn't possible. They had agreed solemnly that they would never see each other again.

My name is . . .

The guy looked exactly like Matías. What kind of coincidence could that be?

She looked again.

Was she imagining this?

They'd *agreed.* A one-night thing.

It can't happen again.

My name is Matías Sanchez.

The man crossed the bar and went over to the defense table. He nodded at Madden and took a seat, gracefully, in the only empty chair.

Her mind went blank. Someone was talking to her, but she couldn't understand what he was saying. She turned to Madden and said, "Could you repeat that, please?"

"Your Honor," said Madden, "I'd like to introduce an addition to our defense team." He turned and gestured toward the man, who stood now and nodded courteously in her direction.

"Good afternoon, Your Honor," he said in his pleasing baritone, that tiny trace of an Argentinian accent. "My name is Matías Sanchez."

5

Juliana went right to her office, her "lobby" as the state's arcane language called it, and sank unsteadily into her desk chair.

Her head was spinning, and she felt light-headed. She saw little pinpoints of light. She closed her eyes.

Matías from Chicago had said he was a businessman, in venture capital in Buenos Aires.

I'm afraid I was staring at you before.

How could this be? Harlan Madden had introduced the man as if they knew each other, as if they were colleagues.

Matías was a lawyer?

The man who had talked about his wife, his daughter. Who had cried when he came.

Was sitting at the defense table.

She was beginning to feel prickly hot and a little nauseated.

The man she was *never going to see again*, ships passing in the night as she'd put it, cliché or no cliché.

Two very separate worlds were somehow colliding, worlds she had been so meticulous about keeping apart.

After Matías had introduced himself, she could hear nothing but the thudding of her heart. Glenda Craft's eyes had narrowed as she waited for Juliana to speak.

For a moment, she'd lost her train of thought. Then it came back to her. Wondering whether she was flushing visibly, she cleared her throat and said to Madden, "By Monday, I'd like to see all of the Slack chats between Ms. Meyers and Mr. Allerdyce and any that mention Ms. Meyers. I'll then rule on the motion. I think that does it for today."

She was slowly beginning to understand that she'd been used, seduced.

Set up.

He must have known she was the judge on the Wheelz case. She felt humiliated, disgusted.

She found herself running through her options. Maybe she should have said something as soon as the man walked into the courtroom. But what could she have said? She had no standing to protest an addition to the defense team. They had the right to add whomever they wanted, especially in the pretrial phase of a case.

He had the right to be there. It was their call.

And what if she'd said something like, *Who are you, and why are you here?* Matías would have produced credentials, no doubt showing him to be a member of the bar in good standing, and then what could she have said?

Aren't you the guy I slept with one night last week in Chicago?

That would be the end of her marriage, the destruction of her reputation.

She could say exactly nothing.

There was a knock on the door. She could see a silhouette of a figure through the clouded-glass panel in her door.

"Come in."

"Excuse me, Your Honor?"

Her clerk, Kaitlyn Hemming, a waifish woman in her mid-twenties with a pixie haircut, a recent Suffolk Law grad, stood there with a sheaf of papers in her hand. Juliana shared her law clerk with another judge.

"Got a minute?" Kaitlyn asked.

"Come on in," Juliana said.

Time to get back to work.

6

The Bostonia Club was one of Boston's grandest private clubs, located in a large, handsome brownstone on Commonwealth Avenue with a highly polished black-painted front door and brass fittings and a doorknob that gleamed. It was a club for lawyers, primarily, a place where they could socialize, play poker, shoot pool, have dinner. And talk law, if they wanted, without being accused of being boring. There were a few nonlawyer members, and civilians were brought in all the time, usually for dinner and a predinner talk. One Juliana attended recently had been titled "Great Defense Attorneys in Film (Besides Atticus Finch)."

It was funny, she had to admit, that she belonged to this fancy club, given that her mother had worked in one. Her mother, Rosalind, had been the operations manager at another exclusive private club in Boston, the Clarendon Club. She was a staff member—not very well paid—and not a member, of course. But she was a fixture at the club and much-beloved (or so she always said, herself). Yet not one of the members attended her funeral.

Juliana remembered coming up with the idea, in the year after her mother's death, of a memorial service at the Clarendon Club. She mentioned the idea to her mom's boss, the gloomy Mrs. Cooper. Mrs. Cooper took young Juliana's hands in hers and gently disabused her. "Such a sweet thought!" Mrs. Cooper said. "And I know that's how your mom saw this place sometimes. But I gotta tell you. When Mr. Carducci retired after half a century as caretaker, I could barely get six people to sign a going-away card. I mean, folks were like, 'We'll miss him—bet we can hire a replacement for half the cost.' I mean, that's just the reality of this place."

With a sinking in her stomach, Juliana recognized the truth.

"Your mom," Mrs. Cooper went on, "bless her heart, preferred her own reality."

Tears had come to Juliana's eyes. She left in a dazed state, a little sickened. Mrs. Cooper had nailed it: her mother invented, lived in, her own reality. She'd told Juliana how the members would say, *What would we ever do without you, Roz?* And she would believe it.

She remembered talking to her mother, shortly before her death, about her brother, Calvin, two years younger, who'd died when he was twenty. "You know," Rosalind had said, "your brother was an extremely talented musician. A poet, really." Juliana nodded, too weary to point out that Calvin had been a mediocre guitarist at best. "You remember that song he wrote, the one about a lady who's buying a stairway to heaven? That was so beautiful. *So* much talent." She was starting to slur her words. If she was at home, she was inevitably drunk.

Juliana couldn't take it anymore. "Mom, Calvin . . . didn't write that."

"No?"

"It's Led Zeppelin."

"Well. 'Great artists steal,' T. S. Eliot said. Calvin put his own touch to it, is my point."

She lived in her own world.

Linda Zucchetti already had dinner plans at the club but agreed to meet her for an after-dinner drink in the club's library at eight o'clock. Linda was around her age, in her early forties, and had been a judge on the Superior Court for six years—a good friend and a good person to share a cosmo with. So first Juliana went home at five thirty, arriving at an empty house, and defrosted some lasagna in the microwave for Duncan and Jacob. She herself had some leftover chicken tikka masala from their favorite Indian place, on Boylston Street, while distractedly checking her e-mail.

She washed her face, put on toner, then her eye cream and some tinted moisturizer. Her mind was replaying the image, over and over, of Matías walking into the courtroom. She had recognized the walk even before she'd seen his face. It was definitely him. She brushed on some blush and stared at her reflection in the mirror. What had she done?

"Idiot," she said aloud. She turned away from the mirror, disgusted, her stomach cramped with anxiety. *What a terrible mistake.*

She drove her blue Lexus sport-utility vehicle the mile or two into downtown Boston, lucked into a parking spot on Exeter Street, and entered the club at seven thirty.

Linda was standing in the foyer, in the middle of an extended goodbye with another woman who was probably her dinner date. The two of them stood underneath the John Singer Sargent portrait of Lucius Graham, the Boston lawyer who'd founded the Bostonia Club early in the nineteenth century. He had a handlebar mustache and wore his collar up with a black tie and black coat and looked sort of raffish, leaning back on his chair with his hand dangling casually in the air.

Juliana caught Linda's eye, smiled hello, gave a little wave—she didn't want to interrupt and didn't feel like being introduced to someone she'd probably never see again—and wandered upstairs to the library. It was lined with books, like a library, but it was also the customary gathering place for club members to have drinks before and after dinner. She found a table as far away as possible from a raucous gathering of members seated in mismatched easy chairs around the unlit fireplace, waved at a few she knew, and told the waitress she'd wait to order until she was joined by her friend.

Linda arrived a few minutes later, apologizing for keeping her waiting, and put a hand on Juliana's shoulder. She was an attractive woman who looked easily ten years younger than she was. Linda and she had had their issues in the past—for a while, when they were both in the US Attorney's office, they were competitive—but now they were allies. They'd even done SoulCycle together. Linda was wearing a suit of pale green silk. Her hair was light brown with blond highlights. *I work in a sack all day,* Linda had once said. *When I dress up I want to look nice.* And she had the figure to pull it off.

Juliana stood and gave Linda a hug, inhaling her wonderfully sultry perfume.

"You're still on civil, aren't you, poor thing," Linda said with a big smile.

Twice a year they rotated between civil and criminal cases, and Linda made no secret of the fact that she much preferred criminal, where the action was, even though some of the homicide cases they had to hear could be wrenching. The criminal session, Linda had once announced, was heartache; the civil session was headache.

"I like it," Juliana said. "You know that."

"Even the endless Wheelz case?"

She shook her head. "Well, except for that," Juliana admitted.

Linda sat in the chair next to her, rather than across from her. When the waitress approached, Juliana ordered a cosmo and Linda ordered a Grey Goose vodka martini. Juliana was determined to limit her drinking to one cosmo tonight.

"You sounded concerned on the phone, Jules. Is everything okay? The family, the kids?" When Linda crossed her legs you could see the effects of her daily Pilates sessions.

"Everyone's fine. Ashley's in Namibia and loving it." Well, as much as you could "love" taking care of terminally ill people; she couldn't even imagine what that was like, those poor women infected with AIDS by their husbands.

"Ashley's *still* in Namibia? God bless that child."

"We have to schedule Skype sessions once a week. I miss her."

"Of course you do. And Jake?"

"I wish he'd go off to college already."

Linda laughed. She knew that Juliana was kidding, mostly. They both complained, jokingly, about their kids, knowing that they loved and appreciated their children, while agreeing that having teenagers in the house was a special kind of stressful. She didn't know what she'd do if it weren't for Duncan, who was like the Teen Whisperer. He and the kids always seemed to be tuned in to the same frequency. But she worried about Jake a lot recently, his apathy, his dropping grades. It was like he was floating through life, blowing with the winds. Whereas Ashley had always been the straight-A student. Maybe girls were just easier to parent.

"I know you worry about him," Linda said. "That's not going to change. I get it. After all you've been through, my God. But you know you've gotta fight that. You can't have that in your head every day."

"I know. You're right. You're absolutely right."

"You had something you wanted to hash out?"

"Yeah, it's this weird situation. On the Wheelz case, in fact. So Wheelz just added another lawyer to the defense, and it turns out to be a guy I know."

"Okay?" Linda blinked a few times: *What's the big deal?*

Juliana knew she was treading a difficult path here. She obviously couldn't tell Linda the full truth, that she'd actually slept with the guy. That was the sort of thing that became hot gossip. Also, she didn't want to tell her what had happened because it felt like just saying it aloud would make it real.

Instead, she said, "We had a drink, last week in Chicago."

"At the bar conference?"

Juliana nodded. "I don't know if I should say something."

Linda shrugged. "Isn't Harlan Madden the lead?"

"He is. And Glenda Craft for the plaintiff."

"You've socialized with Craft and Madden both, I assume."

"I have."

Linda tipped her head to one side and peered at her strangely. "The new defense lawyer is with Batten Schechter?"

"I assume so."

"A drink?" Linda said. She smiled again, cryptically. "You had a drink with him. Fine, we'll go with that. A drink. Honey, no reason to be ashamed. You would be shocked at how many married women have affairs. Quiet little affairs on the side." Linda had been divorced since her late thirties.

Juliana flushed. Was she that transparent? Was there something about the way she'd talked about Matías that gave it away? "Oh, come on," she said.

"Marriage is dull and grinding and constraining, and you know it."

Well, that's why you're divorced, she thought. "Can be," she said.

"We idealize marriage, and turns out the actual thing is a crashing disappointment."

"Not for everybody," Juliana protested.

"I've got a friend, I'm not going to tell you her name, she's one hundred percent faithful to her husband except when she's out of town on work each month. You can love your husband and still have unmet needs."

"Maybe so."

"Listen: since 1990, the number of women who report they've cheated on their husbands has gone up forty percent. Forty percent."

"What about the number of men who admit they've cheated?"

"Stayed flat. See, women are turning to infidelity as a way to stay in their marriages! Because married life is boring and constraining."

"Okay," Juliana said. This was not the conversation she wanted to have. And she certainly wasn't going to tell Linda about Chicago. If she "confided" in Linda, it would be public in a matter of hours.

"Your husband is like your third kid. Another child to pick up after. You're a judge, you're a professional woman with a big career, yet you have to get dinner on the table and do the dishes. Right?"

"Actually, no. Duncan helps out a lot," she said. "He cooks dinner more often than I do. I'll just get takeout from Whole Foods or something."

"Okay, so you had drinks with a lawyer in your courtroom. Correct me if I'm wrong, but you've also had drinks with the defense and the plaintiff's side, right? Why is that an issue?"

"The question is, *Should I be recusing myself?*"

"You know the drill. It's a two-pronged analysis. You examine your own conscience and ask yourself, *Can I be objective?* So, can you?"

Juliana nodded. "For sure." She wasn't going to let what had happened between her and Matías factor into the court case. That night—it was over. It was one and done, as far as she was concerned. But what the hell was he doing on the defense team? Why had he lied about being in venture capital?

"And is this a situation where your impartiality might reasonably be questioned?"

Questioned by whom? she wondered.

Her stomach tightened.

She knew she wasn't biased, but would others have reason to wonder? Only if they knew the truth. But if she didn't say anything, who was going to know? Yet if she told anyone the truth, her life would change forever.

"Sorry, what did you say?" She'd lost her train of thought.

"Is there any reason to question your impartiality?"

"No, I don't think so."

"Then what's the problem?"

She looked away, feeling slightly relieved.

And then she noticed a man sitting in a plump leather club chair in a dark corner of the library.

It was him. Matías.

Jesus Christ.

She was overcome by vertigo. It felt as if she were falling through space.

The man was stalking her.

By now Linda was taking note of the shift in her expression, probably the color she could feel spreading across her face.

"I don't know," Juliana said at last.

Matías was sitting about twenty feet away.

Why is he here?

"Most people would say you're making a big deal out of nothing," Linda said softly. She seemed to mean it as a question. She looked at Juliana hard; she seemed to know more than she was saying. "Myra Silver's death means the federal judgeship is open; you're aware of that, right?"

She was barely listening. "I suppose."

Linda smiled. "You suppose? Word on the street is that you're being seriously considered for the job. I *suppose* you're aware of that too?"

Juliana nodded. "You're not the first to say so," she admitted.

"You want to be very careful about the decisions you make these days," Linda said. "You know, you look at some of the recent Supreme Court appointments—I mean, these are people who always put every foot right. They made the right friends and executed every move perfectly. It's like some giant quadrille, and it never stops."

"Does that sound like me?"

"You've always got to play the long game. The higher you climb, the thinner the air gets, and the ledge you walk on gets narrower and narrower. So be careful."

7

She walked Linda downstairs, embraced good-bye, went back upstairs.

Had she imagined him? Had that been some kind of hallucination?

But Matías was still sitting in the club chair in the corner. She looked around. No one was sitting nearby.

"Your Honor," he said quietly.

She felt something like a kick in the stomach.

"What the hell are you doing?" she whispered, closer to a hiss.

"Juliana. I'm sorry about this." He looked genuinely sad.

"I don't know who you are or what sort of game you think you're playing, but I'm not going to be trapped or coerced or manipulated."

"Juliana, don't try to resist. For your own sake." He didn't say it menacingly; there was even something like tenderness in his voice.

"What do you think you're going to accomplish?"

"You'll grant our motion for a protective order. You will say that the company has the right to protect confidential and proprietary information. That they can withhold certain chats." He shrugged. "All quite reasonable."

She laughed, low and rueful. "Oh, I see. You're trying to blackmail me, is that it?"

He was still for a moment. When he spoke next, it was in a whisper. "There's a video."

"I'm sorry? What did you say? A—"

He nodded once. "Yes, Juliana. A video. Of that night."

Her mouth went dry. "Bullshit. Matías, or whatever the hell your real name is."

He leaned to one side and pulled out a laptop from his shoulder bag. He opened it and clicked an icon. A video started playing in a large window on his screen.

"Oh, my God," she said.

It took her a moment to orient herself, but then she could see her naked torso crisply, the roil of her breasts as she moved up and down, riding him. It was unmistakably her. Over her right shoulder, his face. Also clear. The video was playing on some kind of video-sharing website. Next to the window a box was checked: "Private."

"All I have to do is click the 'Public' box, and your life as you know it is over." A member of the rambunctious fireplace party was walking by, probably on her way to the restroom. Matías closed the laptop and put it back in his shoulder bag. "You can already imagine what the tabloids will call you. The Love Judge, right? But the thing is, nobody ever needs to see this video. The choice is yours."

Disgusted, her lip curling, she said, "What would your late wife think about this?"

Matías gave her a pitying look.

She felt faint. Of course: the whole thing was a carefully scripted snare. There was no late wife. She had been painstakingly played and seduced. "That picture of your daughter you showed me," she said. She remembered the blond, pigtailed girl, the red-and-white-striped T-shirt, the gap-toothed smile. "You don't have a daughter, do you?"

"I used what they gave me. I assume it was some Google Image grab."

What *they* gave me.

"Well, good for you," she said bitterly. "You must be so proud of the work you do."

"You understand what this means, yes?"

"I'm going to rule the way I'm going to rule. However I decide."

"And if you rule the wrong way, I check 'Public.' But why would you want to do this? You're a judge. Your rulings might be appealed, but the decision-making behind your choices? *Your* choices? Nobody will ever second-guess that. Nobody will ever have to know."

She was silent.

"Or, Juliana? If you defy them, you get in their way—then the judgment will come. No appeals. No mercy. No justice. You'll be ruined."

"You're threatening an officer of the court."

"I am only telling you the truth."

Juliana was momentarily stymied. She couldn't find the words. Finally she said, "What's to stop me from picking up the phone and calling *The Boston Globe*?"

"And telling them what? That your career on the bench is over? That for law firms you've become untouchable? And as for your personal life, your kids, your husband, your marriage—you'll need to decide how much you value it. I'm sure the *Globe* would love to run a piece about the sordid fall of a Massachusetts Superior Court judge. But is that really in your interest?"

She looked at him long and hard. Finally she said, "I don't accept this."

"I advise you to see it through," said Matías. "You have no idea who you're dealing with."

"Neither do you," she said.

8

The house was quiet when she arrived home, but deceptively so. She knew Jacob was upstairs in his room, headphones on, listening to music, and maybe even doing his homework. Duncan was probably in his home office working on his journal article.

And the kitchen was still a mess.

Juliana put on an apron and set to work carrying dishes to the sink, rinsing them, and loading the dishwasher—a mindless exercise that allowed her to think about what had happened.

The scene at the Bostonia Club had blotted out everything else. Matías Sanchez sitting sedately, almost regally, in the leather wingback chair, reading a copy of *The Economist*.

If you defy them, you get in their way—then the judgment will come. No appeals. No mercy. No justice. You'll be ruined.

Them.

He had seduced her in Chicago in order to entrap her. To blackmail her. And she had willingly, and thoughtlessly, gone along with it.

He was, had to be, working for Wheelz. To force a verdict favorable to the company. Why in the world go to such lengths for a sex-discrimination case? She didn't get it.

If you defy them, you get in their way—then the judgment will come. No appeals. No mercy. No justice. You'll be ruined.

Well, they weren't going to get what they wanted. She scraped crusted cheese off a plate.

Her reply—*I don't accept this*—had been piddling and inadequate, but she'd been stunned into near silence. Almost paralyzed from fear.

She didn't know what to do. She only knew she had to do something.

Washing the dishes she noticed that her hands were trembling. As she was rinsing, a wineglass slipped from her fingers and shattered in the sink.

"Shit," she said.

"Hey, let me do that," she heard Duncan say, entering from his study. "I'm sorry, Jake and I got into a discussion after dinner, and then I had an idea for my lecture tomorrow."

"That's okay." Washing dishes gave her an excuse not to have to look him in the face. "I'll take care of it."

"No, honey," he said, and gently nudged her aside. "I just need some wet paper towels." She shrugged, stepped out of his way. He dipped a couple of sheets of paper towels in the running water, then used them to carefully pick up the broken pieces of glass. When he was finished, he rinsed the sink and dried his hands.

Then he said, "Can we talk?"

Her stomach dropped. Did he know something?

But then she noticed he was holding something small in his right hand.

She turned off the water, wiped her hands on her apron, and turned to look.

"What's that?" she said. The thing he was holding was a short cylinder with a mouthpiece on it.

"Our son is vaping."

"Like, smoking?"

"Marijuana." Duncan looked like he was trying hard not to smile.

For an instant, Juliana felt an enormous sense of relief. Vaping? So Duncan didn't know about Matías and Chicago? This wasn't about that. This was a problem she could deal with. As he closed the door to the kitchen so Jake couldn't overhear, she took in a deep, calming breath.

Duncan sat down at the kitchen table, and she sat down next to him.

"Was this what you were talking to him about tonight?"

"Yeah. He says he does it with friends, on the weekends, when they're playing video games. He says he never gets high before school."

"So you . . . You know, I wish we could have talked about this all together."

Duncan nodded slowly. "I found the cartridge, the pen top, on the floor next to the washing machine, and I didn't even think. I yelled for him, and we started talking. But I should have, you're right."

It was an old story. Her long hours at work often meant that Duncan played a kind of first responder to the kids.

"I don't know what you said to him, but I really don't want him smoking pot."

"I don't think we can stop him."

"Why not?"

"Because we're not with him twenty-four seven. We have to be realistic about it. And, look, he's self-medicating, that's what's really going on here. He does it to unwind, relax. He says he's got all this anxiety about grades and getting into college and stuff, and this is how he copes. I mean, I smoke weed once in a while myself, right? I also take an SSRI. And you and I have our vodka martinis, our cosmos. I'm in no position to complain about his use of marijuana."

On the counter she found a three-quarters-full bottle of pinot noir and uncorked it. She poured a glass for Duncan, took a sip, and handed it to him. "Dunc, how do we know it's even safe for him?"

"Safe?"

"Given his—you know." She didn't even like saying it. "His health."

Jake had been eleven when he noticed a lump on his neck. He'd been tired a lot. Juliana at first suspected something like strep throat, only his throat didn't hurt. The doctor ordered a biopsy. They got the news a few days later: their son had Hodgkin lymphoma, stage 3.

The diagnosis hit them like a freight train. "Is it curable?" she asked the oncologist.

"Highly treatable," the oncologist replied. They never said "cured." No such thing. Juliana remembered feeling as if she were walking through fog. Her child had cancer; it was as plain and as horrible as that. They were now in a world of blood tests and chest X-rays and bone-marrow biopsies.

He was given three cycles of chemotherapy, a cocktail of drugs in an IV drip every two weeks that made him sick to his stomach. But it worked. He was in remission, the oncologist happily announced. "Thank God he's cured," Duncan said.

"Well, he's in remission," the doctor replied. "We don't say 'cured.'"

"Why not?" Duncan wanted to know.

"Relapse is always possible."

"Jesus."

"But most of the time the lymphoma stays in remission."

Juliana, who had wept when she got the diagnosis, wept again at the good news. But life was never the same. Whenever he got a cold or a sore throat, whenever he complained about feeling tired, it was always there, like a shark's fin in the water, the possibility of a relapse.

Now, she said, "There's all kinds of reasons why he shouldn't do this."

"I don't want him living like the boy in the bubble."

"I just want him to stay well."

"You think I don't?"

"Of course not. But it's illegal in Mass. Adults may possess and use marijuana. And he's not an adult."

Duncan nodded, shrugged.

She went on, "It's like finding a fifth of vodka in his room. He shouldn't be drinking booze either. The point is, he's not allowed to use marijuana. First, because he's still got a developing brain and it's not good for him. Second, because we just don't know if it's safe, given his history. And third, I'm a judge, and I—I'm not going to let my son use weed as long as he's living in our house."

"As long as it's not interfering with his schoolwork and he's not getting high during school hours, it doesn't bother me."

"Well, it bothers *me.* And I think it *is* interfering with his schoolwork. Look at his grades. If he's got anxiety, he should . . . I don't know, do a sport. Row. Get back on the crew team." She could feel herself falling back into the old patterns. They'd dealt with it in couples therapy. She sometimes tended to be . . . *judgy.* That was the word Duncan and Jake used. Which was perfectly appropriate for a judge, she thought. Whereas Duncan tended to be hands-off, easygoing, permissive. "How did you leave things with him?"

"I said I had to talk to you."

"Okay," Juliana said. "Because we obviously have a problem."

Duncan carried his wineglass to the bedroom—he'd opened a new bottle and poured himself some more. He appeared to be a little tipsy. He laughed louder than usual. He was telling a story about his dean, a man he took keen pleasure in mocking. She listened, making grunts of agreement, laughing at the right places, not hearing what he was saying, thinking all the while of Matías and his threats, her mind racing. Meanwhile she got undressed, and so did he.

She was lost, thinking about Matías, and must have missed a cue, because he said, standing naked with his arms folded across his chest, "Earth to Jules?"

"Sorry," she said. "Long day."

He came up from behind her and put his arms around her. He kissed the back of her neck, the hollow at the clavicle.

"You know," he said softly, "I was looking at you earlier when we were talking, and I couldn't stop thinking what a beautiful woman you are." She could feel his hot breath tickling her neck. He caressed her shoulders, his hands then moving down slowly along her arms and then brushing, gently but purposefully, against the sides of her breasts. She flushed, tasted something sour coming up from her stomach.

Then she gave him a kiss, quick and brisk. Turning him down, but gently. She thought of the trap she'd walked into and felt sick. "I'm sorry, honey," she said. "I need to get to sleep."

9

Being a judge was a kind of performance art, Juliana had often reflected. Every word you said was being recorded, so you had to be absolutely fair and make sure to sound that way. You had to act and talk with dignity. You had to look and sound engaged.

You wore a costume: a black silk robe—actually 100 percent polyester and made by a company that provided caps and gowns to graduating seniors in high school and college. No one could see what you were wearing underneath the robe. At least she didn't have to wear a white wig, as they still do in France and the UK. When she had first started as a judge, she walked out into the courtroom a number of times without her robe, forgot to put it on. On some level she disdained the formalities. But eventually she decided there was a purpose to the robe. It showed respect for the legal process. That was important.

Above all, you had to live your life with probity. Juliana never broke the speed limit. She never broke the law. And that requirement extended to her family as well. She couldn't have a son arrested for marijuana possession, and at his age he could be arrested. He had to get rid of the pot. Yes, he would resent it, and yes, he'd be oppositional, but tough luck. Judges' kids had to be better behaved than other kids. That was the deal.

You also weren't supposed to let your mind wander during a hearing, but it was happening this morning anyway. She found herself listening to the defense attorney in a medical malpractice case, trying to focus, when she decided there was just no way around it: *I have to recuse myself in the Wheelz case.*

Otherwise, she was trapped. If she stayed on, she had to rule in favor of Wheelz or else that blackmail video would go public. But she couldn't permit herself to be blackmailed. She wasn't going to be anyone's puppet. She couldn't live with herself that way.

Recusal—that was the solution. It was the only way. She had to get out.

Superior Court judges in Massachusetts rotate every six months between criminal and civil cases; they also move to other counties in the state. Her last rotation had been spent way out in Lowell, thirty miles away, working in the run-down Lowell Courthouse, in its Greek-temple magnificence, the great front steps cheaply patched with concrete, the limestone stained with rust from a century of auto exhaust.

Now she was presiding in the historic, only slightly less run-down Suffolk County Courthouse in Boston. Because judges move so often, they have no permanent office. You don't really decorate your office, because you leave it every six months.

Juliana's lobby was sparsely decorated with a few plants that didn't require much sunlight and a framed certificate from the Attorney General of the United States appointing her an Assistant United States Attorney for the District of Massachusetts. On the wall was also a colorful hand-painted sign, a gift from the previous occupant who'd left it there, that read PEACE in large letters and underneath:

It does not mean to be in a place where
there is no noise, trouble, or hard work.

It means to be in the midst of those things
and still be calm in your heart.

On her desk were two computer monitors, a gold Tiffany clock, a jar of hand cream, a phone, a printer, a couple of neat stacks of papers fastened with binder clips, and a collection of brass clips in the shape of miniature hands.

Her father had kept one on his desk, which she used to play with when she was a kid; after he died, she took it for herself, knowing that he would have wanted her to have it. She then went on eBay and found another couple of brass hands, from an antique store in the UK, to keep Dad's hand company.

Her father, George, had been an admired, if unloved, English teacher at a renowned private school for Boston's 1 percent, where she'd gone too. George Brody's students at the Carlyle School in Boston were the offspring of some of the richest people in America. Whereas at home, Juliana and her brother and their parents ate Salisbury steak, purchased on special at the Star Market. With coupons.

She was raised in frugality and still lived that way. Usually she brought lunch from home, a sandwich. Once in a while she'd send her clerk downstairs to grab a chicken Caesar salad or a tuna sandwich from one of the places near the courthouse, or *bánh mì* from the pho truck. She'd eat at her desk while writing an opinion or revising her jury instructions, almost always working through lunch. That was when she was able to get some reading done. There was always plenty to read.

Her lobby was crowded with tall stacks of paper. Every day a packet of motions would come in, and her clerk would line them up for the week. Medical malpractice motions. A motion ordering a hospital to release a guy's medical records. You'd think in the age of the Internet and the cloud that you wouldn't need so much paper, but the piles kept growing.

Today, instead of lunch, she took the elevator up to the thirteenth floor of the courthouse building. Up here it was hushed and still. There was a floral arrangement on the marble table at the center of the elevator lobby, a pretty spray of lilies and roses. This floor wasn't open to the public. The Superior Court's administrative offices were up here, including the office of the chief justice, a woman she knew only slightly.

But the chief wasn't in her office, so Juliana moved on to plan B and stopped by the office of the deputy court administrator, a few doors down the corridor. If she couldn't talk with the chief, she could sound out her administrator.

"Justice Brody," Sam Giannopoulos said, looking up from his crowded desk. He was a small, gaunt bald man with heavy tortoiseshell glasses, around sixty. "What brings you up here?" Giannopoulos's shoulders were stooped. He was an affable introvert, always pleasant to deal with, probably something of a clock-puncher. He was there to serve out his time until retirement.

"A scheduling thing. I have a question about the calendar." She sat down in the chair next to his desk.

He gave a nervous smile. In front of him was a half-eaten sandwich, which he was slowly pushing away.

"Okay. What's the question?"

"I'm considering recusing myself from *Wheelz*. And I'm wondering if it's going to be a problem to assign it to another judge."

She expected little more than a shrug. Judges recused themselves fairly often. Another judge would be assigned. It happened.

Instead, Giannopoulos looked wary and tense. His brows furrowed, and his mouth jutted open. "But is—is there a problem? Something I should know about?"

She was surprised at his response. Giannopoulos took care of the court's calendar, but he didn't normally get involved in judges' decisions on whether to step away from a case.

"A possible conflict with a member of the defense team." She didn't want to say much more than that, and she'd already told him more than she was required to.

But others would ask, other judges on the circuit. And what could she tell them? That she'd once had a drink with one of the lawyers on the case? How could she possibly justify her decision if she was pressed for details? It was something she'd have to figure out after she recused herself.

She was surprised by his reply. "Everyone else has crowded schedules," Giannopoulos said, taking off his glasses and polishing them with his tie. "This wouldn't be easy for another judge to take over after—how many months?"

"Two or three."

"Three months. Wow. That's a lot of water under the bridge. I'm not— I'm not so sure it's a good idea. You should think seriously about this."

"Which is exactly what I've done." Something about his response seemed a little off. He was normally so deferential, so accommodating.

Giannopoulos seemed to study his desktop for a moment. "For a number of reasons, I think it would be better if you made no changes to your schedule."

"I understand that," she said. "But there are also strong reasons to recuse." She said it as much for herself as for Giannopoulos's benefit. She didn't *have* to give a reason if she decided to withdraw from a case and pass it on to another judge. She could just do it.

A long silence passed.

Finally Giannopoulos spoke again, his voice hardening. "I think you'd be well advised to see this through," he said. He quickly looked away, glancing down at his keyboard.

Juliana felt ice freeze in her abdomen.

See it through.

Those were the words Matías had used.

"What's that supposed to mean?"

Giannopoulos wouldn't meet her eyes. He got up and closed his office door. Then he returned to his desk, his face now chalk-white. He folded his hands, interlacing the fingers. He cleared his throat nervously. "Just—just see it through. It's better this way."

"Sam, what's wrong—what happened to you?"

He shook his head slowly. His phone rang, and he lunged for it, seemingly grateful for the interruption. "Will you please excuse me, Judge?"

10

In the elevator down to the ninth floor, she could feel her heart thudding in her ears. She was still numb from her encounter with Sam Giannopoulos. Her blood tingled.

The man had spoken to her in a way he never had before. He was a member of the court administration; he had no right to tell her what to do. He wasn't her boss. But now he seemed to be warning her: *Just see it through. It's better this way.*

She felt queasy, her stomach tight.

Sam was frightened himself; that was clear. They'd gotten to him. They'd threatened him somehow.

Whoever *they* were.

Shakily, she returned to her lobby, and keyed open the door. Kaitlyn, her law clerk, had picked up lunch from the Middle Eastern place on Cambridge Street. Juliana was touched: she hadn't asked for it. Kaitlyn was thoughtful that way.

She glanced at her watch. Twenty minutes till the afternoon session started. She wasn't hungry but knew she had to eat. She unwrapped the salad and forked some chicken into her mouth, chewing pensively. She barely tasted the food.

She gave up trying to concentrate on the document that was on her monitor, her mind flitting from the videotape she'd seen at the Bostonia Club to Sam Giannopoulos's blanched face.

Her life was on the verge of being ruined. One wrong move, one mistake, and it was over. She was petrified and couldn't think clearly.

Suddenly her cell phone rang. Not many people had that number. Duncan, Jake, a few other people. The caller ID read PRIVATE CALLER. Apprehensively, she picked it up.

"Listen to the man," the caller said.

"Who is—"

"You are not to recuse yourself. That would be a serious mistake. Do it, and the video goes public, and thousands, maybe millions will watch it. Your life as you know it will be over."

She heard the accent and was pretty sure it was Matías.

"Who is this?" she said, but the line had gone dead.

A knock on the door. "Judge?"

She looked up. Kaitlyn.

"You okay?"

Juliana didn't reply.

"You're late for oral arguments," Kaitlyn said. "Do you need me to postpone?"

11

When she arrived home that evening, thumbing her temples, trying to massage away the headache, Duncan was in the kitchen, making a spaghetti sauce, which was bubbling away in a big pot. The house smelled great: sautéed onion and garlic and olive oil and tomato. He was washing a frying pan.

"Hey, hon," he called. "I'm making Mom's Bolognese."

"Smells great," she managed. Actually, it did smell wonderful.

"I'll do that," she said, reaching for the skillet. "You cooked."

"It's okay," he said. "I've got it. So how was your day?"

Juliana looked away, pretended she hadn't heard the question. She could hardly level with him, couldn't exactly tell him about the meeting with Sam Giannopoulos, the threatening phone call she'd gotten on her cell. "Where's Jakie?" she asked.

"Where else?" He shrugged. "His room. You okay? You look—I don't know, tired."

"Just a headache."

"Take any Advil or something?"

She shook her head. "I didn't have any."

He put the pan in the drying rack, then opened a cabinet and pulled out a little bottle of pain pills. He opened it and handed it to her.

She took it gratefully, smiled thanks.

See it through.

She could see Sam Giannopoulos's chalk-white face, tight with fear. *I think it would be better if you made no changes to your schedule.* Then that unsettling call from Matías. *Your life as you know it will be over.*

"Are you okay enough to talk to him tonight, or do you want to put it off till tomorrow?"

She closed her eyes, took a deep breath. "No, let's do it tonight." She wanted to take control of *something* in her life, at least. But she was finding it hard to concentrate, to think about anything other than the video and its awful consequences. She felt it like a physical weight, like she was wearing a backpack full of bricks. It slowed her down and hollowed her out.

In a strange way, she was actually looking forward to talking with Jake, even about something as thorny as this. This was her family life, her home life. It was real life. Not that nightmarish other life.

"So shall we go up?"

"Sure. But—wait, though. First let's make sure we're on the same page, okay?" she said.

He crossed his arms. "Honey, I'm not sure we are."

"Let's set aside the law for a moment. Illegal or not, if smoking pot is causing him problems, I think we both agree we have to intervene."

"Sure. But he said it's not. He does it to calm himself down. Takes the edge off."

She groaned.

"Careful about the Judge Judy thing," he said.

"I know." She laughed hollowly. It was an old gibe, sort of an inside joke between them, which normally she didn't really mind. When she got too *judgy*, when she became like the famous TV judge who could be so outrageous and provocative and comically stern—all he had to do was say *Judge Judy.* Right away she'd get it, she'd back off some, modulate her tone.

The truth was, *Judge Judy* was annoying and completely unrealistic. She hated that schtick, all those courtroom zingers, the way she abused witnesses. "You're an idiot!" Though occasionally Juliana *wished* she could mouth off that way.

She took his hand. "I promise I'll do my best."

"All I ask."

They trudged up the stairs, side by side, and stood outside Jake's bedroom. All the way out here she could hear the percussive notes from his headphones. Duncan thudded his fist on the door. No answer. He thumped again, yelled, "Jake?" and then opened the door.

Jacob whirled around in his chair, took off his bulky headphones. He looked at his father and then his mother. A wary look appeared in his eyes. "What's wrong?"

"We need to talk about the vaping," Juliana said as they both entered.

"You told her," Jake said angrily. "Thanks a lot, Dad."

"I told you I would," said Duncan.

"We're concerned," Juliana said. She sat on the edge of his bed, and then Duncan sat next to her. She crossed her legs. "Who are you getting high with?"

Jake looked around helplessly, glanced at his father, who nodded. Then he said: "Tyler and Ryan, mostly. Sometimes other guys."

Duncan said, "Do you get high by yourself?"

Jake hesitated. He had his father's dark Italian looks, the brown eyes and brown hair, but with a light sprinkling of acne across his nose and cheeks. His face began to redden. "Hardly ever. Why?"

"*Hardly* ever?" Juliana said.

"You did it once as an experiment, right?" said Duncan.

"Just that one time," said Jake.

"Dunc, let Jake tell me. How do you get your hands on it?"

"I mean . . . There's a kid at school. I think his parents buy it for him.

It's totally legal, by the way. This is so not a big deal, Mom. What's with all the drama?"

She ignored his attempt to make this about her. "When did you first start using it?" she asked.

Jake sighed, turned away. "I don't know, maybe a couple of months?"

"Why?"

"Wh—why did I start?"

She tilted her head to the side. "Why do you use it?"

"I don't know." Another sigh. "I like it, that's all. It relaxes me. It takes the edge off."

Takes the edge off. Duncan's exact phrase.

Jake's open laptop reminded her suddenly of Matías and the video. Her memory was flooded with images, like screenshots. Of Matías's hand on the small of her back. Of him walking into her courtroom. Sam Giannopoulos's pale, scared face. She tried to push it all away.

After a moment, she said, "Do you get why we're concerned?"

"Sure I get it. You're worried about your career, 'cause you're a judge."

"Come on, Jake," Duncan said. "That's totally not true."

It was partially true, though. She wouldn't deny it. But only partially.

"This is not a big deal," Jake said. "Like, eighty percent of my friends get high. Some of them get high with their parents."

Juliana's eyes widened. "What?"

"You heard me. With their parents."

"Look," she said, "we don't know if it's even safe for you, given . . . your medical history."

"I'm fine!" Jake said.

"Right, but . . ." She drifted off. He hated to talk about the Hodgkin's. He resented the way she so often asked how he was feeling, how overly solicitous she was. He wanted to be treated like a normal kid.

"Here's the thing, Jakie," she said. "Marijuana is a colossal ambition-buster. I want you to do well in school, because you're smart. You have a bright future if you keep your grades up."

But Jake wasn't hearing it. "Sometimes if I vape a couple of puffs it makes me feel smarter and more creative." He laughed. "Last week I got an A on an English essay, and I was totally high when I wrote it."

"Great," she said sourly, not laughing.

"Jake, listen," said Duncan. "We don't want you getting high alone. That would worry us. If you're going to use it, use it with your friends and don't do anything stupid."

"I don't do stupid stuff," Jake said. "Dad, you know that."

"I saw a serious medical study, an Israeli study," Juliana said. "Cannabis has been found to cause schizophrenia in teenagers, it said."

"Oh, please," Jake said.

Duncan had stopped nodding. He was watching. Not objecting, but not really joining the fight.

She felt a flash of annoyance. The old division of labor in the family: she played the heavy, while Dunc got to be Cool Dad.

Maybe she was just more worried about their son than Duncan was. She worried about how he'd fare in a world where a million kids his age in metropolises on the other side of the planet were being drilled to succeed as Western-style meritocrats. She didn't care about four-point-ohs, he didn't have to go to an Ivy League school; she just wanted him to have the best possible chance of making the life he wanted to make, whatever that was. Not to have to settle. She'd read a statistic she couldn't shake: for the first time in American history, kids had just a fifty-fifty chance of doing better, financially, than their parents.

Whereas Duncan considered the world a giant trampoline. You're falling? Well, you'll bounce back, and it'll make for a great story. When Juliana thought about trampolines, she thought about broken necks and traumatic brain injuries, because those things happen too. You can land on the hard metal frame or on the ground. And sometimes you don't get up.

"Don't worry about Jake," Duncan said later, when they were in their room, preparing for bed. "He'll be okay."

"But he's so apathetic," she said. "He just doesn't care about anything. And it's got to be the weed."

"I don't think so."

"Then what is it? He doesn't like school; he never talks about soccer anymore. I mean, if only he had a passion for something. But from what I can tell, he's interested in nothing."

"Are you afraid Jake's going to get into some kind of trouble that might spill over onto you?"

"That's the last thing I worry about." *If you only knew . . .*

"Sweetie, you've always been the good girl. The rules girl. You always keep your nose clean."

The huge irony of that loomed before her like a shipwreck: Matías and that night in Chicago, the one time she had thrown away caution.

"Remember when Rosa got sick, and Keith and Judy offered us Sofia?"

Their nanny, Rosa, had once been briefly hospitalized with pneumonia, which caught them shorthanded. Juliana had court and couldn't miss it, and Duncan had classes to teach and faculty meetings to attend. Their next-door neighbors had offered their wonderful Filipina housekeeper to babysit for them, and at first it looked like a lifesaver. Until Juliana had discovered that Sofia's papers weren't exactly in order. She was not going to hire an undocumented nanny, even for a couple of weeks. Nanny problems had kept two women from becoming Attorney General of the United States a few years back. It could keep you off the Supreme Court. Why borrow trouble?

"You know I couldn't hire an undocumented worker."

"And my home office deduction on our taxes? You said ixnay to that."

"That's just a red flag."

"Sometimes I think you live your life like there's a constant goddamned Senate confirmation hearing going on."

She looked away. The truth was, there was a spotlight on her. And if she ever wanted to move up in the judicial world—even though she tried not to think too much about that stuff—she had to stay clean. That was just the reality of it. At confirmation hearings, they went after you with all kinds of ammo.

Meanwhile, Duncan was a tenured professor. He lived in the academic equivalent of a gated community: nothing could touch him. His rebellious streak didn't cost him anything. But things might be different for Jake. Maybe his dad's high-wire rhetoric about smashing the system just gave Jake a rationale for screwing up.

Duncan could coast, and Juliana was pretty sure he'd already begun coasting. Whereas she had further to go.

And more to lose.

12

She lay in bed in the dark next to Duncan for a long while that night. She'd waited for his breathing to even out and wondered if she was keeping him awake with her periodic sighs, the way she was flopping around in the bed, trying to get the sheets around her just right. He'd buried his head in his pillow, bracketed by his bent arm.

They hadn't made love in a while now, partly because she felt guilty about Chicago. They'd usually read in bed, kiss each other goodnight, flick off the light. Or Duncan would come in late from working in his home office, after she'd fallen asleep. She was still attracted to him—in some ways more than when they first met—and she wondered if he still felt the same way about her. She worried that maybe he didn't—and what happened three years ago didn't exactly reassure her.

She tried to blank out her mind, to blot out all vexing thoughts, to turn her mind into a large white screen that would allow her to slip off to sleep. Instead, she thought about Jake and his marijuana vape pen and how negative she'd been toward him and even toward Duncan. She didn't want to be that kind of parent, constantly harping on the criticisms.

And she thought about that night with Matías, which now seemed so long ago, and she felt ill. She'd stepped right into their trap without thinking. She had jeopardized her career, was on the verge of destroying her family.

She was frozen in place. If she didn't rule in favor of Wheelz on their protective-order motion by Monday, the world would see her having sex with a man who was not her husband. An item about her would appear in one of those judicial gossip sites, like UnderneathTheirRobes.com. Then it would spread from there. She didn't know how, but it would. That was how things worked these days.

Yet if she did rule in their favor because of the blackmail, she'd be betraying everything she believed in.

And what would happen once she did rule in favor of Wheelz? Would there be more orders? Maybe this was just the beginning of a long series of extortionate demands. She was a prisoner, all because of one awful mistake. She hadn't been able to resist Matías, and not just because of his looks, his handsomeness, and his lithe body. The way he'd talked with her, his apparent sensitivity, which had turned out to be well-rehearsed psychological tricks. And she'd fallen for them.

And what if she recused? Her mind reeled at the thought of what would happen. She didn't think her marriage would survive it. And obviously her career as a judge would be over. She'd have to resign from the bench. She'd be unhireable. Everything she had worked all her life for, at work and at home, would vanish in an instant. That federal judgeship? A soap bubble.

She couldn't imagine what she would say to Duncan, whom she loved so much. How it would slice into him. How devastated Ashley would be when she found out. And what it would do to her already fraught relationship with Jacob.

How she'd ruined everything.

It was funny, almost: she desperately wanted to talk to Duncan about what happened, to get his advice on what to do. But of course she couldn't. He could never know what she'd done.

She looked at her watch, noted the date. Her friend Martha Connolly, who'd been out of town for a few days visiting relatives, was back by now.

Martha Connolly had recently retired as the chief justice of the state's highest court, the Supreme Judicial Court. Now she was of counsel to a big Boston law firm and extremely well connected. Martie had been an important mentor to her. If anyone would know what to do, it was Martie.

13

Late afternoon the next day, Juliana was sitting in the Bristol Bar in the Four Seasons, at a table that overlooked the greenery of the Public Garden.

Martha Connolly wore a beautiful Chanel suit, navy blue with white piping, and a necklace of black pearls. She was in her early seventies, a handsome woman with a halo of white hair and clear blue eyes that could turn serious and judgmental without warning. Martha had authored a number of important and controversial Supreme Judicial Court opinions and was regarded, in the legal community, as something of a demigod.

She also had a salty tongue and a bawdy sense of humor. She was even known to smoke cigars, on occasion. And she was responsible, more than anyone, for Juliana's being a judge. It was Martie who kept urging her to think about it. She'd guided her through the whole arcane process, from the seventy-page application to the appearance before the Governor's Council. That had been intense, the Governor's Council thing. She'd been interviewed by twenty-one influential people, at some downtown law firm, where they threw all kinds of questions at her, trying to get a sense of her judgment, her temperament. The ridiculous application asked you to list every trial you'd done for the last twenty years, and to name every single defense lawyer you ever worked with, or against.

And it was Martie who had pulled the strings to make it happen, urging Governor Wickham to appoint Juliana to the Superior Court. Her advice was good and plentiful. Martha was childless and seemed to consider Juliana her substitute daughter. She could be as intrusive as a Hollywood parent, which Juliana sometimes found annoying, but she did her best to suppress her annoyance. Martha was a hero to her.

Juliana started the conversation by saying, "I'm seeking legal advice."

Martha understood at once, of course: what Juliana was about to say was between them only and was protected by attorney-client privilege. Her eyes twinkled agreement. "Got a dollar?"

"Sure."

"Fork it over. Otherwise a single peppercorn will suffice."

Juliana took a single dollar bill out of her purse and handed it ceremoniously to Martha. Then she told her story, leaving nothing out. She had always thought of Martha as unshockable. She'd seen it all. But now she was registering astonishment.

"It was definitely you on the tape?"

Juliana nodded.

"Dear God." She took a swallow of her Knob Creek.

Juliana exhaled, nodded again.

"Honey. And you're always the good girl. Aren't you full of surprises."

For just one night, I did what I never do. Juliana, who did everything right; Juliana, the obeyer of rules, had gone and done one single incautious, impetuous thing. And it was just like she'd always feared it would be: everything she worked so hard for had been overturned.

"It's a serious problem," she said.

"Oh, it's worse than that, Jules." A waiter came by, but Martha dismissed him with a quick smile and a head shake.

Juliana groaned. "I think the simplest thing to do would be to resign from the bench. Face the consequences—the tape, the public humiliation, everything that follows. Face Duncan and beg for his forgiveness. Maybe he'll understand."

"He sure as hell should. After what happened with that law student."

Juliana had forgotten that she'd told Martha.

"That was a long time ago. And we've moved past it," Juliana said, though she wondered if that was the truth or a mantra she simply told herself.

"I'm just saying, sauce for the gander."

"It's not . . . It's not like that."

"Listen, it's not just that a woman has to work twice as hard and be twice as smart; she also has to be twice as clean. Don't forget, it was Caesar's wife, not Caesar, who had to walk the straight and narrow. Caesar, he could do whatever the hell he wanted."

Juliana closed her eyes for a moment. She wanted to teleport herself out of there. To make it all go away somehow.

"Men are allowed to screw up," Martha continued. "Women are not. This is the God's honest truth. The guy who sleeps around is sowing his wild oats. A woman does the same, she's a pathetic slut. What did George W. Bush say? 'When I was young and irresponsible, I was young and irresponsible.' Imagine Hillary Clinton trying that line." She sipped some more bourbon. "You're Teddy Kennedy, you can survive Chappaquiddick. You're Joe Biden, and a couple of plagiarism episodes fade from memory like they never happened. And you wanna talk about Bill Clinton?"

Juliana put a hand over her eyes, nodded. "I know."

"But if you're a woman and you don't walk the path of the straight and narrow? You're a punch line, and then you're history. Was the tinsel of Camelot tarnished by the revelation that JFK had an assembly line of mistresses? No, it was *burnished*. Honey, the passage of time treats men and women differently in all sorts of ways. When men make mistakes, the mistakes are forgotten. When a woman makes a mistake, the *woman* is forgotten."

Juliana shook her head. "It's not like that anymore," she said. "All the 'Me Too' stuff, all those powerful men dethroned . . ."

"Tip of the iceberg," Martie said. "A few high-profile sacrifices to the media gods. Then attention shifts and everyone moves on. You think we all hit Reset and men have actually reformed? Everyone keeps different ledgers for men and women."

"Maybe. But how exactly does this help me?"

"Do you want me to lay out your options for you?"

"Yes."

"You recuse yourself, and your career is torpedoed right out of the water."

"And my marriage—"

"Only you would know that."

"It's possible we'd survive this."

"Okay. Or you don't recuse yourself, you stick with it, but you don't rule the way they want. They release the tape, and your career is torpedoed, and your marriage is damaged, maybe irreparably."

"Or I go the third way, and I do what they say. I become a marionette. It's a breach of my judicial responsibility. But then at least Duncan and I aren't arguing over child custody."

"Child custody? Honey, you could be *taken* into custody. As in, jail time. If anyone can demonstrate that your judgments were suborned, that's a major felony conviction."

"What the hell can I do, Martie? I'm screwed any way I go."

Martha was silent a long time. Juliana could hear the clink of silverware against china, the tinkle of ice in water glasses, the murmur of people around them. Then Martha reached over for her purse, lifted it onto the table, took out her wallet, and began going through it. Finally she seemed to have found what she was looking for. She took it out and held it up. A small white business card, its edges frayed and soiled. "There's one other way," she said, handing Juliana the card.

Juliana took it and glanced at it. It read PHILIP HERSH, PRIVATE INVESTIGATOR, and listed an address in the Park Colonnade Building in downtown Boston and a phone number.

"A private investigator?" she asked. "And you trust him?"

"With my life. Because I have . . . Trusted him with my life."

There was a long silence. Neither woman spoke for a while. Finally Juliana said, "Do you want to talk about it?"

"No," said Martha. "I don't. It was a long time ago."

Juliana nodded. It felt like she was on the verge of something life-changing, something permanent and irreversible. She put the card face-down on the table, touched it with her fingertips, feeling the cardboard as if it were warm and alive. She drummed her fingers on it for a few beats.

"What do you think he can do for me?"

"You are being extorted," Martha said. "Blackmailed. You have to fight fire with fire."

"That's not who I am."

Martha sighed. "Do you know how hard people have worked to help you get where you are?"

They both knew Martha was referring to herself. "I know," Juliana said, "and I'm incredibly grateful."

"You have so much at stake. You're being mentioned in the right circles now. Governor Wickham is behind you. You're being talked about for other judgeships. And maybe one day not too far in the future—who knows. The high court. You have a bright future ahead of you. And you need to play this right. We need to make this *go away*."

"And how can this PI make it go away?"

"I can't tell you that. Maybe by turning the tables on this—what's his name?"

"Matías."

"Right. Track him down. Find out who he's working for. If you're trying to outplay a blackmailer, you need to get the goods on him."

She nodded.

"Honey, everyone has a little smudge on them," Martha said. "Why do you think our robes are black? So they don't show the dirt."

14

The Park Colonnade Building had been built in the 1920s and still had a vague sort of Roaring Twenties feel to it, all the swooping gold paint on the ceiling, the high-gloss tile floor, the gold letter boxes. Juliana half-expected flappers with feathered headdresses to be thronging the lobby and a newsboy in a flat cap shouting, "Read all about it!" On the third floor, down a long, gloomy corridor, she found Hersh Investigations, gold-leaf letters on a frosted-glass panel inset in a heavy oak door. It looked period-appropriate. Ironic. Like a film noir prop. She knocked on the door, then went to turn the knob. It was locked. In a few seconds a shape loomed behind the glass panel and then the knob turned and the door opened.

The man she assumed was Philip Hersh wore horn-rimmed eyeglasses and was balding, with a short gray fringe above his ears. He looked like a shrink from the days of the old *Bob Newhart Show.* Or a 1970s talk show host. Despite the heat, he was wearing a corduroy jacket over a mock turtleneck.

Her second impression was that he was a very unhappy man. You could see it in his eyes, in the lines in his face.

"Judge," he said. "Come on in."

It was a tiny one-room office, not much more than a closet, with a crowded desk in one corner. *Not promising*, she thought. Certificates and plaques in black frames adorned one wall in a haphazard arrangement; the other walls were lined with bookcases filled with criminal law volumes and law dictionaries and journals.

In front of the desk was one ladder-back chair piled high with magazines. The visitor's chair. He hoisted the magazines away and said gently, "Please, have a seat." He sat behind the desk and moved aside a stack of books so he had a direct line of sight to her. "Tell me how I can help you."

"I'm being blackmailed," she began.

Hersh asked dozens of questions about that night in Chicago, things she was embarrassed to talk about, especially with a total stranger. She was surprised at the range, the granularity of her recall. No, he had no tattoos that she saw. No, she was sure she hadn't seen him before that evening in the rooftop bar. Yes, she would have noticed him; he was an attractive man. Not in the lobby, not in an elevator; no, she'd not seen him before.

"Do you know whether he is in fact a lawyer or not?"

She shook her head. "Not for a fact, no."

"Did you ask to see his credentials when he introduced himself in court?"

"Of course not. That's not my job."

"Do you think he lives in Boston?"

"The lead defense attorney said he's in the Chicago office of his law firm. So I assume he lives in the Chicago area. Do you think Matías Sanchez is his real name?"

"We'll see. It's pretty simple to figure out if Matías Sanchez is admitted in Massachusetts. Just look in the Red Book. Won't take long at all. When will you see him again?"

"I'm not sure."

"When he threatened you, did he give you a deadline?"

"A ruling in their favor once I receive and review all of the Slack chats the defense wants withheld." She shifted in her seat. "What can we do to neutralize his blackmail?"

"We find out who he is and who he works for. That's where we start. Then, if we're very lucky, I catch him in the act of blackmailing you."

"Is that possible?"

"No guarantees. I'll do what I can. How did you get assigned this case? Did you choose it?"

"It was randomly assigned to me."

He smirked. "Randomly," he said. "I wonder. Are you being followed?"

"Followed? How would I know?"

"You might not." He was quiet for a long while. Then he said, "Well, you might start to notice the same person in different locations. Or cars that seem to be lurking in your neighborhood."

"If they're any good, I suspect I wouldn't see any trace of them, right?"

"Unless they want you to know they're there."

"Huh."

"Can you summon Matías and the other lawyers in on some pretext?"

"I suppose I could. But why?"

"The more you interact with Matías, the better, from my standpoint. The more opportunities for me to follow him, trace him."

"What happens when you do? If you do?"

"Then we'll have some decisions to make."

"All right. Let me ask you something, just putting it right out there. Do you think they'll release the tape, make it public? Could that really happen?"

He shrugged, scowled. "Look, you take every precaution to prevent disaster. Knowing you may fail."

"Dark," she said.

"But what do I know?" he said with a hollow laugh.

15

Saturday night was the big St. Jude's fundraiser, which everyone in the Boston political world attended, a black-tie benefit at the Copley Plaza Hotel. Duncan didn't do black tie; he wore his black suit with a black necktie—he wore the same thing to funerals—and considered that a major concession to the powers that be. Because he'd gained a little weight in the last couple of years, he wasn't able to button the suit jacket.

Neither Juliana nor Duncan especially liked black-tie affairs, but Duncan particularly disliked them. She wondered if it was because most of the time, they were invited because she was Judge Brody, and maybe he didn't enjoy being Mr. Judge Brody instead of Duncan Esposito. But he'd never admit it.

And who could blame him for feeling that way? In his world, at the law school, he was the great Professor Esposito. Funky Dunc. The editor of a widely used anthology on critical legal studies. He had groupies.

She remembered one in particular.

Three years ago he started leaving carbs on his plate, working out regularly, paring his mini-paunch. He took the stairs two at a time. He started wearing cologne. He was looking especially good, and she told him so.

Then one day his phone made a text-message alert sound when he was out of the room, having left his phone on the hall table next to hers. She wasn't sure whose phone had just pinged. She picked up her own, saw nothing, picked up Duncan's, and saw a message from a "Jenna" that contained an emoticon of a blushing smiley face.

She called Duncan's name and handed him his phone. Her facial expression told him she'd seen something.

He noticed and glanced at his phone, and his face went red.

"Is there something you wanted to talk to me about?" she asked.

To Duncan's credit, he said, "Yeah."

His voice sounded faraway. She became hyperaware of her surroundings, of the dust motes floating in the sunbeam that transected the hallway, the ticking of the house settling, the distant throaty snarl of a snowblower. She thought, *This moment is the divider between before and after.*

"Look," he said, "I guess this girl has a crush on me. One of those 'hot for teacher' things, God help us. I mean, what am I supposed to do? I can't kick her out of class." He sounded casual yet at the same time slightly . . . *rehearsed.*

And there was something evasive about the way he was acting. He folded his legs in a way he rarely did, and he kept avoiding her eyes.

So that was his story—a law student named Jenna had fallen in love with him, and there was nothing to be done about it.

Part of her wanted to be content with that. Because she knew that sometimes foraging around for the marital truth was sort of like thrusting your hand down a jammed garbage disposal to retrieve a paring knife. Maybe you grasp it by the handle. Maybe by the blade. And maybe the damned thing starts grinding again.

But she couldn't leave it alone.

She ferreted out the girl's name, went through her Facebook and Instagram feeds. She asked Duncan to show her the text-message thread before the one with the blushing-smiley-face emoticon. She knew that couldn't have been the first time they'd exchanged texts.

He took out his phone and found the one from Jenna and handed the phone to her. She looked, saw that there were no texts before blushing smiley face, and she suddenly felt cold. He'd deleted all the earlier ones.

Which meant that he had a reason to do so.

A few days later she brought it up again. He admitted that maybe he hadn't totally discouraged Jenna.

"So what are we talking?" she said. "Anthony Weiner–style crotch shots?"

"No, *God* no, nothing like that."

"Just friendly flirtation, then?"

He closed his eyes momentarily, looked down for a long time, then looked up. "I'm so sorry. But *nothing happened*. That's the truth. *Nothing happened*."

Nothing happened.

Maybe.

Yet she knew that Duncan had been transforming himself for a reason. He was thinking about this girl, about the possibility of an affair, all the time. *Nothing happened.* That was one truth. Another was: *everything happened.*

Soon the conversation turned to trust. Duncan said, "If you can't trust me, our marriage has problems a lot more serious than a student with a crush on me. I'm telling you that nothing happened, and that's the goddamned truth, and if you think I'm lying to your face right now, I'd like to know. Because I'd like to know how things really are between us."

He was aiming the big guns at her now, and she backed down. "Okay," she said.

He came close and stroked her hair. He was close enough that his beard tickled her face. "You know I love you, right?" he said. "You know you're the most important thing in my life, right?"

"I know," she said, because she didn't know what else to say.

That had been three years ago.

At the gala, Juliana knew she looked good. She was wearing her Michael Kors suit. She'd just gotten a manicure. She wore her hair up in a chignon. She and Duncan entered the ballroom arm in arm, and she searched the crowd for a familiar face.

There were plenty of familiar faces. The owner of the New England Patriots was talking to the CEO of Fidelity Investments. The CEO of Liberty Mutual Insurance was picking shrimp from a large ice sculpture. A guy she'd worked with years ago at the US Attorney's office was chatting up someone she didn't recognize. At a distance she spied Martha Connolly, talking with the governor.

She found herself next to Noah Miller, a senior partner at a big Boston law firm she knew only casually. A real power lawyer. Miller was a portly, rumpled man in his mid-fifties with curly black hair ringing a large bald spot and penetrating brown eyes behind rimless glasses. He was holding a rocks glass of bourbon, most of it gone.

"How's it going, Noah?"

"Can't complain, and no one listens anyway. So what's on your docket these days?"

She sighed theatrically. "About a thousand cases."

"I heard you have a sex-harassment suit against the CEO of that start-up Wheelz."

"Yup."

"You haven't granted summary judgment already?" A standard motion, made regularly but seldom granted. She had the power, theoretically, to dismiss the case. Shut it down. Wheelz's lawyers had filed a motion asking for summary judgment at the start, and she'd denied it quickly. Rachel Meyers had a real case and had the right to a trial.

"Nope," she said.

"Huh." Like he found that puzzling.

She gave him a sharp look. How much did he know about this? Had he been following the case for some reason? "Well, we'll see where it goes."

"Because, you know, it's a Porta-Potty. Nobody comes out smelling good."

She nodded, alert. Why did he care?

"How's Chandra?" she asked, changing the subject.

"Chandra's spending the week at Canyon Ranch. Something about a purge?"

"You sure you don't mean a cleanse?"

"Either way, you want to get that steaming pile of whatever off your docket ASAP. Purge it. Or cleanse it. Colonically irrigate it. You'll feel so much better." He grinned. "Just my avuncular two cents, huh?"

She smiled tightly. "Got it, thanks."

She wondered why Noah Miller was so emphatic about flushing the Wheelz case. Did he have some connection to Wheelz, or to the CEO? Maybe she was just making too much out of nothing.

A guy from the US Attorney's office waved her over and introduced her to the new US Attorney. They chatted for a few minutes, and then a text came in on her phone.

It was from Hersh, and it read, Found him. Meet me in the Dunkin' Donuts on Stuart Street in 15.

She knew where that Dunkin' Donuts was, just a block away from the hotel. She needed to escape from the fundraiser and meet Hersh, find out what he knew about Matías. Which meant temporarily abandoning Duncan.

Someone suddenly grabbed her by the shoulders, startling her. As she spun around, she realized she was facing the governor of Massachusetts, a blandly handsome sixty-year-old man. He was with Martha Connolly, looking elegant and austere in a black satin sheath, and the senior senator of Massachusetts, looking very blow-dried.

"This is the woman I was telling you about," the governor said to the senator. "Not just a brilliant legal mind but no shortage of common sense. Book smart *and* street smart."

Juliana took the senator's hand and introduced herself. She was so distracted, thinking about Matías and what she could possibly do now, that she had to ask him to repeat himself even though she could hear him just fine. She had a hard time concentrating on the conversation.

"In *Commonwealth v. Scofield*," the senator was saying. "Am I right?"

Both Martha and the governor laughed, so Juliana did too, a beat late.

There was a pause, as the governor waited for her to reply. Scrambling for something to say, she said, "Sure."

Another pause, and then the governor, who was apparently a bit disappointed in her performance, gestured at the wineglass in her hand. "I think you've either had one too many of those, or one too few." Everybody laughed uncomfortably, and Juliana joined them. Duncan was looking at her strangely. Normally, Juliana knew her lines; she could charm on cruise control. But tonight she was drying, as stage actors say. The lines weren't coming.

She excused herself a few minutes later, having waited as long as she could bear, and whispered to Duncan that she was going to find the girls' room. She left the ballroom, ran down the carpeted steps as fast as she could in her heels to the lobby, and hurried past the concierge and out onto Dartmouth Street.

The sky was dark, but the streetlights cast the sidewalk and the slick pavement in a sickly greenish tone. She walked down the street, turned left onto Stuart Street, and then a moment later she was startled by a voice right behind her.

"Good evening, Judge."

It was Philip Hersh, but it took her a moment to recognize him. He was wearing a Boston Red Sox warm-up jacket over a Red Sox T-shirt, jeans, and sneakers. No glasses. He was no longer a talk show host from the seventies; now he was, convincingly, a townie.

She breathed out.

"Found him," Hersh said.

16

They sat at a table in Dunkin' Donuts away from the window.

"Where is he?"

"In an extended-stay corporate hotel," Hersh said.

"Where?"

"Allston."

"How'd you find him?"

"Combed databases for social links, credit card use, that sort of thing. I did what I did and it worked, let's put it that way."

"I'm impressed."

"He doesn't seem to leave his hotel room. It's strange."

"But you know he's there?"

He nodded.

"He's a lawyer in Chicago, and he really is from Argentina. Went to St. George's school in Buenos Aires, undergrad at Tufts, law degree from Northwestern. And he has a twin sister in Miami who's hooked on opiates. OxyContin, that sort of thing. About a month ago, she was arrested, charged with forging drug scripts for OxyContin. Which is a felony offense. Would have meant prison time."

"*Would* have . . . ?"

"Right. Here's what's interesting. Two days ago, all charges against the sister were dropped. Without prejudice."

"Without prejudice," she repeated.

"Yes." That meant the charges could be reinstated at any time. "So what does this tell you?"

"That she's on the hook. Maybe he's being coerced. By some powerful forces."

Juliana looked at Hersh for a long moment. His mournful eyes, lines deeply carved around them. Finally she said, "What's his address?"

He gave it to her. "But I don't want you going there—in fact, I strongly advise you not to see him alone."

"Why?"

"The man may be dangerous."

"It sounds to me more like he's desperate."

"Desperate people can be dangerous. That's exactly my point."

Juliana took her phone out of her purse and stood up. "I hope you're wrong."

17

On the way—she hailed a cab in front of the Dunkin' Donuts—she texted Duncan: very sorry, got caught up in a thing. will see you at home.

Duncan didn't immediately text back, which was good, because it probably meant he was in conversation with someone. He wasn't a particularly shy man. As a law professor, he had plenty to talk about with lawyers and judges, but tonight's crowd was heavy on financial types. He would no doubt be pissed off that she'd left him there that way, but she'd deal with that later too.

The cab wound through the downtown streets and through the Back Bay, then a few blocks past Boston University to the Home Stay Inn, an all-suite hotel mainly for businesspeople. It was a four-story brick building, handsome in a sort of bland corporate way, located in a desolate neighborhood near gas stations and auto dealerships. She entered the lobby and took the elevator to the third floor and found room 322. She heard her heart beating loud and fast, felt it hammering in her ears.

There was noise inside the room, she immediately realized. Music. No, not just music, but television—music, an announcer, applause—a show of some sort, muffled but loud behind the door.

She reached up her fist to knock on the door but found a doorbell. She pressed it a few times.

Nothing happened. Just the muffled sounds of the TV.

She was oddly unafraid. She was angry, that was the main thing. What this man had done; how he'd used her, manipulated her.

She could hear his words. *I don't know you, but I feel as if I do.*

And *I saw a sense of a light inside you.*

She asked herself why she was even there.

But she already knew the answer. Knew that she needed to confront this bastard, force the truth out of him. Shame him into telling her what was going on, what he was up to, why he did what he'd done.

She rang the doorbell again, a few times.

A minute went by. The TV went quiet. She heard movement inside the room. Then nothing. She rang again. Finally she pounded. "Open the door."

Nothing.

She pounded harder. "Open the goddamn door!"

She raised her fist to pound again, and the door came open.

For a moment she thought she'd rung the wrong doorbell. An unshaven man in a soiled white T-shirt stood in the shadows. It took her a few seconds to recognize Matías.

He stared at her blankly for a moment; then recognition set in. "Why are you here?" he said.

"You goddamned son of a bitch," she said. The blood jumped in her veins.

"This is a mistake. You shouldn't be here."

"You twisted bastard. I know what you're doing, and it's not going to work."

Matías sighed. "Do what they tell you to do and all will be fine."

She was surprised at the way he looked, so much sloppier and more unkempt than the polished, well-dressed man that night in Chicago. Worn down, it seemed.

She took a deep breath. What was the point in venting at the man? Instead, she could try to get him to talk. Before she became a judge, she was a highly regarded litigator. Before that, an acclaimed prosecutor. She knew how to work a witness. She used to do it for a living.

"We need to talk," she said. "We can either do it out here or in there; it's up to you."

After a beat, he stepped back and held open the door. She entered the generic-looking living room of a one-bedroom suite. Nearly every surface—couch, chair, coffee table—was covered with take-out cartons or soda cans or beer bottles. A large TV was on but muted. There was an odor hanging in the air, a sour fermented smell with a sharp note of perspiration.

This is not normal, she thought. The man was not a slob; he had to be operating under stress. Her phone made a text-alert sound, but she ignored it. She looked at him and could see the tension in his face. Why hadn't she seen it before? This was a vulnerability, and she'd go right at it.

"Okay," she said. "Let me be very clear with you. I'm not going to be manipulated, I don't care what it costs me."

"All they want you to do—"

"I know what 'they' want, and I won't do it. Here's the bad news for you, Matías. I'm willing to sacrifice my marriage, if that's what it takes. But I'm not going to be blackmailed."

"You are in so far over your head," he said. "You have no idea." He didn't say it in a threatening way. He sounded defeated.

"And you," she said. "What do you think happens to your sister now?"

He winced visibly.

"Yes," she said, "I know about Bianca."

He shook his head slowly. Now she realized something else: the man was frightened. His eyes widened. "What do you know about her?" he demanded. "*How?*"

Her phone made another text sound, and she ignored it again. "I have my judicial sources. I know the Miami authorities dropped charges without prejudice, meaning that they can charge her again at any time."

"These people—please, just do what they say. You have no idea what they're capable of. These people will do anything—stage an accident, a suicide, whatever they need to do if they think you're an inconvenience."

"And who *are* they? Wheelz? Are they working for Devin Allerdyce?"

Matías laughed mirthlessly. "Devin Allerdyce knows nothing."

"Then who?"

"I have no idea. They have people inside the Justice Department in Washington. They have people all over. It's so much bigger than one corporation."

"And they got their hooks into you through your sister?"

He nodded sadly.

"The opiates. I'm sorry to hear that."

"Our father was killed in the Dirty War, and she has never gotten over his murder."

"You're from Argentina."

He nodded. "I went to law school in Chicago, and my sister went into a master's degree program to become a physician's assistant. In Miami. She worked at a spine clinic, and she started to have problems. She started to forge prescriptions to get OxyContin and that sort of thing. A couple of months ago she was arrested by Miami police. She was charged with obtaining a controlled substance by fraud, which is a felony offense. Meaning prison time. So I flew to Miami—I'm all she's got—to be her lawyer, help her through the process. And that's when they contacted me. They made me an offer."

He hesitated. In the long silence she said, "Yes?"

"They would drop the charges against her if I did as they instructed."

"How were you contacted?"

"A phone call."

"And who was it?"

He shrugged. "I wasn't given a name. He knew who I was, where I was. He knew all about Bianca's legal situation."

"What did they promise, exactly?"

"That all charges would be dropped. Just that."

"And if you didn't do . . . *as instructed* . . . ?"

"She'd be prosecuted to the fullest extent of the law."

"So you—what? You forced yourself to seduce the old bag?"

"Oh, please. You're an attractive woman. You know that perfectly well. That's not the point."

Her face turned hot. "Why is my ruling so important? What's the evidence they're trying to conceal?"

"I don't know. I don't know anything. I just keep my head down and do what I'm told, and my sister remains free."

"I'm sorry I can't help you. But I'm not going to be controlled. I have no idea how I'm going to rule," she said.

"You don't have a *choice*! They're going to release that video. Listen to me. You and I, we're just . . . chess pieces. We're being played. Fighting them is pointless."

She looked at him for a long moment. "Well, they picked on the wrong woman," she said. "I will not be played."

18

Outside the hotel, she looked at her phone and saw a series of texts that had come in from Duncan.

8:47: Where'd you go?

9:16: Hello?

9:23: Where r u?

9:36: going home.

At 9:36 a call had come in on her phone, no voice message left.

He'd looked around for her, texted and texted, and finally had given up. He was probably furious and justifiably so.

And what could she possibly tell Duncan by way of explanation? She couldn't tell him the truth, of course. She scrabbled around for something to say, came up with a story about a college friend she'd run into who was in a very bad way. Yes, she should have checked the text messages as they came in, but she didn't, she couldn't tear herself away from a very difficult conversation. She mentally rehearsed this lie, this one lie atop a pile of lies, and she felt terrible about it.

But what else could she do?

At 10:30, her cab pulled up to her house. Some lights were on, on both the first and second floors. Presumably Jake was awake, but she wondered about Duncan. She'd tried his mobile a few times but had gotten no answer. Either he'd turned his phone off, which would be odd, or he was ignoring her calls. Which would be even odder.

When she entered the house, she called out quietly for Duncan and Jake but got no answer. Upstairs, she saw that Jake was in his bedroom—she could see the light under the closed door—and Duncan was in bed with the lights off. She entered as soundlessly as she could, navigating by the moonlight that filtered in through one of the windows, where he hadn't closed the curtains all the way.

"What happened?" Duncan's voice in the dark startled her.

"Oh—I'm so sorry about tonight. I ran into an old college friend who was in really bad shape. We got into an intense conversation."

She left it vague and hoped he didn't ask more. She'd met her in the women's room, she'd say, if he pressed. This old friend was attending some other function in the hotel, that's what she'd say.

She undressed, placing her clothes neatly on the chaise longue.

"You didn't get my texts?"

"I'm sorry—I heard my phone and ignored it. I didn't want to be rude to this poor woman. I should have looked. I'm really sorry."

A long silence. "A lot of people asked about you."

"Oh?"

"Lynn Golding."

"She was there? It was like I fell into a black hole. By the time we were done talking I checked my phone, and I saw you'd left. God, Dunc, I'm so sorry."

She got into her nightgown, then went to the bathroom, brushed her teeth, and washed her face. By the time she got into bed, Duncan was softly snoring.

When Juliana arrived at her lobby the following Monday, Kaitlyn was already there. "I didn't think you'd want them on top of your desk," Kaitlyn said.

Juliana saw what Kaitlyn was talking about: four bankers boxes of documents were piled next to her desk, taking up valuable (and scarce) floor space.

"From the defense?"

Kaitlyn nodded. "It's printouts of all chats that mention Rachel Meyers's name."

"That's a lot of mentions."

"In these boxes are actually two sets of documents. One is redacted, one's unredacted. With a privilege log."

Somewhere in those four boxes was the answer to the question of why she was being blackmailed. "Where's the log?"

"On your desk."

Juliana saw the manila folder on her desk next to the keyboard.

"Have you looked through the documents yet?"

"No, I wanted to wait for your instructions."

"Okay." She took off her jacket and hung it on the coatrack next to her black robe.

Sitting down at her desk, she opened the folder and began skimming through the privilege log. It listed all the chats the defense wanted to withhold, identifying each chat by date and time, sender and recipient, subject, and, most important, the reason they wanted to withhold it. Assembling a privilege log was tedious grunt work, probably done by some poor young associate.

At least one of these chats contained something so important, so explosive, that someone was willing to go to great lengths to bury it. So the privilege log was a useful tool. It singled out the important chats, the ones she had to pay attention to. She could ignore the hundreds—thousands?—of other chats in those cardboard boxes.

All she cared about right now was finding what was being concealed—why she'd been targeted. She glanced at her watch. She had forty-five minutes before the morning malpractice trial began.

She started reading.

19

The first chat appeared to be between Devin Allerdyce, the CEO, and the chief operating officer, Andrew Westerfield, who was Rachel Meyers's boss.

ALLERDYCE: how's rachel meyers working out?

WESTERFIELD: She just started. But she's smart. Harvard Law.

ALLERDYCE: dude, who cares about smart? she's smokin hot. she involved with anyone?

WESTERFIELD: Not married, all I know.

ALLERDYCE: i'd tap that.

The next one was between the CEO and his CFO, Eugene Brod:

ALLERDYCE: you check out our new gen counsel?

BROD: The blonde?

ALLERDYCE: hands off dude

BROD: Yes sir!

There was a long series of chats between Rachel and her new colleagues in the company, mostly introducing herself. A few more between

Allerdyce and other executives calling attention to the attractive new general counsel and warning the other execs away from her. How serious those warnings were was hard to tell. It was totally frat-like behavior, and Juliana was surprised at how unrestrained the CEO was. He clearly lusted after Rachel Meyers and wasn't shy about letting people know it.

Then there were chats between a couple of engineers that were all marked CONFIDENTIAL on the privilege log. Their chat was mind-numbingly hard to follow, with phrases like "standard back propagation algorithm" and "adjusting the *n* values" and "high degree of feature extraction in high-dimensional spaces." And here and there were sprinkled mentions of the new general counsel. *What is it with men and blondes?* she wondered.

ALLEN: u c the new general counsel?

OSTROVSKY: No, what abt her?

ALLEN: blond, hot as hell

OSTROVSKY: Didn't see her.

ALLEN: Rachel . . . Meyers? Allerdyce, that hound dog, is prob already doing her

So clearly the CEO had a reputation for going after attractive women in his employ. No wonder the company wanted to suppress so many of these chats. It didn't look good. She couldn't help but think of all the crap she'd had to deal with. Her boss, the US Attorney, now the state attorney general, was a toad named Kent Yarnell who was always telling raunchy jokes or sizing her up physically, making comments about her bust size—sometimes it was just plain gross. "When are you going to ask me out, Juliana?" he'd say. Or he'd say things like "Weren't those the clothes you were wearing yesterday? Walk of shame, Juli-girl . . ." That was stuff she preferred to forget.

She read on with fascination tinged with disgust. Until she came upon an exchange between Rachel and her boss, the chief operating officer, that was marked, in the privilege log, "confidential." It made her sit up and reread.

MEYERS: How do I access the Mayfair Paragon files? They're password protected.

WESTERFIELD: Why do you need them?

MEYERS: For the SEC. The new bond issue. I'm reviewing all the paperwork, etc., making sure all the forms are in good shape.

WESTERFIELD: What forms do you need?

MEYERS: accredited investor forms for Mayfair Paragon going back 10 yrs.

WESTERFIELD: I'll see what I can do.

This was followed by an exchange between the CFO, Eugene Brod, and the COO.

WESTERFIELD: Gene—Meyers wants access to the Mayfair Paragon files.

BROD: Why?

WESTERFIELD: Document prep for SEC. What do I tell her?

BROD: What does she need?

WESTERFIELD: Accredited investor forms going back 10 yrs

BROD: Answer No, she can't access those files.

The next day Rachel messaged her boss again.

MEYERS: Just following up re Mayfair Paragon files—any luck?

WESTERFIELD: I can't get you access.

MEYERS: But the SEC specifically requested the accredited investor forms.

WESTERFIELD: I'll handle.

MEYERS: This is a problem. I can't certify without access to those forms.

WESTERFIELD: not to worry

Juliana made a note on a legal pad: *Mayfair Paragon?* Then: *accredited investor forms?* What was that? Was this the reason she was being blackmailed? Did it have something to do with this?

A knock at the door.

"Come on in," Juliana said.

The door opened. Philip Hersh entered, holding a paper bag. He closed the door behind him, crossed the room, and set the bag down on her desk. "You like chicken Caesar salad, right?" he said. "Light on the dressing?"

"How'd you know?"

He shrugged. "I understand this is your lunch break. Mind if I take a couple minutes of it?"

"Please. And thanks for the salad."

"I have a bit of information on Matías Sanchez."

"So do I. I saw him after we spoke."

"I know." He looked annoyed. "I asked you not to. Urged you not to."

She was surprised by his tone. She said, "Well, I'm here, aren't I? What information do you have?"

"It's interesting. Harlan Madden doesn't know much about him."

"How do you know?"

"Harlan and I had a good chat this morning."

"You talked to him?"

"Apparently *American Lawyer* is working on a piece about Boston's Top Defense Legal Eagles." He smiled. "Harlan's a superlawyer."

"And he fell for it."

"Vanity knows no bounds. So he says that the client, Wheelz, insisted that Matías Sanchez be added to the defense lineup."

"But why?"

"He has no idea. Sounds like they're not coordinating, not working together at all. Madden's not sure what he's there for. It sort of pisses him off, I could tell, but he wouldn't say that out loud. Okay, so your meeting with the guy. Was it really worth it? Did you find out something useful?"

"What I learned was that he's not a player. He's a pawn. And he's scared." She opened the bag, took out a clear plastic box and a plastic fork, opened the box, and speared a piece of grilled chicken.

"He said so?"

She nodded. She took a bite, chewed.

"Pawn of who?"

She shook her head. "I'm not sure he knows. Which reminds me." She checked her notepad. "I need you to dig into something called Mayfair Paragon."

"What is it?" He took out a pocket notebook and wrote it down.

"That's what I want to know. It came up a number of times in the chats they want to withhold. The Mayfair Paragon file."

He pointed at the pile of boxes. "The chats are in there?"

She nodded.

"Can you show me?"

"I can't. Legally, only my law clerk and I can look at the discovery materials."

"Who's gonna know?"

"Me. That's the problem. Sorry."

"Then at least give me context."

"I can't right now. I have to finish reading for the afternoon's motion session." She glanced at her watch. "Back to work."

JUDGMENT

"All rise," the court officer called out. He was a tall man of forty with a gray crew cut and a large pear-shaped protruding gut. His name was George, and he'd been working in the Suffolk courthouse since forever.

She entered the courtroom, laptop under her arm. She took her seat at the bench, put down her laptop, and looked over the courtroom.

Glenda Craft and Harlan Madden were there, along with their second chairs, but not Matías Sanchez.

"Uh, Mr. Madden?" she said.

"Yes, Your Honor?" He rose.

"I see your whole team isn't here."

"I'm sure Mr. Sanchez will be here any moment. Traffic, I bet."

"Do you have any objection to our proceeding without him?"

"No, Your Honor."

"Then let us begin."

Matías Sanchez never showed up.

20

Right after the afternoon session, Juliana left the courthouse, got her car from the garage across the street, and picked up Jake in front of his high school. He had to get to his SAT prep class in the farthest reaches of Newton. The sun was still out and bright; it hung in the air, burnt orange and enormous. Jake got into the car, shrugging off his backpack, looking sullen.

"How was school?"

He didn't answer.

"That bad, eh?"

"Where's Dad?"

"Faculty meeting. You're stuck with me." She pulled away from the curb. She glanced in her rearview.

Are you being followed? Hersh had asked.

"How was the history exam?"

"Fine." His tone invited no follow-up.

"How do you like Mr. Bertone?"

No reply. Out of the corner of her eye she could see him shrug.

"He's got to be better than Ms. Thomas." Ms. Thomas was his seventh-grade history teacher with whom he had repeatedly clashed.

She signaled left and merged into heavy traffic on Route 9. From time to time she checked her rearview mirror. Jake was looking at his phone.

"Whoa," he said.

"What?"

"You're famous."

"Me?"

"Well, not you, but the Wheelz case. Wow, there's this whole subreddit about the trial."

"A what?"

"It's on Reddit—anyway, what's her name, Rachel Meyers? Wheelz employees are really sliming her."

"How so?"

He read from his phone. "'That skanknasty bitch should be on her knees saying thank you to Devin for putting her in a big job she wasn't ready for.'"

"Lovely."

"'Skeevy ho wants millions for every bj she gave.'"

"Jake."

"Sorry. I didn't write it."

"It's a swamp of trolls out there."

"It says Wheelz offered her millions of dollars for a settlement and she turned it down. That she's just some greedy pig, and it's all 'cause Devin Allerdyce asked her out on a date."

"It went a lot further than asking her out on a date, Jake. She was subjected to all kinds of abuse. Sexual harassment. So she reported it to the head of HR, who's a woman. She figured, you know—"

"The sisterhood."

"Instead, the head of HR turned right around and told the CEO. Who fired her on a totally bogus pretext. Performance issues. Bad advice. Like that."

"You don't sound very neutral."

"In the courtroom I am. Totally. You know that. But I'm also a human being, and I have opinions. Can't help it."

In her rearview mirror she noticed a black Suburban with a tinted windshield, the same one that had been behind her since leaving the high school.

There was a long silence, and then she said, "Was Tyler back in school?" Tyler was one of his best friends and had been out sick for a while.

"Yeah."

"I'm glad he's better. His mom was worried. Speaking of which, you don't still have a sore throat, do you?"

"That was one day, and it wasn't even really sore."

"You'd tell me if it was getting sore, wouldn't you?"

"*Jesus!*" He hated questions about his health.

She knew she tended to be alarmist and think the worst, fear a return of the Hodgkin's, but what could she do? When he went through that ordeal, she did too. She'd seen the fragility of life. She'd seen her son go partly bald during chemo; he had the rest of his hair shaved off. She remembered how skeletal he looked, his skin fish-pale. She'd seen her son hooked up to an IV for more than two months because his intestines had stopped working and he could no longer eat. No longer would a fever or a lump ever be routine.

Yet her overprotectiveness invariably incited his anger, as if she were pointing out some kind of weakness.

"All right, all right," she said. She glanced in the rearview again and saw the same black Suburban, a couple of cars behind. Opaque windows, a Massachusetts plate.

She felt her insides twist. That had to be *them*, following her for some reason. Some reason she didn't want to know.

"Why do I have to go to this stupid class anyway?"

"Because it's important." She could barely concentrate on the argument, she was so anxious.

"It's pointless."

"If you . . . If you do well on the SAT you won't have to take it again, think of it that way."

"Lots of colleges are SAT-optional now. It's not like when you were in high school."

"Okay," she said. She didn't want to argue. Her mind was stuck on that black Suburban a couple of cars back. What the hell was it doing, were *they* doing—just intimidating her? Reminding her that she couldn't make a move unobserved?

"If I don't get my homework done, you're just gonna be pissed off."

"If you . . ." She wanted to say, *If you don't waste your time on Instagram or whatever,* but she caught herself in time. *Don't be Judge Judy.* "You'll get your homework done," she said.

"It's *tedious.*"

"What is?"

"This pointless SAT prep class. It's a waste of my time."

"And we know how valuable your time is," she said. She changed lanes, and so did the black Suburban. Anxiety sent ants crawling up the back of her neck. What the hell? If they were trying to intimidate her, it was working.

"Dad says this whole ridiculous system is just designed to turn us all into sheep. Excellent sheep."

She sighed. Duncan had a well-thumbed copy of a book called *Excellent Sheep* on his bedside table.

He went on, "Bionic hamsters. The whole thing is a factory that turns out conformists who get perfect grades and are good at taking tests. Dad says it's all bullshit."

She didn't want to argue about this either. The grim fact was that

Jake's grades had been dropping, and he didn't seem to care. His father's attitude had infected him, she was fairly sure. She wasn't a tiger mom, but she knew how the world worked, and she wanted Jake to have every opportunity.

"My brother, Calvin—"

"Not Calvin again!" Jake protested.

Her younger brother, Calvin, had been a loser whose life had been a series of failures, until the day he died in a collision with a tractor-trailer that probably wasn't an accident. He was a Bukowski-reading romantic who prided himself on being edgy and interesting. He'd dropped out of college after his freshman year.

He smoked a lot of dope—another reason she wanted Jake to stop. The friends he made were the kind who encouraged him in the worst way, brought out the worst in him. One of them turned him onto something stronger. He started a garage band that wasn't very good. Once she'd even helped him get a booking at a local club in Allston, and then his band showed up totally stoned and barely able to play.

Calvin's life, and death, haunted her. Her parents never recovered. Calvin was like an object lesson to her: what could happen, how your life could be derailed, when you made reckless choices.

She hated using Calvin as a parable, a metaphor for bad judgment, but she did it anyway and always felt guilty when she did.

"You need to have a plan, that's all. When people don't plan, life makes plans *for* them."

"Dad says, 'Man plans, God laughs.'"

She smiled. "But you can't just coast, honey. Look, I see the real world. I have people coming into my courtroom who come from good families and end up in trouble, make bad decisions. I see it all the time."

"Oh, God."

"You're at a really crucial point in your life, Jake. It's not the time to slack off."

They had arrived at the modern red-brick office building where the prep course was held. She pulled up to the curb, and Jake opened the door and hopped out.

As he entered the building, she glanced in the rearview mirror and saw the black Suburban again, idling at the curb, and something in her finally snapped. She was more angry than scared. How dare they follow her. How dare they intrude on her family. She shut off the car and got out. She felt a tightening in her chest. They would never do anything to her here, not out in the open, not with people around.

She strode up to the Suburban, feeling hot, prickly with anticipation.

She rapped her knuckles on the tinted driver-side window, her heart pounding in her ears.

The window powered down, and an Asian woman in a business suit was looking at her, puzzlement in her eyes. "Juliana? Everything okay?"

The mother of Soo Jung Kim, a kid in Jake's class.

"I'm sorry, Chae-won," she said. "Wrong car."

21

Jake would be in class for the next two hours, which meant that Juliana had a choice: she could find a Starbucks nearby and work while she waited for him, or she could drive home and then come back to pick him up.

She decided to drive back to the courthouse and pick up a stack of documents to read at home. As she drove, she replayed her conversation with Jake and regretted how she'd somehow gotten sucked into an argument. He didn't like talking about school or schoolwork anymore. She remembered when he would chatter excitedly about his day when she picked him up, about his teachers and what he was learning and what happened in recess. But that was long ago; he must have been no older than ten. Now, everything was grist for a potential fight. He didn't argue nearly as much with his father. Jake was hyperarticulate, unusually so for a kid his age, and scary smart.

Unfortunately, he'd started coasting, it seemed, at just the wrong time. He just stopped caring. Was it weed? Was it something else? His grades had dropped this year. He was screwing things up for himself. She couldn't shake the feeling that he was doing a Calvin. How could you motivate someone like that? He was so different from Ashley.

Jake was also so different from the way she'd been when she was his age. She'd been the real grown-up in the house, not her alcoholic mother or her recessive father. She made sure Calvin got to bed on time and did his homework.

And Calvin, of course, came to resent it.

Everyone always thought she was so together, so on top of everything, so in control. When the truth was, she always feared she was one stumble away from becoming Calvin. Or Rosalind. She knew it was a lot easier to judge them than to acknowledge how easily she could have been them.

How baffled poor Chae-won Kim had looked when Juliana had stormed up to her. And she still couldn't stop looking in the rearview mirror from time to time to check whether she was being followed. Even if she were being followed—what would they find? That she went from home to courthouse and back, with occasional jaunts to Jake's school. That was about it.

She lucked into a space on Cambridge Street and entered the courthouse.

"Judge, isn't it kind of late for you?" said one of the security guards, waving her through.

"No rest for the wicked," she said, an old line they batted back and forth. *If you only knew.*

"I hear you."

She took the elevator to the ninth floor and walked to her office. The hallway, normally bustling with people going to court, was empty and still.

She unlocked the door, and before she switched on the light, she noticed light seeping in from the adjoining courtroom. *Strange,* she thought. *Who could be in the courtroom at this time of day?* She switched on her office light and then strode across to the courtroom door, which she opened.

A janitor was vacuuming the floor of the courtroom. A light-skinned black man with a shaved head, wearing steel-framed glasses. She knew the maintenance and custodial staff, always greeted them by name. But this one she'd never seen before.

Her nerves were really frayed, her suspicions out of control. The janitor looked up at her; she nodded, and he went back to vacuuming. She closed her office door.

She located the place in the pile of printouts where she'd stopped reading—she'd marked it with a sticky note—and grabbed about an inch-thick pile of documents, looking around for a file folder.

She heard a key turn in the door lock and, surprised, looked up. The janitor was opening the door.

She smiled. "I'll be out of your way in five or ten minutes," she said.

He entered her office anyway, holding a broom.

"Excuse me," she said a little louder. "I should be out of here in five or ten minutes."

But the janitor kept walking toward her. "This will only take a minute, Judge Brody," he said. She was surprised he knew her name. She felt a pulse of fear.

He leaned the broom handle against her desk, then picked up a delicate glass object, blindfolded Lady Justice holding up her scales.

"Judge of the Year," he said. He had a pronounced, jutting jaw and was staring at her intently.

She felt the breath catch in her throat. He was a tall, powerfully built man wearing a tight, tan T-shirt. She could see the ropy muscles along his shoulders and his arms.

"I'm sure you were worthy of the prize."

She didn't trust herself to speak.

"It's fragile," he said. "Like everything we most love in life."

He looked as though he could crush the glass statuette in his giant bare hands. Then abruptly he let go, and it smashed on the floor, shattering.

She gasped and stepped back, terrified, as he picked up something else from her desk, a silver picture frame. Her favorite picture, of her and Duncan and the kids in the middle of a pumpkin patch in autumn. He admired it for a few seconds.

"Excuse me," she said, "what the hell do you think you're doing? Put that back!"

"A precious thing, a family," he said.

"Please," she said quietly. Her heart hammered. "Put it down."

"A lot of things are more fragile than you realize, Judge. It's so much easier to break things than to put them back together."

"What the hell do you want?" she said desperately.

"I know people like you; you think you can just turn the page, not be haunted by the past. What happens in Chicago stays in Chicago, right? But maybe that's not how it really works."

"What do you *want?*"

"Some people say who we are is the sum of everything we've ever done. In other words, no backsies. No hitting the Delete key in life, right? All you have is what you've done and what you're gonna do. When you make one rash decision, the only way out is to make a smart one. You ready to make the smart choice?"

He tossed the frame toward her, casually. She surprised herself by snatching it out of the air, a perfect catch.

"Is there a problem?" he said in a soft voice.

Her heart was pounding wildly. She set down the frame carefully on her desk.

"I'd like to know if we have a problem."

She just looked at him. He pointed at the broken glass strewn on the floor. He began to sweep it up. "Don't worry about that," he said. "That'll all be gone in a minute." He swept the jagged pieces into one neat pile. "You have a decision to make," he said. "You don't want to make the wrong one."

22

For a long while after the man left, she sat at her desk, heart racing, adrenaline pulsing through her body, as the sound of the janitor's bucket thumped along the hallway, one squeaky wheel, faded away. She felt light-headed. She wondered whether the man had intended to go through her office, her files, after hours, when she was usually gone. Had they sent someone to go through her files and notes at home too? Or had he come here just to threaten her? Because if that's all it was, it had worked perfectly. The guy hadn't needed to pick up the picture frame; she'd gotten the message. They could go after her family. No longer was the threat just her public shaming, discrediting, through the release of a video. Now her family was in the crosshairs too.

She waited for her heart rate to steady, then picked up her phone, texted Duncan.

Just checking in. All good here, you?

She waited, staring at the phone, for the three little dots that meant he was typing a reply. A long time went by, but no return text.

Then she called Duncan's phone.

"Hey, what's up?" he answered.

She exhaled, long and hard. "Just checking in," she said. "Everything good?"

"Sure, just making dinner."

"Okay. See you soon."

"Okay."

She hit Philip Hersh's number.

He answered after a few rings: "Judge Brody."

She heard loud noises in the background, the cacophony of a crowd. "Can you run fingerprints?" she said.

"It's not something I usually do, but theoretically I can. I've got a buddy on the police force. Why, what do you have?"

"A picture frame," she said. "Some guy just threatened me. Threatened my family. If I don't make the right decision." Just telling him brought it back to her. It was starting to sink in, what had happened. She could almost see the man: the steel-framed glasses, the shaved head, the ropy muscles. *Is there a problem?*

"Physically?"

"Sort of. I mean, he didn't touch me, but he could have. He broke some glass. Point is, they're escalating, whoever these people are. Now it's not just some video. It's— I don't know, you just—"

"Hey, Judge," Hersh said quietly. "I'm here, okay? I'll do anything I can."

For a moment she thought she might burst into tears from the tenderness in his voice. "Thank you, Philip."

He said nothing.

She said, "Did you find out anything about Mayfair Paragon?"

"No. No trace of it online. You say it's, what, a company?"

"Must be. Wheelz's general counsel said she needed 'accredited investor forms,' whatever they are, on something called Mayfair Paragon. But she kept getting turned down. Something about those documents she wasn't allowed to see."

"So it's an investor in Wheelz?"

"I assume so, yes."

"There's no mention of Mayfair Paragon in any of the business databases, nothing in social media, nothing. Nada."

"That's not possible. There has to be a record of it somewhere."

"Here's what I know," he said. "Five years ago Wheelz almost went out of business. Ran out of money. People talked about Uber, about Lyft, but no one ever mentioned Wheelz, because it was never a real competitor. Not even an also-ran. It was a company on its deathbed. Then three years ago, all of a sudden, everything turns around for Wheelz. Suddenly they're loaded. Some British firm sinks a billion dollars into it in exchange for fifty-one percent of the company."

"Which British firm?"

"It's called Harrogate Capital Partners. A venture capital firm."

"So they own Wheelz."

"Right. Most of it."

"And who are they? I want to know who they are. These people who are threatening my family."

"Understood, Judge. I'm on it."

Her phone chimed a text-alert sound. "I need to go," she said. "Thank you, Philip." After she ended the call, she looked at the text. It was from Duncan:

Don't pick up J, he's at home.

She was confused: the SAT prep class went on for another half hour. She called Duncan.

"Where are you?" he said when he answered.

"Courthouse. I forgot something. What's going on with Jake—did the class end early?"

"Jake bailed."

"Bailed?"

"He took an Uber home. Just showed up here. He says he doesn't want to sit through it anymore."

"He can't—just do that."

"I don't know how we force him to take it."

She sighed into the phone. "I'll see you soon," she said.

Half an hour later she arrived home, put down her stuff, then went up to Jake's bedroom. She stood for a moment outside his closed door and tried to focus. She was distracted and tense and kept thinking about the man who'd threatened her. *Is there a problem?* How bizarre was her life, she thought, that she had to cope with such different problems at the same time, problems of such different scale. Jake and his apathy, whatever he was going through—and now a threat to her family, a matter of life and death.

But at the same time, she knew she could never just stop caring about her kids, no matter what. She was determined to focus on what was in front of her, even if it was a struggle. *Focus*, she told herself. *On your family. On what matters.*

She could hear him talking. She waited a moment, couldn't make out what he was saying, then knocked. She waited, then knocked again, harder. She heard him say, "Oh, shit." Finally he opened the door.

"Yeah?"

He stood there, headphones around his neck, a look on his face somewhere between ashamed and defiant.

"What happened to SAT class?"

"It's bullshit."

"Excellent sheep, I got it." She paused. "You don't think the class is helping?" she said, as reasonably as she could. "It's supposed to be the best prep class you can take."

"I'm talking about the SAT. It's a scam. It doesn't predict how well you'll do in college. It just measures how good you are at taking the SAT!" He appeared to be primed for an argument, but she didn't want to give it to him.

Juliana sighed. "Okay," she said. "Do your homework. Your dad and I have to talk."

She closed the door and headed downstairs. She wanted to tell Duncan about what had happened earlier, the intruder at the courthouse, but of course she couldn't. That would involve telling him about Chicago, and that was out of the question.

He was downstairs watching *Game of Thrones*. Everyone in the world had seen it, it seemed, except her. She had no interest. He was sparing her.

When he saw her, he paused the show—someone was being decapitated—and looked up. "You talk to him yet?"

"Just did, a little. Honey, what are we going to do?"

"Like I said, we can't force him to take the course."

"So we just let him blow off the SATs?"

"If that's what he wants to do . . ." He shrugged.

She came over to the couch and sat next to him. "Did you see that e-mail from Mr. Wertheim?"

He nodded. Mr. Wertheim was Jake's despised math teacher. "He flunked the big test."

"It's the damned marijuana."

"He's just rebelling."

"Against us?"

"Against Mr. Wertheim, against high school, college, the whole thing. It's a goddamned pressure cooker."

She shook her head, heaved a sigh. "Excellent sheep."

"Exactly."

"It feels like he's just throwing away his chance to go to a good school."

"He'll get in somewhere. Some place that's right for him, where he belongs. With other kids who don't believe that perfect SAT scores are the holy grail. Maybe he's enjoying life. It's like Baba Ram Dass said—'Be here now.'"

She gave a tight smile. "He can be here now as soon as he gets into college."

Be here now. That had a double meaning, didn't it? That was what it meant to keep living. You might know there was an asteroid hurtling toward your neighborhood. That didn't mean you didn't have to floss. Maybe the asteroid would veer off course. Maybe it wouldn't. Life was about handling different threats on different scales. She remembered how scared her mother had been after receiving her breast-cancer diagnosis. But an hour later, Rosalind was on the phone with the carpet-and-tile shop, pestering them about a delivery date.

"He's almost an adult," Duncan said. "In some societies, he *is* an adult. We can't control him. Maybe you can control what happens in your courtroom, what happens in your life, but we can't control *him*."

Control? she thought. Her life had spun out of control and all because of that night in Chicago. And that second drink. *One slip,* she thought. One mistake. Nobody got points for walking a tightrope with a little detour into thin air.

Maybe he was right; maybe she was trying to control Jake because she couldn't control what was happening to her and she didn't know what to do about it.

"You okay, Jules?" Duncan said. "You seem really distracted. Anything wrong?"

"Me? No, I'm fine. Just—worried about Jakie." She stood up. "Okay, I have some reading to do. Enjoy the decapitation."

23

While Duncan was downstairs watching TV, Juliana went to the bedroom to read more of the Wheelz chats. She'd closed the door so she couldn't hear the TV. She needed to be in her own head.

She had a pile of the documents on her lap, and at first she just skimmed through the chats, dipping in here and there in no particular order. But soon she found herself in the zone, focused, and she started reading them in chronological order. She was following Rachel Meyers's short career at Wheelz.

She was surprised to see that barely two weeks or so after starting at Wheelz, Rachel was already in conversation with the CEO. Their first exchange began with an invitation by Allerdyce.

ALLERDYCE: rachel it's devin a.

MEYERS: oh hi!

ALLERDYCE: settling in OK?

MEYERS: Yes, thanks!

ALLERDYCE: we're different from most companies—don't worry if it takes you a while to get up to speed

MEYERS: OK, good to know.

ALLERDYCE: i'm here to help, whatever you need. why don't you come by my office sometime and we can talk about the carras lawsuit

MEYERS: sure

ALLERDYCE: come by at 5 today

MEYERS: great, see you at 5!

No surprise that the CEO wanted to talk with his new general counsel. But a couple of hours later Allerdyce contacted her again to change the plan.

ALLERDYCE: OK if we meet at madrigal at 7 instead?

MEYERS: OK, cool.

Madrigal was famous, the most expensive restaurant in Boston. Juliana had been there once and remembered their copper menus and the superpricey wine list. Madrigal was a major change in venue—from a meeting in his office to a meeting over dinner at an over-the-top restaurant. That altered the dynamic of the meeting quite a bit, and Rachel must have known it.

An hour later he messaged her to change the time.

ALLERDYCE: moved our rez to 8pm—busy till then

MEYERS: Fine, see you then.

The next exchange between Allerdyce and Rachel came the next morning. Clearly something had happened between the two of them, something awkward.

ALLERDYCE: hey sorry if we got our signals crossed

MEYERS: No problem.

ALLERDYCE: ok cool

Whatever had transpired between the two of them, it was never mentioned again, as far as she could see in the chats. "No problem," she'd told him, after whatever had happened the night before. Words that would no doubt come back to haunt her if they went to trial. Though she probably had said "no problem" because she was talking to the CEO of the company, no matter how she really felt.

Then she found a chat between Rachel Meyers and someone in the company named Karen Heraty, who was probably a friend.

MEYERS: Devin hit on me again

HERATY: Another dinner at Madrigal?

MEYERS: No, we were at the 4 Seasons in Palo Alto last night—road trip to meet with Silver Lake and Elevation. he asked me to come to his room for a meeting and when i got there he was in his bathrobe!

HERATY: !!!!! what did you do???

MEYERS: told him I wasn't comfortable meeting with him in that situation and left.

HERATY: this the 2d time he hit on you?

MEYERS: basically he hasn't stopped.

HERATY: you gotta do something. Report to HR?

MEYERS: not going to help

HERATY: who's your boss? Andy Westerfield?

MEYERS: right. But Andy was in Devin's frat!—he's not going to stand up to DA

HERATY: maybe. but worth a try I think.

She thought about the powerlessness that Rachel Meyers must have felt, the relentlessness of her boss's boss. The arrogance of the guy, the sense of privilege, assuming his beautiful new general counsel would be interested in him sexually—or would at least relent—because he was the founder, the boss.

Well, that sure as hell wasn't new. She'd had to deal with all kinds of crap when she started working as a lawyer. She would never be sure why, for instance, she didn't get that associate job at the law firm where she interned one summer, where Spence Murchison, a senior partner, kept hitting on her until he gave up, embittered. "My boyfriend wouldn't like it," she'd deflected with a fake smile. But her heart was pounding, and her face was hot. She didn't have a boyfriend.

The firm didn't hire her, and she'd never know why. Were the other applicants just stronger? Maybe. Or did Spence Murchison decide it would be too uncomfortable to have her around?

She just took it for granted that you had to deal with all that crap. Her male colleagues never had to.

Juliana put down the stack of documents. So far nothing she'd read gave her any indication of who might be blackmailing her, who it was who so badly wanted to keep the chats from being made public.

She switched off her bedside lamp, and the bedroom went black. *I'm in the dark*, she thought. *I'm still in the dark.*

24

No matter what stresses had intruded into her life—the struggles with Jake, the terror of the impostor janitor threatening her, the blackmail threat from Matías Sanchez—visitors to her courtroom would have thought everything was going on as normal. The parties in *Meyers v. Wheelz* were off doing depositions, which freed some afternoons to write. The malpractice trial was coming to an end, and Juliana had to write instructions for the jury.

She'd woken up that morning feeling as though the incident with the janitor was a terrible dream. It wasn't as if things were returning to normal. Maybe they never would. But the terror she'd felt, that awful sense of powerlessness: that had dwindled. In its place was a low-level buzz of anxiety that wouldn't go away.

She pulled up a set of jury instructions and began to edit, make changes.

By the time she finished revising, her jury charge began:

Members of the Jury, you are about to begin your final duty, which is to decide the fact issues in this case. Before you do that, I will instruct you on the law. These instructions are in three parts . . .

Some of it was basic stuff, Jury 101. *You must follow the law as I give it to you whether you agree with it or not. That's not just because I'm the judge. It's because every person who comes before the court for trial is equal and is subject to the same law.*

She even threw in some country music. *Don't outsmart your common sense.* (Lee Brice.) And she was done.

At two thirty there was a knock on the door.

"Come on in."

Kaitlyn Hemming entered. "There's a call for you on line two—it's both counsel on the Meyers case."

"What's it about?"

"They're in the middle of deposing the defendant and they have a dispute. They need to talk to you."

"About what?"

"The plaintiff's lawyer is asking the CEO—Allerdyce?—if he's ever settled any sexual harassment claims before—"

Juliana nodded. "And the guy is refusing to answer because he says any such settlements, if there are any, are confidential."

"You got it."

She told herself to focus. Part of her mind was cycling again, obsessing over what was happening to her. Uselessly rehearsing the nightmarish situation she'd found herself in. She closed her eyes for a moment.

"Okay, put 'em on," she said.

She imagined for a second the CEO of Wheelz, Devin Allerdyce, and saw his rodent face. She had no doubt that guy had harassed other women who worked for him, that there'd been other claims against him that the company had settled quietly, the terms of the settlement kept confidential. But of course she couldn't say that aloud. She had to maintain a pose of fair-mindedness.

Kaitlyn put Juliana's phone on speaker. Juliana said, "This is Judge Brody. Is everybody here?"

A female and a male voice said yes at the same time. She said, "Can you please identify yourselves?"

"Harlan Madden for the defense, Your Honor."

"Glenda Craft for the plaintiff, Your Honor."

"Stenographer?" she asked.

"Terri Rhodes, stenographer."

"Anyone else?"

"No," said Madden.

No Matías.

"Okay, let me see if I can help you. Ms. Craft, can you give us some background as to what the issues are here?"

"Sure. I asked Mr. Allerdyce about any prior claims made against him and Wheelz regarding sexual harassment. This information is highly relevant to establish a pattern and practice of discriminatory behavior at Wheelz. It's also relevant to whether or not the company's practices and policies provided effective remedial measures to prevent harassment—"

"Judge." Harlan Madden.

"Let her finish, please."

"Effective remedial measures to prevent harassment," Glenda Craft went on. "The plaintiff's claim in this case is that they did not, and evidence of other claims will help establish this."

"Mr. Madden, what's your position?"

"Not only is this information irrelevant, Judge, but to the extent that there are prior claims that have been resolved, those claims were resolved subject to confidentiality agreements, and the company is bound by these agreements not to divulge the nature of the claims or the terms of the settlement. To require them to produce this information would be forcing them to breach confidentiality agreements that they may have entered into with other employees. The company is not at liberty to disclose those terms. That information is privileged and not discoverable."

Juliana wasn't surprised, of course, that Harlan Madden didn't want his client talking about any sexual harassment claims that might have been made against him in the past. That made sense. And he had a point: if Wheelz had settled claims made by other women, it had surely required the terms of the settlements be kept confidential. That was fairly standard. Wheelz didn't want those details made public.

On the other hand, it was perfectly legit for Rachel Meyers to know if the CEO had harassed other women before. That strengthened her case.

What made the dispute interesting was that Rachel had refused to sign any confidentiality agreement with the defense. Probably for the same reason she had persistently refused to settle: above all, she wanted her story told. She wanted everyone to know everything that happened in the courtroom. She wanted a public trial.

Juliana thought for a moment about requiring both parties to submit briefs and then make oral arguments. But she realized she didn't need to make them go through all that. She had a pretty good idea of what the right solution was. A compromise of sorts.

"All right," she said, "here's what I'm going to do. Courts in our jurisdiction have found that this information is relevant and discoverable. At a minimum it speaks to the policies and practices of the company and whether they were effective in remediating these disputes. So I'm going to compel the defendant to produce this information, but I'm going to impose some confidentiality restrictions. Access to any settlement agreements is restricted to Ms. Meyers, her attorney, and her experts, and these individuals cannot make any further disclosure."

"Judge," protested Madden.

"We're done here," she said.

When she finished for the day, she locked her lobby, left the courthouse, and walked over to the parking garage. Normally, she tried to make it home by six, but tonight she was going to be a little late. She texted Duncan to let him know.

She was going to make a detour. She was going to try to find Matías Sanchez.

25

Maybe Matías had left town, gone back to Chicago, his work done. But she had no other way of reaching him than to try his hotel. If he was gone, he was gone. All she could do was try.

Was it foolhardy? Was she sticking her head back in the jaw trap? Maybe so. But she needed to find out what he knew, if anything, about Mayfair Paragon. He'd called himself a chess piece in a game whose players he claimed not to know. But her instincts told her that he knew more than he was letting on. Maybe a lot more.

Not that he would readily cooperate with her. She'd have to force a deal. There was a way out of this nightmare, and she was determined to find it.

As she drove, she checked her rearview mirror from time to time, looking for a following vehicle, feeling sheepish about it, ruefully recalling how she'd nearly torn into Chae-won Kim. The fact was, several cars had been behind her since Kenmore Square, three or four of them. None, as far as she could tell, since leaving the courthouse.

Legally, of course, she was putting herself in a compromising position just meeting with a member of the defense team. For her to do so without the other side there was considered ex parte communication. If she was photographed meeting with Matías, she could face all sorts of questions. And if the truth ever came out, that would be sure grounds for impeachment. Her career could be over in a flash.

She found a parking space easily, on the curb a block beyond the Home Stay Inn. Just as before, she entered the hotel lobby with purpose and turned left to the elevator bank and took it to the third floor. As before, no one tried to stop her or ask where she was going. Look like you belong and most people won't bother you. But just in case she was recognized, she wore sunglasses and a hat.

She passed an open door and a housekeeper's cart in the hallway. When she came to room 322, she could hear noise inside, what sounded like the television on, fairly loud. For a moment she hesitated, listened for other voices, then finally rang the doorbell. Right away she sidled away from the door, along the wall, out of view of the peephole. If he looked out and saw her, he might not open the door. She waited. The TV blared, muffled-sounding. The door remained closed. She waited some more.

Was it possible he hadn't heard the doorbell over the noise of the television? She slid back over to the doorway, her face hidden behind the brim of the hat, in case he was looking out the peephole—and rang again. Then she knocked. The TV remained on. She waited another minute; then she pounded hard on the door.

Coming down the corridor was the housekeeper, diminutive and Latin-looking, pushing her cart. She avoided Juliana's eyes. It wasn't her business.

But then Juliana had an idea.

"Excuse me," she said to the housekeeper.

The maid looked up reluctantly.

"My husband forgot to give me a key. Could you let me in?"

She was wearing her blue suit and looked respectable. She lowered her sunglasses, her back to the camera. Sure enough, the housekeeper looked her over, her eyes moving up and down Juliana, sizing her up. She said, "Is three-two-two?"

"That's right. I'm positive."

The woman approached, gave her a questioning look, pulled out a keycard, and beeped the door open. She didn't seem happy about it. It was probably against the rules: hotel guests who'd misplaced their keys probably had to go to the front desk and present ID. But she pushed the door open for Juliana, and a split-second later she made a strange yipping sound, a high-pitched scream. "*Ay Dios mío!*"

Juliana pushed her way into the room and saw what had so frightened the housekeeper.

In the twilit gloom, she could just make out a naked male body slumped on the floor, unmistakably dead.

26

It took her a few seconds to recognize Matías Sanchez, and by then she'd collapsed to the floor, her purse tumbling beside her, its contents spilling onto the carpet.

"*Dios mío! Dios mío!*" the housekeeper keened, clutching her hands to her bosom. "*Llama a la policía!*"

Juliana got to her feet unsteadily, looked again, confirmed that what she had first thought was in fact the case. Sanchez had been strangled, or maybe hanged, by the black electrical cord around his neck. He was seated and leaning over, his head canted all the way forward. The electrical cord that had served as a noose was wedged between the bathroom door and the door frame.

Her heart fluttered in her rib cage. She felt dizzy, weak-kneed, as if she were about to pass out. The housekeeper was retreating slowly down the hallway.

She looked away, but not before registering the lolling tongue and the red staring eyes. She searched for the toilet, found it, rushed there, and, before she reached it, vomited into the sink.

For a long moment she kept her head bowed, willing herself not to lose consciousness. Her field of vision sparkled. She gripped the front edge of the vanity.

She remembered the note of desperation in his voice. *These people will do anything—stage an accident, a suicide, whatever they need to do if they think you're an inconvenience.*

Slowly she raised her head, saw herself in the wall-to-wall mirror. Her face was red, a splotch of vomit on her chin.

She had to leave this room, this hotel. Suddenly that realization hit her, filling her with panic. She couldn't risk the police arriving, her presence here impossible to explain. She had to leave before the housekeeper summoned hotel security or the Boston Police.

She hesitated before rinsing out the sink carefully, running the water until all trace of her vomit—her DNA—was gone.

She wondered if the housekeeper had already called for help, though there was nothing to do. The man was dead.

She knelt down on the carpet, began picking up all the objects that had fallen when her purse fell to the floor and stuffing them back. She moved quickly, her hands reaching and grabbing, hurrying. Finally, when she'd retrieved everything she could see, she got to her feet and raced out of the room and into the carpeted hallway. Then she forced herself to slow to a walk to avoid drawing attention.

She emerged from the elevator into the lobby. A few people were gathered at the reception desk. Not the housekeeper.

Maybe she didn't call for help, Juliana thought. She ran away. Maybe she was an illegal immigrant, afraid she might be so identified by the police.

Juliana increased her pace, striding down the block and to the next. Her blue Lexus SUV was still there as well.

She drove in a dazed state, barely noticing where she was going, navigating home by instinct. Should she find a pay phone and alert the Boston Police about the death? But not only were pay phones ridiculously hard to find anymore, she couldn't take the risk of being traced and then connected to the murder.

And she had no doubt it was murder. The man had been frightened, not suicidal, when she'd last seen him. He'd known what might happen to him. Had his unseen controllers learned he had talked to her? Was that what had happened? Matías was a gigolo who had betrayed her, but he was also pitiable and a victim.

Her thoughts were jumbled, chaotic. She couldn't suppress a wild panic. Lost in desperate thought, she nearly passed her street. With a jerk of the steering wheel she turned off Beacon Street and pulled into her driveway.

Glancing at her watch—it was nearly eight—she got out and slammed the door and for a moment stood there next to the car and looked at the side door to the house. The lights were on, upstairs and down. The men were home. She badly wanted to talk with Duncan.

But she was stuck. She obviously couldn't talk to him without revealing what she'd done and what kind of trap had closed on her.

The door swung open as she approached, startling her. It was Duncan.

"Everything okay?"

A slight pause. She stepped in. "Sure."

"I saw you standing out there— What is it? What's wrong?" He tipped his head to one side, peered at her. Was it that visible? Was it really in her face?

And then she couldn't hold it in: her throat tightened, and the tears started rolling down her face.

He put a hand on each of her shoulders and brought her into him. "What happened?"

She shook her head, put up a palm. She struggled to gain control of her emotions, hating herself for losing it when she needed to keep things together, but the stress, the jangled nerves, the sheer terror, of the last hour had all at once overwhelmed her.

"We need to talk," she said.

27

They sat at the kitchen table, the door closed.

Duncan had betrayed no emotion at first, not anger or upset. He nodded a lot. But he avoided her eyes. "I'm glad you told me," he said a few times, as if her belated candor was the main thing.

"Look, I know what I did," she said. "And all the clichés are true—it didn't mean anything, all that. And they're pointless, because it isn't even up to me to say what it meant. I'm a horrible person, Dunc. I did something horrible; you have every right to hate me."

He was looking off into the middle distance, almost contemplative.

"Say something. Yell at me. I deserve it. I've got it coming."

"That's not who we are."

"Not who we are?" she echoed.

"You want a big blowout? Like . . . a *cleansing storm?* That's not how it works, not with us. Or I should say, not with me."

But she could see him fighting to control himself. She thought of the yoga nostrum about one-nostril breathing. It was as if he was trying to detach himself from his body, to float free. With exaggerated casualness, it seemed to her, he went to the sink and filled his glass with water, turned back around, took a sip. His hand was shaking slightly. The imperfect exertion of control. "I'm glad you told me."

She wiped away tears with her hand. "That's all you're going to say?"

"It's a lot to process, okay?" He breathed slowly, blinked a few times.

"I understand."

He lifted his chin but still looked away from her. "Which means . . . I can't be with you right now."

"Will you look at me, Duncan? Please?"

But he couldn't. "I can't be under the same roof as you."

Realizing, she whispered, "Please don't leave, Duncan. I mean, I need you. You know that. *We* need you."

"These things take time." His words had a styptic, almost clinical edge.

A little louder, she said, "Please don't do it. Don't move out."

"Oh, I'm not moving out." Finally his injured eyes settled on hers, like the red dot of a weapon's laser sight. "You are."

28

Martha Connolly had a four-bedroom condo in the Ritz-Carlton with floor-to-ceiling windows and a glittering aerial view of Boston. It wasn't purchased on a judge's government salary; her great-great-great-grandfather was Samuel Colt, the gun maker. Once in a while she jokingly talked about her "blood money." She was anti-gun, but not enough to turn away Mr. Colt's bequest.

She had a dog, a small, wire-haired Jack Russell terrier with pert ears and heart-melting brown eyes. Her name was Lucy. Tonight Lucy was seated at Martie's feet, chewing on a dog toy that looked like Donald Trump.

She poured each of them a strong drink, a few fingers of bourbon over ice. Juliana was still on her first Buffalo Trace when Martha finished her second. She told Martie everything, held nothing back. About finding the man's dead body. The horrible conversation with Duncan.

"He let you leave the house while you're under this kind of threat?"

"He doesn't know—I didn't get a chance to tell him." She'd told Duncan about Chicago, but before she could go any further, tell him about everything that had happened since, he'd cut her off. *"Okay, I can't hear anything else."*

"I'm so sorry," she'd said.

"I can't be around you right now," he'd replied.

Martie came over and enveloped Juliana in a tight hug. Her tears were hot on her face.

"Honey," Martie said. She was wearing a T-shirt and pajama bottoms. She'd been in bed when Juliana called. Sure, Juliana could have gone to a hotel, but she was in desperate need of support. "You must be terrified."

Juliana thought. "You know, there's so many different kinds of terror, I'm coming to realize. There was what I felt when I saw the body—I felt like screaming and running. And there's what I feel now, which is more like a dull ache. Worse than that. God, I'm such an *idiot*!"

"You've made some mistakes," Martie said briskly. "Was it at least a relief to have it all out with Duncan?"

Juliana shook her head. "It was awful."

"And his law student chippy—that didn't come up at all?"

"That was three years ago, and again, he didn't sleep with her."

"So he says."

"So he says. But I believe him." Well, she didn't know for sure, of course. But she had to believe him.

"What about your kids? Have you talked with them?"

"Haven't had a chance. I dread it. I mean, Ashley could maybe deal with it, but this is the last thing Jake needs, his parents splitting up."

"Hmm." She clasped and unclasped her hands. Juliana could hear the steady ticking of the grandfather clock in the foyer. The walls were painted pale yellow and hung with fine antique oil portraits of relatives.

"What does Philip say?"

"I haven't told him yet."

"You haven't? Tell him at once. If you're right, and it wasn't a suicide—if what you saw was a murder—you may have something to worry about."

Juliana nodded, put down her drink, and reached for her phone. She sent off a brief text to Hersh, telling him about Matías and that she needed to speak with him tomorrow.

She saw a photograph in a silver frame on a side table and picked it up. A woman in her fifties or sixties wearing a black-and-white-striped shirt, like the gondoliers in Venice wear. She had an impish smile. A boathouse in the background. It looked like Cambridge and the Charles River, probably the Harvard boathouse. "I'm sorry I never knew Iris," she said.

Martie's face clouded. Iris, who'd died of cancer ten years ago, had been the love of Martie's life. She had been a Shakespeare scholar at Harvard and an avid rower.

"Me too," she said. "You would have enjoyed her. She'd have admired your mind."

Juliana looked at the picture a moment longer and then put it down. "Not only have I wrecked my marriage, but I've put my family in danger. Now I don't know what to do."

"I wouldn't say you've wrecked your marriage. It's probably a good deal more resilient than you give it credit for. But you're cornered. They can still release that video."

"It's already done its damage."

"Oh, there's a lot more it can do. That . . . gigolo was a party to a case you're presiding over. You could be sanctioned by the CJC, and worse." The CJC was the Commission on Judicial Conduct, the secretive body that investigated all judges accused of wrongdoing. "It would destroy your public standing, love. It would end your career. We don't want this video made public. You can't be associated with this man."

"Oh, God, what have I done?"

"I know this looks bleak, but there's nothing to be done about it tonight. Right now, what you need is rest. Let me show you to your bedroom and get you some towels and whatnot. You're welcome to stay as long as you want."

"You're the best."

She thought of something and retrieved her purse from the floor next to her chair. She rifled through the purse, groaned, looked up. "Oh, God."

"Anything you've forgotten I'm sure I can provide."

"My sunglasses." Her stomach went tight.

"That I can't help you with. You'll have to stop home tomorrow, pick up some clothes while you're at it."

But Juliana's thoughts were elsewhere. "My purse fell when I saw his—body. I nearly fainted, and everything went flying. My sunglasses must have gone under the desk or something. I must not have seen them."

"Is your name on them? Are they in a case?"

Her head was pounding. "My name's not on the case, but—" She pulled her car keys from her purse and stood up, her eyes throbbing.

"What are you doing?"

"I need to get them back before the police declare it a crime scene."

"What if it is already?"

"Then I'll turn around."

"Don't go back there," Martie said. "Plus, you've had a drink. I don't think you should drive."

"You're right about driving," Juliana said. "I'll get a Lyft. But I have to get over there now."

29

It was past midnight, but she was wide awake. A terrible panic had seized her, electrified her blood. The Honda Accord hurtled along the Mass. Turnpike. It was not the route she'd have taken, but she was too distraught to say anything to the Lyft driver. Was she leaping to conclusions? Might she have dropped her sunglasses in her car? She was pretty sure she hadn't. She kept her car tidy and would have noticed. No, she was increasingly certain that they'd fallen out in the hotel room and were still there, probably under the desk.

Assuming the police hadn't been called, she was then faced with the problem of getting into the hotel room. That was a tough one. All the housekeepers would have left for the day. Hotel security? A low-cost, bare-minimum hotel like the Home Stay Inn probably didn't have security. Just someone at the front desk.

Well, there had to be a way. She would figure something out.

From a block away she saw the flashing blue lights of the police cruisers double-parked in front of the hotel.

Her mouth went dry. "I've changed my mind," she said. "Can you take me back to Boston?"

The driver, a Vietnamese man with an unusually wrinkled face, gave her a baffled look and pulled a U-turn on the deserted street.

Her thoughts raced. The housekeeper must have notified her manager, who called the police. She was pretty sure it would be treated by the police like a possible homicide, the room designated a crime scene.

Her sunglasses. Even a rudimentary search of the room would turn them up. But they wouldn't know whose they were, would they? There was no way to connect them to her. Was there?

Fingerprints. Her prints were all over the sunglasses. And her ten prints had been in the system since she joined the US Attorney's office, however many years ago. It might not happen immediately, but the crime scene techs would put the glasses in an evidence bag and run the prints, and her name would come right up. Maybe tomorrow, maybe in the next few days. Then she would be connected to Matías Sanchez no matter what she did.

She stared out the window at the whizzing cars, the streaking lights. What a goddamned rookie mistake it was to go back to his hotel room! She was finding it hard to think clearly. Were there any strings to pull? Somehow she had to keep her name out of this investigation. Was that even possible?

The worlds of the Boston Police and the Superior Court barely overlapped, except when a cop wanted a warrant approved. She wouldn't know whom in the police to call. And what could she hope to accomplish? The police would want to know why her sunglasses were there. The housekeeper had surely already told the police that she'd discovered the body while letting in a woman who claimed to be his wife. It wouldn't take long for the police to figure out she'd been in his room earlier that day. They'd want to question her; she couldn't get around that. They'd want to know why she'd been there.

What kind of an answer could she give them? Anything she told them would drag her in, force her to disclose what had happened, and that had to be avoided at all costs.

If she made calls to anyone, she'd just be incriminating herself. There was nothing she could do.

By the time she arrived back at the Ritz and took the elevator to the seventh floor, it was almost one in the morning. Martie, who'd given her a key, had left a few lights on for her. Lucy barked a few times, shrilly, but then, fortunately, stopped. She flipped off the lights and found her bedroom, and very quickly she was asleep.

30

The jury in her morning trial was out, luckily, so she was able to work quietly with Kaitlyn in her lobby. She'd barely gotten a few hours of sleep and was grateful for the slow pace of the day. She skipped lunch, had no appetite.

Every time her phone rang her first thought was that it was the Boston Police. But the call never came.

The afternoon was busy, with a number of oral arguments and motions. But she was glad to be busy. It distracted her. She kept seeing the man's body, his grotesquely contorted face. The man had been murdered.

What did that mean about her? Might she be a target too?

She entered the courtroom, and everyone stood. She sat down in the high-backed leather chair and looked around. She felt a low-grade dread. She was finding it hard to concentrate. She said, "Are we all here?"

Harlan Madden kept looking back at the door.

Juliana said, "Should we wait for your co-counsel?" She felt dry-mouthed and tense and wary.

"Well, frankly, Your Honor, he hasn't been answering messages, so let's just continue without him."

Juliana felt her stomach drop. She had to be careful about what she said. She needed to think clearly. Coffee would help, but she had to avoid drinking too much: caffeine would make her even more anxious.

That afternoon the two sides in the Wheelz case were presenting oral arguments. A few weeks earlier, the defense had asked Rachel, in the form of an interrogatory, to describe all "sexual and romantic relationships" she'd had in the last five years. Glenda Craft wouldn't let her reply. That was an outrage, she said. So Harlan Madden had served a motion to compel her to answer. Then both sides filed briefs. Today they would go at it full bore in the courtroom, arguing over whether the defense had the right to grill Rachel on her sex life before she started working for Wheelz.

When she first became a judge, Juliana was astonished at how different it was from being a trial attorney. It was like going from mono to stereo, from black-and-white to Technicolor. All of a sudden she had to listen with both sides of her brain, understand dueling arguments at the same time. You had to see three-hundred-sixty degrees. You had to keep an eye on which juror was sleeping. You also had to make decisions with alarming speed, sometimes. You saw a lot of suffering and felt the stress of wanting to get every decision right. You had to be extremely empathic. You had to understand the humanity, the greed, or the sorrow of the defendant and the anguish of the victim's family.

Make one bad decision, and the whole thing gets flipped on appeal.

"Good afternoon, counsel," she said. "I've read the papers. Mr. Madden, it's your motion; I'll hear you."

Madden stood at the counsel table. "Judge, as you know, this is a sex-discrimination suit. We've propounded interrogatories to the plaintiff, but she has declined to answer questions regarding her romantic history, which are clearly relevant." He looked at Glenda Craft. "Part of the plaintiff's burden here, Your Honor, is to show that the work environment at Wheelz was hostile or offensive, to show it was unwelcome. We think if Ms. Meyers is required to answer these questions, the evidence will show whether the atmosphere at Wheelz was in fact unwelcome, which is the plaintiff's burden of proof at trial. We believe that Ms. Meyers's prior sexual history will show that the conduct she encountered at Wheelz was something she was accustomed to. We think this information is directly relevant."

Juliana stifled a yawn, exhausted yet tense. "Thank you, Mr. Madden. Ms. Craft, what do you have to say to this?"

Glenda Craft stood. "Your Honor, the defense's goal here is nothing less than to embarrass and humiliate the plaintiff. They're just trying to defame her. They're trying to imply that Ms. Meyers had a bad moral character—which has no bearing on the conduct within the company. Her sexual history has no relevance to what happened at Wheelz during her tenure there. This is just character assassination, plain and simple."

Glenda Craft paused, and Juliana broke in, "Thank you, Ms. Craft. It was helpful to hear from both of you." There was no point in letting them both go on at length. She already knew what they were going to say, they'd said it in writing, and she'd made up her mind anyway. She was tired and finding it hard to concentrate.

"As I said, I've read the papers, and I'm familiar with this area of the law. So I'm going to rule from the bench." Both lawyers looked at her sharply, surprised. "I'm going to allow the motion in part and deny it in part. I'm going to deny the motion with respect to any sexual or romantic relationship not connected to the workplace. Anything that happened while she was employed at Wheelz, any sexual relationship with a fellow employee, is relevant and discoverable. It's fair game." Madden half rose to object, and Juliana—tired and stressed and needing to get the hell out of there—shut it down: "Thank you, all."

31

How much longer is this going to go on?" Juliana said on the phone.

"I don't know," Duncan said. "We have a lot to talk about, but I'm not ready to talk."

"Well, can I come home for a while tonight so we can all talk as a family?"

"I'd rather you didn't."

"We need to tell Jake what's going on."

"I already did. He asked where you were this morning, and I told him that we'd had an argument and you were temporarily staying with Judge Connolly."

"That's all you told him?"

"Just that. He asked for details, and I said we'd talk later. He wasn't happy to be kept in the dark."

"I'll give him a call, if you don't mind." She thought, in pique: *He's my son too.*

As soon as she hung up, she called Jake's phone, but it went right to voice mail. She texted, Call me. A moment later, she typed Matías Sanchez's name into Google to see if his death had been reported anywhere. Not so far as she could see. She was about to call Hersh when her office landline phone rang. She picked it up.

"Yeah, I'm looking for Judge Brody," a man said. "This is Austin Bream from *The Boston Globe*."

She recognized the name. Bream was a columnist with a reputation for breaking scoops, usually having to do with city government fraud or abuse. He was trouble. She hesitated a moment, thought about pretending to be someone else, a clerk or a secretary. "Speaking," she finally said.

"I assume you've heard about Matías Sanchez."

So it begins. It was out there. "I'm sorry, who?"

"A lawyer from Chicago named Sanchez. He was in town on a case before your court."

"What about Mr. Sanchez?"

"He was found dead last night in his hotel in Allston. Police are calling it a suicide. I was wondering if you had any comment."

She quickly weighed the pros and cons of talking to a reporter. And realized there were no pros. Speaking to Bream would just feed the beast, make a story where there didn't need to be one. "I'm sorry, Mr. Bream, I really can't comment. This is the first I'm hearing of it. I'm sorry to hear of this man's death, but I can't say anything further." She disconnected the call.

So the death had probably appeared on the police log overnight. Maybe the hotel had identified Matías Sanchez. His only connection to her was that he had argued in her court. His appearance in court was a matter of public record. Apart from that, no one would connect him with her, she was sure. She was fairly certain she hadn't left fingerprints.

But what if they found the sunglasses?

Her cell phone rang.

"Yes?"

"I'm outside the courthouse." Hersh.

"I'll be out in five minutes or so," she said, standing to leave even before she'd hung up. She'd left him another message first thing in the morning and had been waiting all day for a call back.

She didn't recognize him at first. He looked like an old pensioner, down at the heels, wearing a threadbare herringbone scally cap and smoking a cigarette in front of the courthouse. Maybe he changed looks for different jobs. She tapped him on one shoulder, and he turned slowly.

"I didn't notice you smoked."

"I don't." He exhaled, his grin wreathed in smoke. "Well, not often. What can I do for you, Judge Brody?"

"Didn't you used to be a police detective in Boston?"

He nodded.

"You still know people?"

"A few. Why?"

"I have a feeling the Boston Police may be contacting me."

"Why?"

She hesitated. "I'm pretty sure I left my sunglasses in his hotel room."

She could see recognition dawn on his face.

"That would be unfortunate. Is your name on them?"

"No. Just my fingerprints. Can you get them back for me?"

"From a crime scene?" His eyebrows shot up. "I'm afraid there's nothing I can do about it. I can't stop them from doing their job. You know that. Anyway, by now I'm sure they've already been logged in as evidence."

"Maybe I got lucky and they didn't find them."

He shrugged, took a drag on his cigarette. "Maybe. Are your prints in the system?"

"I used to work in the US Attorney's office."

"So they are. Well, we can hope that the death is treated as a suicide, in which case they're not likely to run prints." Twin plumes of smoke unspooled from his nostrils. "Did you happen to notice any CCTVs in the hotel, in the halls and lobby?"

"Cameras? A few. But I wore a hat and sunglasses."

"Then you're still on tape. Let's hope you can't be identified."

"Let me ask you something. Candidly. Should I be afraid?"

"Because of what happened to Sanchez?"

"Right."

"Look," he said. "You take every precaution to try to prevent disaster—"

"Knowing you may fail," she cut in, recalling his exact words.

"You got it."

"What the hell is that supposed to mean, anyway?" she said.

"You don't agree?"

"It doesn't exactly help. It's just a very dark vision. Pretty extreme."

"Is it? You've got kids; I don't. Aren't parents always reassuring their kids there's no monster under the bed?"

She just gave him her skeptical look. When she did it on the bench, she unnerved whichever lawyer she aimed it at. But Hersh seemed unmoved. "Well, guess what. You've been lying to them and to yourself. Hell, yeah, you bet your *ass* there's monsters under the bed."

Juliana shook her head.

"One day you step into the elevator and it's just a shaft," he said. "One day you take a slip and fall and you hit your head, right? And you're never the same. Or one day that little tiny filament in your head just pops, right? And for the rest of your life you're dragging the left side of your body around like it's a corpse."

"It's always possible."

"Friend of mine, a lovely man, woke up one day with the worst headache he'd ever had. And when he went to the hospital he learned he had inoperable brain cancer." He shrugged. "How do you explain that?"

"Shit happens."

"That's the reality of it."

"Is it?"

"Yep. That's the reality. Which is that we're all standing on a thin, fraying crust above a deep pool of magma. We're one random fissure away from being incinerated. One day the car behind you doesn't stop and you're smashing your windshield with your skull. A sniper in a hotel room with an assault rifle and a grudge, half a block away, starts shooting out the window. Whatever. Shit happens, and complete control is always an illusion, the way I figure. There's always magma underfoot."

"O-kaay," she said.

"But what do I know?"

"And how is this supposed to help?"

"Thing is, you can't live this way," Hersh said, a little more softly. "The only way we get through life is by looking away. Wresting our attention away from the fact that there's always sharks in the water. Or the hellmouth might open right in front of you. You can't think about it. You have to will yourself not to know."

"Thanks for the inspirational lecture," she said.

"Now, in answer to your question. Should you be afraid? Damned if I know. I mean, I assume Sanchez was a risk that had to be eliminated."

"Because?"

"Maybe they were afraid he wasn't reliable. That he might tell you too much."

She didn't like thinking this way, but it couldn't be avoided. "So . . . what does that mean for me or for my family?"

"I think you know how I feel."

"Great," she said with a bitter twist of a smile. "What about that guy who threatened me—the janitor?"

"He's an ex-Marine sergeant, dishonorably discharged."

"Okay."

"Name is Donald Greaves. Certified level two in Russian kettlebells."

"What does that mean?"

"He's a beast. Employed as a contractor for Fidelis."

"Fidelis?"

"One of the big security companies. Fidelis Integrated Security."

"So he's hired muscle."

"That's what it looks like."

"Hired by Wheelz."

He shrugged. "Not necessarily."

"Then can you find out who he's working for?"

"All I can do is try."

"You said *dis*honorably discharged. Any idea why?"

"Not yet. I'll see what I can dig up."

"I want everything you can get on this guy."

"Everything? Like where he went to high school? Instagram pictures of his dog?"

"Everything."

"Do my best."

She gave him a long, steady look. "You say there's no guarantees, you can't promise, you may fail—I don't like hearing that."

Another shrug. "I'm not going to lie. I never lie to a client. This isn't someone you want to mess with."

32

Martie Connolly had sent down for dinner from the Ritz kitchen: beef tenderloin with braised leeks and mashed potatoes served in silver domes. "I can't tell you how nice it is to have company for dinner," she said.

"If I have to be kicked out of my own house, I can't think of a better crash pad," Juliana said.

But it was more than a crash pad. It felt like a sanctuary. Up here on the twenty-third floor, with security guards at the entrance, she decided she was safe, for the moment. But she didn't *feel* safe. In some part of her mind, a shadow-puppet theater was playing out scenes in which faceless figures menaced her kids, her husband, anybody she cared about. Really, it was more like one of those endlessly repeating GIFs: she imagined black-clad figures emerging with outstretched, taloned claws.

When she became a mother, she realized that her children would always be phantom limbs. That wherever they were, however far away, they'd feel attached to her, a source of vulnerability. Being a mom meant she could never turn off the phone. And now she herself had raised the family's threat level. To come after her, her enemies could well come after them. She felt her mind eddying in anxiety.

"As long as you want, honey, as long as you want." She poured them each a glass of pinot noir. "So has Philip found you a way out of this?"

"No. Not yet. But it's become clear to me that the documents Wheelz is trying to suppress have to do with the ownership of the company."

"They're trying to conceal it for some reason?"

"It looks that way."

"Why is it a big secret?"

"I don't know. Philip doesn't know. He's looking into it."

Martie looked off into some middle distance and spoke almost to herself. "So if you allow them to exclude the chats, or some of the chats, whatever they want, you're off the hook. But if you don't, they're going to release that little movie."

Juliana nodded, cut a piece of tenderloin, chewed thoughtfully.

"So the death of this lawyer gives you an opportunity to delay your decision," Martie said. "Buy yourself more time. String this out."

"Yes. Good idea." She took a sip of wine. "I got a call from that *Globe* columnist Austin Bream."

"Avoid at all costs. What does *he* want?"

Juliana's phone suddenly launched into the distinctive, bubbly, syncopated Skype ringtone. "It's Ashley, calling me back. Hold on." What time was it in Namibia? Six hours later, so it was after midnight. She'd been trying to reach Ashley but couldn't get through.

She answered the call. "Ash, is everything good with you?"

"What do you mean? Of course."

"I—I just wanted to hear your voice."

"Mom, what happened?"

"What happened what?"

"Jake told me you moved out!"

"Sweetie, it's nothing permanent."

"That's not what it sounds like. Are you and Dad getting divorced?"

"Oh, sweetie, no, no . . . We just needed to take some time apart."

"What happened?"

"Nothing serious. We'll talk when the time is right, you and me, okay? Who's that in the background?" She'd heard a male voice, sounding close by.

"That's Jens."

"And who's Jens?"

"He's the director of the mission. He's Danish. He's amazing."

"Are you—seeing him?"

"'Seeing him'? What's that supposed to mean?"

"Are you two a couple?"

"I guess. Sort of." Ashley paused. "When the time is right, we'll talk."

"Fair enough," she said, smiling. "Just be careful."

"About what?"

After a long pause, she said, "Men."

"Oh, so now you're going to offer me *relationship* advice?" Ashley said. "That's hilarious, Mom."

In the morning, when she got to work, she found a note tented upside down atop her keyboard in her lobby. It was a message left by Kaitlyn, printed in architect-style all caps, her neat hand.

TROOPER MARKOWSKI/STATE POLICE
WANTS YOU TO CALL.

She didn't return the call.

In the afternoon, both sides in *Meyers v. Wheelz* were seated in their usual spots in her courtroom. They were there for a status conference, scheduled long in advance. Administrative, nothing more.

"I want to start off today by expressing my condolences on the untimely death of your colleague," Juliana said to Harlan Madden.

"Thank you, Your Honor. It, uh, came as a shock."

"Obviously, this is going to create some difficulty for the defense."

"Actually, no," Madden said. "We're okay."

That she hadn't expected. "Well, I want to make sure the defendant is adequately represented. I know you're doing a very capable job of representing the defendant, Mr. Madden, but I can't ignore the upheaval this must have caused."

"But, Your Honor—"

"So out of an abundance of caution, I think we ought to put the brakes on a bit. Why don't we push out the tracking order ninety days to give everyone time to catch their breath? Make sure you all have adequate time to process this and get things in order."

"We actually don't need more time, Your Honor," Madden said.

The door to the courtroom opened, and a couple of middle-aged men entered and took seats at the back. She could tell right away that they were cops, despite their civilian attire.

"Your Honor," said Glenda Craft, "we would rather move forward with the schedule already agreed upon. Respectfully, the defense counsel here before you is more than capable, and they're not asking for more time. So I don't think there's any basis for the court to delay. Both sides are in agreement on this."

"I understand," Juliana said, "but I have to take into account this is obviously a significant and troubling event, and I don't want anyone to look back on this a year from now and feel that we rushed."

"Both sides want to keep moving full steam ahead," said Madden.

"All right," Juliana said reluctantly. She couldn't push any harder.

Shortly after she returned to her lobby, there was a knock on the outside door.

"Come in," she said.

The door opened. It was the two men from the back of the courtroom.

"Judge Brody," one of the men said, tall with swept-back gray hair and a gray goatee. "I'm Trooper Markowski from the State Police, with the Attorney General's office, and this is Detective Krieger, with the Boston Police. We're sorry to bother you, but we have a serious matter to discuss."

33

Juliana showed the two cops into her lobby. She sat behind her desk while the men pulled up chairs.

"Detective Markowski, is it? Or Trooper?"

"Either is fine," said the taller man with the swept-back hair. "I'm a trooper with the State Police. I'm also an investigator with the Attorney General's office, and Detective Krieger is with Boston Police homicide. Judge Brody, we're really sorry to be taking your valuable time, but we're investigating the death of a man named Matías Sanchez, who as you probably know is a defense attorney who had a case before you." He sounded genuinely regretful about the imposition.

She nodded. "I've heard about it. A suicide, as I understand it?"

"An apparent suicide, yes, ma'am, but we're treating it as a suspicious death."

"What sort of death was it?"

She knew this was exactly the sort of question that homicide investigators normally would never answer. *They* ask the questions. But she was a judge. They had to treat her with respect. It was an awkward situation.

"He hanged himself. If it was suicide."

"Hanged himself? Why is there a question about whether it's a suicide?"

"It's standard procedure in cases like this."

"Like what?"

"Well, there was no note found, for one. And other aspects of the decedent's body. It's being treated as suspicious."

"How can I be of help?"

Her brain was whirring at top speed as she spoke. How had they connected her to Sanchez? Was it just the Wheelz case? She knew they wouldn't be talking to her, a Superior Court judge, without first having done all their homework.

"We just want to know what type of relationship you had with the decedent."

"Relationship?"

And then for an instant she froze. She realized suddenly she was at a point of no return. She could either tell the truth, or she could lie. Whatever she decided to do, the choice was irrevocable. Lying to a law enforcement officer was, for her, for an officer of the court, nearly unthinkable. She'd never done it.

"As you said, he's a defense attorney in a case I'm presiding over. He appeared in my courtroom for the first time about a week ago, just once, and never appeared again."

"Yes, Your Honor, but did you have a relationship with him outside the courtroom?"

"Trooper Markowski, what are all these questions about?"

"Detective Krieger?" the man with the swept-back hair said, turning to his colleague, a small, worried-looking man with advanced male-pattern baldness.

Krieger, the Boston Police homicide investigator, spoke for the first time. "Yes, ma'am, we found a pair of glasses, sunglasses, in the decedent's hotel room. I ran the latents myself and found your prints on them."

Detective Krieger paused, giving her a furtive look.

"Sunglasses?" She looked back at him, met his eyes, furrowed her brow. For a moment, she was stymied as how to respond. She mentally tested out several replies before saying, "How bizarre."

"Are you missing a pair of sunglasses?"

"I am."

"Were they stolen?"

"Stolen? Not that I know of. I'm sure I just misplaced them."

And there it was: she'd just lied to law enforcement. But . . .

"When did you notice they were . . . misplaced?"

"A couple of days ago."

"What kind of sunglasses were they?"

"Oliver Peoples, tortoiseshell."

Krieger nodded. She'd given the right answer. But what the hell else was she supposed to say?

"How much did you pay for them?"

"Around three hundred dollars or so."

"Wow."

"Prescription."

"Did you file a police report?"

"On sunglasses? No, of course not."

"Why not?"

"Because I figured they'd turn up eventually."

"And so they did," said Detective Krieger pleasantly. "Were you in the decedent's hotel room at any time?"

Had they pulled the surveillance video from the hotel's cameras? If they had, they'd have seen her on the tape, entering the hotel—maybe entering his room, if there were cameras in the hallways.

She felt a single bead of sweat roll down the back of her neck. Was her perspiration visible? She hoped not.

She shook her head.

"That's 'no'?"

"No."

"Were you in his hotel?"

"No. I don't even know which hotel he was staying in."

"Well, do you have any idea how your sunglasses might have ended up in his hotel room?"

"No."

"No?" he repeated skeptically.

"I wish I knew. Last I knew I had them with me in the courtroom."

A long, full silence followed. Krieger looked at her for five or six seconds, a puzzled expression on his face. It felt like an eternity. "Where did you last wear them?"

"I'm not sure. Probably on my way to work, a couple of days ago."

"How do you get to work? Do you take the T? Do you drive?"

"What is the big mystery?" she said. "I probably left them in the courtroom, and someone, this lawyer, must have picked them up to give to me."

"Really?" said Markowski with a smile.

She had lied to them, and then that lie had generated more lies, little ones, but lies all the same. That big shellacked bench that separated her from the criminal defendants who came before her? That was the biggest lie of all.

She wished, desperately, that she could come clean about the sunglasses. *They fell out of my purse because I freaked out upon discovering this guy dead, and the reason I was there . . .*

"Is this really necessary, all these questions? I have a lot of work to get to."

"I'm sorry for taking up your time," said Krieger. "But I'm afraid we have a lot more questions for you."

34

Duncan had texted her asking if she'd pick up Jake after school, since Duncan had his afternoon class. She was happy to do it and left right after court was adjourned. Jake didn't seem so happy about it. He gave her a brief surprised look when he saw her pull up and got into the car with a surly expression.

"Where's Dad?"

She couldn't help but feel a pang of jealousy. Considered making some sarcastic remark—*Sorry, you're stuck with me*—but decided against it. "He's meeting with students. Have you been getting my texts?"

He shrugged. "I've been busy."

"How was soccer practice?"

He shrugged.

"Okay?"

"Fine."

Okay, so he didn't want to talk about soccer. "What do you think Mr. Wertheim wants?"

"What do you mean?"

"He wants to meet with your father and me."

"Asshole."

"Mr. Wertheim?"

"He's a terrible teacher."

"What do you think he wants?"

Another shrug. "How do I know?"

"How are you doing in precalc?"

"I don't know."

Of course he knew; he just didn't want to say, which told her all she needed to know. He'd begun bending the fingers of his left hand backward as far as they'd go, a long-standing nervous habit. During chemo he did it all the time. He bent his fingers so far back they nearly broke. It must have hurt a lot. Maybe the pain was a needed distraction.

"What's going on, sweetie?"

"Nothing's going on. What do you mean?"

"I'm sorry I haven't been around."

He shrugged. "Doesn't bother me. You don't have to pick me up, you know. I could Uber. I know how busy you are."

"But I like picking you up."

He continued bending his fingers back, looked out the side window. They fell into silence for a minute or two. Finally she said, "You talked to Dad."

"He told me."

"We're just taking some time apart."

"You guys getting a divorce, is that what's really going on?"

"No, sweetie."

"This family is nothing but silences."

"How so?"

"You think I can't tell? You guys don't hold hands the way you used to. Or kiss."

Was it that obvious? Did he really notice that much, barricaded in his room with his giant recording-studio-quality headphones on?

"Is that true?"

He looked away.

"We can talk about anything you want to talk about," she said.

But he said nothing. He kept bending back his fingers, staring straight ahead. His face was set in an adolescent scowl, but his eyes were a child's.

She remembered one Saturday afternoon when he was ten, memorizing a poem for a school competition, helped by Duncan. Jake was marching up and down the stairs, declaiming, "O Captain! My Captain! Our fearful trip is done."

And Duncan marching with him, saying, "Big gesture, big gesture—no, *bigger*!"

"The ship has weather'd every rack, the prize we sought is won!" Jake called out.

"Yes!" Duncan said. "Outside!"

Jake and his father went out into the backyard, and Juliana followed, just watching, enchanted.

"O Captain! My Captain!" Jake said. He marched on the lawn, his arms swinging wildly. "Our fearful trip is done!"

Duncan marched alongside him, his arms swinging in sync. "Your body has to know it better than your mind does, you see? So you make it rhythmic to yourself by running while you shout it out—*Here Captain! Dear father! This arm beneath your head!*"

"Dear father! This arm beneath your head!" Jake shouted.

Duncan was playing coach, but at the same time it was as if they were really two boys playing together, Jake giggling sporadically, Duncan fighting to keep a straight face. He'd always had a bond with his father, she remembered. Different from the relationship between Jake and her. Duncan and Jake always seemed to be in sync, to just get each other. That had never changed. It probably never would.

Martie was having her dinner when Juliana arrived, eating a salad in front of CNN. "There's salad and some chicken if you want it. And

Sancerre." She gestured toward some take-out boxes on the kitchen table.

"I had to pick up my son and decided to get some more clothes."

"As long as you want. It's a pleasure having the company."

"I don't want to turn into the houseguest from hell. It shouldn't be for much longer. Duncan and I still need to hash things out."

Martie muted the TV and put down her salad container. "Any more from Austin Bream at the *Globe*?"

Juliana shook her head, told her about the visit from the cop and the state trooper.

"This went all the way up to the AG's office?"

She nodded.

"Boy, that must have been a hot potato. The cops find your prints on a pair of sunglasses and their supervisor must have freaked out. Bounced it all the way up to the Attorney General. Nobody wants to handle a case involving a Superior Court judge."

Juliana winced as she told her about how she'd lied to the State Police detective. Martie listened, nodding, and didn't react one way or another. "You had to do it," she said. "You had no choice. Your connection would have become a matter of public record. You're just in a terrible position. An unenviable position."

"You know Kent, right?"

"Sure. But you don't want me to call him. It's not going to help, and it's just going to backfire—shine a light on you—and you don't want that."

"No, you're absolutely right."

"Can they place you at the hotel?"

"If they have surveillance video they sure can."

"Did they mention video?"

Juliana shook her head.

"Call Philip. Ask him to find out if the police took the video yet. They should have."

"And if they have it?"

"If they have it, if they can see who entered his room, they probably have the identity of the killer. Assuming the guy was in fact killed and it's not a suicide."

"And they'll also know I was in the guy's hotel room too."

Martie was silent for a while. At last she nodded. "Let's hope they don't find out."

35

Juliana slept badly most of the night. It was the unfamiliar bed, as comfortable as it was, with high-thread-count sheets; it was the strange room, the heavy sweet smell of the potpourri on the nightstand. She found herself reliving her conversation with the homicide investigators, the lies she'd had to tell, their suspicious expressions. She mulled over Jake's anger. She thought about what would happen to her if the hotel had surveillance tape and the State Police detective saw her enter the hotel not once but twice. How would she explain that? Before going to sleep she'd e-mailed Philip Hersh and asked him to meet her at the courthouse in the morning. She thought about Hersh, wondering how good he really was, whether he'd be able to find out more about Mayfair Paragon or—what was the name of the British firm that was the lead investor in Wheelz? Right, Harrogate Capital Partners.

Then something popped into her head, a free-floating phrase: *accredited investor form*. Whatever the hell that meant. She'd come across that phrase in the Wheelz chats, and she remembered jotting it down. *Accredited investor form.* Rachel Meyers was trying to get access to them and was shut down. Her boss didn't want her to see this form, these forms, for some reason.

By the time she got back to sleep there were pale orange brushstrokes in the sky. The alarm on her phone jolted her awake after what seemed like only minutes.

Hersh, dressed in a gray suit and loafers and looking like a shabby courthouse lawyer with not a lot of clients, was waiting outside her office door when she arrived. He handed her a cup of coffee from the gourmet coffee truck out front. Which she didn't expect but appreciated. She always accepted coffee. Then, when they were sitting inside her lobby, he gave her a file folder.

"The dossier on Greaves, old-school style. I can also e-mail it to you if you want. Using WhatsApp."

"Who?" She'd momentarily blanked on the name.

"Donald Greaves. The muscle. The enforcer. The guy who threatened you."

"Right. Do you know who he's working for, who his client is?"

"I don't have that yet. But I have a bit more on Harrogate Capital Partners."

"Okay?"

"It's not much. Let's see, it's based in the town of Harrogate, up north in England, in Yorkshire. Sort of a posh town. One member of their board of directors is an earl. The Earl of Wenfield. He's vice chairman."

"Okay."

"I poked around some, and I found out that the Earl of Wenfield went bankrupt a few years ago. Guy's name is Charles Arthur Bertram Hogg, known as Cab. Next thing you know, Cab becomes vice chair of Harrogate Capital Partners."

"Huh."

"What a lot of these British firms do is, they name someone fancy and titled to their board of directors. It bestows cachet. My guess is that the earl doesn't actually have to do anything. Lend his name, go to cocktail parties, maybe give a party for the company at his grand house once in a while. Vice chairman is probably a title without responsibility."

"So what do they invest in?"

"Not clear. It's a private company; they don't have to reveal their portfolio to the world. Here and there you find mentions of Harrogate investing in European high-tech companies."

"But whose money is behind it?"

"No idea. All I know is that it wasn't so long ago that Wheelz was burning through their cash like crazy, they were desperate for money, and all of a sudden this English venture capital firm swoops in and saves their ass."

"Okay. What about Mayfair Paragon? Any more on that, who's behind it?"

He shook his head. "I don't have any more leads. But I found an article in a pretty obscure newspaper called the *British Virgin Islands Advertiser* about the Wheelz deal. It talked about some local BVI bank getting involved with this financing arrangement along with a much bigger bank in Cyprus."

"I don't understand—what can I do with that? What does that mean?"

"You gather facts until you have enough facts to recognize a pattern."

"And what does this tell you?"

"I don't know."

Frustrated, she sighed. "What about the 'accredited investor forms' that the plaintiff was trying to get and kept getting blown off? Any idea how we find these?"

"Nothing on that either. I'm sorry to disappoint. I found out what they are, though. When you make a private investment in a company, the government makes you fill out a form. You've got to put down your name and the names of all investors. There are no anonymous investors. Everyone has to list their name. It would be huge if we could find these forms. They probably contain all the information you're looking for."

"What about the surveillance video at the hotel?"

"I checked with hotel security. The investigator from the Attorney General's office asked for the tapes, and they found something kinda screwy when they tried to make a copy for the police."

"Yeah?"

"There's no video for the entire past week. Some kind of freak malfunction. All of the hotel's cameras, down the whole week."

"Meaning someone got to them."

"What I assume. But it's good news for you."

"Yes." Without videotape, it would be that much harder for the investigators to prove she'd been there. Though not impossible. They could interview people who might have seen her. They might talk to the housekeeper who'd let her into the room. It would be easy to connect her, if the police pursued it.

"Why does it not feel like good news?" she said.

36

A few minutes before the morning's court session was to begin, her mobile phone rang.

"Judge Brody, this is Trooper Markowski from the Attorney General's office. A couple things have come up, some things we'd like to talk to you about."

Her stomach seized. "Happy to talk."

"Does this afternoon work for you?"

"I'm in court until four."

"We can come by your office at four."

"I have a meeting at my son's school. Let me get back to you in a few minutes about my schedule."

"Sounds good."

She hit End, glanced at her watch—so she'd keep the courtroom waiting a minute or two—and hit Martha Connolly's number.

"Martie," she said, "the AG's investigator wants to talk to me again. They have some follow-up questions."

"That's not good. But remember, you don't have to talk to them."

"I'm not talking to them without a lawyer."

"Who're you going to use?"

"You," Juliana said.

There was a pause. Juliana wondered if Martie was taken aback.

"Let them know they are welcome to talk to you in my home," Martie said. "And let me give you a warning I used to give all my clients, which I heard from an old Boston political boss: 'Never write if you can speak, never speak if you can nod, never nod if you can wink.'"

"And never put it in e-mail," Juliana added.

During lunch a large envelope had been hand-delivered to her lobby by a courier for Wheelz's lawyer, Harlan Madden. Inside were a DVD and a short document. As soon as she glanced at the document she understood what it was. The two parties had been in the middle of depositions, with Rachel Meyers being questioned by Madden, when a dispute broke out. She looked at the paper. It was an emergency motion filed by Harlan Madden "to compel answers to deposition questions and to preclude counsel from improper coaching." He said they were going to have to come back for a second day of deposing Ms. Meyers and wanted the plaintiff to cover the costs. She skimmed the rest of the motion, then put the DVD into her computer's disk drive.

She hit Play. A wispy blond woman in her early thirties, Rachel Meyers, was sitting nervously at a conference table, looking directly at the camera. A male voice off-camera was asking her questions. That was Madden.

She couldn't help but think about Trooper Markowski and what might possibly have "come up." What the hell else could they have found? But at the same time she had to pay attention, because what she was doing was important. And there was nothing she could do about Trooper Markowski until later.

She fast-forwarded to a couple of minutes before the point in the time code where the controversy erupted. The offscreen voice asked, "Ms. Meyers, have you had a lot of boyfriends?"

Rachel Meyers looked to one side, probably at her lawyer, and said, "A lot? No."

"How many, would you say?"

"I don't know. I don't keep a count."

"More than ten?"

"No."

"Twenty?"

"Much less."

"Then how many?"

"Maybe four or five."

"And are you seeing someone at the present time?"

"No."

"And, Ms. Meyers, are you a member of any online dating sites?"

"Yes."

"Which ones?"

"Uh, OkCupid and Bumble."

"Have you had many dates as a result of these online dating sites?"

"I don't know."

"Well, can you give me your best estimate? Would you say fifty?"

"Fifty? No way. Maybe five or six."

"Ms. Meyers, Devin Allerdyce is the CEO of Wheelz, is that correct?"

"Yes."

"Did he invite you to dinner?"

"No—"

"No? When he said to you over chat, 'OK if we meet at Madrigal at seven,' were you aware that Madrigal is a restaurant?"

"Yes."

"An invitation to a restaurant at seven o'clock in the evening is not a dinner invitation?"

"Well, I mean, it was supposed to be a business meeting. He said he wanted to talk about the Carras case."

"A business meeting at the most expensive restaurant in Boston?"

"No, at first he asked me to come by his office. Later he changed it to Madrigal."

"Ms. Meyers, did you know that Devin Allerdyce was single?"

She seemed to hesitate. "I think I'd heard that, but I don't remember."

"Ms. Meyers, when a single man invites you to dinner at an expensive, romantic restaurant like Madrigal, wouldn't you assume that was a date?"

A female voice broke in: "Objection! This is ridiculous; this is improper and totally irrelevant and intending to harass the witness."

Madden said, "Counsel, are you instructing the witness not to answer the question?"

"No, I'm not instructing her not to answer, but this is a highly inappropriate line of questioning. You can answer the question, Rachel."

Rachel Meyers's eyes slid from one side to the other, from her lawyer to Madden. "No, I did not assume it was a date," she said. "He's the CEO of the company. I thought it was business."

"Ms. Meyers, is it true that you changed your clothes before dinner?"

A pause. "Yes."

"What did you change into?"

"I—I don't remember."

"Have you been to Madrigal many times?"

"No, just that one time."

"And you can't remember what you wore that night?"

Glenda Craft's voice broke in again. "Objection, this is completely irrelevant. How is the fact that she changed her clothes relevant? This was almost two years ago! How would she remember what she was wearing on one night two years ago?"

"Objection," said Harlan Madden. "Coaching the witness."

"Go ahead and answer, Rachel," said Craft.

"I don't remember," Rachel said.

"Thank you," Madden said. "Ms. Meyers, did you order wine at dinner?"

"He did."

"Did you drink wine?"

"Yes."

"How many glasses of wine did you drink?"

"The waiter kept filling my glass. I don't know."

"Really? Do you think it was at least two glasses?"

"Probably."

"More?"

"Possibly."

"Three glasses?"

"I don't know."

Another pause. "Ms. Meyers, were you intoxicated at your dinner with Devin Allerdyce at Madrigal?"

"That's it!" Glenda Craft, loud and angry. "Time-out. We're taking a break."

"We're not taking a break until I finish this line of questioning."

"No, we need a break, and we're taking one right now!"

"I'm not going to allow you to take a break and go off the record until I finish this line of inquiry."

"Come on, Rachel, let's go."

Rachel looked uncertainly at her lawyer and slowly got up, walking off to the left of the camera. Now all Juliana could see was an empty side of the conference table and a white wall. The time code kept racing along.

Madden raised his voice. "If you guys get up now, I'm going to suspend the deposition, and I'm going to go to court and file a motion."

Craft: "Do what you want. Come on, Rachel, let's confer out in the hall."

Madden: "I am suspending this deposition based on improper conduct by the plaintiff's counsel, and I intend to file a motion to ask the court to intervene and instruct the plaintiff's lawyer to allow me to conduct this deposition as I'm allowed under our rules of civil procedure, without improper coaching and interruptions."

The blank table, the white wall stayed on-screen for another ten seconds, and then it went dark.

She understood why the defense lawyer was pissed off: he was on a roll, he'd gotten the plaintiff in a corner and wanted to keep her there. And the plaintiff's lawyer, Glenda Craft, had in fact been coaching the witness. In her objection to Madden's question, about what Rachel wore that night at Madrigal, she'd all but supplied Rachel's answer. On the other hand, she shouldn't have interrupted the deposition, taking a break while a question was pending and meeting with her client. You didn't do that.

Juliana figured she'd wait for the plaintiff's lawyer to submit her opposition, and then she'd make a ruling quickly, which meant within the week.

She ejected the disk and packed up her files. She had a meeting at Jake's school to get to. Her regular life went on.

Duncan picked her up outside the courthouse for the conference with Jake's math teacher. They'd decided to go together.

She got in, said, "Hi." Wary.

Duncan said, "Hi." Same.

They avoided each other's eyes. Juliana watched the road.

Duncan's 2014 Prius was littered with coffee cups and empty Diet Coke cans. The cans rattled around, sliding front to back and side to side as he drove. For a long time, she listened to the uneven clatter. Once again she was distracted by that obsessive part of her brain that kept cycling. She kept seeing the dead body of Matías Sanchez. The man with the shaved head and the steel-rim glasses: Greaves, and his terrifying threats. Trooper Markowski and—what was his name, she'd forgotten. What would happen to that video that Matías had shown her, the blackmail video?

"Doing okay?" Duncan said.

"I'm okay," she said. She was grateful he asked about her.

"Do we have a strategy here?"

"I don't even know what's going on with Jake in math. Did he tell you? He wouldn't tell me. He said he didn't know how he's doing."

"Oh, he knows."

"Does he?"

"I'm sure. But he won't tell me either."

"Wild guess: not so good."

A long silence passed. She started thinking again about the police and what they wanted. She hated being this scattered and willed herself to think about Jake and his damned math class. "Has he been doing his homework?" she asked.

"I assume so. He goes upstairs to his room and puts on his headphones and taps away at the keyboard. Sometimes I hear him talking on the phone."

Another long silence.

Then she said, "He hasn't stopped vaping, has he?"

"I don't know."

"I don't smell pot, but you wouldn't, with a vape pen, right?"

"That's right."

Another pause.

"So our son is vaping to take the edge off, and lo and behold, he's flunking math. I guess that's taking the edge off, all right."

Duncan rolled his eyes.

Sometimes, she thought, Duncan acted more like his son's pal than his father. But he was a warm and loving father, and that was the most important thing. He was born and bred to it: he came from a big and loving Italian family, where (at least as she imagined it) there was always a pot of marinara bubbling on the stove. He and his brothers and sisters bickered constantly but always came through for one another.

The Espositos could not have been more different from the Brodys. Her mother practically mainlined her martinis after work every night. Her father was what today you'd call emotionally unavailable. He was an articulate man, a brilliant teacher, but he rarely spoke at home except to complain about the administration at the school where he taught. A general fug of disappointment always surrounded him. He was always working on his novel, which no one ever saw. It was never published, and as far as Juliana knew, it was never completed. All he'd say about it was that it was "literary." He was recessive, a shrinking violet: always removed, always distracted. He was barely even there. He emerged from his shell only to grouse about something. Follow his rules and leave him alone.

Her mother only drank at home, never at work, or so she insisted. But she drank a lot at home. To the extent that dinner would usually burn in the oven. Twice she'd almost burned down the house. It got so bad that Juliana started making dinner. Then, since her mother always slept late, Juliana had to start making Calvin's lunches every morning. She remembered putting in those little red boxes of raisins for him instead of the fun-size Kit Kat bars left over from Halloween, being the responsible mom-type figure; she also remembered Calvin's howls of protest. There were plenty of times when she wanted to go into a sulk, to throw a fit, to act like a kid. To be a moody adolescent. But that felt like a luxury she couldn't afford. That *they* couldn't afford.

Everything in the Brody house went unsaid; everything was distant and swaddled in batting. She'd grown used to the silences.

She'd looked at her parents' lives and thought: *I want no part of that.*

Her dad, desperately unhappy and unloved in his job. Her mom, living in a world of pretend. And then if you rebelled against them, like Calvin, you got yourself killed.

So it was Duncan's family-centric warmth that had really attracted her to him, even more than his brown eyes and his long lashes and his perfect butt. More than his passion, his intellectual stubbornness. In a way, it came down to how much he loved his mother.

Jake's math teacher, Mr. Wertheim, was a clumsy, overweight man in his late twenties with thick glasses and an inability to look you in the face. Juliana had forgotten what his first name was. He was just Mr. Wertheim. He opened the door to the classroom with a surprised look that implied that he'd forgotten they were coming. The classroom was otherwise empty. They sat in chairs with tablet arm desks, facing one another. Mr. Wertheim cleared his throat and looked down at the desktop. He wore a green tartan plaid shirt. His big belly barely fit behind the desk. He traced a figure eight on the desk with his index finger and cleared his throat and said, "Um, I think Jake is a really smart kid with a lot of potential, but he's failing math."

"Failing?" Juliana said.

"The last three tests he's gotten an F. And he hasn't turned in the last six homework assignments."

Juliana looked at Duncan, who looked rattled. "What can he do about it?" Duncan said, ever the optimist.

"That's the thing. I don't know. I've offered to stay after school to work with him, but he has yet to take me up on it. I figured he'd have time after school since he's quit the soccer team."

As they left the classroom, Juliana said, "He quit soccer?"

"I'm stunned. Jesus."

"Wow. So what's he doing after school every day?"

He was silent for a beat. "Not his math homework, clearly." He laughed painfully.

They walked for a while in silence. Outside the building they said hi to Jake's history teacher, Ms. Howland. Juliana wondered whether he was flunking history too. She looked at her watch. "We're fifteen minutes early to pick him up. From whatever he's doing. You want to wait with me?"

"I do. Thanks."

They sat on the wooden bench outside the main entrance, where kids waited for their parents.

She said, "Our son's flunking math, and we're flunking parenthood."

After a long silence, they both started talking at the same time. "You know," Duncan said as she said, "Can I say something?" and then "Go ahead."

Finally Duncan collected himself. "I'm not ready for you to come home yet," he said. "We built something together—it's not me and it's not you, it's something else, and maybe we have a responsibility to it. Now, I'm not the perfect husband, I know that. This isn't all on you."

"Thanks," she said. "But it kinda is."

He hesitated. "Yeah, it kinda is," he said, and he smiled. A pause. "So we'll talk to him?"

"Whatever good that does. He keeps telling me soccer is 'fine,' and he doesn't elaborate, but that's sort of typical of the way he is these days, with me anyway."

A few minutes later, her phone rang. It was Martie Connolly. "I just got a heads-up," she said. "The two police detectives are on their way. When do you think you'll be back?"

Her stomach knotted. "Give me half an hour," she said.

Jake showed up a while later, his heavy backpack looped over his right shoulder, his big headphones around his neck.

"How was soccer?" Juliana and Duncan said in unison, unintentionally.

Jake looked from one to the other, realizing something was up. "I didn't go to soccer," he admitted.

Gently, Juliana said, "What'd you do, Jake?"

"I worked in the library."

"Uh-huh." She didn't persist, because she was fairly certain he was lying.

They were all getting much too good at that.

"We need to talk," Juliana said.

37

She tried Lyft, but the app said there were no drivers available and she didn't want to be late for the interview with the detectives. So she requested a Wheelz black car, and the app said the driver, whose name was Mohammed, would be arriving in seven minutes. Gradually the time counted down to one minute and then "arriving now," and a moment later a black BMW 7 Series limousine pulled up to the curb. It glinted in the watery light of dusk. She said good-bye to her husband and son and got into the back of the car.

She greeted Mohammed. The BMW smelled new. She sat back and tried to relax, checking her e-mail on her phone. The sedan pulled into the rush-hour traffic on Beacon Street.

Jake had been understandably defensive. He said his math teacher was "overreacting" and that he promised he'd do better in math. No, he didn't want a tutor. He apologized for "kinda lying" about going to soccer practice, but he was doing homework in the library and working on a "project" that he didn't want to talk about.

Unfortunately, she hadn't been particularly engaged during their talk with him. She'd been far too distracted. She kept mulling over what the state trooper had said. *A couple things have come up.*

That could be any number of things. He had sounded reasonable and accommodating, but that was the pose of a guy with a winning hand. It made her nervous.

"Judge Brody, it's time," the driver said.

She looked up. Surely she had misheard him. For an instant she wondered how the hell he knew she was a judge. As far as he knew, her name was Juliana, no last name. That was the most information Wheelz gave the driver, the passenger's first name and a number, the average score other drivers had given her.

Then she recognized the man's face, and an electric charge crackled down her spine. Greaves.

"Pull over," she said. "Now."

"I'm afraid we have something to discuss."

"I have nothing to say to you. Pull over."

"My employers are running out of patience. You've already hit your deadline. Tell me why we should give you any more time."

"I have nothing to say to you." She grabbed at the door handle and tried to yank it open, without success. She tried again. It was locked from the inside.

"You think you're calling the shots, but you're not."

"Are *you*?" She inhaled sharply. Her heart was racing.

"I'm a messenger. Nothing more."

"I know who you are. You're Donald James Greaves, dishonorably discharged from the Marines twelve years ago for assaulting your commanding officer. Employed by Fidelis Integrated Security for eight years. You've lived in Jacksonville, North Carolina, and Memphis. You're certified, level two, in Russian kettlebells, you take Lipitor for high cholesterol, and I know who you took to your high school senior prom."

Greaves was silent for several seconds.

"So pull the goddamned car over and let me out now."

"We're almost finished, Judge. Plus, we'll be arriving at your destination in a few minutes."

"We're finished."

"I think you need me to explain your situation. As clearly as possible. You have not been cooperative, and my employers are not happy about this. So the requirements have escalated. Listen to me closely, please. The defense will be filing a motion for summary judgment. You will respond in the usual way. You'll schedule an oral argument, you will take the motion under advisement, and then you will issue a written decision granting that motion, thereby ending the case. This will all happen quickly: once the defense files the motion, you will have no more than a week to grant it."

"And if I deny the motion?"

"First up would be a scandal that totally incinerates your career."

"Maybe I can live with that."

"Oh, but that's the thing. You *can't*. After a very public disgrace like that? No one's going to question your decision."

"My decision."

"You'll have it easy. It's your husband and your children—they're going to have to live with it. You—who knows how it happens. Is it an overdose of pills? A leap out the window of a tall building? Suicide by motor vehicle, like your brother? Do you want to write it, or shall I?"

"What the hell are you talking about? Write what?"

"Your suicide note." He was silent for a beat. "You have some pondering to do."

38

The two detectives gawked at the view as they entered Martie's condo. They all shook hands. Juliana smiled at them politely while her mind raced through her horrifying exchange with Greaves. Detective Markowski, the state trooper, was wearing a mismatched suit: a blue jacket and lighter blue pants. Detective Krieger, the Boston policeman, was the nattier dresser, in a sharp gray suit with a purple tie, looking like a network anchorman.

Lucy, the Jack Russell terrier, growled at them, sitting alert. As if she sensed their hostility.

Martie showed them to her living room and offered them coffee, which Krieger declined but Markowski accepted gratefully. While Martie went to her kitchen to prepare the coffee, the two cops made awkward small talk with Juliana. They understood they couldn't ask Juliana anything of substance until her attorney returned with the coffee.

Once Detective Markowski had his coffee, cream with two Splendas, Martie sat at a high-backed chair and folded her arms. She had a large presence, even though she was petite. When she walked into a room, you noticed her.

"It's good to meet you," she said. "I'm Martha Connolly. You probably don't remember that I was chief justice of the Supreme Judicial Court back in the day."

"Of course we do, Your Honor," said Markowski.

"It's an honor to meet you," added Krieger.

"Now, Judge Brody is not only my client today, but she's an old, dear friend. She's one of the finest judges I know, and not just in Massachusetts. She is a woman of impeccable character. But you know what they say, a lawyer who represents herself has a fool for a client, and Judge Brody is no fool." Both detectives were watching her closely. "In light of her stature as a public figure and the sensitivity of this matter, I'm here to be sure that the integrity of this process is maintained and that her rights are fully protected."

They both nodded, and Markowski said, "Understood. We'd like to apologize, first, for taking your time on this matter once again, but we've received some new information we'd like to ask you about."

Detective Krieger busied himself writing on a clipboard.

"Let's start with the decedent's hotel, the, uh, Home Stay Inn in Allston. We've had a chance to review the hotel's surveillance tape, and we wanted to clear up a couple of points. Did you say you've been to this hotel?"

"Asked and answered," Martie said, before Juliana could say anything.

Markowski feigned a confused look. He'd already asked her, and she'd denied ever being there. He was trying to entrap her. They wanted her to think they had her on videotape, so she'd no longer dare try to deny it.

But she knew better. They had no tape. He was bluffing.

"As I've already told you, I have not been to that hotel," Juliana said.

Martie scowled but said nothing. She obviously didn't want Juliana to talk.

Markowski seemed to be studying his notepad, as if the right answer were there. The other man looked from his partner to Juliana and back again.

Markowski said, "Judge, have you recently taken a trip out of town?"

"I went to Chicago last week for a conference," she replied, and she thought: *They've pulled my credit card records.*

"Which hotel did you stay at?"

"The Peninsula." Which they must know if they'd done their homework.

"Did you at any time encounter the decedent during your stay at that hotel?"

She suddenly felt a chill. *They've pulled my credit card records and know that Matías Sanchez and I were at the same hotel at the same time, the same bar at the same time,* she thought. Were there eyewitnesses? All she and Matías had done in public was to sit and talk.

"You don't have to answer this," Martie said.

"That's all right. No. I had no idea—was he there?"

She remembered: *We were both on the rooftop terrace at the same time, having drinks. Did we use our credit cards at the same time too?* That she didn't recall. Had Matías paid for the drinks? She thought so, but she wasn't sure. She had been on her second glass of wine by then.

That made her think of her mother, reliably soused at night after work or on the weekend, and she wondered again whether she should maybe stop drinking. She was fairly certain she didn't have the alcoholic gene, but growing up with Roz Brody as your mom, you had to wonder if her drinking problem might have been passed on.

"That's what I found interesting, that you both stayed at the same hotel at the same time. Quite the coincidence."

Martie smiled at Juliana, then turned to Markowski. "Two lawyers at a national legal conference." A frosty smile. "Some coincidence. Gentlemen, do you have anything else for Judge Brody?"

"We're still trying to figure out how Judge Brody's sunglasses ended up in Mr. Sanchez's hotel room."

"Well, best of luck with that, and do let us know when you have an answer. Are we done here?"

"That's all we have," said Markowski.

"If you're done processing the sunglasses," Juliana said, "I'd like them back."

"You didn't need me," Martie Connolly said later.

"No. But it was good to have you there. For moral support."

"If they could place you there at the hotel consorting with Sanchez, they would have said so."

"True."

"I don't think they're going to be able to connect you with him outside the courtroom. And I don't think they're coming back."

Juliana nodded. "I hope you're right. But as long as I have that sex tape hanging over my head, this isn't over."

She went to her room a short while later to check e-mail one last time and get ready for bed. When she opened her laptop and signed into her e-mail, she found a new message from an address she didn't recognize. The sender was a Richard Donegan, followed by a string of numbers, at Gmail. The subject was "Your Recent Visit." Curious, she clicked on the link in the e-mail. It opened slowly, and she saw that it was a color photograph, large and high-resolution. She had to reposition her cursor several times to get to the center of the image.

She was instantly overcome by dread. It was an image capture from a surveillance tape. Her face was half-turned toward the camera, clearly recognizable despite the hat. Her right hand was poised in midair, knocking at a door whose number, 322, was also clearly discernible.

"Oh, dear," Martha said when she saw it, a few moments later. "So the surveillance video wasn't missing after all."

"I assume the police don't have this."

"Yet."

"A way to remind me of the leverage they have over me. They can prove I lied to the police."

"Exactly."

"I've dragged you into this, and for that I'm deeply sorry."

"Honey, I'm retired. There's nothing that can be done to me."

"Your reputation. You know I lied to law enforcement."

"I've done worse. Someday I'll tell you." She put a hand on Juliana's. "But we don't know who's doing this to you, do we?"

Juliana shook her head.

"Philip hasn't found out who's behind all this?"

"Nope." She fell silent for a long time. She could hear the ticking of Martie's grandfather clock in the foyer.

"You'd tell me if you knew, wouldn't you?"

Juliana looked at her sharply. "Of course. But I think I know someone who does. Someone who might know what's really going on."

Martie raised her eyebrows.

"Marshak," Juliana said.

Martie's eyes went wide, an incredulous look on her face. "Ray Marshak? That's crazy. That man is your mortal enemy."

"Maybe so. But no one knows more about financial subterfuge."

"With him you may be putting yourself in even greater danger, Juliana. From what I've heard, anyway. What are you thinking?"

For a long time, Juliana didn't reply.

Then she said, "I'm desperate, Martie. Do you understand that?"

Martie nodded slowly. "And desperate times call for desperate measures. I get it. But please, Juliana. Be careful."

39

Raymond Marshak had made his fortune in something called risk arbitrage, though the real secret to his success was illegal insider trading. It was an open secret. For years he had gotten away with it. Until Juliana Brody came along.

As a young assistant US Attorney, Juliana had heard the rumors and decided to do something. But Marshak was a slippery bastard. Getting anything on him seemed impossible. Everyone was afraid to testify against him. He went around in a low-hanging fog of suspicion, yet he repeatedly eluded prosecution. Finally Juliana was able to nab him on a technicality: he'd sent confirmation slips through the mail that didn't disclose the fact that a commission was included in the price. Piddling, but that constituted mail fraud. A felony.

Her boss, the US Attorney, Kent Yarnell, wanted her to drop the case. She couldn't win, it would look bad; Marshak was too high-profile, too well connected. Yarnell was always most concerned about his scorecard. Better a guilty man go free, he probably believed, than be embarrassed by an acquittal. He wouldn't go ahead with a case unless he had 95 percent certainty that it would result in a conviction. And Juliana admitted there probably was only an 80 percent chance she'd win.

So instead of going up against Kent and getting fired, Juliana reached out to a law school friend in the Justice Department in Washington, Aaron Dunn, who worked in the Securities and Financial Fraud Unit. Dunn's unit was supremely interested in bringing down the notorious Ray Marshak, however they could do it. Hell, they got Al Capone on tax evasion; if mail fraud was what it required to take down Ray Marshak, go for it. Now she had the air cover to pursue her case against Marshak, no matter how Kent Yarnell felt about it. Kent was pissed off, but he'd been neutralized. He couldn't stop her.

Going above your boss's head was normally a firing offense, but Juliana got the conviction. Her boss wouldn't dare fire her for cooperating with Main Justice, with headquarters. So she kept her job—and even though he got to take some of the credit, she'd nonetheless made an enemy in Kent Yarnell.

And, of course, Ray Marshak, who went to prison for five years. When he came out, he returned to his wife, his mansion in Chestnut Hill, Mass., and a good chunk of his ill-gotten fortune. And an abiding animosity toward Juliana Brody, who by then had gone into private practice.

So it was no surprise that he kept her waiting for almost fifteen minutes in his front sitting room, a space as large as the entire downstairs of her house. The bigger surprise was that he'd agreed to see her in the first place. She sat on a hard sofa that was probably a valuable antique and anxiously checked her iPhone. At last a petite young woman in black-and-white livery sidled into the room and asked Juliana to follow her.

The housekeeper walked out into a harlequin-tiled hallway, Juliana close behind, her heels clicking on the floor.

Ray Marshak's study was lined with leather-bound books he'd never read or even opened. He sat at a delicate antique secretary in a cone of light and looked up as the servant knocked at the open door. He raised his hands like a priest offering a benediction, but he didn't get up. "Why, Judge Brody, how long has it been?"

"Thank you for seeing me, Ray." The housekeeper left, and Juliana sat in a chair facing Marshak.

"How could I possibly resist?"

Five years in prison had aged him ten. He had never been a good-looking man, with his moon face, pockmarked cheeks only partly camouflaged by a scraggly gray beard. Now he looked frail, his shoulders humped. He was in his midseventies but looked much older.

"I was intrigued to hear from you, Judge Brody. You've come to ask a favor. It almost sounds like a joke, does it not?"

She noticed a cluster of framed pictures on the desk, facing the visitor, of him with George Bush the younger, golfing with Trump.

"I suppose it does," she said.

"But I'm honored by your visit. I've always admired your pluck."

"My pluck."

"Against all odds, you've managed to climb the greasy pole, haven't you?"

"I wouldn't say the odds were against me. Not at all."

"Well, you certainly made an enemy of Kent Yarnell."

"That I did. But Kent wasn't on the Governor's Council. He wasn't able to blackball me."

"Lucky you. You were quite clever, the way you went after me."

"Just doing my job."

"Well played. You probably imagine you're on the side of the just and the righteous, don't you?"

"I wouldn't say that," Juliana said.

"I think you do." She could see anger tighten his face. "You had a career to make. Another check in the win column. You didn't care what it might do to a family, the shame it would bring to my wife. And to my son. That didn't figure in your moral calculus at all, did it?"

Juliana didn't reply.

"And using that absurd technicality to prosecute me. Because you couldn't make an honest case. How is that justice?"

"I did what was right," Juliana said. "If I could have gone after you with bigger weapons, I sure would have."

"The United States versus Ray Marshak," he said. "Does that sound like a fair fight to you?"

"It's not meant to be."

"You're here because you want something from me, and—even stranger—you actually think I'm going to give it to you."

"All I can do is ask," she said.

"So, Judge Brody, I am all ears." He folded his arms and smiled.

"Yes, I'm here to ask your help."

"Me?"

"There's no one more qualified," she said.

"I'm listening."

"Do you know anything about a company called Mayfair Paragon?" she said.

He shook his head. "Should I?"

"What about Harrogate Capital Partners?"

He paused. "Aren't they some investment firm in the north of England?"

"Right. They bailed out a company called Wheelz, and now they own most of it."

"And Wheelz is one of the cases you're presiding over, am I right? One of your cases?"

"It is."

"I vaguely remember—Wheelz was almost declared dead; then this English firm shows up and saves it. I remember wondering what lunatic would sink a billion dollars into a failing Uber competitor. Insanity. I mean, in a world with Uber and Lyft, who needs Wheelz?"

"Here's what I want to know," she said. "Whose money was behind it?"

"Behind Harrogate Capital Partners?"

"Right. Who's the investor?"

"Why do you want to know?"

"I have my reasons."

"And what makes you think I have the answer?"

"I don't. But I think you know how to find it."

"Do I?"

"You know how money is hidden. You're a master of financial engineering."

"You flatter me."

"It's not flattery, Mr. Marshak. In this realm you have no equal."

"I'm fascinated," Marshak said. "This is so inappropriate—for a judge to be conducting a private inquiry like this."

She shrugged, said nothing.

"I wonder what they have on you."

She immediately blushed and hoped it wasn't too visible. She shook her head slowly, disapproving.

Marshak continued that line of thought. "Probably a hell of a lot more substantial than what you had on me. In fact, I have a feeling that you're walking on the dark side yourself. I'm speculating that you're no longer quite so high and mighty. Those pretty little hands of yours, with that pink manicure—there's dirt in those nails, isn't there? Sure, you like to pretend that you're better than me, but I can tell those hands aren't quite clean."

"I understand," she said. "You don't know the answer, but you can't bring yourself to admit it. That's all right. If you don't know, you don't know."

For a brief instant, he looked stung, but he quickly recovered. He sighed with exasperation, then laughed. He was being manipulated, and he knew it.

"Tell me, Judge Brody," he said after a moment. "How much do you know about the money behind Harrogate? Do you know anything?"

"Very little. I know the financing for the Wheelz deal was done by a bank in Cyprus."

"Ah."

"And a bank in the British Virgin Islands."

He gave a crooked grin. "I see. Well, here's the first thing to know. There's no such thing as total anonymity," Marshak said. "Everyone leaves tracks."

"What sort of tracks?"

"For instance, if they're the lead investor in Wheelz, you can be certain of one thing: they will certainly have installed their janissaries."

"Their *what* now?"

"Janissaries. The sultan's bodyguards."

"Bodyguards. I don't understand."

"A lead investor will insist on placing two or three of their own people—his janissaries, I call them—in key positions throughout the company. To make sure things are done right. To report back. His *people*." He nodded a few times. "So the rumors are true," he said, almost as if to himself.

"Rumors?"

"It's the Russians. That's the Russian pattern. The Cyprus-BVI structure—that's classic oligarch. Their offshore havens. How these Russian billionaires keep their honeypot away from the Russian bear. The tax collectors. You are dealing with an oligarch. Quite likely *chorniy krug*."

"Which means—?"

"Hell if I know. It's what they call Putin's inner circle, the oligarchs who remain directly connected to the Kremlin and the Russian security services. Most slavishly loyal to Putin. The ones who'll do the Kremlin's dirty work when asked, without hesitation. This is the sort of people you're going up against."

"Okay."

"If your plan is to go bear hunting, be my guest. I'd love to see you try." He smiled tightly. "Because I know how it ends."

"Do you."

"Oh, yes. I can see the glistening red viscera around the bear's mouth."

"So how do I find out the name of my oligarch?"

"Go for the soft underbelly in their security. The weak spot. It's always the lawyers. Law firms have the worst IT security. It's laughable."

"But what can the lawyers tell me?"

"The lawyers have to fill out all the tedious paperwork."

"Like the accredited investor form?"

Marshak's eyebrows shot up. "Very good. I'm impressed, Your Honor. Yes, find the lawyers and you'll find the names of their clients. Of course, if you had any sense, you'd just let this thing lie. But that's not your way. You are not the type to ever back down. Which I'm counting on."

"Why is that?"

"Because it's a throne of blood, and I'm happy to take you to it. Because when you go up against some of those *chorniy krug* oligarchs, you're putting your life on the line."

"That right?"

"If I were a betting man, and I am, my money would not be on you. You're playing Russian roulette. But I rather enjoy the prospect. Because sooner or later that bullet is going to wind up in the chamber. *Click.* And I won't shed a tear." A thin smile. "Your Honor."

40

Philip Hersh was wearing his ratty gray suit, looking again like a down-and-out courthouse lawyer. His shirt collar was frayed. He handed Juliana a cup of coffee from Tanner Roast in downtown Boston and sat down in the old wooden chair next to her desk in her lobby. His was the gloomy expression of a man who didn't much like his life.

"The Russians, huh?" he said.

"So Ray Marshak says. An oligarch."

"He didn't have a name?"

She shook her head. Her mobile phone began to ring. She glanced at it, saw it was a judge friend of hers.

"Hold on," she said, and she answered the call.

"Juliana, it's Nina Ernst."

"Hi, Nina. What's up?"

"The strangest thing. Last night I was approached by a state trooper, an investigator with the AG's office, requesting a search warrant on *you*."

Her heart started to skitter. "You're kidding."

"Your lobby, your home. They want files, computers."

"They have probable cause?"

"Weak, I thought. I turned it down. But I thought you should know. Any idea what might be going on?"

"I'm as baffled as you are. More so. But thanks for the heads-up, Nina. Morrie doing okay?"

"He's great, thanks. He's, like, ten times as energetic since the bypass."

She hit End and looked back at Hersh. "The AG's office is requesting a search warrant. On me."

He nodded. "Did they get it?"

"Not from this judge."

"Well, that's good, anyway. So Marshak didn't have any names?"

"No. But he says focus on the lawyers. Find out which law firms are involved in the Wheelz deal."

Hersh nodded. "Ropes and Gray, and Miller and Payson, were the two firms I remember reading about."

"Miller and Payson—right, that's Noah Miller's firm."

"Noah Miller represents Harrogate Capital Partners."

She remembered Noah Miller coming up to her at the St. Jude's fundraiser. The curly hair, the big bald spot, the rimless glasses, the staring eyes. He was the one who'd suggested she flush the Wheelz case from her docket, get rid of it, grant the defense's motion to have it dismissed. Of course: he represented the investor, Harrogate Capital Partners. There had been something about the relentlessness with which he'd pursued the subject. Something about the fake casualness, the way his eyes hadn't left hers. Yeah, she was pretty certain that hadn't been random.

She told Hersh about her conversation at the fundraiser, then wheeled her chair around to her computer and typed Miller's name into Google. The first search result was his page on the Miller & Payson website. She found a flattering studio picture of Miller, smiling wisely. She scanned the anodyne bio and read aloud to Hersh: "White-collar criminal litigation and complex business litigation, a range of criminal and civil litigation matters, blah blah blah. Nothing useful here."

But she had a feeling about the guy.

"Marshak said that lawyers have the worst IT security."

"Often true."

"Can you get into his e-mail?"

He looked surprised and took a breath. But her phone rang again. Duncan. She said, "Excuse me," answered, "Hey."

"There's some cops here, searching the house!" He sounded panicked. "They handed me a warrant, and it looks legit."

"Boston Police?"

"State Police. What's this about, Jules? Is this about that goddamned lawyer—?"

Just then she heard a loud pounding on her office door. "Hold on," she said to Duncan. She got up and opened the door. "Shit. They're here too."

Duncan said something, loud and rushed, but she wasn't listening anymore. Four state troopers stood in the hallway. She recognized the one with the goatee and the swept-back hair, Markowski.

"Judge Brody?" he said. "We've got a warrant to search your office. May we please enter?"

"May I see the warrant first, please?"

"Of course." Detective Markowski handed her the thatch of papers. The search warrant, the application, the affidavit. The affidavit was a page long and sworn by State Police Detective Markowski. She skimmed it quickly. It mentioned the sunglasses found in the deceased's hotel room, her stay at the same hotel in Chicago as the deceased, all that. Written in a careful, just-the-facts manner. She looked over the search warrant application and saw that it was signed by a famously hard-ass Suffolk Superior Court Judge named Warren Hogan. She'd met Hogan, though she wouldn't call him a friend.

Everything in the warrant seemed to be in order. She noticed the box was checked where you had to say whether you'd submitted this affidavit to another judge previously. Markowski, turned down by Judge Nina

Ernst, had next approached a judge who was rarely known to say no to law enforcement.

She put the iPhone back up to her ear and said, "I'm sorry. Let me call you back." Then she said to Markowski, "Come on in. I have to get into court, but, Philip, can you stay here while they search?"

Hersh looked at her. There was something new in his gloomy expression, maybe an *I told you so.* "I can stay for another half hour, but then I have another appointment."

"Whatever you can do," she said.

Markowski and the other one, Krieger, small and bald and worried, nodded at her as they entered. There was barely room for them in her lobby along with herself and Hersh.

"Is this really necessary?" she said. "You said I'm a person of interest. Not a suspect."

Markowski pointed to her computer. "If you're in the middle of any documents, you might want to save them now."

"You're taking my *computer*? For God's sake, why?"

But she knew why. The attorney general was looking to tie her to the murder any way he could. She was furious, but she managed to stay silent. They'd find nothing on her computer. They were wasting their time and hers. She steadied her breathing, and looked at her watch. She was three minutes late for court, and she liked to start on time.

41

When court was out for lunch, Juliana returned to her lobby, took off her robe and hung it, and sat behind her desk. She could see the big dust-free rectangle in the middle of her desktop where her computer used to be. Her phone indicated a voice mail from Hersh. Without bothering to listen to it, she called him back.

"They took some files from your file cabinet," he said. "That and the computer, that's all."

"Thanks for staying."

"That was totally unnecessary. Just a brutal show of force."

"I told you, the AG hates me, has for years." She hesitated. "So I have a question for you, but I'm not sure we should be talking about it on the phone."

"It depends. Are you talking on your office landline or your mobile phone?"

"Cell. My iPhone."

"I'm reasonably confident your iPhone is secure, and I know on my end I'm clean."

"Well, I'd rather be careful. I'll come by your office when court's out this afternoon. Will you be there?"

"Call first, but I should be. Meanwhile, I think I found your 'janissary.'"

"Really?" She remembered what Ray Marshak had told her, about how the new owner of a company might plant his own soldiers, his guys, in the company. Janissaries, he'd said. "Excellent."

"I searched every executive hire made *after* the company was sold. And one of them caught my eye—the CFO, a guy named Eugene Brod."

"I remember him. He's the guy in the chats I read who wouldn't let Rachel Meyers see the paperwork on Mayfair Paragon."

"He's Russian—his name originally was *Yevgeny* Brod; he worked in the Moscow office of PricewaterhouseCoopers, the accounting firm. A graduate of Moscow State Forest University."

"Interesting," she said.

"It makes sense for the owner to plant the CFO. He's the keeper of all data and all knowledge. I may follow him home from work one day, see what I find."

"Terrific. Thank you."

She ended the call. She was hungry, and she also needed fresh air, so she took the elevator down and lined up at the pho truck in front of the courthouse. The line was long, but it was worth it. A guy got in line behind her, and then a woman. The pho truck had only recently started coming around, and it was a smash hit; it was like she and the other people in line shared a secret.

She worried about what the attorney general might do. Sure, he was probably out to get her, but what could he actually find? Then the thought hit her: *Is it possible I left my fingerprints somewhere in the hotel room?*

"Worth the wait?"

The guy in line behind her, in a black leather jacket.

She smiled. "Oh, for sure."

"So, long line for a reason."

"It goes fast."

"Got to be better than the crap they're peddling inside, the café on the second floor." He had a very slight accent. Middle Eastern? Russian? She wasn't sure. She smiled politely, looked at her phone, trying to discourage further conversation.

But the man wasn't done. He had gray-flecked black hair, a neat part, a long, sharp nose. Black crewneck sweater that looked like cashmere, over a gray shirt. He wasn't dressed like a lawyer. "I once got a chicken parm sandwich inside, had a hair in it. Last time I ever ate there."

"Yuck." She kept looking at her phone, hoping he'd take a hint.

"Always gotta be careful, all you judges. Minefield out there. Cross your eyes at the wrong person and the CJC opens an investigation, right?"

Her bowels clenched. The Commission on Judicial Conduct went after errant judges.

She looked directly at him, studying his features. Who the hell was this guy? He was in his forties and somehow gave off an air of prosperity and confidence. Brown eyes, heavy eyebrows. Strong-looking.

"Do I know you?" she said.

"You're Judge Brody, right?" In a quieter voice he went on, "Sleep with the wrong lawyer, CJC's going to come after you all hot and heavy, right? It's crazy."

Blood rushed to her face. Suddenly it was as if the sound had cut out. All she could hear was the beating of her heart. She watched the man's mouth move.

"What do you want?" His hands were strong and callused, capable of anything.

"Once they got their hooks in you, they don't let go. I mean, it can be career-ending stuff." He shook his head.

Nobody in line, nobody around her, had the slightest idea anything was wrong. Even on this busy street corner, she realized, this crowded place, she was all alone. She noticed a man leaning against the courthouse, holding a wrapped sandwich. The man smiled at her and nodded. At her? Or at somebody else? Was he a stranger? An enemy? The line seemed to be blurring. She felt light-headed.

The guy in the black leather jacket glanced at her casually, then looked at his watch. "My, look at the time," he said. "Enjoy your lunch, Judge Brody. I hear the *bánh mì* sandwich is the thing to get."

And then he walked away.

42

Later that afternoon, Juliana knocked on the Hersh Investigations door, and it came right open. Philip Hersh nodded as she entered the tiny office. He had already cleared off the ladder-back visitor's chair. She sat down. "Here's what I didn't want to ask you over the phone. Do you have a way to hack into Noah Miller's e-mail?"

He was silent for a couple of seconds. "Hack in?" He looked troubled. "Not really in my skill set. Also, I could lose my license. It's illegal."

"But surely you have someone who can do it. Someone you work with."

He hesitated. "No, I don't."

"You don't?"

"*I* don't."

"But—"

"Off the record, I can give you a name. But it's got nothing to do with me."

"Okay . . ."

"You can talk to the guy, see if he'll do it. But you might not want to tell him who you are. A judge."

"You mean, I can't trust him?"

"It's not in his interest to tell anybody about you. But I'd give him as little as you have to."

"Who's your guy?"

Hersh smiled wanly. "Ukrainian, I think. He's just a computer PI who does pen testing and vulnerability assessments. I think he used to be a hacker, but he went legit. Mostly legit. He needs the money—I don't think he has a lot of clients—which is why he's willing to overlook his morals, and the law, for some cash. And if he won't do it, I got other names."

"Why are there so many Ukrainian hackers?"

"Because hacking is legal in Ukraine. There are whole buildings full of people who generate spam and send it out to make money."

"But you say he's good."

"He knows what he's doing. Again, just to be clear, this doesn't go through me. You hire him, you deal with him, my hands are clean."

"Understood."

"I'm happy to look over whatever he finds." Hersh scrawled a name—"Sasha"—and a phone number on a Post-it pad. He pulled the top note off the pad and handed it to her. "Long as I don't know where it came from. Why do you want to hack into Noah Miller's e-mail?"

"I want my life back."

He nodded. "What do you hope to get?"

"Who knows. Information is power."

She heard herself. *Information is power.* Who had she become, what kind of person? There she was, planning to hire someone to break the law for her. Which meant, of course, that *she* was breaking the law.

She was doing something that she'd sent people away for doing.

"In the meantime, I talked to a buddy of mine on the job who got a look at the medical examiner's report on Sanchez's death. The ME's ruling it a homicide, based on the autopsy."

"Not surprised."

"The lack of contusions around the neck or petechial hemorrhages—it's pretty clear evidence the guy was already dead when he was hanged. He was strangled. And then hanged."

She took in that sobering detail, nodded.

"So that's who you're dealing with here, Judge. A guy's been murdered. You have to make sure you're not next."

She closed her eyes, exhaled. "Then I need protection."

"Correct. But not a gun."

"No. But I need . . . something."

He nodded, pulled open a desk drawer and took out something small and dark, about five inches long and an inch wide. He held it in his right hand, and with his thumb he pressed a metal button. A long blade shot out, gleaming and sharp. "You want protection, here's protection." He pulled out something on the knife's handle, and the blade retracted.

"Jesus. What is this, a switchblade?"

"No. A tanto-point Microtech." He handed it to her. "Be careful with this. You could really hurt yourself."

He showed her how to use the knife, giving her painstaking instructions.

She said, "Thank you. As you're always saying, prepare for the worst."

"Yeah, you take every precaution to prevent disaster but know you may fail."

She smiled. "The elevator shaft."

"Yeah, the elevator shaft."

"Mr. Sunshine, as usual. I'm assuming your wife is used to it." She'd noticed his wedding ring, a fat gold band.

His smile faded. "My wife's gone. She died."

"I'm so sorry," she said. "She must have been young. What—happened?"

"What happened is what happened."

She waited for a long moment. Then she said, "Okay." She didn't want to pry into his unhappiness. "Thank you," she said, wagging the knife. "May I never have to use it."

43

After she left Hersh's office, she called the phone number he'd given her and got voice mail. It was a company called Boston Digital Forensics. The voice on the message was male and didn't sound very professional. He had a strong foreign accent, presumably Ukrainian.

Next she called Martie Connolly and told her she'd be coming "home," to Martie's apartment, on the late side. Tonight was parents' night at Jake's school. She and Duncan would arrive separately.

Her phone trilled. She recognized the number as the one she'd called from the Post-it. "Hello?"

"Yeah, I'm looking for—Rosalind?"

"This is Rosalind. Is this Sasha?" She wasn't going to use her real name with the guy if she didn't have to.

"Yes."

"I got your name from Philip Hersh. I need some computer assistance."

"Uh-huh."

"Where's your office? I'm not comfortable talking about this on the phone."

Sasha gave her an address on Newbury Street in the Back Bay.

She didn't have a lot of time—she had to be at Jake's school at seven—but if she hustled, she'd be able to do this. She found a resident parking space on Comm. Ave., where she'd get a ticket if the parking police nabbed her, but she didn't have time to look for a legal one.

The office was in a building whose street-level floor was occupied by a coffee shop. She took a small elevator to the fifth floor and walked down a narrow corridor lined with small offices, past a massage therapist's studio, an accountant, and a financial adviser. The office of Boston Digital Forensics was at the end of the hallway. She knocked on the door and pulled it open.

A small man in his thirties—black hair, beard, hunched shoulders, thick glasses—was sitting at a receptionist's desk right by the entrance, a cup of coffee in his hand. He stood up, shook her hand limply.

"I'm Sasha."

"Rosalind." She felt odd using her mother's name.

He pointed to a couple of couches perpendicular to each other against the walls of the reception area. He waited for her to sit, and then he sat on the other couch and opened a small laptop computer. She could smell the man's sweat and whatever Indian food he'd just eaten. His fingers were poised over the keys.

"So—"

"Can I get name?"

Hersh had told her to give as little as possible. She'd already told him her first name was Rosalind. She used her mother's maiden name. Rosalind Winter. Sasha typed.

"What is it you want?"

"I need access to someone's e-mail."

He nodded as if she'd asked him for an insurance quote.

"Name?"

"Noah Miller. He's at a boutique firm called Miller and Payson." She spelled Miller's name.

More typing. "Law firm."

"Right."

"Should not be a problem." His fingers flew over the keyboard. He worked in silence for a minute, then peered closely at the screen. "Actually, is a problem."

"What kind of problem?"

"The IP address doesn't trace back to the law firm. It traces back to G Suite. Google. Gmail for business."

"What does that mean?"

"Means someone is smart. They take precautions. They don't use exchange server. The system is stovepiped."

That was gobbledygook to her. "Why is that a problem?"

"Usually you can send phishing e-mail to anyone on company's network, and you're in everywhere. But the way the Miller and Payson network is set up, every employee has separate e-mail container. Hosted internally at company. No internal exchange server."

"Does that mean you can't do it?"

He shook his head. "It means if you want to get into this man's e-mail, you have to send him something directly. Not anyone else. Just him. Every e-mail account is in its own silo. So it becomes social engineering problem. If you want this Noah's e-mail, you have to send him e-mail that he will open. Some people are very suspicious and they don't click on anything unless it's from someone they know."

"He knows me."

"Ah. Maybe this is possible, then. But is not cheap."

"How much are we talking about?"

He told her. It was actually less than she was expecting. Hersh had said it wasn't complicated, that all the software could be downloaded, prefab.

"Okay," she said.

"You can send him an e-mail and he will open?"

"I'm sure he will."

"He has to download PDF. You think he will do this?"

"I'm not sure."

"Will he click on link you send him?"

"I don't know. He's more likely to open a PDF, but I may need to prepare the ground first. I have an idea for that."

"Okay. You write e-mail with attached PDF. This is payload."

"The payload."

"Keystroke logger. Credential harvester. It comes preloaded with the Kali Linux social engineering tool kit."

Juliana wasn't totally ignorant about computer stuff, even though her son probably knew a thousand times more than she did. She wanted to understand what was about to happen. "A 'credential harvester' records everything he types?"

"Right. It creates its own internal mail server on his computer and sends keystrokes in file to location we specify. Passwords and everything."

"What do you need from me?"

"An e-mail and the document you're going to send as an attachment. I'll embed the payload in the PDF."

"I can get you something tomorrow." She looked at her watch. She had to get going. "But can you assure me that this will be undetectable?"

"Yes."

"Absolutely?"

"Yes," Sasha said. "One more thing. I need payment in cash."

44

On her way to Jake's school, she spotted an ATM on Comm. Ave. She pulled over and withdrew the maximum, four hundred dollars, and then used a second bank card to withdraw another two hundred. She got to the school a few minutes late. Signs pointed parents in the direction of the auditorium.

Duncan had saved her a seat next to him. They nodded to each other as she took her seat.

The head of the school, Dr. Cole, was speaking, an introductory welcome. "A place devoted to diversity, equality, and inclusion," she was saying in her deep contralto.

She saw, under Duncan's seat, a laptop bag. It was a Macbook Air that he hadn't used in four or five years, but it still worked. She caught his eye, mouthed, *Thanks.*

He nodded, didn't smile. He handed her a sheet of paper with their names on it that listed the classrooms they were to visit this evening and the times.

"A safe space for everyone," Dr. Cole said. "An atmosphere of mutual respect."

Then finally the headmistress was finished, and parents were getting up out of their seats, some men in suits and neckties, others in windbreakers. The auditorium was filled with voices. Juliana and Duncan remained seated, talking to each other quietly, each looking straight ahead. It could not have been more awkward.

"Did they take anything?" she asked.

He shook his head. "They were searching for, like, two hours."

"File cabinets and the like?"

"I don't know what the hell they were hoping to find, but they sure as hell didn't find it. This about the death of that Argentinian sleazebag?"

"Yes." She'd filled him in on everything, how she'd been blackmailed and her decision to hire a PI rather than give in to their demands.

"What are they looking for?"

"They want to know if I communicated with the guy. If I had a relationship with him." She continued to stare straight ahead as she talked, at the now-empty stage. She couldn't look at him.

"What, they think they have to take the computer to read the e-mail? They do all that stuff remotely now."

"I think it was a display."

"Of?"

"Like an alpha gorilla's display of dominance."

"Who's the gorilla?" he asked.

"Kent Yarnell."

Duncan smiled unpleasantly. "How did that asshole get involved in this?"

"The DA kicked the death investigation up to the AG's office because it tangentially involves a judge."

"How much do they know?" he asked.

"About me?"

"Yeah."

"Not much. But Yarnell must think there's blood in the water."

"Maybe because there *is* blood in the water."

"They can't prove I had a . . . connection to this guy." A long silence passed between them. Then she said, "Listen. I think we should go back to Dr. Ross." Helen Ross was a therapist who did couples counseling. She was good, but Duncan didn't like her. He thought she took Juliana's side far too often, a kind of female-solidarity thing.

"I'd see somebody else. Not her." He got to his feet, and she did too. A woman took her forearm—Juliana smelled Jo Malone—and said excitedly, "You look fantastic."

"Hey, Suz." Susan and Barry Marshall were both friends of theirs. They both worked at Fidelity and had a son in Jake's class he didn't like, which was a little awkward. She gave Susan a hug. The husbands shook hands. They had a superficial friendship based entirely on basketball.

"Are you still seeing that trainer?"

"No time," Juliana said.

"Well, whatever you're doing, keep doing it."

"Thanks." Juliana couldn't resist giving Duncan a quick look. He gave a smile that left out his eyes. He'd told her he wasn't near ready to let her back in the house. It both stung and pissed her off, that he got to say who lived in their house. A house they owned jointly, the house she loved and had found and insisted they buy. On the other hand, she could only imagine how Duncan was feeling about her, the resentment he was accumulating the way a bear stores up on food before he hibernates. And there they were, acting like a happily married couple for the sake of appearances.

"We should have dinner!" Susan said.

Just then, Juliana's phone rang: Hersh. She excused herself and walked off to a dark corridor where the school administration's offices were located, all of them closed. "Hi," she said.

"The janissary," Hersh said.

"Eugene Brod, right?"

"Right. I followed him home from work this afternoon, but he made a detour before going home. He went to the Mandarin Hotel, went right up to someone's suite there."

"Whose?"

"I don't know. No luck on that yet. But there were a couple of bodyguards sitting outside the hotel suite, talking to each other in Russian."

Martie Connolly was lying on her sofa reading Jane Austen when Juliana returned. Martie gave her a wave. "How was parents' night?"

"Fine. His English teacher is pretty great. I'd even be willing to read *All Quiet on the Western Front* again if I had a teacher like that. Too bad Jake's not doing the homework."

"So what is he doing?"

"Drugs, I think. I don't want to talk about it. Hey, Kent Yarnell is on the warpath."

"How so?"

She told Martie about the search warrants.

"That's ridiculous," Martie said, sitting up and putting the book down. "That's harassment."

"That's what I think." For a few seconds she was quiet, contemplating. She and Martie were dear friends who trusted each other completely. It wasn't right for her to hold back.

She told her about her meeting with the hacker.

When Juliana finished, Martie said softly, "Well, now I'm starting to worry."

"About . . . ?"

"I think you've just crossed a line. With hackers and whatnot."

"You do?"

Martie nodded. She looked sad.

She didn't like hearing it put that way, but she knew Martie was right.

She'd crossed the border into some foreign country where the rules were different. Where she was different. What she was doing, what she was willing to do. How far she was willing to go.

But it hadn't just happened. She'd crossed that border the night she met Matías.

"You know," Martie said, "you stare too long into the abyss . . . Point is, honey, you go down this path and they've done what they wanted to do. They've corrupted you. Turned you into an ends-justify-the-means type."

"It's not like I've got a lot of choices," Juliana said.

"Honey." She shook her head slowly, a disappointed woman. "Do you really think the law is for other people?"

In the guest bedroom later that night, she took out Duncan's old laptop and turned it on. While it was booting up, she noticed the knife in her purse. She took it out, grasping it in her right hand, feeling its weight. Gingerly she pressed the button, and the blade shot out the front with surprising force. She touched the blade, amazed at how sharp it was. It glinted. Then she pulled at the nub in the handle and retracted the blade. A dangerous instrument. She was scared of the thing. She wondered whether she'd ever have occasion to use it, whether she'd need it, whether she'd ever have the courage.

It took her a few minutes to get onto Martie's Wi-Fi—password *certiorari*—and then she checked her e-mail. She'd heard back from an old friend from Albany giving her the thumbs-up on the favor she was asking.

She was breaking the law, and she knew it. She was a Superior Court judge who was about to commit a crime, paying for a sketchy computer hacker to try to break into someone's e-mail. That wasn't much different from hiring a burglar to break into someone's house. If she was caught, that would be the end of her judgeship, and that was the least of it. But if she didn't do it, she knew the blackmail wouldn't end. Her life wouldn't be hers anymore.

And she'd gone too far to stop now.

45

In the morning, shortly after she got to her lobby, she picked up the phone and called Noah Miller's office. It wasn't quite eight thirty. His secretary put her right through. Of course he was in already.

"Judge Brody," he said, picking up. "This is twice in a month. To what do I owe the good fortune?"

"I'm glad I ran into you," she said. "Your name came up in an interesting conversation I had recently with an old sorority pal of mine."

"Yeah?"

"I had dinner at Nine Park with my old Sigma Kappa sister Joan, who was visiting from Springfield. So Joan runs a state pension fund, I'm sure you haven't heard of it, the Massachusetts Teachers' Retirement System, out of Springfield? Anyway, it's this enormous fund, assets of almost two hundred billion dollars or something. She's the chief investment officer."

"Oh, I've heard of it." He sounded suddenly alert.

"Joan's just not happy with their legal representation, especially the compliance part. You do compliance work, right?"

"Absolutely."

"Anyway, Noah, I told her I really shouldn't make any recommendations, given my position, but I said the conversation starts with Noah Miller."

"That's very kind of you."

"Oh, it's the truth. Nothing but the best for Joan, I figure."

"I'm sure we can do better for your friend—what's her name?"

"I'll send you her bio and CV. The e-mail address on your website?"

"Right."

Her sorority sister, Joan Pollock, was indeed the chief investment officer at a huge pension fund in Springfield, Massachusetts. It wasn't true that Joan was dissatisfied with her legal representation, but she was willing to pretend so for one phone conversation.

On the phone last night she'd told Joan, "Hey, this is complicated, but you're gonna get a call from Noah Miller—yeah, that Noah Miller. I told him that your fund might be interested in pursuing new legal representation. Just a possibility. So just take the call, hear him out, and say you need to confer with your colleagues. Like that. And that's the end of the road."

"What, are you pranking the guy?"

"No. It's actually kind of a long story. Let's have drinks in a week or two and I'll fill you in. Meanwhile, I owe you big time."

Juliana looked at her watch—twenty minutes until the morning trial began. She turned her attention to other matters for a bit—another decision, in a long queue, that needed more work—and after a respectable amount of time, she wrote a brief e-mail to Noah Miller, attaching the PDF that Sasha the hacker had prepared. The payload, he called it.

There was no chance in the world that Noah *wouldn't* download and open the attachment. He would probably do it immediately, the moment he saw her e-mail. It would be irresistible. Greed was fairly predictable.

A few minutes later, she glanced at her watch, then stood up and put on her robe.

As she was about to enter the courtroom, her phone made an unfamiliar sound, a sort of outer-spacey chime.

A WhatsApp text. Sasha had instructed her to install the secure messaging app on her phone.

She read the text.

Her heart started thudding.

It was from Sasha.

We're in.

During a recess, she was back in her chambers when there came a knock on her door.

"Come in," she said.

Her clerk, Kaitlyn, entered, holding a thick manila envelope. "Judge, plaintiff in the Wheelz case just asked for an emergency hearing."

"Emergency?"

Kaitlyn held aloft the envelope as if it were the answer. "This is unbelievable. This is revenge porn."

"Revenge porn? What are you talking about?"

"Take a look."

She handed Juliana the envelope. It was from Craft & Connors, the firm that represented Rachel Meyers, the plaintiff. Juliana slid a hefty sheaf of papers out onto her desk.

The first thing that caught her eye was a photograph of a nude young woman. You could tell right away who it was: Rachel Meyers.

Underneath was another nude photo, with Rachel in a different position, but her face still visible. Then came printouts of text messages between Rachel and someone named Jason.

She read one page:

RachelMeyers: then you take me from behind or hold me down while you tease me.

JasonCooke: I'm thrusting into you and you scream my name and you're coming so hard.

The ones that followed were more explicit.

"What the hell?" she said.

"Jason Cooke was her longtime boyfriend, but I think they're broken up," Kaitlyn said. "Most of those texts are between her and Jason. Some are texts she sent on Tinder. Sent on her personal account—but on the laptop Wheelz gave her for work."

"So it's company property. Isn't it kind of sloppy of her to leave all that on a work computer?"

"She wiped the disk. But the Wheelz legal team hired a digital forensic expert to recover all the deleted files."

"And turned it over for what reason?"

"Plaintiff asked for all correspondence to and from, and mentioning, Rachel Meyers."

"What the hell?" she said again.

"You see what's going on? They're trying to slut-shame her."

Juliana nodded. It was a threat. A way to pressure Rachel Meyers to settle. By handing those highly personal, embarrassing files over to their opponent, Wheelz's attorney was implicitly threatening her: Who knows, maybe something'll leak to *The Boston Globe* or get filed as an exhibit to a motion. One way or another, it'll get out there. Settle, or the world would see the most personal details about Rachel Meyers's sex life.

Meyers had refused to sign a confidentiality agreement, because she wanted the world to see what had happened to her at Wheelz.

So now Wheelz was exacting its revenge.

You won't sign a confidentiality agreement, they were saying, fine. But it's going to cost you big time.

You will be completely and utterly shamed and humiliated before the world.

46

Juliana called both sides into her courtroom for the emergency hearing. Rachel Meyers was seated in the second row, wearing a green suit over a white blouse. Unusual for the client to come to motions, but it was her right. Her face was tight, and she looked exhausted. There were purple circles under her eyes. The poor woman. The trial hadn't even begun.

"All right," Juliana said, "I've had the chance to read the papers. Plaintiff, what's the issue here?"

She knew what they wanted, of course. Glenda Craft, Rachel's lawyer, had filed a motion for a protective order. They wanted this set of personal texts to be declared confidential, so they couldn't be released to the public, couldn't be used in any other case. But she wanted the argument on the record.

Craft stood up. "We just received supplemental discovery material that contains highly personal and private e-mail exchanges between my client and a couple of male friends of hers. Some of them were messages exchanged on the dating app Tinder. And we are concerned about what the defense is planning to do with them."

"Which is what?" she said.

"This is a deliberate move to pressure my client into settling."

"Your Honor—" said Madden.

But Juliana cut him off. "All right. I have your motion to protect."

"Yes, we—"

"Okay, I'll hear from the defense."

Harlan Madden stood up, cleared his throat. He spoke in a bland, guarded tone. "Yes, uh, in response to the discovery request made by the plaintiff, we engaged the services of a computer forensics specialist to recover all deleted files on a laptop used by the plaintiff while working for the Wheelz Corporation. We have provided the plaintiff with those recovered files, as requested."

"Hold on, Mr. Madden," Juliana said. "I have looked at the discovery materials, and I saw sexually explicit text messages and nude photos, and I have to say, it made me wonder what you're planning on doing with all that."

Madden gave her an even look. "We're simply complying with the plaintiff's discovery request."

Juliana thought: *Oh, please.* She said, "I recall you were extremely concerned about confidentiality when it came to any past legal settlements of sexual harassment cases."

"Yes, Your Honor, but these aren't business records. Also, the plaintiff clearly wasn't so concerned about keeping her correspondence confidential, because she used a laptop that is the property of the Wheelz Corporation. She should have been under no illusions that what she put on this laptop would remain private to her."

"So what are you planning to do with these documents?"

"We have no plans to do *anything* with them."

"Judge, this is a brazen threat that the defense is holding over my client's head to compel her to settle and not go to trial. Frankly, they're trying to embarrass her. We want all of these personal text messages and photographs to be designated as confidential."

"All right," Juliana said. She saw no reason to postpone a decision. She didn't need to take a week to think about it. This was easy. "I am granting the plaintiff's motion for a protective order. I hereby order the defense not to use or disclose any of these documents and materials produced by the defendant, which are Bates labeled 5539 to 5884, to any parties outside this litigation. I can't imagine this is a problem for you, is it, Mr. Madden?"

"No, Your Honor," he replied meekly.

"And one more thing. If any of these private text messages see the light of day, I'm going to hold you and your client accountable for the violation of her privacy. Do I make myself clear?"

"Yes, Your Honor," he said.

Her phone buzzed, and she glanced at it. "Let's take a recess," she said.

When she emerged from the courtroom, she saw another WhatsApp text on her phone. She opened it. From Sasha again: **Call me.**

She tapped on the phone icon on the top right of her screen, then tapped Voice call. They were on an encrypted line now.

He picked right up. "Where is your office? I come over now," he said.

"No." She didn't want to be seen with him, a hacker, someone sketchy and marginal, at the Suffolk County Courthouse. "I'll come to you."

"Call and text only on the WhatsApp," he said. "Or Signal. Only."

"Okay, but why?"

"Because we are dealing with some kinda bad guys. Some scary players."

Her throat felt tight. She swallowed. "Scary how?"

"You'll see what I'm talking about."

"What do you mean, you think someone's . . . bugging my phone?"

"At this level anything is possible."

Hersh had told her that her iPhone was probably secure. Maybe Sasha knew more.

"This level . . . ?"

"Um, do you have my payment?"

"I do."

"Cash, yes?"

"Yes."

"It's not that I distrust you . . . Judge."

Judge. So much for the Rosalind ruse. "You know who I am," she said. "Why am I not surprised?"

"Rosalind Brody, formerly Winter, born in Billerica, Mass. The Social Security Administration says she died some years ago. And that she has one living descendant, a judge."

"Well done," she said, and she said good-bye and hung up.

Then her phone made a curious little electronic bleat, and a text came up in a different window. The text contained only a link, which she clicked on. She had to trust him; she had no choice.

The link took her to a Gmail home page that looked like her own. There was an inbox that showed a long stack of e-mails, one column showing the name of the sender, next to a subject line. All very familiar. But she didn't recognize the names of the senders.

She was looking at Noah Miller's inbox.

47

"Your Ukrainian friend did it," she said.

There was a long silence on the line. Then Philip Hersh said, "That was fast."

"Are you still okay to help me go through the—"

"I'm going to send you a link and a password," Hersh interrupted.

"Do you have an app called Signal or WhatsApp installed on your phone?" she asked.

"Uh, yeah," said Hersh. "*You* do?"

"Your Ukrainian friend recommended it."

"He tends to be on the paranoid side. Occupational hazard. But in this instance, I actually think it may be wise."

She remembered the phrase the hacker had used—"scary players"—and wondered whether that was nothing more than the manifestation of a paranoid mind-set. Or whether there was something to it. It filled her with dread.

And something else: she was in possession of someone's stolen private e-mail correspondence. She had been party to an illegal act.

It was funny, she reflected: she waited for a Walk sign even when no cars were coming; she'd never cheat on her taxes; and back when she was in private practice, she never rounded up her billable hours. Yet she'd broken her marriage vows, and she'd just broken into someone's e-mail, and she wasn't so sure she was in the wrong.

She remembered once reading about a thought experiment: A man's wife is dying. There's one drug that can save her life, but it's prohibitively expensive. The pharmacist won't lower the price, and the man doesn't have the money. What should the man do? Should he steal the drug?

To Juliana, the real question was, who *wouldn't*?

Sitting every day at that vast judicial bench, a big hunk of oak separating her and the defendants and plaintiffs who came to her courtroom, it was easy to imagine she belonged to a different tribe. But it was a reassuring lie. Because she knew that they were separated only by circumstance, by situation, by a cascade of decisions. The person wielding the gavel, the person in the dock—how hard, really, was it for them to trade places? Martha Connolly liked to quote somebody, Juliana didn't know who: life is a garden of forking paths.

"I could use your help going through it," she said to Hersh. "You'll know what to look for."

"Understood."

When they hung up, she launched Signal and was about to send him the link, when there was a knock on her door.

"Come in," she called out.

Kaitlyn was holding a thick manila folder. She handed it to Juliana. Inside was a bundle of papers. The top page was titled "Motion for Summary Judgment."

If she granted the motion, that meant the case was over. She'd be saying there was no case, no cause of action, no material facts at issue. No trial.

Just as Donald Greaves had promised. She had one week, he'd said, to allow it. One week to do the right thing.

48

She had a message on her phone from Hersh.

"We need to talk," he said. "Come by my office as soon as you can."

She looked at her watch. If she left now . . .

She found Hersh in his office, hunched over his computer, a yellow pad next to the keyboard. He looked up, held up the yellow pad as she walked in.

"Noah Miller is in even deeper than I thought."

"What do you mean?"

"He has clients in the People's Liberation Army in China. Chinese generals. Two Saudi princes, the minister of foreign affairs in Zimbabwe, the president of the Philippines . . . Jesus, it's an all-star cast of global dictators."

"I always thought the rumors were just rumors. What about Russians?"

He nodded. "I searched his e-mails for *Wheelz* and came up with a very interesting exchange."

"Okay."

"Let me print you out a set." He turned back to his computer, tapped at a few keys, and then his laser printer hummed to life. As they fed out of the printer, he reached over and began handing them to her.

"Here," he said. "Start with this one."

It was an e-mail dated two years earlier.

> Noah
>
> Hope all is well. We understand Wheelz is doing a round of financing. Can you find out who's representing them? Still Goldman Sachs? We may be interested. I'd like to see the book.
>
> Cheers,
>
> Charles
> Charles Finch, Partner
> Harrogate Capital Partners
> 6 Victoria Avenue
> Harrogate, United Kingdom

"Okay," she said, looking up. "Do we know anything about this guy Charles Finch?"

"Cookie-cutter finance guy. Went to Cambridge, then Harvard Business School, worked at a private equity firm in New York, now based in the English town of Harrogate."

"And 'the book' is . . . ?"

"That's the document they give prospective investors. Keep reading."

She did. Then came Noah Miller's response:

> Charles,
>
> It's Joe Quintanilla in Goldman's Boston office, and they're looking to raise $500 million, primarily from new investors. I can get you the book as soon as you

sign the attached NDA. Sounds like they're trying to move quickly. It's on a short fuse.

Noah

"A short fuse means everyone wanted to get this done immediately, I assume," she said.

Hersh nodded. "Wheelz was in big trouble, I remember. Bleeding cash. People thought they were going to go out of business."

"Okay."

She skimmed the next couple of pages. A few back-and-forth volleys about possibly investing in Wheelz. Noah Miller sends Charles Finch a nondisclosure agreement. Finch makes some edits to the agreement, signs it, sends it back. That sort of thing.

"No," Hersh said, watching her read. "Don't skip past those. You see where the British banker says, 'We might be interested in doing the whole round'?"

"Yeah?"

"That means that Harrogate Capital Partners is considering investing the entire five hundred million bucks. The whole enchilada."

"Okay."

"Check out how Noah responds."

She scanned the pages and found an e-mail from Noah Miller to Charles Finch, the next day. She read:

Noah Miller
to Charles Finch

Charles,

Joe Quintanilla at Goldman has said he will make the Wheelz management team available to meet with you and your team at your convenience next week.

But one question: your fund size is $1 billion. Half a billion represents half your fund. We don't understand how you can do the whole round.

"Okay, got it," she said. "Reasonable question."

"Look at how Finch replies."

She read further.

Noah

One of our LPs in Harrogate Capital Partners is particularly interested in this and he will cover anything, up to half a billion, that our fund does not invest itself.

Charles

Noah Miller
to Charles Finch

Who's the LP?

Charles Finch
to Noah Miller

Let's discuss on phone. What's the best number to reach you on?

"Ah," she said. "This guy Finch won't put it in an e-mail."

"Right. There's one unnamed investor with some very deep pockets. He uses the word 'he.' One person."

"Is the investor's name anywhere in these e-mails?"

"Not that I can see. It would take me a while to go through the e-mails and look more closely. But from everything I've seen, they never mention his name. They're really careful about that."

"Huh. Bizarre."

"Now take a look at the exchange I printed out between Noah Miller and this guy Joe Quintanilla at Goldman Sachs. Quintanilla is the point man in charge of the Wheelz financing."

She skimmed the next few pages.

Joe Quintanilla
to Noah Miller

Noah—OK, before I take this to the company, how do I know this is credible? Who are we talking about?

—Joe

Joe—It's a Caymans-based insurance company, Antilles Windward Insurance.

We're talking half a billion. Who the hell is Antilles Windward Insurance?

LTL

"'LTL'?" she said.

"Stands for 'let's talk live,'" said Hersh.

"So the investor isn't a person, it's some insurance company I've never heard of?"

"It's an insurance company *nobody* has ever heard of. And there's no such insurance company. There's no record of any insurance business it does. It's based in the Netherlands Antilles, and it's probably just a front for this one very wealthy investor. A shell company."

"A shell company that owns half a billion dollars' worth of Wheelz," she said.

"No. *More.* Keep reading. The next bunch of pages. Noah e-mails another lawyer, a partner at Ropes and Gray in Boston named Sidra Evans, because this *unnamed client* wants to acquire a controlling interest in Wheelz. He wants to sink even more money into it. More than the half-billion dollars."

"Okay." She shuffled through the papers until she located the exchange he was talking about.

Noah Miller
to Sidra Evans
(Sidra.Evans@ropesgray.com)

Sidra,

To recap the conversation we just had, our Client would like to increase the size of their investment in this Wheelz round to $1 billion. We add the following terms and conditions to the agreement as discussed.

—Agreement sets board of directors at 5, of whom 2 board members will be named by the Investor.

—Company cannot impair the assets in any way—

She skimmed through the rest. Boilerplate language; even she recognized it, from reading contracts. She looked up. "So 'let's talk live' is because no one mentions the big guy's name in an e-mail, right?"

"Look," said Hersh, "these are major players in a very big deal. They want to make sure they know where the money's coming from. And that the money is really there."

"So they want to know actual names. Of people."

"Right."

"But the real name, or names, is never written down in an e-mail."

"Right."

"So this guy Finch, at Harrogate Capital Partners, is the point of contact for this rich investor. Who uses a bogus insurance company to hide behind."

"Right."

"And Finch gets on the phone and tells Noah, and Noah tells the Goldman guy on the phone as well, and it never appears in any paperwork."

"Except the . . . accredited investor form."

"Right."

"But you can't get access to that form?"

"They belong to the government. The Securities and Exchange Commission, in some locked file, probably."

"Okay." She thought. "And still nothing on Mayfair Paragon?"

"Right. The owner of Wheelz is this phony insurance company, Antilles Windward. Which owns fifty-one percent of the company."

"That's in the e-mails?"

"Right. And here's what's interesting." He swiveled in his chair to face his computer monitor, tapped at the keys, stared at the screen for a few seconds. Then he swiveled around to face Juliana. "The lead investor for the last couple of rounds—the one before Antilles Windward invested a billion dollars?"

She felt a chill. "Don't say it."

"Sorry," Hersh said, "but it's true. He's dead."

"What do you mean—he died recently?"

"Couple of months ago. A Silicon Valley private equity guy, Kevin Mathers, who would have been the largest investor in Wheelz. Forty-six. Died in a tragic skiing accident in Aspen. In the woods on Ajax."

"So? Accidents happen," she said. Though in fact she didn't know what to think. Could this be true?

"Yeah," he said. "People die in skiing accidents, it happens."

"But?"

"But you take Kevin Mathers, and then you factor in Matías Sanchez, and it becomes a coincidence, and I don't believe in coincidences."

49

She was silent for a long time. She watched the traffic on the street below, the shadows of dusk settling on St. James Street. Then she went back to the pile of printouts. A few seconds later her eye was snagged by another e-mail thread. An exchange between Noah Miller and someone named Fiona Charteris.

> Fiona Charteris
> FCharteris@Linklaters.com
> to Noah Miller
>
> Noah
>
> One further addition to the terms and conditions discussed in our phone conversation of yesterday afternoon. Our mutual client requires that all the Wheelz software code be kept in escrow.
>
> Fiona

She read it aloud. "Any idea what that means?"

"Yeah. It means that the client has gotten a look at the financials and knows the company is in deep shit. So if they go out of business, the company's software, the engine that makes everything run, is held separately, and it belongs to them."

"I see. And who's this Fiona Charteris?"

"I didn't get around to her. I know that Linklaters is a law firm—a member of what's called the 'Magic Circle,' one of the big five law firms in the UK. So she's probably a lawyer."

"I'm guessing she represents Harrogate Capital Partners."

"Right. Let me do a quick search."

She went back to reading the thread of e-mails between Noah and Fiona Charteris, mostly boring stuff concerning the Wheelz deal, and then one e-mail caught her attention.

> We're finishing our work on the Wheelz round, and I have some serious concerns.
>
> I am concerned that our co-investor, Antilles Windward Insurance, is not actually the investor. Based on my read of their financial statements, Antilles does not have the funds. The money is coming from 'an affiliate' of theirs, Mayfair Paragon Ltd., via a Russian subsidiary bank in Cyprus which is under US sanctions. Based on United States law, this transaction is illegal. I am confused and concerned.
>
> Fiona

"She's discovering that there's Russian money behind the Harrogate firm. Russian money that came in from a Russian-owned bank in Cyprus. Which is illegal."

"Exactly."

She turned the page.

"Oh wow," she said.

"What?"

"Noah forwards her e-mail to her contact at Harrogate, and listen to this."

She read the next exchange aloud:

> Noah Miller
> to Charles Finch
>
> We have a problem regarding a lawyer in this deal. I need to talk to you soonest. Please call me on my cell.

She looked up. "Something the two lawyers couldn't talk about over e-mail?" she said. "Something about this woman Fiona."

Hersh was no longer listening. He was staring at his screen, reading something.

"What is it?"

"What's the date of that e-mail?"

"November 28, 2015."

He let out his breath slowly.

"Mother of God," he said. "I'm reading an article in the *Daily Mail.* A British tabloid."

"What?"

"Fiona Charteris, City solicitor, twenty-seven . . ." He fell silent. His eyes were moving back and forth, rapt on the screen. "Killed in gruesome bus accident near Moorgate Station . . . crossing the street . . . Charteris, a third-year associate at posh law firm Linklaters, was going home to shower and change after staying up all night at her law firm. . . . A witness says she was probably pushed. . . ."

He looked at her.

Juliana felt light-headed. She felt droplets of sweat breaking out along her hairline. “Oh, my God,” she said. “Who knows I’m your client?”

He nodded. “Nobody. I never reveal the names of my clients.”

“Philip, listen to me.” Her stare burned into Hersh’s sad eyes. She leaned forward and put a hand on his forearm. “I have a family. I have kids.”

“Of course. I understand. As I was saying—”

“I want you to do everything you can to make sure my name is not connected with this investigation. That nobody knows what I . . . know.”

He looked miserable. “You know what I’m going to say. I will take every precaution—”

“*No!*” she exploded. “You make goddamned sure of it. Make a *hundred* percent certain.”

Now he looked away, toyed with a stapler on his desk. “Okay,” he said. “I’ll do everything in my power. But I think we’re in agreement: we’ve gone as far as we safely can.”

She nodded, not sure what to think. It felt like an insoluble problem, a terrible dilemma. Keep digging, keep peeling back the layers of the onion, and maybe you’ll figure out a way to keep your family safe. But—to shift clichés—the more they poked at the hornets’ nest, the greater the chance of being stung. “I don’t know what the hell to do,” she said.

“And what do you plan to do about this new deadline, that legal decision you mentioned?”

“The motion for summary judgment. Yes. It would end the case.”

“How are you going to rule, or am I not allowed to ask that of a judge?”

“I haven’t ruled on it yet.”

“You going to meet their demand?”

“I can’t. I’m going to deny the motion,” she said. She kept thinking of the plaintiff, Rachel Meyers, and the harassment she’d faced at Wheelz. The ugliness. The young woman wouldn’t settle, wouldn’t take a multimillion-dollar payment from Wheelz. She wanted justice to be done. There was something heroic about that. "But I'm terrified about what's going to happen when I deny it."

"Honestly?" Hersh said with a sad little smile. "I don't think it makes any difference what you decide."

"What the hell does that mean?"

"Let's say you grant the motion. Once you give them what they need—well, they'll probably bide their time, but they'll get to you."

"*Get* to me," she said. "What are you saying?"

"You're probably safe as long as they need you around to make a decision. Which means you're okay until you make that decision, thumbs up or thumbs down. Because once you do—they don't need you anymore."

She shook her head, not wanting to hear this.

"It'll be you and your family, skiing in Aspen on winter break, and maybe none of you come back."

"Hersh."

"Or a scuba-diving accident in Costa Rica. Or there's a car accident."

"Enough."

"Don't think I'm just speculating. I'm trying to warn you away. I mean, there are so many ways this thing could go down. Do you really think they can tolerate your presence on this planet? If they find out you know what you know? There's always going to be crosshairs on your forehead. A dancing red dot, wherever you go. The marksman's bindi dot."

She felt sick, dull, and headachy. The court provided judges with additional security when needed. The State Police. There were lunatics out there, tempers flared in the courtroom, and a lot was at stake. A judge always had to be careful. "Maybe I should ask for extra protection."

Her phone chirred. Duncan. She let it go to voice mail.

"Yeah, I suppose a squad car parked in front of your house might work for a while. But does that mean that you and your family are going to have to live like that—bodyguards and police escorts, maybe private security—the rest of your life? Being terrified all the time about some minor security glitch? That's no way to live."

Tears had come to her eyes. She whispered, "So what the hell am I supposed to do?"

Hersh was quiet for a very long time. Finally he said, "I may have an idea."

50

At a minute before nine o'clock the next morning, just as she was about to walk into the courtroom, her phone buzzed. A text. She was on edge, with everything that was going on, and anything could be urgent. She grabbed her phone.

From Duncan. **Call me immediately.**

He picked up the phone after less than one ring.

"Duncan," she said, her heart pounding. "Everything okay?"

"You've got to get over to Jake's school. Now."

"What?" she cried. "Is he all right? Did he get hurt?"

"No—no, he's fine. I mean, he's not fine at all. He is in serious trouble here."

"Oh, God. What'd he do?"

"He's being expelled. For drugs."

"Drugs? For weed? Shit. What—?"

"Can you get over here now? I know you're in court."

"I'll be there," she said.

She hated to cancel court. Especially when she had a jury in the box. Sixteen average citizens had disrupted their lives for this. The jury was deliberating in the medical malpractice case, and the stakes were sky-high. An obstetrician was fighting for his reputation, for his livelihood.

And a young couple had lost a baby because of his failure to detect distress, they believed.

But she had no choice.

She called Kaitlyn into her lobby. "Can you call the lawyers, advise them that I'm unavailable, and reschedule?"

Then she got her car from the parking garage across the street. As soon as she was on her way, she called Duncan over speakerphone and talked as she drove. A bad habit, and something she would ordinarily never do. But she was worried, and she wanted to arrive at Jake's school with a plan.

It was good to have something else to worry about for the moment, she thought. Was she being a bad mom, she asked herself, to think of her son's situation as a diversion, a distraction from far more consequential things? She felt protective of Jake and concerned about him, about how lost he seemed to be. It was actually strange the way she was feeling. The blank, helpless terror seemed to have abated and given way to a kind of ferocious focus. She was a lioness protecting her brood.

"What did he do?" she asked.

"They found a vape pen and a couple of pen tops in his backpack."

"Pen tops are . . . ?"

"Cartridges of marijuana extract. THC oil. Cannabis concentrate."

"Shit, Dunc. So he didn't give it up, as promised."

"Did he promise us? I don't think so. We didn't exactly tell him to quit the stuff. It was kind of left hanging."

"Great."

"They're saying he was dealing."

"*What?* Was he?"

"He says he wasn't."

"You believe him?"

"Yes. I do."

"They're expelling him?"

"Right."

"I want to talk to Dr. Cole." Dr. Cole was Pamela Cole, the head of the school. She was always "Dr." Cole, though she wasn't a medical doctor. Juliana had met her, talked to her at school events, but didn't really know her. Dr. Cole sort of floated above things. "If they intend to expel our son, at least we can hear it directly from the head of the school."

"I'm on it."

"Tell them Judge Brody wants to talk with her right away."

"I know," he said. She could hear the smile in his voice. "I know how it works."

"Okay."

"He brought THC concentrate into school," Duncan said. "That was not bright. But I'm more pissed off at the school."

"Because?"

"Because if they're going to expel a kid for something as minor as this, they should let you know."

"They probably do in the student handbook, and we just haven't read it."

"Okay. Maybe you're right. But let me take the lead in there, with Dr. Cole."

"Why?"

"I don't want you doing your Judge Judy routine in there, tangling with her. Being the pit bull."

"It'll be Judge Juliana, and I will be the velvet hammer."

"Maybe better if you don't. Let me handle it. Let me do the talking."

She let out a huff. "Okay," she said.

She met Duncan in the school parking lot. When they arrived at the headmistress's outer office, they found Jake slumped in a chair. His face was red, and his hair was wild. He looked as though he'd been crying. He eyed Juliana warily as they entered.

"I'm really sorry," he said.

Juliana felt warring impulses. She wanted to hug him, console him, tell him everything was going to be okay. He was her baby. She was also angry, wanted to tell him off. But she wasn't a yeller, and this wasn't the place anyway. So she gave him a hug and murmured to him, "You are in such trouble."

Pamela Cole emerged from her office. She was a short, stocky woman, a Sherman tank with platinum blond hair, cut short in a modified pixie. She wore oversize round blue-framed eyeglasses.

She had an unnervingly deep voice. She had been the head of the school for seven years and was said to be a master fundraiser. She favored knit pantsuits. Today she was wearing a navy suit with white piping.

She took each of their hands and said sadly, "Judge Brody, Professor Esposito." She was a very formal woman, dignified, remote. Not a natural people person, Juliana had always thought. But somehow great at fundraising. "Let's sit over here," Dr. Cole said, walking them into her book-lined, high-ceilinged office, flooded with light, and over to a long oak library table. Jake was left in the outer office.

Dr. Cole sat at one end, the head of the table. Next to her, Juliana and Duncan sat on opposite sides from each other.

She folded her arms across her chest. "This is very difficult for all of us," she began. "We're never happy to expel a student, particularly one as bright and well liked as Jake." She gave them a long, disappointed look. "As you know, we have a zero-tolerance policy on drugs." She seemed to be directing her attention to Duncan, who, with his head of long curly hair, probably looked like a hippie to her. Which wasn't far from the truth. "Now, I realize I'm talking to two lawyers here, and I'm of course aware that possession of small amounts of marijuana has been decriminalized in this state. But it is still illegal for anyone under the age of twenty-one to possess or use marijuana. And more to the point, it's against school rules."

Duncan was nodding, attentive.

"A search of Jake's backpack yielded several electronic vaporizer pens as well as a number of vials of what appears to be a highly concentrated form of marijuana. These vaporizer devices look like thumb drives, easily disguised. It seems that Jake has been selling this equipment to his fellow students. And the school's policy on this is quite clear. The penalty is expulsion."

There was a long silence. Dr. Cole looked at each of them, one after the other.

Duncan was shaking his head. He sighed. "Look, I get it. In my day you were technologically advanced if you had a roach clip."

Dr. Cole chuckled, and some of the tension in the room seeped out. He had the ability to do that, to connect with people, put them at ease. Dr. Cole didn't look like someone who might have gotten high when she was young. In fact, she didn't look as though she had ever been young.

Duncan went on. "All these—what did you call them, 'electronic vaporizer devices'?—freak me out a little too. So here we are, the grown-ups, with our rules, and here's this kid who, you know, thinks rules mean 'strongly consider.'"

Dr. Cole smiled and nodded.

"I totally get the frustration," he said. "Jake hears his old man going after the 'rules' of neoliberal patriarchy and—I gotta own this part—he gets mixed messages. So you, you're stuck in a situation where you've got an institution to protect. School kids to protect. Rules to lay down. That's heavy. That's your truth. But can we talk for a moment, parent to parent?"

Juliana thought: *That's where Jake gets it.* The art of blarney. She kind of admired it.

Dr. Cole said, "Of course."

"One thing all of us here know is, Jake's a kid with a good heart. So let's figure this out together. God bless the rules. But he really *belongs* here. How do we get to *that* truth?"

Dr. Cole looked at Duncan for a long while and kept nodding. She seemed to be mulling something over.

Duncan said, "I think this is a teachable moment for Jake."

"I hope so." Dr. Cole smiled.

Juliana remembered all those times when Dunc talked his way out of a traffic ticket, or into the head of a line, or into possession of Toys R Us's last Marvel Legion action figure, which Jake had once desperately wanted.

He'd even coaxed a smile out of Dr. Cole.

Dr. Cole cleared her throat. "Alas, we're not able to make an exception for one student, as much as we might like him. That's why we have a zero-tolerance policy. This . . . *vaping* or *dabbing*, or sometimes it's called *Juuling*—these e-cigarettes, the marijuana use—it's an epidemic at this school, and the only way for us to stop it is to be firm in our response. Challenging us only makes us the best we can be."

Duncan nodded again, looked thoughtful, and Juliana could see he was trying to figure out another approach, another way to Dr. Cole's cold heart. But she could also see that it was useless. Dr. Cole would not be swayed. Duncan's approach was falling flat.

Juliana spoke up.

"This drug use at the school, you said it's 'epidemic'?"

"There's a high baseline incidence of drug use, an increasing use of this sort of equipment, yes. So Jake's recent academic troubles all begin to make sense."

"A 'high baseline incidence,' is that right?"

"Yes, quite disturbing. Quite widespread."

Duncan glanced at Juliana, alarmed at whatever she was doing.

He knew she was a shark smelling the chum in the water. Or a pit bull.

"Huh," she said. "So essentially you've just confessed to me that this institution has utterly failed in its responsibility to—how do you put it in the student handbook?—'create and maintain a safe and optimal educational environment.' I'm pretty sure I've quoted that accurately."

Dr. Cole sat up straight in her chair. Her eyes were angry. "Judge Brody—"

"And that fascinates me, because I'm thinking of your remarks on that recruitment panel in Boston last spring—the one that was on YouTube?—when you indicated there was no drug problem at this school." She looked directly at Dr. Cole. "It makes me wonder whether this school has changed drastically overnight—or whether you simply don't know what's going on here."

The headmistress started to speak, then thought better of it.

"That would suggest that this issue desperately needs outside intervention." She took her iPhone out of her purse. "Now, the state Commissioner of Elementary and Secondary Education, as you should be aware, released a statement earlier this year proposing that *receivership* be considered for any school—I have it on my iPhone here—'unable to ensure a safe and drug-free environment for its pupils.' From your own account, it sounds as if this school should receive a Level 5 designation. Receivership. Meaning they take over control of the school. Do you follow me?"

"Yes, but—"

"Good. So should we report the situation to the Massachusetts Department of Education? Should we talk to Lester Milbank about launching an inquiry? Or the Boston Police?" She paused, took a breath.

Dr. Cole's cheeks had reddened, as if she'd been slapped.

Juliana went on. "I can either infer that you are publicly lying about this institution—or that you have simply lost control of it. It's difficult to see any other explanation."

"Judge Brody," said Dr. Cole.

But Juliana was on a roll. "So you're telling us you've made a decision to expel our son. And looking ahead to what's going to happen as the result of his expulsion, I'm sure the good name of this school will recover, though it may take a few years. And it won't be under your leadership, of course. But challenging us only makes us the best we can be, right?"

"That was very sexy in there," Duncan said.

They were standing outside of her car, in the front parking lot. They'd left Jake behind at school, to begin serving his sentence of detention, which was about three rungs down the punishment ladder from expulsion. Her son had looked at Juliana with stunned disbelief, as if she had just walked on water right in front of him.

"You don't think I was too hard on her?"

"Not at all. She was going to expel him. You had to get serious. You were a goddamned tiger in there."

Lion, she thought. *Lioness*. It had felt good, actually, laying into the headmistress that way, taking control of something finally, when she felt so otherwise helpless.

"Maybe the thing about 'challenging us' was a bit much," Juliana said.

"I enjoyed it."

"Okay, then."

"Hey," he said softly, "so I've been thinking a lot. I've cooled off a bit. I mean, we're in this thing together, and we've got to work it through together."

She nodded and said, "I'd like that."

"We need you at home. Jake clearly needs you. And I miss you."

She nodded again, not trusting herself to speak.

"I still want to work out our marriage," Duncan said.

"Me too."

"Come on home. Okay?"

51

Martie Connolly came in, with Lucy jingling her tags. Lucy's tail started wagging metronomically when she saw Juliana. Martie unleashed the dog and hung up the leash on a peg. Then she noticed Juliana's suitcase.

"You're leaving," she said.

"Yeah, it's time," Juliana said. "Thank you so much for letting me crash here."

The dog trotted over to her bed and picked up dog-toy Donald Trump. She had destroyed much of the yellow hair. Now she began industriously gnawing on the face.

"Well, I'm sad you're leaving. But if this means things are better for you at home, I'm happy for you."

"We still have a lot to figure out, but Duncan and I finally talked. And with everything going on, I really need to be with my family."

Juliana found herself looking at a painting on the wall, a fine oil portrait of a grim-looking bearded man that had to be a hundred and fifty years old. "Is that Samuel Colt?"

"The Peacemaker himself. I wonder how he'd feel knowing that his money now pays for dirty martinis for a liberal gun-control supporter in the Commonwealth of Massachusetts."

"He'd have every right to be pissed off, don't you think?"

Martie's eyes crinkled. She looked away. "It's none of my business, of course, and I'm not foolish enough to get involved. But with this, this business between you and Duncan—let me remind you of something. We're all flawed. Don't forget that. We've all done things we regret, and nobody is perfect."

"I sure know that."

Juliana hesitated, but then she reminded herself that she and Martha were always candid with each other. She wasn't going to stop now.

"Listen," she said, and she told her about what Hersh had said. How he at first wanted her to stop, to push no further. And what he had discovered. She told her about Noah Miller's e-mail reporting a "problem" with the lawyer in the UK. And how a few days later that lawyer was dead.

Martie looked stricken. Her normally sparkling blue eyes had gone dark. "What does Philip think you should do?"

"He had an idea, but I have to tell you, it's pretty bleak."

"He can be a gloomy Gus." She reached down and picked up Lucy, put her in her lap. Lucy's pert ears twitched as she wriggled against Martie. "But he has his reasons. So what's the idea?"

Juliana told her.

Martie listened, her face composed and neutral. Then she spoke, gently at first. "My dear, please don't be brave. My mother used to say that 'bravery' is how clever people get simple people to do their bidding. Right now you're on a trolley car bound for parts unknown." Looking directly into Juliana's eyes, she said heatedly, "Get off that trolley. Get off as soon as you can."

52

Juliana arrived home after nine and put down her suitcase. Home, at last. Right away she heard a door on the second floor open and Jake come thundering down the stairs. He was wearing a black T-shirt with the cartoon head of a crazy-looking angry guy and the words IF THERE'S A GOD, IT'S ME! The T-shirt was from an animated show Jake liked.

"Hey, Mom," he said, and he gave her a hug. Tears came to her eyes. It was so out of character for him. Normally he'd be barricaded upstairs in his room with his headphones on.

"Sweetie."

"That was really cool, what you did with Dr. Cole."

"What do you know about what I did with Dr. Cole?"

"Dad told me."

"Listen. We need to talk."

"I know."

They sat down at the kitchen table, round and old, oak and solid. He wasn't fighting it. She folded her arms, even though she knew the body language was bad, defensive. "What I did with Dr. Cole today, I'm never going to do again. I got you out of something I'm not going to get you out of again. I just want us to be clear about that."

"I get it."

"Were you in fact dealing drugs?"

"No! My friend Arthur was paying me back for— I mean, I gave him one of those pen tops—"

"Oh, God."

"No, I'm not a *dealer.* That is so ridiculous."

"Jakie, you claim you want to be an adult. Well, you're growing up, you're being treated like an adult, and that includes taking responsibility for your actions. I saved your bacon this time, but it won't happen again."

He hung his head, his face gone stony.

They made eye contact. She reached out and mussed up his hair, a gesture of affection he'd become uncomfortable with. "I understand," he said.

"It is legal in our state to possess and use marijuana," she said, "if you're over the age of twenty-one. You're sixteen, last I checked. Now, personally, I think it's a bad idea for you to use the stuff at your age—later, I'm agnostic—but I don't want you using it at home or at school. That's all."

"Okay."

"Agreed? This is the deal."

"Agreed."

"And if they catch you with drugs again, you can be certain they'll throw you out, and then you're going to have real problems. And I won't be there to help."

"I understand," he said.

She looked up as Duncan entered the room. He came over to her, gave her a hug and a kiss. "Hey," he said softly.

"Hey."

He was wearing a white button-down shirt with a button missing on the right collar. She flicked at the unbuttoned collar point and considered saying something, then decided against it.

Duncan looked at Jake. "I overheard. I agree with your mom."

She looked at Duncan, surprised. She couldn't help it.

Jake's reaction was swift. He was annoyed. His parents were agreeing;

his dad was no longer his co-conspirator. He shook his head, rolled his eyes, and got up. "I hear you," he grunted, and he left the kitchen, clomped up the stairs.

"Thanks," she said.

"Don't thank me. I'm glad you're back."

"Me too."

She went over to the kitchen door, which was almost always left open, and closed it so they could have some privacy.

Sitting down at the oak table, she said, "There's stuff you need to know." She started talking.

When she finished, they sat in silence for almost half a minute. Duncan's fingers were tracing the swirls of the grain on the tabletop. Finally he said, "All right, that's it. I want a gun."

"A *gun*? You?" Duncan was a gun-control zealot. She couldn't believe he was talking this way. "You're the most anti-gun person I know."

"We need protection," he said. "I'm not going to let anything happen to us."

"Where are you going to get a gun?"

"What about that private detective? Maybe he can loan us one."

She shook her head. "He won't."

"You asked?"

"I was exploring options." For some reason she didn't want to admit that he'd given her a knife.

"Well, I know people."

"Okay."

"Okay." She didn't want to argue. It was extremely hard to get a gun license around here, and it took forever. She doubted he'd actually be able to buy a gun on the black market. He didn't know the right kind of people, she was sure. He knew law professors.

Her phone bleated a text message, and she glanced at it. Philip Hersh: Call me ASAP.

53

Duncan went upstairs, to his study, while she sat at the kitchen table. She reached Hersh on his cell phone, using WhatsApp.

"I know it's late," he said. "I'm sorry. But I think I figured out Mayfair Paragon."

"What did you find out?"

"I had this little brainstorm. I Googled the Earl of Wenfield."

"Who is—?"

"The vice chairman of Harrogate Capital Partners."

She remembered: the British firm that invested heavily in Wheelz. "Right."

"So Lord Wenfield gives parties for Harrogate Capital Partners. That's basically his job. He gives a party at Henley every year for the firm, for instance."

"Okay."

"I found an article in a British magazine, *Tatler.* About a shooting party at Derwent House, the earl's grand estate. It's an annual event for Harrogate Capital Partners."

"Okay."

"Remember, his given name is Charles Arthur Bertram Hogg? Who can forget, right? So I caught a lucky break. He has a daughter, twenty-one years old. Olivia Hogg."

"Lucky break because . . . ?"

"Because I knew the daughter, like everyone else in her goddamned generation, would overshare on social media," Hersh said. "And sure enough, she does. At this shooting party, Olivia's Lamborghini goes into a pond on the earl's estate. A couple of months later, I found another article, this time in *The Sun*, about how Olivia Hogg was arrested in London for cavorting nude in one of the fountains in Trafalgar Square, at four A.M."

"Not sure I see—"

"Along with her boyfriend, Arkady Protasov. You recognize the boyfriend's name?"

"Protasov, sure. You mean, he's Yuri Protasov's son?"

"That's the guy," Hersh said.

Yuri Protasov was a well-known Russian businessman and investor as well as a major philanthropist. There was the Protasov Pavilion at New York Presbyterian Hospital. A wing of the Tate Modern in London, the Protasov Building. The Protasov Fellowship at the Harvard Business School. He was a generous, revered man.

"So Olivia Hogg posts on Instagram a lot," Hersh said. "She put up a picture of herself with her boyfriend, Arkady, and wrote something about how she met Arkady on his dad's yacht because, quote, 'our parents are doing a deal.'"

"Huh."

"Protasov, the dad, is, like, the hundredth richest person in the world, supposedly worth fifteen billion dollars. Owns a couple of football teams in the UK, owns one of the world's largest yachts. Bought a house in the Silicon Valley area, Los Altos Hills, for a hundred million bucks. Big investor in Facebook and Twitter. Once, he flew in Prince and Beyoncé to perform at his New Year's party on St. Barts."

"And his son goes out with the earl's daughter. You think . . . Protasov is the money behind Harrogate Capital Partners?"

"Gotta be."

"He's the guy who owns Wheelz."

"Right. That guy."

"So where does Mayfair Paragon come in?" she asked.

"Yuri Protasov owns the largest private residence in London, called Paragon House. In a part of London called Mayfair."

"Mayfair Paragon."

"Mayfair Paragon is probably one of his private investment vehicles."

"Wow," Juliana said after a moment, nodding to herself. "Genius work. I'm impressed."

"Thank you. So the woman who's suing Wheelz, Rachel Meyers, starts asking for the files on Mayfair Paragon. Because she's the general counsel, and it's her job. And maybe those files are the only place where Yuri Protasov's name appears."

"Maybe."

"And she's not allowed to see them. Because for some reason Yuri Protasov doesn't want anyone to know *he's* the secret owner of Wheelz."

"But why the hell would he care?" said Juliana. "So he owns an Uber rip-off. So what?"

"That I can't figure out. But it's obviously something he's willing to kill to protect."

"And you still think it's safe to keep kicking at the door? Knowing that?"

"I'm doing it, right?" Hersh said.

"You're not answering my question."

"I'm a professional," said Hersh. "I'm not an easy target. Don't worry about me. Worry about yourself."

Later she Googled Protasov. There was a lot, mostly philanthropic. She saw that in 2017 he had given fifty million dollars to Yale to establish the Protasov Fund for Innovation at Yale, and the very next year his daughter was admitted to Yale College. One of those happy coincidences. She found his Wikipedia page and saw that Protasov was on the International Steering Committee of Doctors Without Borders.

Along with Martha Connolly.

54

Juliana got up early the next morning and went for a run. It cleared her head and calmed her down, better than any sedative. And she needed it, badly. But as she ran her usual route, around the reservoir at Cleveland Circle, she found herself paying close attention to the vehicles she passed, wondering about vans that looked somehow suspicious. About other runners who might be following her. But as far as she could tell, she wasn't being followed.

Part of her wanted to stay in the house, hide downstairs. She was terrified. But she couldn't give in to the fear. Instead, she was almost defiant. She wasn't going to be a victim, a prisoner of fear.

By the time she got back to the house, the men were awake. Duncan was making scrambled eggs; Jake was upstairs in the bathroom, where he spent ridiculous amounts of time. She was ravenously hungry, probably because of the run, but she wanted to get to her lobby early. So she scarfed down some eggs, grabbed her briefcase, and went out to the car. She arrived at her lobby just before eight.

She did some searching online for an e-mail address for her old law school classmate Aaron Dunn, who worked at the Department of Justice in Washington. She found out quickly that Dunn was now chief of the

Criminal Fraud division. That was excellent. He'd have some juice in the department. She needed allies.

But she couldn't find his phone number or his e-mail address. She called the main Justice Department line and asked for him by name. She was put right through to his voice mail. She left him a brief message, told him it was important, gave him her cell number.

And she went back to work.

A motion had come in from Glenda Craft, the plaintiff's lawyer in the Wheelz case. A bundle of paper all in support of a motion to compel the defense to turn over a document. Sure enough, the defense had responded with a motion of their own. Another bundle of paper. This afternoon they'd be arguing it live, and she wanted to refresh her memory.

The damned Wheelz case—already ugly—had gotten even uglier. First, the defense had tried to pressure the plaintiff into settling by threatening to release her nude photos and sexts. All under the name of "discovery." She'd shut that down, but now the defense was refusing to hand over documents. The games never ended.

She spent half an hour rereading Glenda Craft's motion and Harlan Madden's opposition, and then her iPhone rang. A 202 number: Washington, DC.

"Aaron."

"Judge Brody! Long time!"

A long time ago, back in law school, Aaron Dunn had been interested in her, romantically. He'd asked her out persistently, even though she'd politely rebuffed him. It took him a long time to get the message. Not all persistence is rewarded. But eventually they got past it and became friends.

"Nice to hear your voice. You're, like, chief of the division now."

"Yeah, you keep to yourself and mind your own business, and look what they do to you. How's Duncan?"

She glanced at her watch. Court started in ten minutes. She had to get right to it, didn't have time to chat and catch up.

"Aaron, let me tell you why I reached out." She gave him a quick summary of the Wheelz lawsuit she was presiding over.

"Wheelz is that Uber competitor, right?"

"Right. And because of various documents that have come to my attention, I've learned that Wheelz is secretly owned by a Russian businessman you might have heard of. An oligarch named Yuri Protasov."

"Sure, I know the name," said Dunn. "He's a dual national."

"A citizen of Russia and the US, you mean?"

"Right."

"Well, for some reason, he's trying to keep his ownership stake a secret. He's done it through a series of shell companies."

"Interesting."

"And something else," she said. "This is going to sound like a—thriller, a movie, whatever. But the last principal investor, before Protasov took it over, was killed on the ski slopes at Aspen. Kevin Mathers."

A pause. "Okay." He sounded dubious.

"One of the defense lawyers in the Wheelz case died last week—ostensibly a suicide, but very likely a murder. Their British lawyer, or should I say solicitor, was killed a few years ago in a bus accident in London."

"Wow. I don't know what to say."

"I need to contact the FBI. At the right level. And I thought you might know some FBI agents."

"Of course I do. You want me to give someone a heads-up?"

"If you could."

"I'd be happy to."

She thanked him and hung up; then she stood up and put on her robe.

55

All right," she said as soon as she sat down. "Ms. Craft, this is your motion. I'll hear you first."

Glenda Craft stood. She was wearing an elegant black suit over a white top and pearl earrings. A perk of being a judge, she reflected: no one expects a judge to look especially put together. Judges should look dignified. Dignified, with a black robe on, was easy.

"Your Honor," Glenda said, "a couple of months ago, we served a request for the production of documents. We requested copies of any and all e-mails that mention Rachel Meyers, including e-mails to and from her. But the defense is stonewalling us once again. Now, Mr. Madden and I have discussed this, and we were unable to arrive at a satisfactory resolution."

"How many e-mails are we talking about?"

"Well, it's a string. A chain of e-mails. The chief operating officer, Andrew Westerfield, forwarded an e-mail he'd gotten from Rachel Meyers to his boss, the chief financial officer, Eugene Brod. For some reason they're withholding that."

"For what reason?"

"They claim it's 'proprietary and confidential,' Judge. And—"

"Hold on. Let me talk to you, Mr. Madden. How many e-mails are you withholding?"

"Five, but they're all part of one conversation, one thread, between Mr. Brod and Mr. Westerfield."

"And the basis for your claim of privilege?"

"Your Honor," Madden interrupted, "the e-mail correspondence back and forth between the CFO and the COO contains proprietary and confidential business information that has absolutely no bearing on this case. Which is, let's remember, alleged sexual harassment."

"All right," Juliana said, her hands up, palms out. "Let's make this easy. I'm ready to rule right now. Mr. Madden, I want you to produce that entire e-mail thread for me to read in camera. And I don't want to see pieces of paper full of black lines. I want to see the whole exchange. And show me what you propose to redact, and why. Are we clear?"

"Yes, Your Honor," said Madden.

"Yes, Your Honor," said Craft.

"I want it within one week," Juliana said.

She wondered what the Wheelz Corporation might be withholding. Was it the identity of the principal investor? Was that it? How could the top officers not know who owned their own damned company?

Or were they withholding something else?

When she returned to her lobby, she found a couple of phone messages. One was from an assistant to Attorney General Kent Yarnell asking her to join General Yarnell—she actually called him *General!*—for a drink that night at the Bostonia Club. She was too intrigued by how sociable it sounded—was Yarnell trying to make nice?—to be put off by how last-minute it was. She was amused that Yarnell didn't extend the invitation himself but instead had an assistant do it. That was officious, of course, and probably meant to send her a message, to remind her of her place in the ecosystem.

The second message was from her old friend Aaron Dunn at the Justice Department.

"Jules, okay, call this number," he said, and he gave her a Boston-area phone. "He's a good guy. Works in the FBI in counterintelligence. I told him about you and said you were going to call."

She was glad the guy was in the Boston office of the FBI. She wanted to talk in person, not over the phone, and preferred not to go to DC if she could avoid it. Rescheduling her court obligations was a massive pain.

She wrote down the name—Special Agent Paul Brickley—and the number on a pink message pad and called it.

56

At 4:45 she pulled up in front of a new eight-story building in Chelsea, outside Boston, in front of which was a giant stone seal and the words FEDERAL BUREAU OF INVESTIGATION. She parked in the small visitors' lot and approached the guard booth. The man asked her to put her driver's license against the bulletproof glass so he could see it. He told her she should lock up her phone in her car because she wouldn't be allowed to bring it into the building. He buzzed her into a small glass-walled room, where she had to empty her pockets and put her metal objects in a bin and walk through a metal detector. (She'd left Hersh's knife in the car along with the phone.) Then she entered the main building and handed over her driver's license in exchange for a small plastic clip-on badge with a red V for *Visitor* on it. While she waited, she looked over the wall display of the FBI's Ten Most Wanted Fugitives. Nobody she knew.

A few minutes later a door opened, and a man in his midforties emerged. He wore a gray suit and had jet-black hair with a prominent white part. He reminded her of a TV anchorman.

"Judge Brody, I'm Special Agent Brickley." He had a deep, rumbling voice.

She stood up and shook his hand. He led them to a conference room just off the lobby. There was a table with an Avaya phone on it and a couple of chairs.

"Aaron Dunn speaks very highly of you," Brickley said. "It's an honor to meet you."

"Very nice to meet you. I'm sure you're busy, and I know it's the end of the day, so I'll make this brief. I'm in a difficult position here. I have a concern about a case I'm involved with. I've never done anything like this before. But I've never confronted a case like this before."

She gave him a rundown on Wheelz. She concluded: "So it appears that the biggest investor in Wheelz is a Russian oligarch named Yuri Protasov."

He nodded. He knew the name.

"The financing for the deal secretly came from a bank that's under US sanctions. So it's illegal. Which may be why he's going to such lengths to keep his name a secret."

Agent Brickley nodded again.

"And one thing more," she said. She felt faint, queasy. "I just have to say it, no matter how farfetched it may seem to you. A couple of people who've found out about this have been killed."

His expression morphed from skeptical to concerned. He paused a few seconds. "Obviously you've found something quite interesting. Maybe even alarming—*I* think so, for sure."

"Okay."

"But this isn't really our area of concern. It's really more a matter for the State Department."

"The State Department?"

He nodded, smiled sadly. "Yeah, they're in charge of sanctions. Sorry to make you come all the way in here."

"I see." *Why*, she wondered, *did Aaron Dunn give me this guy's name?*

"But come to think of it," he went on, "the State Department shut down their sanctions office a while ago. So there really isn't anyone at

State who deals with it. It may be a matter more for the Treasury Department."

"Treasury, now? Hold on a sec. The FBI is charged with enforcing US law, and we're talking about a US law. Am I right? How is this not the FBI's business? The guy's breaking the law. That seems pretty clear-cut to me."

"I know, I know. But candidly and off the record? We're not in the business of going after Russian oligarchs."

"You're not? Even Russian oligarchs who break US laws?"

"It's a new era. The Russia stuff—you know, our enforcement powers have been whittled away. We just don't have the staff anymore."

"How come?"

"I used to be in CD, Counterintelligence Division, in Russian affairs, but most of us Russia experts have taken early retirement or left. Not many left. So Russia is no longer so much of a focus."

"Seriously?"

"And, you know, the FBI isn't exactly the apple of anyone's eye these days, when it comes to funding and personnel and such," said Agent Brickley. "It's a new world."

She returned to her car and sat in the FBI visitors' parking lot for a few minutes. She took out her phone and called Aaron Dunn in Washington. This time she got right through.

"He said that?" Dunn remarked.

"Yes," Juliana said. "'Russia is no longer so much of a focus.'"

"Oh, Jesus. Listen, is there any chance of you coming to DC?"

"If I need to, sure."

"I found someone who'll see you. Can you get here Monday?"

"It can't be any earlier?"

"I'm afraid not. He's out of town before then."

I have court, she thought. "I'll be there."

57

She stopped at home before going out to the Bostonia Club to meet Kent Yarnell and found both her husband and her son. She was hungry, and Duncan hadn't made dinner or picked up any takeout. She'd grab something from the refrigerator.

But first she made a point of chatting for a couple of minutes with both Jake and Duncan. She wanted them to think of her as *living at home* again, not the wife and mother who was sent into exile at Martha Connolly's. Her exile was over. Going out tonight, to the Bostonia Club, was an exception. She preferred to be home with them.

Once again she and Duncan were walking on eggshells with each other, back to being polite and formal and distant, and she realized it would take some time before relations got back to something approaching normal.

Then she got into her SUV and headed into town. As she drove, she called Hersh.

"Safe to talk on the phone?" she asked.

"As long as it hasn't been out of your hands."

She thought for a moment. She'd left it in the car when she was visiting the FBI. But the FBI parking lot was probably the safest place in the city to park. "Okay. You think you have a source on Protasov?"

"Not quite. Someone who may be able to get into that British lawyer's e-mail for me. Legally or at least semi-legally."

"At Linklaters."

"Right. Fiona Charteris, her name is. The woman who was killed. She was basically doing her due diligence, closing a financing deal, and she obviously found out something she shouldn't have about Mayfair Paragon and the money behind the deal. I want to know what else she found out. I wonder if she figured out about Yuri Protasov. It'll be in her e-mails, I'll bet."

"Can you do this remotely? You don't have to go to London, do you?"

"What, you worried about my travel costs?"

"I'm worried about *time*."

"Well, I'm just making phone calls."

"On Monday I'm going to DC for the day." She explained about Aaron Dunn at Justice. "Let me ask you something. How do I know if I'm being followed?"

"I don't know how to answer that over the phone. Beyond the obvious. You're driving. You *think* you're being followed?"

"Maybe."

For the last couple of minutes she'd noticed a car behind her with a figure of a horse in its grill. A Mustang. Even she, not exactly a gearhead, knew it was a Ford Mustang. It was dark blue and new, and it had been behind her all the way down Route 9, for the last couple of minutes. And even before she turned onto Route 9, she remembered.

Odds were it was a coincidence. She knew that. She didn't want to surrender to paranoia. On the other hand, she didn't want to be oblivious.

"I want to know if you really think you are being followed, okay?" said Hersh. "Call me right away if you are."

She next called Martie Connolly and told her about DC. "Do you know anyone at the CIA, by any chance?"

"I do—an old, dear friend," Martha said, "who is not only an excellent person, but he's as discreet as they come. I suppose that comes with working for the CIA. Anyway, he's a real character. You'll like him. Let me put in a call."

"Thanks," she said. She turned left onto Brookline Avenue, and the Mustang turned left as well.

At the next major intersection, she decided at the last minute to turn left onto the Riverway instead of going straight as she'd normally do.

The Mustang behind her turned left too.

Was she in fact being followed? Or was the Mustang simply heading into Boston the same way?

Because if this car was following her, it was not being subtle about it. It was following in an overt, obvious way, as if to taunt her. Or intimidate her.

She felt her nerves prickle.

At the light, at the intersection with Park Drive, she hit the stored number for her law clerk, Kaitlyn. "I need to be out of town on Monday," she said. She asked Kaitlyn to continue her cases and "take off" the motions. She hated to do it, but she knew she had no choice. Trials are scheduled up to a year in advance. Motions are set up weeks in advance. She would be inconveniencing a long list of attorneys and witnesses, and she wasn't happy about it.

The Mustang was still following her.

When she backed into a parking spot on the same block as the Bostonia Club, she saw the Mustang pass by.

She shut off the car and called Hersh again. "Okay, I really think that car might have been following me."

"Did you get a look at the driver?"

"I didn't, not really. A guy."

"You'll have to do better than that."

"If I see the Mustang again, I'll look more closely."

"A Mustang?"

"So?"

"Good acceleration. A good chase car."

"Wasted on me. I generally keep to the speed limit. One of the drawbacks to being a judge."

"But more to the point, a Mustang's also instantly recognizable. They wanted you to know you were being followed. Let me know if you see it again."

"I will."

She pushed at the beautiful brass knob on the gleaming black front door.

Attorney General Kent Yarnell was standing in the lobby, alone, underneath the John Singer Sargent portrait, waiting for her.

The General, she thought.

58

Kent," she said. Juliana and Kent Yarnell exchanged quick, social kisses. "Good to see you," she said. "Been a while."

"Juliana," he said. He had never called her "Jules." Always "Juliana," and he liked to overenunciate each syllable, annoyingly.

They were both pretending to like each other. He disliked her, she knew, and the feeling was mutual.

"Library okay?" he said.

"Sure." That meant a drink, not dinner. Good.

They found a nook in a far corner of the library, dimly lit. The attorney general sat on a green leather couch, and Juliana took the chair next to it.

Kent Yarnell had a high forehead, a ridiculously large dome, and small, deep-set eyes. He wore frameless glasses. His eyes, she'd always thought, were beady. He was dressed in a well-cut gray suit with a red tie. But with his long limbs and his slender wrists and his liquid movements, he'd always reminded her of a spider.

They chatted awkwardly for a few minutes. He mentioned someone they both knew from the US Attorney's office. But Juliana didn't really remember much about the woman. She said, "That was a long time ago. My memory's hazy."

"I know what you mean," he said with a smile.

The server came, and they both ordered drinks. She ordered a chardonnay, and he ordered a Diet Pepsi.

"Well, I imagine your feminist sisters are proud of you."

"Excuse me?"

"Sexual *harassment*," he said. He flicked two fingers of each hand to make air quotes. He shook his head. "What a racket. You start handing out major awards, you know what's gonna happen, don't you? People start filing major grievances. And when one employee starts, another one joins in, and pretty soon you get a riot effect. It's like looting. Once the storefront gets smashed, everybody wants to grab a stereo for themselves."

"You aren't really going to debate the Wheelz case with me, are you?"

"It's the criminalization of, what did we used to call it? Nookie?"

"Kent, come on. We're not going there."

He crossed his legs and tented his hands atop his knee. "The reason I wanted to see you, Juliana, was to give you some advice. Consider it advice from a friend."

She nodded, awaiting whatever came next.

"I think we both know what we're talking about," he said.

"I'm not sure I do, Kent."

They looked each other in the eyes. She wasn't going to make it easy for him.

"In the course of investigating a possible homicide," he said, "the Boston Police found evidence indicating that you may have had a relationship with the deceased. An attorney who argued a case before you."

"Are we talking about a pair of sunglasses, for God's sake?"

He shrugged. His eyes were dead. "My investigator now has the deceased's mobile phone records. Wouldn't it be interesting if they found a call between you and Mr., uh, Sanchez."

Her stomach did a twist. Did she ever call the guy on his cell phone? She didn't think so.

Then she remembered—a call she'd *received* from him. *You are not to recuse yourself. That would be a serious mistake.*

Yes, he'd called her, to threaten her. That call established a link between them.

"And what on earth does this have to do with investigating a homicide?" she said. She thought about how she could explain the call from Matías. She could say the guy called her, and she told him this was an ex parte communication, and she got off the phone right away. That was all.

Maybe.

"Juliana, let's put our cards on the table. If we can establish that you had an intimate relationship with Matías Sanchez, an attorney who appeared before you, and you did not disclose this or recuse yourself . . . well." He shrugged broadly. "I'm going to recommend that the matter be brought before the CJC."

The Commission on Judicial Conduct. Which investigated judges. "Oh, for God's sake."

"And I'm going to recommend your removal from the bench. I'm sorry, but I don't see a choice."

She felt the blood rush to her face. She felt both trapped and angry. "I think what you're talking about," she said, "is that a pair of sunglasses with my fingerprints on them was found in the deceased lawyer's hotel room. Fine. How my sunglasses ended up in his room, I have no idea. It's peculiar. Did he find them? Did he take them? Who knows. But how that indicates that I had a relationship with him—is that the best you have? Seriously? That's pathetic. Kent, don't embarrass yourself."

There was no longer any need to pretend they liked each other.

"Trooper Markowski is one of our best. If there's something to be found, he'll find it. He always does."

"Hold on, is he investigating a crime of some sort?"

"As you well know, you're a person of interest."

"Kent, we know each other. I know you. If your Trooper Markowski had found something in the deceased's phone records, you'd have told me already."

"Trooper Markowski has requested the phone logs. He'll get them tomorrow."

"Then you should have waited before asking me out for a drink."

"I'm offering you an opportunity. To resign from the bench with dignity, on your own terms."

"On my own terms," she said, shaking her head.

"You can avoid all the ugliness, all the publicity, by choosing to resign from the bench." He spoke quietly, somberly. "Oh, and the disbarment that will inevitably follow. I think a resignation, for personal reasons, would be better for all concerned."

They locked eyes.

He said, "Am I making myself clear?"

"You are," she said.

"And I mean resign now, tomorrow morning, and not at the end of the year."

"I understand."

"I'm sure we can work out something that doesn't damage your reputation." He was not negotiating. He believed he had her trapped, that he was in control of the situation.

But he was bluffing. He was also going on instinct. He'd guessed that something had happened between her and Matías Sanchez.

But he doesn't know for sure.

Tomorrow, the phone records would come in, and Trooper Markowski would let his boss know a call had indeed been made between Judge Juliana Brody and the deceased.

And the attorney general would file notice with the CJC. Would circumstantial evidence be enough to get her thrown off the bench?

Maybe.

"Kent," she said, "the funniest thing. Your kind 'advice to a friend' is reawakening my own fond memories of working for you. I'm remembering all sorts of things."

He cocked his head.

"I think we both know what I'm talking about."

"I'm afraid I don't."

"The Ray Marshak case."

"I remember it well too, Juliana."

"And since you brought up the topic, we found your phone number in Marshak's phone records. Quite a few times. When you know you shouldn't have been in contact with him. But I didn't see any reason to tell you. Nor anyone else, of course—at the time. Anyway."

He blinked, then pursed his lips. She could see the realization dawn in his eyes, beady though they were. The fear that contorted his face. "Are you threatening me?" he said.

"I don't know. Do you feel threatened?"

In a very low voice he called her a very bad word.

She gave him a large, gladiatorial smile, as if she was enjoying this. "So I *am* making myself clear, then?"

The waitress arrived with their drinks. Juliana lifted hers from the tray and raised it in mock salute. "I'm going to take mine to go, Kent. So glad we had this little chat."

59

On the way home from the club, she kept her eye out for the dark blue Ford Mustang, but she didn't see it this time. No one seemed to be following her.

Hersh had left her a text message asking her to call him if and when she saw the Mustang again, "or any other car that looks like it's following."

By the time she got home, he'd sent her another text message: I want to sweep your office in the morning—OK?

"Sweep," she assumed, meant look for bugs, surveillance devices. The idea of someone planting a listening device in her lobby creeped her out, made her nervous again. She texted back: Sure.

The building's maintenance staff had keys to her lobby. It wasn't exactly high-security, ordinarily. There was no reason for it to be.

But then there had been the fake janitor. Maybe she could use some security.

In the morning, Hersh was waiting for her in front of the courthouse. He was holding a bulky aluminum briefcase.

"You been here awhile?"

"Half an hour, maybe. Thought you'd be in earlier."

"Sorry. Late night."

"I know. This briefcase is going to bum out the security guards. I'm going to need you to pull strings."

They got in line.

"What's in it?" she asked.

"TSCM equipment."

She didn't know what "TSCM equipment" was, but she didn't want to ask. Something to do with sweeping her lobby, that was all she needed to know.

When they entered the building, she took one of the guards aside. He was a pudgy African-American guy named Lamar. "Morning, Judge," he said.

"Morning, Lamar. This gentleman here is doing some security work in the courthouse."

"He's still going to have to put that case through the scanner."

Hersh got through security without a problem. She led him to her lobby. He watched as she keyed the lock. When they were inside, he said, "I could pick that lock inside of a minute and a half."

"I know. It's not exactly high-security around here."

"This is going to take me several hours. Is that too long a disruption?"

"Not if you do it while I'm in court."

"Okay. Listen, don't use my name after we enter your chambers—"

"'Lobby.'"

"*Lobby*, right. I don't want them to know I'm there."

"Let who know?"

"Whoever the hell is following you. Where were you when you made the plan to meet the attorney general last night?"

"In my office. On my landline."

He nodded. "Then I know where to start."

After they'd entered her lobby, he inspected the bookshelves while she checked her e-mail.

"You a big Trollope fan?"

"Trollope? I like him well enough, why?"

He reached over to the shelf in the bookcase where she kept the many crimson volumes of *Massachusetts Practice.* He plucked a leather-bound copy of *Barchester Towers.* Then, looking directly at her and not at the book, he opened it, revealing the hidden compartment. It was a hollow book, a book-safe, in which she kept a small stack of cash and a pair of pricey pearl earrings Duncan had given her on her fortieth birthday. Sometimes she went out in the evenings right after work and needed to style up.

"You should give *Barchester Towers* a try."

"Very good," she said, grinning. He was good. Then again, the leather binding was uncreased, and the novel was out of place among all the legal volumes, right next to the *Massachusetts Guide to Evidence.* So it was more than a lucky guess. He closed the book and put it back on the shelf.

"I should have been a burglar," he said. "Woulda been good at it."

After the morning's court session, Juliana returned to her lobby to find Hersh sitting at her desk holding up a sign on a clipboard. DON'T TALK TO ME.

She nodded.

He pulled the top sheet from the clipboard, revealing another sign: I'M GOING TO SHOW YOU SOME STUFF. WE CAN TALK OUT IN THE HALLWAY.

Then he stood up and walked to the other side of her desk, where he knelt. She came around to look. He pointed at something small and off-white plugged into the back of her computer where her keyboard plugged in.

He nodded at her.

She felt her stomach jolt. She didn't know what it was, but she could guess. Some eavesdropping thing.

She nodded back: *I see it.*

Then he reached onto the desk for her landline phone console, turned it around, and lifted its case, exposing the guts of the phone. He pointed his pen at a small black plastic device, about two inches long and a half an inch wide, that was wired in place. He nodded; she nodded back. He took out a screwdriver and screwed the case back on to the phone.

He began packing up equipment—a long black wand with a little screen at the end, something else that resembled what she imagined a Geiger counter to look like—and went into the hallway. She took off her robe, hung it up, and then followed him out into the hallway and then to the bank of elevators.

"Step outside the courthouse for a bit of fresh air?" Hersh said.

"I'll take you to lunch."

"Deal."

They didn't talk again until they were outside the courthouse. She said, "The Killarney?" That was the Irish restaurant at Two Center Plaza, right nearby.

"Sure."

The Killarney was dimly lit; what little light there was was absorbed by all the dark wood. They were seated at a booth. Hersh ordered a Guinness, and she ordered a Diet Coke.

"Okay," Hersh said when the waitress had left. "The thing I showed you on your keyboard is called a key logger," he said. "It captures every keystroke you type."

She nodded. "How long do you think it's been there?"

"I have no idea. That device on your phone line broadcasts a signal using your Wi-Fi."

"And that thing inside my desk phone?"

"A transmitter. They also did some internal rewiring for room audio monitoring. Meaning they could hear whatever you said in the office, or on your landline, and read whatever you typed."

"Do you know who put them there? Can you tell from the devices where they're from?"

"Well, it's not the FBI. I can rule them out."

"How do you know?"

"Every surveillance device used by law enforcement is required to have a serial number marked on it, either engraved or on a sticker."

"No markings on the devices you saw?"

"Right. So I think we're talking spies."

"But which spies? Russian? Is that . . . paranoid of me to ask?"

"I'm not comfortable hazarding a guess. The absence of any identifying marks tells me it's very likely *some* government espionage agency."

"Why did you leave them there?"

"Because I think you have more options if you're one up on them. We may find the opportunity to use it."

"Use what?"

"You can say things on the phone, or type out phony e-mails, that mislead the bad guys."

"You're serious about this?"

"Dead serious."

"Isn't that what's called disinformation?"

"Right. If you want me to remove them, I'll gladly remove them. The bugs, I mean."

She shook her head. The waitress came with their drinks, her Diet Coke in a tumbler and his Guinness in a pint glass.

"I'm starting to feel really scared," she said.

"Starting?" he said. "I guess somebody really cares what you say in chambers."

"I have till noon on Tuesday to grant the motion for summary judgment," she said. "Which, if I say yes, would mean that the lawsuit's over and the bad guys win."

"The bad guys."

"Wheelz."

Hersh arched his eyebrows in surprise.

"I'm allowed to have opinions," she said. "I just don't express them."

"I'm honored to hear your opinions."

"And you don't think it makes a difference how I decide."

He looked somber, didn't reply.

There was a long pause. "Philip, your wife. It's none of my business, of course, but—what happened?"

He was quiet for a few long seconds, and she immediately regretted asking him.

"It's not a happy story."

She said nothing. Waited for him to speak.

He was silent a little longer. Then he said, "I was working a case involving the Albanian mob."

She nodded.

"I started getting threats. Turns out I was actually a step ahead of the FBI's own investigation. I was getting messages, you know—*You'll be sorry, you're making a mistake*—and naturally I took all precautions. My wife, you know, I told her that just until this thing cools off some, I want you to go to your sister's in Hyannis."

"And?"

"And she did."

He fell silent. She could hear her own heartbeat, felt it in her throat, her ears. "They grabbed her on her way out of town."

She looked at him. He was just narrating his story, telling it matter-of-factly, as if he was talking about cyber security or something. "So, they found her body on a construction site outside of town."

"Oh, my God," she whispered. She reached across the table and took his hand. Tears came to her eyes.

"Yeah, they'd poured gasoline over her and set her on fire." He was looking off to the side, into the middle distance, remembering. "I thought I'd never get that smell out of my nose. So much burnt flesh."

"I'm so sorry." Juliana felt a well of sadness.

"The pathologist said she'd—" There was a catch in his voice. And tears in his eyes as well. He put his hand up like a policeman stopping traffic.

She wanted to comfort the man; she gripped his forearm, but he sat back, rigid, his right hand still up in the air, palm out. A single tear rolled down his face.

A minute of silence passed. She felt helpless. Time had stood still. A car horn sounded outside.

"We say 'safe as houses.' But, you know, you can latch every window and bolt every door, and then the whole damned thing catches fire and burns up with you inside. Or an earthquake strikes and the ground beneath opens like the portal to hell. Or a flash flood sweeps the thing from its foundations and drowns everyone. So, yeah, like I said. You take every precaution to prevent disaster. But disaster is a cunning beast."

"Dear God," she said. She was silent for a long moment. "So what are you saying? There's no point to doing anything?"

"Oh, no," he said. He looked at her almost tenderly. "You do something. You do everything. You do everything you can. But don't assume that everything is going to be enough."

60

That night she told Duncan she was going to Washington for the day on Monday, and why.

He listened closely. "You're going to cancel court?"

"For one day. I'm not happy about it."

"Guy can't see you over the weekend?"

"Monday's the soonest."

He nodded, but he seemed increasingly troubled.

"What is it?" she said. "What's wrong?"

"I worry about this. It bothers me, and I know it bothers you too."

She nodded. "You mean, talking to the FBI, talking to people in Washington?"

"About a case you're presiding over."

"I know," she agreed. "But I have no choice. I think this is the only way we're all ever going to be safe. I have to keep digging." Her head throbbed when she thought about the upcoming hours she'd have to spend poring over the discovery exhibits again. But she'd learned that the tiniest of crevices could sometimes provide a needed handhold.

Hersh's voice played in her head like a tape loop. *You're okay until you make that decision, thumbs up or thumbs down. Because once you do—they don't need you anymore.*

"You're right."

"It doesn't make any difference how I rule, what judgment I put out."

He nodded, listened.

"Kent Yarnell wants to bring me up before the CJC," she said.

"On what grounds?"

She shrugged. "He eventually backed off. But whether he does or not, I've made my decision. It's clear I have no choice but to resign from the bench. When this is over, I'm stepping down."

"Jules, no," Duncan said. "That's—"

"I have no business judging others. You *know* that—"

"Damn it, that's crazy. You're not going to throw away the life you've built for yourself, Jules."

"It's a *career*, Duncan. That's all. I can find another line of work."

"Bullshit. It's never just been a career for you. It's a goddamned *calling*. What you live, eat, and breathe. And you have a great future."

"Had." Her voice was flat. "That future is in flames. I don't know why you can't see that."

Duncan just shook his head. "Stay focused on the now. Get through this, leave the long-term choices for the future. You hear me, Jules? It's the only way."

61

When her flight landed at Reagan National Airport in Washington, she made a point of observing her fellow passengers as they got off, and the people waiting for the next flight, and people walking near her. It was near crazy-making. It made her anxious. Plenty of people looked suspicious, if you were inclined to look at people that way. She also realized that looking people in the eyes often made them nervous. You generally avoid people's eyes out in public.

Situational awareness, Hersh had instructed her. "Look for patterns. And anomalies. If they're following you, they'll probably use a team, to do handoffs and keep you unaware of the followers."

In the cab on the way to Lafayette Square, to a steakhouse near the Treasury Department and the White House, she looked back a few times, but that seemed pointless. She wasn't a spy or a detective; this wasn't her expertise, checking for a tail. So was someone following her? She had no idea.

She entered the restaurant and immediately spotted her old friend Aaron Dunn. Dunn was around her age, early forties, but it seemed that the pressure of his job had aged him. He looked very late-middle-aged. He was bald, with a gray fringe around his ears, the kind of balding pattern that inspires many men to shave their heads. He had heavy-lidded eyes that made him look bored or supercilious, though he was seldom either.

"Judge Brody!" he said. "Hey, at the risk of sounding superficial, you look great."

She smiled, gave him a hug. "Thank you so much for doing this."

"No problem. He's at the table." He pointed. She looked over, saw a rotund guy with white hair, busy tapping something out on a phone. "His name is George Hastings. He's the Director of the Office of Foreign Assets Control in the Treasury Department."

"Okay, wow."

"So he's a guy with juice," Dunn said quietly, leading her toward the table. "He never goes out for lunch, so this is a big deal for him."

"I appreciate it." She looked around. The restaurant was in a hotel located in the Old Post Office building. The decor in the restaurant was interesting: the old steel trusses and struts had been exposed and painted white.

She introduced herself to Hastings, who stood up, a large, bulky man in his sixties with a shock of white hair and a red, chafed face. His demeanor made it plain he had better and far more important things to do. He was clearly doing his friend a favor.

"I already ordered the candied-bacon appetizer," Hastings said. "I'm on a tight schedule." He had a soft southern drawl. "Try it. Great stuff."

She wasn't late; he'd clearly gotten here early. She looked at the menu. The burger cost twenty-six dollars.

She decided to get right to the point. They could be social afterward. She told him that, in the course of presiding over a sexual harassment case, she happened to come across some internal company documents. These documents revealed that the secret owner of the company was a Russian oligarch named Yuri Protasov. "You know the name?"

"Sure. The Protasov Great Innovations Prize." That was the rich prize, worth four million dollars a year to the lucky winner, given to a leading "innovator" in science—physics, chemistry, mathematics, or life sciences.

"That's the one. He's gone to great lengths to keep his ownership of this company a secret."

Hastings shrugged. "So?"

"So the financing for his purchase of this company came from a sanctioned Russian bank."

"Ah."

"Which I figured you might be interested to hear."

"Indeed. Do you know which bank?"

"I think it's called VTB. The VTB bank."

His eyebrows shot up, but he said nothing. "You know, Protasov is not an SDN."

"A *what*?"

"A Specially Designated National. A blocked person. One of the named individuals you're not supposed to do business with." He said it with a slight smile, which surprised Juliana. It seemed to imply it was a rule that no one takes seriously. "Which means he's okay to do business with. And this company—Wheelz, obviously—is not sanctioned."

"Okay, but as I said, the money came from a sanctioned Russian bank. Making it an illegal transaction and one that the US Government can shut down."

"Mrs. Brody—Judge Brody, excuse me—forgive my bluntness, but is it appropriate for you to be doing this inquiry?"

"I don't know," she said. "I'd have to ask a judge."

He smiled. "I see. Well, the thing is, Judge, we're not really doing much by the way of enforcement these days."

"You're not?"

"No, our enforcement and compliance unit is gone."

"How do you mean, gone?"

"No one ever got appointed to run it. The position's been vacant for a few years now. The whole unit—people left, retired early."

"There's really no enforcement?"

"There's self-disclosure. Voluntary compliance. But no—no cops running around arresting people for sanctions violations. Anyway, look." He sighed. "Okay, he's a Russian. All this paranoia about Russia—people are tired of it."

"They are, huh?"

"Enough, already. I wish I could help you, but I don't have the time or the resources or, to be perfectly plain about it, the inclination. I'm not the type of person to go on a one-man crusade, fighting the bureaucracy."

She nodded. "I understand."

She didn't understand, actually, not really, but saw nothing to be gained by arguing with the man. She thanked Hastings, and when he got up to go back to work, she excused herself to use the bathroom.

As she passed the table next to theirs, her eye was caught by the shoes worn by the businesswoman sitting next to them. They were nothing fancy—a pair of black napa leather round-toe pumps, well worn, the heel neither skinny nor chunky. The soles of the shoes were red and badly scuffed.

She had remembered seeing the exact same pair of shoes on a woman at her departure gate at Logan Airport in Boston that morning. She knew that red soles were a trademark of Christian Louboutins. And she remembered because she'd noticed how scuffed-up the soles were. She'd thought: *They must be well-loved, those shoes.*

She looked from the scuffed red soles up to the woman's face. She was a bland-looking person, forgettable—short brown hair, glasses, a dowdy brown suit. The sort of person who blends into the background. She was dining with a man who was equally forgettable.

Juliana's eyes met the woman's, and her stomach clenched and her heart started thudding.

The woman quickly looked away, and Juliana continued on to the restroom. There, she stared at herself in the mirror above the sinks.

It was no coincidence that the woman with the Louboutins was here, next to their table, maybe listening in.

She'd seen this woman before. She was sure of it.

And she wondered how much of her lunchtime conversation had been overheard.

62

By the time Juliana got back to the table from the restroom, the woman in the Louboutins was gone. So was Hastings. Aaron Dunn apologized profusely. "I didn't know it was that bad in the bureaucracy. The so-called Deep State. Plus, back when Hastings and I played poker, he was sort of a no-bullshit kind of guy. Someone who wouldn't put up with crap. I guess staying there too long changes you."

She walked him back to the Justice Department. "Don't worry about it," she said, though of course she'd flown to Washington just for this meeting. "What about Capitol Hill? Do you know any members of Congress, or senators?"

The Walk sign came on, and she was about to step off the curb when a bus came blasting by, through the red light, brakes squealing. She thought of that solicitor in London, killed in a bus accident, and it took a moment for her pulse to stop racing.

"I know some chiefs of staff," he said. "What were you thinking?"

"Anyone you could get me in to see this afternoon?"

"Now?" He shook his head. "Sorry, but that's a very big ask. Which is fine, but I don't have anyone I could call for a favor like that."

Martie, she thought. *She knows everyone.*

After she said good-bye to Dunn, she took out her phone and hit Martha Connolly's number.

"Martie, I need a big favor."

"Anything," Martie said immediately.

"No, this is a big one. I need a few minutes of an influential senator's time."

"Who?"

"Whoever you know who's on the Senate Intelligence Committee. Who has a link to the intelligence community. And has clout."

"Okay. To talk on the phone?"

"In person would be much better. Even if it's just five minutes."

"How soon?"

"This afternoon."

Martha didn't laugh. "Time sensitive, is it? Well, it would be good for you and Senator Hugh Comstock to get to know each other a bit. Let me see what I can do."

Senator Hugh Comstock agreed to be pulled out of a staff meeting for ten minutes to meet with Judge Brody. It was a testament to Martie's remarkable clout.

He had a long, thin nose and a prominent jaw. He sat behind his desk, an antique mahogany hulk, and listened with rapt attention as Juliana talked.

"The lead investor, and the person controlling the company, is a guy named Yuri Protasov," she said.

"Okay," the senator said guardedly, and she could see his interest flag at once.

He was a senator from Illinois, on the Senate Intelligence Committee. Martie thought he'd be interested in what Juliana had to say. Juliana had done some research on her phone, looked up who Senator Comstock's biggest donors were, and didn't see Protasov's name. That had been a relief. If Protasov was a major contributor of his, he'd be unable and unwilling to help. Instead, Comstock's biggest corporate donor was a Chicago-based biopharm company.

"But the reason I think he's taking such pains to keep his ownership a secret is that the money he used to buy Wheelz was wired to his company from a Russian bank that's under US sanctions."

The senator nodded, examined his fingernails. No longer paying attention.

She told him about the deaths that she suspected were connected. He didn't seem to react.

Then she said, "So I have a plan that I think—"

"Okay, let me cut you off here," Senator Comstock said. "Save you a little time."

"Sorry?"

"You're someone who Martha Connolly thinks is worth listening to. She thinks you've got the Supreme Court in your future."

"Martie is sometimes prone to hyperbole."

"So I don't understand why you'd want to throw it all away."

"How would I be throwing it away?"

Her phone started ringing. She ignored it.

"By going after Yuri Protasov. Do you know who he is? Let me tell you who he is. He is the genie who grants your wishes. He is not someone you go to war with."

"I'm not talking about a war—"

"You want to go after him on some, what, grade D SEC misdemeanor? A violation of sanctions that no one pays attention to anymore? This man is an icon. He's a great man. He may be from Russia, but he's become an integral part of American life." Now he was looking right at her, pointing at her, surprisingly impassioned. "My wife was treated for ovarian cancer at the Protasov Cancer Institute at Sibley Hospital, okay? I'm on the board of the Protasov Family Foundation."

"I didn't know that." Dammit, she hadn't checked the list of board members.

"When people put me down, they call me the 'senator from biopharma.' Because my biggest support comes from the pharmaceutical industry. And I don't mind that at all. I'm proud to be the senator from Oncopharm. They're in the business of saving lives."

"Oncopharm is—"

"The majority shareholder is Yuri Protasov."

"I see."

"A man who has given away a *billion* dollars of his own money."

"So I'm told."

"Oh, sure, his rivals have tried to smear him. All those rabidly anti-Russia people. I'm afraid you've been bamboozled by the fake news." The senator shook his head. "It so happens that if you run a charity, a museum, or a hospital, part of your job description is sucking up to a gentleman named Yuri Protasov. So I don't think you're getting the message here, Ms. Brody. You don't go after a man like Yuri Protasov. You send him thank-you notes."

After she left Senator Comstock's office, Juliana checked her phone. A voice message and a text from Martha Connolly. The text read, I've got someone else for you.

63

The Old Saloon, on Fifteenth Street, was a Washington institution, established in the mid-nineteenth century, and known for its oysters and its crab cakes and its rude waitresses. It was the oldest saloon in Washington. The bar was made from solid mahogany, and the antique gas fixtures had been electrified. The Old Saloon was also known as a watering hole for CIA types.

Juliana quickly found the man she was meeting. It wasn't hard; he would stand out in any crowd. He was wearing a blue-and-white seersucker suit and a navy bow tie. He looked as though he'd walked out of another era. She gave him a smile and sat at his two-top. She thought: *What kind of undercover CIA operator actually wants to stand out in a crowd?*

"Should I say 'Your Honor'?" he said. She'd lost count of how many times someone had asked her that, socially. People were sometimes intimidated by judges and dealt with it by joking around.

"You must be Paul."

They shook hands. He was working on a drink already, something brown on the rocks.

His name was Paul Ashmont, and he was some kind of mucketymuck in counterintelligence at the CIA. He'd gone to Yale with Martie Connolly. Besides that, she knew only that he was a Russia expert and pretty high up the ladder. He was in his seventies and looked as though he enjoyed a hard-drinking, hard-smoking life.

She started at the beginning, told him about how she'd been entrapped. Ashmont nodded and smiled. "What the Russians call *kompromat*," he said. "Compromising material. Blackmail. They're skilled at the art. And of course they used a cutout."

"I'm surprised you were willing to meet me," she said. "I'm not exactly getting the welcome wagon in DC."

Ashmont chuckled. "Any friend of Martie Connolly's is a friend of mine." He took a sip of his drink. "Though I understand you tried my friends at the Bureau and got turned away."

"And yet you're here."

"Call it a personal interest of mine. Mention Yuri Protasov and you sure as hell get *my* attention."

"Why's that?" she said.

"How much do you know about the guy?"

"I think I know the basics. Philanthropist, investor, billionaire . . ."

"That's right. Estimated wealth of fifteen billion dollars, which puts him at number sixty-one on the *Forbes* list of the world's billionaires. Owns the largest private bank in Russia. Owns a Siberian natural gas company. Owns the largest private house in London—Paragon House, in Mayfair."

"I know."

"He owns a Manhattan penthouse and a villa in Sardinia and, last I heard, a Greek island. Guy's got houses in California, Aspen, Montana, Nantucket, Paris, Moscow . . ." He counted out with his fingers. "And he's a sailor. Owns the world's biggest superyacht. Two hundred forty meters long. Cost a half billion dollars. Two swimming pools and two helicopter pads on deck. Sorry, I'm kind of a yacht freak. What else? Two kids at Yale—my alma mater, like most Ivy League colleges, sure loves those oligarch kids. Good for the endowment."

"Sure."

He drained his drink and signaled the waitress for another.

"His private Boeing 767 has a dining room that seats thirty, okay? Beyoncé sang at his wedding. *Party like a Russian*, dude. It's a song."

She laughed. "I'm getting the picture." He was an odd duck, but she was starting to like him.

"But here's the thing—he's a good guy. You can't hate him. You go to his business headquarters, and the walls are lined with *books*. Why? Because Yuri loves reading. And he loves dogs, right? He paid for a bunch of kennels to house stray dogs left by the construction workers who did the Sochi Olympics. The guy owns six dogs at his house outside Moscow."

"Okay."

"He's a chevalier of the Légion d'Honneur. His foundation promotes the love of chess among youth. It also supports the elderly and also orphans. He owns the Tottenham Hotspur football club in Britain. He gave a wing of the Tate and too many hospital pavilions to list. And then there's the Protasov Peace Prize, the richest prize in the world, for contributions to peace and amity among the nations."

"I get the point," she said politely.

"No, I haven't even gotten to my point. Which is that Yuri Protasov is a myth."

"A myth?"

"A creation. A notion. A Potemkin oligarch."

She furrowed her brow. "I'm not sure what you mean."

"Okay. Protasov is different from the other Russian oligarchs."

"How so?"

"The other oligarchs basically stole what used to be state-owned enterprises as the Soviet Union was going private. They were all friends of Putin—it was an inside job. The biggest theft in the history of the world. I mean, Putin's stolen hundreds of billions of Russia's wealth and in the process helped enrich his closest friends. The guy is probably one of the richest men in the world. There's a cellist in Russia who's a childhood friend of Putin's, he's the godfather to Putin's daughter, and he's got a Swiss bank account worth two billion dollars."

She nodded.

The waitress set down his drink.

"Whereas Protasov is a creation of Putin. He poses as a brilliant investor, but he's basically underwritten by the Kremlin. The Kremlin secretly owns all these companies like Wheelz, through a straw. A cutaway named Yuri Protasov. Who everyone thinks is worth fifteen billion dollars."

"Okay."

"He's an invention," Ashmont said. "A stooge. He's a childhood friend of Vladimir Putin's, played ice hockey with him. See, Protasov isn't independently wealthy. All his money comes from the Kremlin. And all his investments—all the companies he supposedly owns? All owned by the Kremlin."

"You know this for sure?"

"We have a lot of signals intelligence. And human intelligence—people talk. Then there's our eavesdroppers over at Fort Meade."

"The NSA?"

"Exactly. We discovered some really interesting bank records, the movement of billions of dollars from Russian state banks into thousands of shell companies linked to Protasov. Basically, Yuri Protasov gets to live the life of a stratospherically rich man, one of the greatest philanthropists in history, as long as he does whatever his old judo partner Vladimir Putin asks. He gets to play a combo of Warren Buffett and Mother Teresa, right?"

Juliana was puzzled about something. "Is this the kind of secret the KGB, or whatever, will kill to protect?"

Ashmont cocked his head, looked at her curiously. He gave a quizzical smile, which quickly disappeared. His expression became somber. "What do you know?"

"About what?"

"People dying. Why do you say they'll 'kill'? What do you know?"

"I know that a Chicago lawyer named Matías Sanchez was recently killed." She didn't feel the need to get into who Matías was. Or whether he had committed suicide. "And a lawyer in London named Fiona Charteris."

He nodded. He seemed to know about these deaths. "Yeah, the law's a dangerous profession recently. Then there was Kevin Mathers, who had the misfortune to be the last lead investor in Wheelz and who died in an accident on the slopes." He drained his drink and signaled the waitress for another. "These guys don't mess around."

"These guys being—who? The oligarchs, like Protasov?"

He shook his head. "All the signs say it's their foreign intelligence service. FSB. Which you may know is the reincarnation of the KGB. Roughly speaking."

"You think these people were killed by the Russian intelligence service?"

"That's the speculation. To be specific, URPO." He pronounced it "urp-oh." "The FSB's kill squad. But they're very careful when they're dealing with non-Russians. They have no compunctions about blatantly killing off Russians who get in their way. Feeding them polonium, shit like that. Make them suffer long and painful deaths. But when it comes to foreigners—it always has to be done subtly. With plausible deniability. All done through cutouts."

Greaves, she thought. "But what I don't get is why Protasov is so concerned about keeping his ownership of Wheelz under wraps. Yes, his money comes from a bank under US sanctions—but so what? Doesn't sound like anyone much cares about sanctions, or sanctioned banks, in DC these days."

"No, people care. There's just no capacity to do anything about it. The Russia experts are thin on the ground."

"I see."

"As usual with the Russians, it's all about secrets within secrets. Let's start with this: Yuri Protasov has eighty percent of that investment round in Wheelz. Series D convertible preferred."

"Meaning?"

"He owns the company. But more to the point, *he owns the software.*"

"So the Kremlin owns Wheelz."

"Right."

"But for God's sake, why? What's the big deal about owning another Uber? Why is this so important?"

"Because this is actually all about a secret technology transfer."

She shook her head. "What's the technology?"

"Wheelz has a shitload of proprietary technology for autonomous vehicles. They own a lot of significant patents. Big-time military applications. That's what the Kremlin is after. Valuable intellectual property with significant military uses. The Russian Ministry of Defense wants self-driving tanks and convoys of supply trucks. The future of warfare is *autonomous vehicles*, man. That's the next frontier. Autonomous military vehicles are the backbone of next-gen warfare. Tanks, mobile artillery, logistics trucks. And Wheelz's self-driving car unit is believed to be way ahead of Uber or Lyft. That's really the crown jewels."

"Self-driving cars?"

"And if it could be proved that the Russians secretly siphoned off this technology? You'd have Congressional inquiries up the wazoo. It's a total violation of US export control laws. Starting with the Arms Export Control Act. Plus, apparently Wheelz is in the process of acquiring a Silicon Valley start-up with major defense contracts, and that would certainly come screeching to a halt. Look, we've been lax about the Kremlin's gambits, but a scandal like this would really tip the balance."

She nodded.

"And yeah, the Kremlin also doesn't want it known they wholly own an oligarch. They've invested a lot in the myth that's Yuri Protasov, and they don't want to lose it. So tell me, how did you have the bad luck to preside over the Wheelz sexual harassment case?"

"Luck of the draw. We're just assigned our cases; we don't choose."

"I'm sorry you ended up with it. To me it looks like Yuri Protasov set you up—entrapped you—to ensure he ended up with the right legal decision."

"To keep the documents from being released, you mean."

"Right."

"And I'm alive because—what, I haven't yet issued a decision?"

"They need you."

"For now. And when they don't—" She shrugged and stopped, thought: *They kill me.* She said, "So this is what I want to do."

She told him.

"But can you get yourself in a room with him, do you think?" Ashmont asked.

"I think so. Can you help?"

"Okay." He nodded his head slowly, musingly. The waitress arrived with another drink for Ashmont. He waited for her to leave; then he said, "I'm sure you're aware that we're not supposed to get involved in any domestic spy business. Doesn't exist, we don't do it, we leave that to the FBI."

"Right," Juliana said skeptically.

"I'm not saying it hasn't happened."

"Right."

"Also, by the way, officially this conversation never happened. We never met."

"I understand."

"I'm not sure you do. Things are different these days inside Christians In Action."

"Christians In Action?"

"Sorry. A bad joke. It's what some of us call CIA. Anyway, like I say, the Russia section's been decimated. Russian operations have been cut way back. A big re-org. And these days, no one's going to sign off on an op targeting a Russian oligarch, a Putin crony. Especially involving a civilian."

"A civilian?"

"You. You're not a professional. So that's just not happening."

"I'm sorry to hear it," she said.

"You're not a trained operative. This is against medical advice."

"Medical . . . ?"

"You know how when a patient leaves a hospital despite his doctor's advice to stay, the hospital makes him sign a legal waiver, confirming he's leaving against the advice of his doctors?"

"Okay, I get it."

"You would be putting yourself in great danger. First of all, he's got bodyguards up the wazoo."

"I get that."

"Do you? Because if he finds out what you're doing—well, I don't want to think about it. Bad news."

"If I do it right, that won't happen."

"You know what the motto of the Central Intelligence Agency is? *Shit happens.*"

She thought of Hersh and his fatalism. *You take every precaution to prevent disaster. But disaster is a cunning beast.*

"Let's put our cards on the table. You're saying I'd have no backup, no one covering me."

"You got it. Totally off the books. You do what you're going to do, and then you come to us with the results. A citizen volunteer. You okay with that?"

He looked at her for a long time, waiting.

Finally she said, "I am."

"This is going to sound cold, but if anything happens, if it goes south, if it goes to shit—I can't be connected to it."

"Understood."

"If you're volunteering as a walk-in and willing to assume all the risks and plausible deniability and all that, I may be able to make something happen. But know this: you're messing with some very dangerous people."

"So I've been told. I understand."

"I hope you do," he said.

"So how quickly can this happen?"

"I will make some calls and sound some people out. I know how to reach you. I'll be in touch soon."

"No," she said. "I need to know within twenty-four hours."

He cocked his head: *Why?*

"In two days, a meeting is taking place at Protasov's house on Nantucket. A board meeting of the Protasov Foundation."

"You know this how?"

"I have my sources. Tell me more about Protasov, about these people. Tell me how they think."

"How much time do you have?"

"About another hour."

"Should be enough for a start," he said. He took a long pull of his bourbon. "You know, it's interesting."

"What's that?"

"This case that pulled you into this whole thing. Wheelz. How strange is it that the thing that unmasked this whole foul affair—the thing that exposed this nest of illegal . . . manipulations—was a woman employee who refused to put up with a toxic environment."

Juliana nodded.

"She may have unwittingly ended up exposing more than she

realized," he went on. "But it wouldn't be the first time that sex led to money."

"Which led to lies, violence, and power," she said.

"The usual unholy trinity." The ice cubes in his glass clinked.

"Surprise, surprise," Juliana said.

He leveled his gaze at her. "They underestimated you, didn't they? They looked at you, and they saw a delicate flower."

"I don't know what they saw."

He nodded. "They didn't see the honey bee inside, though. The bee with the very formidable stinger."

"Is this supposed to be cheering?"

"Not entirely," he said. "Bearing in mind that a bee sting is always fatal."

"That's not true," she said.

He drained his glass and put it down on the table with the sound of a banged gavel. "Oh, it's invariably fatal, all right. To the bee."

64

The man from the CIA gave her his mobile number, scrawled on a torn piece of newspaper. He didn't have any business cards.

On the street she hailed a cab to the airport. Sitting in the back seat of the taxi, she looked at her watch. She would make the last flight back to Boston in plenty of time. She had a number of voice mails—from Martie, from Kaitlyn Hemming, from Hersh. Nothing from Duncan. Kaitlyn was just checking in. Martie wanted to know how her meeting with Paul Ashmont had gone.

At the airport, waiting at the gate, she listened to Hersh's voice mail. "I have a file for you," he said. "I don't want to e-mail it—I don't trust your e-mail, frankly. So it's a paper file. I'd be happy to drop it off wherever you are. Happy to bring it to your office. Maybe I'll do that. Or you can stop by my office and pick it up, if that's on the way. But I think you need to see this. Okay?"

I think you need to see this.

She wondered. The businessman sitting next to her caught her eye. "Heading back to Boston?" he said.

She nodded, smiled vaguely. "Yep."

"Looks like your meetings weren't all that successful, were they?"

She looked at him. A business traveler, a generic road warrior, like a thousand others at the airport, with their Mophie chargers and their noise-canceling headphones and their non-iron shirts.

The only thing that was off was the man's fingernails. They were overgrown and a little grubby. Not a road warrior at all. She remembered her father always said you can tell everything about a guy from his fingernails and his shoes.

"What do you want?" she said coldly.

"You're very interested in a friend of mine," he said. "Mr. Protasov."

It was the way he pronounced the name that gave away he wasn't an American. His American English accent had been nearly perfect. But he spoke Russian like a Russian.

"Yeah?" Her heart was thudding.

"Why such an interest?"

"That's my business."

"Well, that's the thing. I'm afraid it's not just your business. My friend, he's a very private person. He doesn't like it when people start asking all kinds of questions about him. Live and let live, he says. You know? Everyone's entitled to their own zone of privacy."

"Even me?" she said.

The man's bland smile faded. "Tomorrow you have a deadline, I believe. On a *motion for summary judgment*, I think it's called. Maybe you shouldn't be so casual about it. Things can happen. Actions have consequences." The more he talked, the more he flattened his As, exaggerating his American accent, too much now.

She took a breath. "I'm sorry, what's your name?"

The man shrugged, as if to say, *It's not important*.

She went on, "You know, I'm actually not so interested in talking to you. *Mister* Protasov sent a flunky? Not for me. Pardon my bluntness. But I'd be very interested in talking to your boss. See if you can set that up, will you?"

Her phone rang. She turned away to answer it. The caller ID gave a number in the Boston area code, 617.

"Yes?"

"Hello, my name is Doctor Kapoor calling from the emergency room at Boston Medical Center. Who am I speaking to?"

"Oh, my God," she said. "This is Juliana Brody."

"The reason I'm calling you is that this number came in with a patient who's critically ill."

"Who is it?" she nearly whispered.

"That's what we're trying to find out. There's no wallet. No ID. Just—"

"How did you get my number?" Her heart was racing wildly.

"It's on a piece of paper, a little sticky note. Just this number."

She closed her eyes. *Please not Jake, please not Duncan.*

"Male or female?"

"Male."

"How—how old is this person?"

Not Jake, not Duncan, please God.

For a moment it felt as if her life was balancing on a precipice, in absolute stillness, poised to turn into a tragedy.

"It's—it's hard to say. Forty or fifty, I'd say?"

She swallowed. "Hair?"

"Ma'am, this patient is critically ill. You need to come to the hospital so we can speak in person. Please get here as quickly as possible."

And then the caller hung up.

The man who'd been sitting next to her was gone.

65

She hit Duncan's mobile number. It rang and rang. She listened to the rings, her heart thumping away, her jaw clenched. *Please not him. Not him.* Three rings, four, five . . . *Your call has been forwarded to an automatic voice message system.*

She didn't leave a message. She hit Jake's number. He picked it up after two rings. "Hey, Mom."

"Jake, where's your dad?"

"He's upstairs."

"You're sure?"

"He's here. Was that you who just called?"

"Yeah."

"Oh, he left his phone downstairs as usual. Want me to get him?"

"No, that's fine. I wanted to make sure he's okay. Thank God."

"Why?"

"I'll—I'm at the airport, on my way home. I'll see you soon, honey."

So she knew who it was, who it had to be: Philip Hersh. What had the doctor said? *This patient is critically ill.*

Who else could it be?

She called his mobile phone number, and it went right to voice mail.

The 10:00 P.M. American Airlines flight out of Reagan National Airport arrived in Boston at 11:30 P.M. Just about everything in the airport, every concession, was closed. Whole sections were dark.

She told the cab to take her to Boston Medical Center. She got there a little before midnight. She had court in the morning and needed her sleep, but there was no choice. She had to see Hersh.

She told the nurse on duty that she was looking for a patient who'd been admitted to the ER within the last few hours, no ID on him.

"And you are—?"

"Juliana Brody."

"Are you a family member?"

She hesitated a second or two. "No. I'm a friend. Dr. Kapoor called me a few hours ago from the ER because my number was in the victim's pocket."

"Ah, yes." She directed Juliana to the neuro ICU. There, she identified herself the same way, and a nurse came around from the counter, a stocky redhead of around forty, holding a metal clipboard. "The patient I think we're talking about was around fifty? Balding? He had no wallet or ID on him, just your number in his back pocket."

"Can I see him, please?"

"I'd first like to get some information."

"Take me to him and we can talk on the way."

"Okay," the nurse said with a shrug. She pressed a disc on the wall and buzzed them both into the ICU.

"How is he doing?" Juliana said.

"He's out of surgery, in recovery."

"Surgery."

"I'll let the doctor fill you in." They arrived at a glass-walled room, a glass box.

The man on the bed looked nothing like Hersh. His eyes were purplish and grotesquely swollen shut. His nose was broken and bloodied, crooked and out of place. There were black sutures on his cheek. He had tubes coming out of his nose and mouth, and more tubes coming out of his head and his arms. His head was covered in white bandages. Each arm was in a splint. Only when she saw the fat gold wedding band on his left hand, the knuckles bloody, did she know it was Philip Hersh.

"Oh, my God," she said.

He had been beaten nearly to death.

But he was alive.

It was oddly quiet, for everything that was going on, the monitors and the IV stands and the tubes and the wires. She heard only the soft whooshing of the ventilator, in time with Hersh's breaths, and a low beeping.

"You're a friend?" the nurse asked.

Juliana nodded.

"What's his name?"

"Philip Hersh." She spelled it for her.

"Do you know where he lives?"

"I can give you his office address. I don't know his home address."

"What about next of kin? Do you know anyone who might—?"

"I don't. I don't really know him that well."

"I'll page the doctor," the woman said, and left.

Tears streamed down her cheeks. She looked at Hersh's brutalized, misshapen face, listened to the whooshing. She wondered what exactly had happened.

She wondered if he'd been tortured.

She thought about his voice message, replayed it in her head.

I have a file for you. . . . I don't trust your e-mail, frankly. . . . Happy to drop it off wherever you are. Happy to bring it to your office. Maybe I'll do that. Or you can stop by my office and pick it up, if that's on the way. But I think you need to see this. Okay?

Did he have this file with him, and had it been grabbed when he was beaten?

Or had he left it at his office?

She noticed a large clear plastic bag in the corner with the words PATIENT BELONGINGS printed on it. The mud-spattered leg of a pair of jeans spilled out. His stuff.

She picked up the bag, pulled out the jeans.

She felt the jingle of keys in his pants pocket. She checked the other pockets. No wallet. No cell phone. Nothing besides clothes in the bag. No file, no pieces of paper, folded or crumpled or anything. If he had a file with him, it was certainly gone.

She had a thought and reached into the jeans pocket and grabbed the ring of keys.

There was a knock on the open door. She looked up. A young man in a white doctor's coat, wearing a tie. Had he just seen her take the keys?

"I'm Dr. Robiano," he said. "I take it you are a friend of the patient's."

"Yes. Juliana Brody. Are you a surgeon?" she asked.

"I'm the neurocritical care fellow," the doctor said, nodding. He was surprisingly alert for the middle of the night. His eyes shone. He had short brown hair and an appealing, very white smile. He also looked like he was about fifteen years old, though in reality he was probably in his midthirties. He reminded her of an adolescent who'd put on his dad's white medical coat and tie.

He took a sip from a can of Coke Zero. "Look, I'm going to be very direct with you. I don't have very much good news. His injuries are such that he could die."

Juliana's eyes flooded with tears. She nodded.

"We have him in a medically induced coma now, but he arrived with a Glasgow coma score of one-one-one."

"I don't know what that means." A plastic bag of blood hung from one stand, fluids from another. A tube came from under the sheet filled with what looked like pinkish urine.

He didn't bother to explain. "He sustained a really serious injury, but for now he's stable."

"So what happened to him?"

"He had injuries consistent with an attack. This is a nonmedical observation, but to me it looks like someone went after him with a tire iron." He finished his Coke and tossed the can into the trash.

"Jesus."

"I'm guessing some good Samaritan called 911. Anyway, there was a lot of facial trauma. His jaw is broken. We put a tube down his throat to protect his airway, then put him on a breathing machine and gave him some medication so he's protected and he's not in any pain."

"Okay."

"Unfortunately, we found a large amount of bleeding in his brain, an intracranial hemorrhage that required surgery."

"Oh, dear God."

"A subdural bleed—under the dura."

"Was the surgery—successful?"

"We evacuated the hematoma, yes. We stopped the bleeding."

"Is there—is there going to be brain damage?"

He looked at her for a couple of seconds. "You don't ever know what the damage is going to be. Just putting all my cards on the table, he has a high risk of death or permanent disability. You just never know. Or he could recover and go back to a normal life."

She nodded hopefully.

"If he does recover, though, there's a good chance he'll never be the same person again."

"My God."

"This is a marathon we're looking at now. It's impossible for us to predict today what the outcome is going to be, and he's going to be in the coma, on the ventilator, for easily another twenty-four hours."

"Then what?"

"Then we wean him out of the coma, and he's extubated. This is a significant and serious injury. I should tell you—I don't know what Mr. Hersh was like, physically, before this. But he gave as good as he got."

"What do you mean?"

"You see what we call 'fight bites' on his hands? That laceration in the knuckles, from punching someone in the mouth. We found a tooth embedded in one of his knuckles. Whoever went after him probably has some serious dental work in his future. You can tell from his hands he didn't go down gently."

She nodded. "When can I—speak to him?"

"When? I don't know if you'll ever be able to speak to him."

66

It was a few minutes after one in the morning, and she was beyond exhausted. She felt jittery and strangely wide awake. She stood on the sidewalk outside Boston Medical Center, stunned, horrified by what had been done to Philip Hersh. She wondered if it had happened because of her. Surely he was also working on other cases.

But what if it *was* because of her case that he was so badly wounded? What if it was over this file he mentioned? The possibility sickened her.

There was a surprising amount of traffic for that time of night. She watched the cars for a moment, then looked at her phone. Duncan had called several times.

His voice messages sounded increasingly worried. *I thought your flight gets in at like eleven thirty. Call me. Where'd you go? Jules, where are you?*

She called him back, told him she'd be home soon, and she'd explain.

Then she hailed a cab to the Park Colonnade Building, in downtown Boston.

Maybe he'd left this paper file in his office. What had he said? *I'd be happy to drop it off . . . you can stop by my office.*

I think you need to see this.

If the file was in his office, she needed to get over there right now and get it. Whatever it was.

The cab pulled up to the Park Colonnade Building, and she got out. It was dark, nobody else around.

That means no one is following me, she thought.

At least no one that I can see.

She took the stairs to the third floor. The hallway was dark, as were the offices, which she assumed were all empty and locked this late at night.

She walked down the hallway in the darkness, her footsteps echoing. At the door to Hersh's office, she took out her cell phone to use as a flashlight and Hersh's key ring.

And began to try the keys, one by one.

The fifth key turned the lock.

She waited for an alarm warning tone, but there was just silence.

No alarm? That surprised her. Hersh would make sure his office was alarmed. He would take security precautions. That was the kind of guy he was.

Maybe the alarm had been turned off. Or hadn't been set in the first place, for some reason.

She didn't want to turn on the overhead lights, which would spill light into the hallway and arouse the curiosity of any passing security guard. Instead, she continued to use the flashlight function on her phone. It illuminated a broad area with a dingy light.

And she saw that his office had been searched. File cabinet drawers were all open, files spilling out of them. His desk was heaped with file folders. Piles of folders were scattered here and there on the carpet. Hersh's office had been untidy, but there was no way Hersh had left it like this. Someone had been here and searched aggressively, not bothering to return it to its previous condition, not caring who knew what had happened. It almost looked as though they were making a point—we can do whatever the hell we want. Not just to the office, but to anyone who gets in our way.

She heard footsteps in the hallway and immediately fumbled with her phone, trying to turn off the damned flashlight, finally swiping up and finding the right icon and pressing it to switch off the light.

The footsteps came closer. She froze, standing there in the dark, in the middle of this tiny office. A security guard? If so, she didn't know what she could say. She had Hersh's keys, which counted for something. *He's in the hospital and asked me to pick something up for him.*

That might work.

She breathed in, and out, and stayed perfectly still.

The footsteps were right outside the door.

She exhaled slowly, silently.

The footsteps moved on. She waited for another thirty seconds or so to make sure the guy was gone.

Then she put the phone-flashlight on and began to search through the chaos.

The first open file drawer seemed to have client files. There was a gap in the B section. Maybe that was her file. If Hersh had made a file with her name on it, someone had taken it.

She went through the other files, looked over the piles on the desk and on the floor. Nothing that had to do with the Russian man, Protasov, nothing that had anything to do with her case.

Either someone had found what he wanted and took it—or he'd searched and given up. But as far as she could see, the file wasn't here.

She didn't get home until after two in the morning. She had to be in court no later than eight thirty. She could push it to maybe a few minutes before nine, if she really needed the sleep. She'd get five hours. That would be fine. In law school there'd been nights when she didn't sleep at all.

But she couldn't sleep. She was wired and tense. She thought about

Hersh, so badly wounded, beat up nearly to death. And about how nervous Paul Ashmont, this CIA career professional, was about her getting close to Protasov.

You would be putting yourself in great danger, he'd said.

Now she found Duncan in their bedroom, awake and distraught.

"Jesus, Jules, where the hell have you been?" he said angrily.

She told him about Philip Hersh and what she'd seen.

"Do you understand how worried I've been?" he said.

"I'm sorry. You're right. I should have kept you in the loop. I'm sorry I didn't."

He exhaled. "Tell me what happened in DC."

She told him about the Russian oligarch and his minions in Washington. About the CIA guy she'd met at the bar and his theory of Yuri Protasov.

And she told him her plan.

After about an hour she was finally able to go to sleep, but it was a light, troubled sleep.

It felt like just a moment later, though it was more like a couple of hours, that she heard Duncan whisper her name. She opened her eyes, saw that he was standing by her side of the bed, in his T-shirt and boxers. She sat up. "What?"

He put a finger to his lips. *Shh.*

She whispered, "What is it?"

"Do you hear that?"

"Hear—what?"

He cocked his head to one side. "Downstairs."

"What?"

"I heard something from downstairs."

"You think it might be Jake?"

He shook his head. "Someone's in the house."

67

She listened for a few seconds, looked at Duncan, shook her head. She didn't hear anything.

"What did you hear?" she whispered.

But he didn't seem to be listening. He walked around to his side of the bed and knelt. He pulled something out from underneath it, something dark in his hand.

She gasped. "No!" Then she whispered: "Duncan!"

He was holding a gun in his right hand, black and squared-off, a semiautomatic pistol. She had very little experience with guns. When she'd tried skeet shooting as a teenager, she had used a shotgun to hit the clays. She'd fired a revolver once—she'd asked her father to teach her how—but was freaked out by how loud it was. She hated it, hated anticipating the explosion, and it always messed up her aim.

"Do you know how to use that thing?" she said.

He didn't reply. He kept moving toward the hall.

"What if it's Jake down there?"

"*Shh.*" He padded out into the hallway.

Her heart was racing. She got up and followed him out. She caught up to him. She put an arm on his shoulder and whispered in his ear, "Duncan, call the cops."

"No time," he said, heading to the stairs. "We can't wait twenty minutes."

"Honey, don't," she whispered again, but he wasn't listening. She descended the carpeted stairs right behind him. At the landing he froze.

"Oh, Jesus," he breathed.

The door to her study—the old pantry that they'd converted into her home office, long and narrow—was open, as it always was. And she saw a pale spill of light.

In her study.

Far off, maybe thirty or forty feet away.

The light was jittery, moving. Like someone was holding a penlight.

Someone was in the house. Someone was there.

They'd nearly killed Philip Hersh, and now they were coming for her. Or for her family. They were professionals, they were assassins, and they'd already killed several people. These were people who wanted something, and she was standing in their way, and they wouldn't hesitate to kill her.

Or Duncan.

He put a hand in the air, signaling *stop*.

He cocked his head. She listened.

And she heard what he heard. She heard a drawer being opened slowly.

Duncan moved swiftly, barefoot, toward her office, his right hand up, the gun pointed. *There is a safety on most pistols*, she thought. Was the safety on? What if he aimed the gun, and it was grabbed from him, turned back on him?

Now he was standing at the threshold to her office, his right hand extended, the gun pointed, and he said, in a quiet but firm voice, "Don't—fucking—move."

And then came the explosion, deafeningly loud, so loud that her ears shrilled a high-pitched squeal. She saw a flash of fire at the end of the muzzle, and then the gun jerked back, nearly coming out of his hand.

And she heard a shout, more like a roar, like the bellow of a wounded animal. She raced to the study, frantic. There was a crash. A gust of cold air hit her. One of the French doors was open, a few small panes of glass shattered, the pebbles of glass on the carpet twinkling in the moonlight.

Duncan came in from outside, panting. “He took off. Bat out of hell.”

“You shot him.”

He nodded. “He pulled out a gun. I had to.”

She heard thundering footsteps coming from the stairs: Jake.

“That was loud. Someone’s going to report it. One of our neighbors.”

“What happened?” Jake shouted, racing across the room toward them. “Was that a gunshot?”

68

Jake, get back upstairs!" Duncan said. The gun was no longer in his hand. He'd dropped it to the carpet.

"What just happened? Did a gun go off?" Jake, like his dad, dressed for sleep in T-shirt and boxers.

"Upstairs! Now!"

"Did someone get shot?"

"Go!" She'd never heard Duncan yell at him that way before.

"Jesus!"

Looking like he'd been slapped, Jake winced, turned, and walked heavy-footed away, back upstairs. But he would be listening at the top of the stairs, lurking at the upstairs railing.

She closed the door to her study. Duncan had walked over to the open French door. He was picking up some papers that had flitted to the floor in the breeze.

"Duncan, that was insane!" she said. "Where—where the hell did you get that gun?"

"I know a guy who knows a guy. I just—five hundred bucks for the gun plus some ammunition."

"This is crazy! I've turned us both into criminals."

He put his arms around her, pulled her close. "Breathe, Jules."

She nodded, closed her eyes. "He wasn't here to kill anybody. He was here to look for something."

"For what?"

"Hersh had a file for me."

"I think I got him in the leg," Duncan said. "I'm not sure." He actually looked pleased.

"You've never fired a gun before?"

"*Call of Duty* on Jake's Xbox. But this was pretty close range."

"God, what if one of our neighbors heard the shot and called the cops?"

"So?"

"And the cops come knocking on our door. Asking about a reported gunshot. If they find out you have a gun and fired it without a license, we're screwed."

"Gunshot? No gunshot here. Maybe from the movie we were watching. Who knows."

"Unlawful possession of a firearm," she said. "That's eighteen months in prison."

"I know the law. And they can get you for discharging a weapon within five hundred feet of a dwelling too. I know. But I wouldn't worry about illegal. The guy pulled a gun on me. He could have killed me. He could have murdered all three of us. How do I know what he's about to do?"

She nodded, closed her eyes. She felt the beginnings of an onrushing panic attack.

"The guy was a threat to my family," he went on. There was something in his voice, something hoarse. Not loud but firm. "Legally, we both know you can twist it this way or that, but what I did? I'd do it again. You think I'm going to let these bastards break into my house, menace my family?"

"Is that blood on the carpet?" she said, pointing at what indeed looked like a darker spot on the gray carpet. "We've got a crime scene. What do we do?" Her voice shook.

Duncan came close and gently caressed her face. "Breathe," he reminded her.

She nodded. "I'm okay." She drew him near. They hugged, hard, and for a fleeting moment she felt safe.

"We'd better hope this guy doesn't check himself into a hospital," she said. "They're required to report gunshot wounds."

"Guy like that? He's not turning himself into any hospital."

He placed his forehead against hers. "The cops are either coming or they're not, and I'm not going to call them."

"But what if we call the cops, tell them about the break-in? Maybe they'll park a cruiser out front for a while."

"Think, honey. Your situation, you sure you want the cops involved? And how long do you think the police can protect us anyway? A day or two?"

"Yeah," she said, neither agreeing nor disagreeing.

"Jules, I'm here, okay? Don't think for a moment there's anything I wouldn't do to keep you safe," he said. "To keep us safe."

Her heart rate began to slow. A curious sense of calm seeped into her like a warm fluid.

They cleaned up the crime scene, as she thought of it, sweeping up the glass, putting packing tape over the holes where the glass panes had been broken. Before they went to bed, they checked in on Jake—amazingly, he'd fallen back to sleep. Juliana wondered briefly if he'd even remember this in the morning, and if so, what they could possibly say.

They both lay there for a long while. She looked at a beam of moonlight across the ceiling and tried to still her revving thoughts, but it was like trying to slap down a spinning top.

"Sweetie?" Duncan whispered.

"Yeah?"

"You awake too?"

"Yeah."

She felt his hand caress her thigh, and then she reached for him. "I missed you," she said. She pulled his face close, kissed him, lightly at first, then ferociously. His hands moved slowly over the swell of her hips, and then his fingertips brushed against her nipples, his lips grazing hers as his hands encircled and caressed her breasts. She pushed him down on the bed, straddled him, slid him inside her. She closed her eyes, felt the pressure building and building, more and more intense, and then the dam burst and an engulfing hot wave came over her, a great flood of pleasure and a hot tingly sensation all over, and she felt herself melting, and then she gave over to it entirely. Her head was spinning and her body began to shake. A surge of heat washed over her, and then a great calm.

They talked for another hour until pinkish light appeared in the night sky and morning began to dawn. She made coffee, took a shower, and got dressed for work.

Her phone made a text sound.

It was from a long series of numbers at T-Mobile. It read only:

12:00 NOON TODAY.

69

By the time it was almost noon, she was dragging. She hadn't slept more than a couple of hours, and the coffee was no longer working, just making her stomach sour.

During the ten o'clock break, Duncan came by her lobby. He said hi to Kaitlyn, who got up when he arrived and excused herself.

"Look," Juliana said, "what we're talking about—what I'm about to do is—you know. There can't be any e-mail trace, no texting, nothing, okay?"

"Okay. I understand."

"Do you know how much money this guy has? Fifteen billion dollars. That's billion with a *B*. He's one of the richest guys in the world. Five *million* bucks is peanuts to him."

"But it's so goddamned risky, babe. You've got the police breathing down your neck, and—"

"Dunc, the way they turned over my life, that's the *least* I'm owed."

They both fell silent. Duncan said, "I wonder if this is something you negotiate with him. Like, you know, start at ten million?"

"Why not? That's *nothing* to him."

A long pause. She said, "What have I become?"

"I think you've become what circumstances made you. I think you don't really have a choice."

Back in court, at two minutes before noon, Juliana checked her iPhone to see if there were any more text messages.

Just that one from the long number at T-Mobile. 12:00 NOON TODAY.

In two minutes, noon was going to arrive. The minute hand on the courtroom clock would click over the twelve.

The plaintiff was sitting in the witness box, testifying about the icy pavement in the privately owned parking lot where he'd taken a nasty fall. She was finding it hard to concentrate.

Instead, she was remembering when Duncan fired the gun. The crash, the man tearing outside through the French doors. She thought about how remarkably calm Duncan seemed when it was all over. He seemed suffused with the certainty of having done the right thing.

And she couldn't help thinking about Philip Hersh. She'd called the hospital before court started for the day and asked how Hersh was doing. Still in the medically induced coma, the nurse said. She wondered how bad his injuries were going to be. And she wondered what the file was he'd left for her somewhere.

She wondered if Hersh had figured out a way to get to the oligarch, Protasov. And if she'd ever know the answer.

At the stroke of noon—she could see the numerals 12:00 appear on her iPhone—the plaintiff's lawyer was asking questions of his client, who was in a wheelchair, paralyzed since his fall on the ice.

At 12:01 a message appeared on her phone:

Time's Up.

She looked up when the door at the back of the courtroom opened and a uniformed deliveryman entered with a large bouquet of flowers. Her heart jumped. *What the hell was going on?*

A few people laughed and whispered. This never happened. The deliveryman, who looked like a gawky teenager, walked down the aisle until he came to the bar, which separates the spectators' gallery from the area where the lawyers and their parties sit.

She watched apprehensively as the court officer, George, leaped up and blocked the delivery guy's path. He grabbed the teenager's sleeve. The deliveryman turned, stopped. The two conversed in low voices. Then George took the bouquet from the delivery guy, who turned and walked right out of the courtroom.

"Nothing further," said the plaintiff's lawyer.

"And we're adjourned," Juliana said.

As the courtroom emptied, she saw George approaching her bench. He was holding the bouquet of flowers, a pastel arrangement of stargazer lilies and pale pink roses, tipping it toward her.

She had crazy thoughts. What if there was a bomb in it, a plastic explosive or something?

"Those were for me?" she asked.

"'Judge Juliana Brody, courtroom 903,'" George read.

"Who the hell told that kid to deliver to a judge on the bench?" Ordinarily all deliveries to a judge went to her lobby.

He held the bouquet in her direction. "Just hand me the card, please," she said.

He pulled a small white envelope off the bouquet and passed it to her.

She slipped a white card from the envelope.

It read:

See you soon.—Matías.

She flushed, her heart suddenly knocking.

She stared at the note.

"It better be your husband," the court officer said, mock-sternly, laughing.

"My secret admirer," she said, forcing a smile. "Thanks, George."

As soon as the lunch break began, she went online and checked a bunch of legal-related websites to see if that video had been posted anywhere. She clicked on sites that ran news about the legal profession, like *Underneath Their Robes* and *Above the Law,* to see if anything had been reported. They wouldn't post the video, of course. They'd post a story about it.

But she found nothing, thank God. At least nothing yet. Finally she Googled herself and waited tensely for a couple of seconds for the search results.

Nothing about a sex tape.

She glanced at her phone. Paul Ashmont from the CIA had left her a message, returning her call. As she was about to call him back, her phone rang.

"Hey," Ashmont said. "You have Signal on your phone, right?"

"I do." That was one of the encryption apps Sasha had told her to install.

"I think we'd better use it."

He called her back a minute later using Signal. She answered the phone out in the hall.

"Okay, you called me. What's up?" Ashmont said.

"This board meeting of the Protasov Foundation—there are a lot of

VIPs coming to Nantucket," she said. She mentioned some of the names: a former prime minister of the UK, a former female Secretary of State, a senator from Massachusetts. "Security's going to be tight."

"Oh, you better believe it."

"I wonder who does security for Protasov. If he contracts it out."

"The Russian *mafiya* does security for most of these guys, these oligarchs," Ashmont said. "Why? What do you have in mind?"

Juliana called in Kaitlyn and asked her to cancel the afternoon session. She had important personal business to attend to, she said. Then she drove over to Boston Medical Center in the South End. She parked, took the elevator up to the neuro ICU on the sixth floor of the Menino building. She stopped at the counter and asked the nurse where she could find a patient, Philip Hersh.

The nurse looked up and then away, said, "Um, yeah, let me ask someone."

She got up and went over to another nurse, who was standing at a desk, a dark-haired young woman. They conversed quietly for a few seconds. Then the dark-haired nurse came over and said, "Hi, excuse me, are you a family member?"

"I'm a friend," Juliana said. "I—my phone number was in Philip's pocket when he was found."

She nodded. "Let me page the neurocritical care fellow, Dr. Robiano. I think he's still on call." She picked up the phone and spoke briefly. Then she hung up and came around to the front of the counter. "Why don't we talk in one of these rooms?"

"Oh, no," Juliana said, her eyes tearing up. "What happened? A few hours ago he was stable."

"I'm sorry, I don't know any of the details."

The dark-haired nurse showed her to a small, stark conference room, a round table with four chairs around it. Juliana sat and pulled out some Kleenex.

When Dr. Robiano showed up a few minutes later, holding a can of Coke Zero—still looking like a fifteen-year-old playing doctor—he seemed genuinely saddened. "I'm sorry to tell you that Mr. Hersh died."

Juliana sighed, her breath trembling. She nodded. The tears were streaming now.

He said, "He had a rebleed in his brain. We took him to the operating room, and he died on the table."

She nodded, couldn't talk.

He sensed that and went on. "It'd been touch-and-go since he got here. His injuries were just too severe."

"When did it—when did he die?"

"About an hour ago. They haven't taken his body away yet, so if you want to go into his room and spend some time . . . ?"

"Thanks," she said. "I do."

When she was able to stop crying long enough to talk, she called Martie and arranged to come by. She didn't want to tell her over the phone.

70

Numbly, she entered Martha Connolly's apartment. She gave Martie a quick hug, leaned over and petted Lucy. The dog had brought her Donald Trump chew toy over, as if to show off how little of it was left: just half a torso and an arm.

"You look terrible," Martie said. "What happened?"

"Philip Hersh is dead."

Martie gasped. "What?"

Juliana told her what little she knew.

"Can I pour you a drink?"

"I have too much to do now."

"Have you talked to the police?"

She shook her head.

Martie seemed to know what Juliana was thinking. "You don't know this happened because of your case," Martie said.

"But it did."

She shook her head. "You *think*."

"It's my fault," she said. "You told me to get off the trolley; that was how you put it. Stop what I was doing. But I didn't stop. I didn't ask Hersh to stop digging, even when we knew it was dangerous."

"Juliana—"

"I need to ask you something," Juliana said.

"Ask away."

She hesitated. "You know Yuri Protasov. You're on a Doctors Without Borders board with him. Yet you never mentioned that to me."

Martie was silent for a long time. She looked down at the carpet. Then she looked up at Juliana. "I knew a woman once who became obsessed with black mold," she said. "Who was convinced she was getting sickened from black mold, that she was suffering from toxic mold syndrome. So she had dehumidifiers installed in her basement. But the experts came to test, and the tests still came back positive for mold spores. So she ripped everything out. When that didn't work, she gutted the first floor. Then the second. Eventually she got rid of every piece of textile she owned, even a quilt that had been passed down from her great-grandmother. She ripped her whole damn house apart, her whole *life* apart."

"And?"

"She ended up moving into some sterile cinder-block house in Brighton. But she still felt something was wrong. So she had the place tested, and it came back positive for black mold."

"Your point?"

"There's no uncontaminated terrain. Or people. Some hands are cleaner than others; none are truly clean. Have I ever met Yuri Protasov? No. Have I ever even been in the same room with the man? I don't think so, but maybe. You want to find moments where I've crossed paths with this villain or that? The harder you look, the more you'll find. And I could explain every one, but that's not the point. Because anyone can explain anything. At the end of the day? You need to ask yourself one question: *Do I trust her?* So do you?"

It was a long, fraught silence. The two women stared into each other's eyes frankly, almost hostilely. And then something in her melted. Because she knew the answer was yes.

"I do," Juliana said.

"Okay, then," Martie said quietly.

"You told me Philip Hersh saved your life. You didn't tell me how."

"You remember who Frank Krupinak is?"

"God, yeah."

Krupinak was a serial killer who'd raped and murdered four girls in Massachusetts, in a particularly grisly manner. "When I sentenced him to one hundred and fifty years in prison," Martha said, "he shouted at me as he was led away. That he was going to kill me. And then his conviction was reversed on appeal."

"Ineffective assistance of counsel?"

"That's right. Plus there was some issue with the lab that did the DNA testing."

"They let him out, right?"

"Right. Awaiting trial. So this rapist-murderer who promised he was going to kill me is out there. At large. And I was terrified—but what could I do? I had to be in court every day. And then a couple of days later I opened my mailbox and found the, uh—this is still not easy to talk about." She paused a long time. Then in a smaller voice she continued, "I found the severed head of my cat."

"Oh, my God."

"This was when I was living in Lincoln, in that isolated old house? And the thing is, Sheba was a house cat—she never went outside. So he'd been inside my house."

"Dear God."

"Then he paid a visit to my mother, who was frail and on an oxygen tank. He unplugged her tube and left her gasping for breath. If I hadn't gone to visit her that afternoon, she would have died."

"You must have told the police."

"The police chief at the time really had it in for me. Saw me as being on the other side. The cops wouldn't lift a finger. Sure, I got one of those useless restraining orders. Changed all the locks. Didn't matter.

"Next night, I woke up in the middle of the night and saw him standing there, in my bedroom. And he said, 'Not tonight. But soon. I've written your death sentence. It'll come. Soon.' That was what he said."

"Oh, Jesus. He wasn't afraid you'd call the cops on him?"

"He knew they wouldn't do anything."

"Why didn't he try to kill you then?"

"Because he got off on my living in terror. Killing me would be too easy on me. This was about feeling the fear. The fear eating your soul. About knowing every day could be your last. You will die, but at a time of my choosing. It was mental torture. So I called Philip."

"Okay."

Martie paused for several seconds, shrugged. "And the problem stopped. It just . . . stopped."

"What—what did Philip do?"

"I never knew. I never asked." A long pause. "But I got my life back."

Juliana looked at her for a few seconds. "Yet you tell me to get off the trolley."

"I told you that several stops ago," Martie said. "But you stayed on it. And now, you have no choice but to see it to its final destination. You play the game and you follow the rules. Like in tennis. But when the game changes, the rules do too."

Juliana nodded. "I'm scared," she admitted. She sounded like a child saying it, a frightened child, because in some ways that was how she felt.

Martie went on, "Someone's lobbing a grenade in your direction; it's not tennis any longer. Point is, honey, you do what you have to do. To stay safe. To keep your family safe. I love the law like my grandma loved scripture. You and I both swore to uphold the law. But a suicide pact we did *not* agree to. Am I clear?"

"Crystal." Juliana nodded, said nothing for a long time.

"You want my considered judgment?" Martie said. "*You get those bastards.*"

71

Fifty Braintree Ridge Park was a generic red-brick office building in a generic office park in the suburbs of Boston, surrounded by plenty of parking and a lot of hulking round pruned bushes. Juliana took an elevator to the fourth floor. She walked past the radio station and the marketing company until she came to an office suite at the end of the hall. The door was marked THE NAZAROV COMPANIES.

She thought: *A criminal enterprise hiding in plain sight.* She tried the door, but it was locked. She found a button on the door frame and pressed it and the door buzzed open.

She entered a reception area that was utterly barren, just a couple of squared-off couches and chairs. No magazines. No TV. No framed maps or prints. Not even a receptionist's desk. She stood for a minute, looking around, and finally decided to sit on one of the couches.

She was waiting for Dmitry Nazarov, a man she knew to be in the higher reaches of the Russian mafia in America, the *mafiya.* He'd once appeared before her in her courtroom, six years earlier, when she was still new at judging. A Russian-American owner of parking lots had been charged with bribery of a state official. Dmitry Nazarov was the parking lot kingpin of Boston.

When she imagined the Russian *mafiya*, she imagined scary-looking guys with large and exotic tattoos. Not the slump-shouldered man in a polyester bowling shirt who had been on trial. His attorney had been able to show that prosecutors had withheld something exculpatory: a statement of a witness that was inconsistent with his trial testimony. Juliana had no choice but to dismiss the charges. A Brady violation, it was called. Nazarov walked out of the courtroom a free man.

And as he walked out, he shouted, "Thank you, Your Honor! Thank you!" He put his hands together as if praying. "Anything I can do for you, ever, anytime, I will do." At the courtroom door he stopped and turned around, a stocky man in a black bowling shirt. He shouted, gesticulating with his hands, "Anything I can ever do for you, you have only to ask!"

But locating Dmitry Nazarov six years later hadn't been easy. Turns out that *mafiya* kingpins don't have websites. Eventually she located an address for the Nazarov Companies in Braintree and a phone number that rang and rang and was never answered.

Now she waited, uneasily, occasionally looking at her phone. Six minutes went by before someone appeared, a guy in his early twenties with a bodybuilder's physique, wearing a gray suit, open collar, no tie. He approached Juliana and said, like a haughty salesman, "Yes?"

Juliana fixed the man with her "objection overruled" stare. "I'm here to see Mr. Nazarov."

"Who?"

"Dmitry Nazarov. Tell him it's Judge Juliana Brody. He knows who I am."

The young guy stared malevolently. After a while he turned and left.

He emerged about two minutes later, and now he was fawning. "Please to come with me, Your Honor," he said with an awkward smile. "Mr. Nazarov is very happy to see you."

He led her along a corridor and then down a hall that ended in a set of double swinging doors that opened into a large, raw space—a big open area with bare concrete floors, steel girders, and a lot of exposed pipes. It looked as though they'd just stopped building the interior. Standing at a steel desk in the middle of the space was a stocky man wearing a black-and-white bowling shirt.

Dmitry Nazarov was wagging his index finger at someone, a young Asian woman with chunky glasses. "No, you see, we bring these two lots together, with the entrances on these two blocks, here and *here*, and triple the revenue! Crunch the numbers, you see!" He looked up, pushed his glasses back up the bridge of his nose, and he saw her. His face shone. He suddenly extended his hands in the air, like a papal benediction. As he came toward her, he said, "Your Honor, it is my honor!" He laughed, delighted to have cracked a sort of joke. "A jurist of your eminence. To what do I owe this great pleasure?"

The woman with the chunky glasses left the room. Juliana sat in a chair next to Nazarov's desk and said, "You once told me that—"

"Yes, that wish to be granted. Of course. I swore this on my babushka's grave. Anything that's within my power." He placed a palm on his chest. "Is a burden to carry a debt. A relief, always, to pay it off. Tell me, Your Honor, what can I do?" He was beaming, like a child who'd just been given a puppy.

When she told him, his smile became a rictus of horror. He looked, Juliana thought, like a child whose puppy had just been run over.

She turned her Lexus left onto Granite Street and looped around to 93 North, the artery that went straight through Boston, thirteen miles of highway. Four lanes of traffic headed north. Traffic was light. Rush hour hadn't yet begun.

She glanced up in the rearview mirror to see if she noticed anyone, any vehicle that seemed to be following. She saw a white car behind her, a Dodge, that she thought she'd seen in the Braintree office park. She saw the car's snout, its aggressive grille.

It was traveling a little close.

Then the white Dodge changed lanes and came up on her left, far too close. She accelerated, and the white Dodge accelerated, and then she felt a heavy thud, heard a sickening metallic crunch.

The Dodge had crashed into her.

In panic mode now, she swerved away, to the right, setting off car horns, nearly colliding with a blue Toyota. But the Dodge had moved lanes and was immediately on her left, again, and moving in closer.

She accelerated even faster, and now the Dodge had pulled up even with her, on her left, and far too close. She swerved her SUV one more lane, into the rightmost lane, but the white Dodge followed her over.

The car was trying to force her off the road.

Another loud crunch. The Dodge had driven right into her again. She swung the wheel hard right, away, into the breakdown lane, and the Dodge was on her again, and she spun harder to the right. With a shrieking of steel, she'd smashed into the steel guardrails, sparks flying, and she slammed on the brakes. A loud squeal and car horns blaring all around, and she came to an abrupt stop.

The white Dodge sped away.

She keyed off the ignition, sat there, breathing hard, trying to steady her heart rate.

Then a beat-up red pickup truck pulled up ahead of her and also came to a stop, its emergency lights flashing. A large guy with long blond hair and a big potbelly, in his thirties or early forties, got out, wearing an old Carhartt work jacket and a "Make America Great Again" hat. He came over to her.

"Hey, lady, you okay?"

"I'm fine, thank you." She was out of breath.

"Looked like that guy cut you off. I saw that! I mean, what the hell?"

"Unbelievable." She was jittery with adrenaline, which had now flooded her system. Her heart juddered, and her face felt hot.

"You want me to call the cops? Call you an ambulance?"

Shaking her head, she said, "Don't bother. No need." The last thing she wanted was to be entangled with the police. She knew there was damage to the vehicle, but from where she sat she couldn't really get a sense of how bad it was. Not without getting out of the car. Which she didn't want to do, not in the middle of traffic where there was no shoulder and cars passing by all the time now.

"But thank you so much," she said.

After another minute or so she'd calmed down enough to start the car back up, and she was on her way home.

72

She was driving on Beacon Street, a mile or so from home, when she pulled up to a traffic light and stopped. Glancing at the sidewalk, she saw a man sitting on a bench waiting for the bus. Something about the man—she looked more closely. If Calvin were still alive, that's what he would have looked like.

In her frayed, sleep-deprived state, she remembered their last argument, couldn't turn her mind away. He'd been hitting her up for money, something he did more and more often. She was finishing law school, living at home with her parents. He was living with his girlfriend, freeloading. She said something about what a mess he was making of his life.

He lashed back, talked about what phonies Mom and Dad were. At least they weren't home to hear his rant. She said something about how he wasn't too proud to take the checks Mom was always writing him. He'd even wheedled her into taking out a second mortgage, and when Dad found out, he practically exploded. And yet he couldn't be bothered to visit her when she was in the hospital with the mastectomy. "Not once," she said. "Not once. You take her money, and yet you couldn't be bothered to visit."

"So what? I was *touring*. And she's fine. She's *fine*. I don't hear *Mom* complaining."

"Oh, playing at Miller's Ale House in Scituate is *touring*? You're unbelievable. You damage people, Calvin. You damage the people who love you, and you don't even know it."

He was wearing a filthy pair of jeans and his crappy leather motorcycle jacket that gave off that skunky pot smell. She looked with sadness at his bitten-down fingernails, one with a death's head on it that his girlfriend had painted with black and white enamel.

If she squinted she could see him as the bouncing eighth grader who led the lacrosse team to victory in the all-district tournament, hoisted up by his teammates to ride their shoulders as they whooped their elation. Neither Mom nor Dad could make it, but Juliana watched it all with a wide smile that seemed to own her face.

But if she squinted again at his once-handsome face, now bloated, she could almost see him as the middle-aged barfly he was on track to be.

The argument grew more and more heated. She said he didn't appreciate the way she was practically a mom to him, all she did for him. "Yeah, and how'd that work out, sis?" he snapped. He called her "*Der Führer*" because she was such a control freak. It got ugly. By the end he was bellowing at her, red-faced. It was terrifying.

"You're nothing!" she yelled at him. "You're nothing. You're a goddamned waste of space."

He stormed out of the house and jumped into his beat-up Toyota. He raced off, leaving skid marks on the driveway.

Her memory of what happened after that grew a little vague and disjointed. She remembered watching TV and the phone ringing. The call from the hospital in the middle of the night. They couldn't save him.

She remembered being brought in to see the body, which she wished to this day she hadn't agreed to. Neither of her parents did.

Later, in that hallucinatory night-into-day, she remembered the police telling her about how Calvin had driven his Toyota through a red light and right into the path of an oncoming tractor trailer.

The truck driver was fine but shaken. He wasn't at fault, no question about it. Calvin was drunk, but most of all he was drunk with rage.

And—this was the most horrible thing of all—she had provoked him into doing it. Why the hell had she gotten it into her head to tear into him that way? She'd told herself she was staging a kind of "intervention." But if it hadn't been for her anger that night, Calvin might still be alive. It was her judgmental nature that had directly resulted in Calvin's death.

She was always bringing up Calvin with Jake, as if Calvin was some parable of all the reckless decisions he made. But now she realized there was more to it than that. It was really about a fateful decision of her own. About hurting those you love.

Sitting in judgment upon herself, she found herself guilty.

The tears were streaming down her face when she was startled out of her thoughts by the loud honk of the car behind her. The light had turned green.

She took her foot off the brake and drove away.

73

My God," Duncan said, standing at the front of her SUV in the garage, his arms folded. "What the hell *happened*?" He'd arrived home from work and was at first surprised to see her there, until she'd explained.

"I told you. The guy tried to run me off the road."

"My God," he said again, and he put his arms around her. "I'm just grateful you're okay. You could have been killed."

She'd been badly rattled, but by the time she got home, she was just weary and numb. "I don't think he was trying to kill me," she said. "Maybe just warn me off. There are easier ways to kill a person."

"Oh really?" He took her by the shoulders and looked her in the eye, visibly furious. "I think this way almost worked. You could have lost control of the car and spun out and—that would have been it."

He opened the door to the house, and she followed him in. "This—this thing with the car, this could just be the first attempt, right?" he went on. "They know where you live, they've already broken in once, next time they come back to finish the job."

They entered the kitchen. His eyes were wide. "We are not safe here. Where the hell is your CIA guy?"

"I've been waiting for his call."

"Well, he's taking his goddamned sweet time, isn't he? We have to go to Nantucket tomorrow. We have, what, eighteen hours!"

"I'll call him," she said. "I'll figure out a way to make this work, with or without the CIA." She realized she was still jittery from the incident on the highway, her nerves still taut. The numbness was wearing off. "Where's Jake?"

"I'm sure he's upstairs," Duncan said.

"Can you make sure?"

She set down her purse on the counter, took out her phone, found Paul Ashmont's number among the recent calls in Signal, and hit redial.

Ashmont answered the phone on the first ring. "Hey. I haven't been avoiding you. I've been striking out all over the place."

"Striking out?"

"Nobody in house wants to sign on to this. Nobody wants a piece of it. Nobody wants to play."

"Because of who it is—Protasov?" Even though their conversation was encrypted, she thought twice before saying his name.

"Too many risk factors."

"I understand."

"And because of what it is. Because of Russia. No manpower. Like I said, most of the Russia experts have retired or been squeezed out."

"But I need help badly. Now."

"I understand."

"I'm not sure you do. I was just nearly killed."

"For real?"

"Forced off the road, outside of Boston."

"When was this?"

"Just now."

There was a pregnant pause before he responded. "All right," he said. "I'm going to have someone from FinCEN contact you."

"What is that?"

"FinCEN is the Financial Crimes Enforcement Network. Part of the Treasury Department. They go after criminals for money laundering and other financial crimes. Dig into terrorist financing and such."

"Never heard of them."

"Which is probably just the way they like it. They've been mostly an intelligence-collecting agency, but ever since Bitcoin markets got established, and Silk Road 2.0 and the like, they've launched a low-profile ops unit. Special Collections, they call it. They plant high-tech bugs in hard-to-reach places, in foreign countries or here. You know, parabolic antennas and all that shit."

"But when? When am I going to hear from them? We have to be in Nantucket tomorrow morning, when people are arriving for the board meeting. So we don't have time to screw around."

"Got it," he said after a beat. "I'll see what I can do."

She put down the phone when the call was done as Duncan entered the kitchen. Something was wrong.

"Jake's not upstairs," Duncan said.

"You call his phone?"

"No answer."

"You didn't pick him up today, right?" she asked.

"He was supposed to take the bus home, as usual."

"But he wasn't home when you got here?"

"I guess I thought he'd made some arrangement with you."

"Me? I told him no more staying after school, he's got to be home doing his homework. Saving his grades. Saving his own butt."

"All right, he didn't tell either one of us he was going anywhere after school," Duncan said. "Right?" He didn't wait for an answer. "So where is he?"

"Oh, God," she said, and she tried not to think about any terrifying scenarios. This is one of the things they don't warn you about becoming a parent, she'd often thought. Realizing your utter powerlessness over fate.

"What are you thinking?" Duncan said. "Don't worry, it's nothing bad." He sounded like he was trying to convince himself. "I'm sure there's a good explanation."

"Let's call Ashley."

"What?"

"If he went somewhere, she'll know. He tells her a hell of a lot more than he tells us."

She hit Ashley's number.

"What time is it over there?" she asked.

"It's, like, eleven, she's probably asleep."

"I don't care if I wake her up," Juliana said. "I want to know she's okay too."

"Hello?" Ashley's voice, pulled out of sleep.

"Sweetie!" Juliana said.

"Everything okay?" Ashley said, alarmed.

"Everything's—everything's just fine, I'm just—"

"Then why are you calling now?"

"We're trying to find your brother," Juliana said, trying to sound casual.

"Jake? Oh, that's easy. Karney's."

"The ice-cream place?"

"Yeah. Working on his podcast."

"Podcast?"

A pause. "Oh, well, if *he* hasn't told you, I'm certainly not going to tell you."

"He's not answering his phone."

"That's not cool."

"Karney's," she said, catching Duncan's eye.

"On my way," Duncan said.

"Sweetie, I'll let you go back to sleep. I just wanted to make sure you were okay."

"But why *wouldn't* I be?"

"Okay, glad you're okay. Love you."

"Oh, hey, wait, Mom."

"Yeah?"

"Strange thing happened this morning. I was in Katutura, and some dude came up to me, I think a South African soldier?"

"Yeah?"

"He said 'Regards to yer mum. Tell her: Just see it through.'"

"What?" She froze. "He said *what?*"

"'Just see it through.'"

Part of her wanted to tell Ashley to get on the next flight home. But she realized that being back home, in Boston, would be no safer. More proximity could mean more danger.

They were sending a message. Protasov's tentacles were everywhere.

74

Karney Kone was a small soft-serve ice-cream place in Newton, a boxy stand-alone building with a red-and-white-striped awning. Duncan parked in the lot, and they both got out, looking in the big plate-glass windows as they walked in. When the kids were younger, she and Duncan used to take them there after movies. Karney's was one of Jake's favorite places.

They found Jake in a booth at the back. Juliana was at the same time tremendously relieved and angry at the kid for just disappearing. He was sitting across the booth from a young woman wearing the tangerine Karney Kone uniform. Her name badge identified her as Megan. In the middle of the table was a small matte-black electronic device about the size of a paperback book. It was covered with nobs and buttons and looked extremely complicated. Attached to it was a funny-looking microphone.

"Hold on," he said. "Um, Megan, these are my parents." He touched a button on the recorder and said into it, "And that's not getting recorded."

"Time to get home," Juliana said. "Time for dinner."

The young woman, a petite brunette with piercing blue eyes, sidled out of the booth. She looked to be a few years older than Jake. "I have to get back to work now anyway," she said.

Juliana took note of Jake's guilty expression—the kid never had a poker face—as he got up and shrugged on his backpack. "I'm not hungry," he said. "I had a burger here."

"You should have told us where you were," Duncan said. "You should have told me you were working on your podcast."

"Why didn't you answer your father's calls?" Juliana asked.

"My phone died," Jake said. "I'm sorry."

"Let me see it," Juliana said, holding out her palm. "Hand it over."

"What?" Jake said, as if he didn't understand, but at the same time he slid his phone out of his pocket and reluctantly handed it over. She glanced at it, saw it still had 16 percent.

"Why would you even lie about that?" she said. "I don't get it."

"I mean—" Jake said.

"And what's this all about? What's with the fancy recorder?"

Jake heaved an impatient sigh. "Dad?"

"Jake has a podcast," Duncan said.

"A podcast?" Juliana said. "Sure, why not? What kind of podcast?"

"It's a huge hit," Duncan said proudly. "It's insanely popular at his school. Very subversive."

"What's your podcast?" she asked Jake.

"It's called *Fleecing Sheep,* and it's about this whole factory we're in, you know? It's just— I'm trying to tell the truth about the whole deal. This whole brainwashed meritocracy, so-called. How we're all born into captivity. How we're supposed to be groomed and regimented and primed so that liberal-arts colleges can do more of the same to us—"

"Okay," she said and thought: *Here comes the verbal diarrhea.*

"And produce a whole generation of overeducated baristas—excellent sheep primed for soul-crushing bullshit jobs, because the system is rigged, and—"

"I get it, I get it," she said.

"I mean, whatever, you're not exactly the *target demographic,* Mom."

They dropped off Jake at his friend Link's apartment. Link's parents did something in tech and had a lot of money, and they lived in one of the nicest modern condo buildings in Boston, on Boylston Street. Link was a nerdy kid, a good friend of Jake's who turned out to be the editor of his podcast. Jake would spend the night at Link's condo. Juliana wanted him to be somewhere safe and protected, somewhere where the bad guys wouldn't be able to find him. At least not easily.

On the way over, with Duncan driving, she said to Jake, who was sitting in the back seat: "Explain it to me slowly. What does your phone dying or not dying have to do with the fact that you didn't tell either one of your parents what you were doing? You didn't answer calls or texts."

"I'm not— It's just— I mean," Jake sputtered. "Dad, you said it was okay."

"Wait, how is this my fault?" Duncan said.

"You know what I'm doing."

"I had no idea where you went," Duncan said.

"The podcast," Juliana said. "That looks like an expensive little digital recorder. Where'd you get it?"

"It's Link's," Jake said. "A Zoom H6. He's letting me borrow it."

"For what?" she said.

"The overeducated fast-food worker."

"But what I don't get is why you didn't tell us where you were," Juliana said. "Or why you didn't answer calls or texts."

"I was recording. I had to turn off my phone."

"Duncan," she said.

"You should have told us where you were," Duncan said.

"Oh, I'm sorry, Officer," Jake said. "Is this a parole violation?"

"No," Duncan said. "You don't get to do this. Not to us."

"So there's an 'us' now?" Jake said.

Juliana set her jaw and turned to look out the window, trying not to smile.

"I want to hear this podcast," she said. It had been preying on her, what was happening with Jake, and she hated like hell that she'd been so distracted. There are things in life you must never take your attention away from, she thought, and one of those is kids. Mothers don't have to be reminded. So whatever Jake was doing wasn't a secondary concern for her.

"Yeah, fine, whatever," Jake said.

"How about right now? Set it up for me."

Once Jake had connected his Samsung Galaxy to the car's sound system, his voice came out of the speakers, speaking more clearly than he ever did in real life. "So there's this village in Guatemala," he was saying. He had a pleasingly raspy voice. It was very Ira Glass from *This American Life*.

"Every year, thousands of high school kids come down there and help build a barn for the villagers, so they can write about it on their college applications. Now, after they've left, the barn gets knocked down again. So a whole new crop of kids can have something to write about on their Common App. That's right, the barn goes up, the barn comes down. It's an industry. It's a racket, okay? For them *and* for us."

He spoke slowly and emphatically, yet conversationally, with lots of pauses, but it worked. "I mean, look, there's a whole generation of kids who actually give a shit, you know, about social justice? But they're told, *Just go build this barn*. The reality is, they don't *want* you to actually give a shit. They just want you to play make-believe with this Guatemalan barn. A big charade. And you gotta ask yourself, how many things they train you to invest your time in are basically one ginormous . . . *Guatemalan barn*?"

Jake shut it off.

Tears were in her eyes. "Wow," she said. "I'm proud of you."

Jake was scowling down at his hands, his face red.

"That's really smart," she went on. "I mean, I don't think college admissions people are going to love it."

Jake shrugged. "They're never going to hear it anyway."

She was relieved. His words were dark and cynical, sure, but they weren't the words of a troubled teenager. They were the words of a quirky, original kid. Maybe his view of the world was a bit grim—well, she wasn't exactly in a position to tell him that everything was unicorns and rainbows out there. They both knew better.

When they arrived at Link's parents' condo building, Jake hopped out and grabbed his backpack. She looked at the building, at the security both inside and out, and was glad he'd be safe for a little while.

And then with a terrible pang she realized: *I might not ever see him again.*

When they got home, half an hour later, Duncan said, "He asked me not to tell you about the podcast."

"But did you know he was at Karney Kone?"

"Of course not. I didn't know where the hell he was." Duncan was eating a cold slice of leftover pizza; she wasn't hungry.

She shook her head. "Without telling anybody. I just about freaked out there when we found him gone, Dunc. I thought something had happened to him. So did you."

"I know."

"He just went to Karney's without telling us, without leaving a note or sending a text or even asking permission. And he thinks it's okay with Dad."

"So?"

"How's he ever going to develop a sense of responsibility? Or accountability? He just does whatever feels good in the moment. And you're clearly okay with that."

"I'm okay with letting the kid enjoy his life," Duncan said.

"He has to learn to be responsible."

"That's called being an adult, and he's not. He's not an adult. He's a kid. Why not let him enjoy his childhood?"

"He's not a child either. He's sixteen. Ashley was never like this."

"Maybe because Ashley's not a boy."

"Jake's not a boy anymore, Dunc; he's a man."

"No," Duncan said.

"And it's time for him to start acting like a man. Like a responsible adult."

"If you had your way, every inch of that kid's life would be planned, no spontaneity, everything scheduled."

"That's not fair, Dunc, and you know it. I just don't want him looking around when he's twenty-two, a college graduate on the job market, wishing he'd made better choices with his life."

There was a long pause. She could see Duncan slowly turning red. "What?" she said.

"God*damn* it, Juliana, you know better!" he shouted. "You've read the fine print! We don't even know if he's going to *see* twenty-two!"

And Juliana was stunned. They stared at each other. There were tears in his eyes and in hers too.

"Don't say that," she said.

He shook his head, the words choking in his throat, for a long while before he began speaking again, in a low voice. He said, "I knew a kid in college who thought he'd beaten Hodgkin's and died of a relapse before he graduated."

"*No*, Dunc. He's in *remission*."

"Yeah, the kid's parents paid for a commemorative bench in the college"—his voice broke—"courtyard."

She was shaking her head. Her throat hurt. She was thinking, *No. No. No.*

She remembered the lines that Duncan had wanted to feature in Jake's birth announcement. It was a passage from a nineteenth-century Russian thinker, Alexander Herzen.

We think the purpose of the child is to grow up because it does grow up. But its purpose is to play, to enjoy itself, to be a child. If we merely look to the end of the process, the purpose of life is death.

She'd objected. It was too somber, too pretentious, she said. Duncan gave in. But the words were meaningful to him, and from time to time they came back to her too. *Its purpose is to play.*

"We both know a recurrence is possible," he said. "We've read the medical cautions, over and over. It could come back at any time."

"It won't."

She was in denial, she knew it—she told herself Jake had been cured. To her it felt like a betrayal even to entertain the possibility that it might come back.

Duncan was blinking back tears, almost furiously. "These years—these years—these months—this *now*—these could end up being the entirety of his time on this planet," Duncan said. "Right now. I want him to love his life, to make the most of it. To get everything out of life. You remember when Jake was in the crisis, and he was shaking and seizing and convulsing, and I held him in the hospital bed, and I told him things would be better after it was over? It'll be behind us, I told him. And then—no more bad days, is what I said, right?"

She nodded. She remembered Duncan repeating that: *No more bad days.*

She could still smell the hospital room, that medicinal odor, hear the low buzz of the unwatched TV set mounted on the ceiling, its meaningless chatter flowing like hot water through a radiator. The fluorescent-hued gelatin dessert cups. Jake's ashy lips and poisoned, jaundiced flesh.

"No more bad days," Duncan said hoarsely.

And for an instant that memory flooded her brain again. She was looking at their sun-drenched backyard, watching ten-year-old Jake marching around the yard, imitating his father imitating Robin Williams in *Dead Poets Society*, chanting, "O Captain! My Captain!"

Her eyes filled with tears. Suddenly her cell phone rang, jolting her. She looked at it, glanced at the number. Didn't recognize it.

She picked it up, said hello.

"Your Honor, my name is Alex Venkovsky. I, uh, got your name from a mutual friend."

"Okay," she said warily. She had no idea who it was.

"He might have mentioned I work for the government?"

"Right," she said. This had to be the guy from Treasury, from FinCEN Special Collections. "Nice to hear from you."

"Tomorrow seems to be a day of opportunity," he said.

"I think so."

"How early in the morning can I meet you? There's some toys I wanted to show you."

They arranged to meet in the morning. He was taking the earliest flight out of Dulles, at zero dark hundred. She didn't have to give him her address. He already knew it. "I'll be at your house at five o'clock," he said.

Another call was coming in. She took it. This number she recognized: Nazarov, the *mafiya* guy.

She said hello.

"Your Honor," Nazarov said, "I think we are all set. If you are really so sure this is what you want."

"I need to find the file Hersh left for me," Juliana told Duncan later. "I didn't have time to look for it in my lobby this morning. And it may have something important in it."

"No," Duncan said. "You're exhausted—we both are—and we have a big day ahead of us. You need to be sharp."

"You're right." Juliana realized there was no use arguing with Duncan, that neither was going to budge. But she needed that file.

She waited until he'd fallen asleep. Then she scrawled a note, telling him where she'd gone, in case he got up before she was back.

75

She parked in the underground parking garage across the street from the courthouse. Finding a space there was no problem at this time of night.

The courthouse was closed, but her ID allowed her to enter after hours. She greeted the security guard, Rodrigo, by name.

"Very late for you, Judge," Rodrigo said.

"No rest for the wicked," she said.

"No, ma'am."

She took the elevator to the ninth floor. It was dark, and her footsteps echoed.

A security guard walked by. She tensed. Not someone she knew. She kept going down the hall to her lobby. She unlocked the door and switched on the light.

She remembered Hersh's words, when he first came to her office: *I could pick that lock inside of a minute and a half.*

Might he have left his file for her here, in her office?

Maybe, maybe not. He'd said he might bring it by. But at the same time, he was less than impressed by the security in the courthouse. Her office was easy to get into, too easy.

She looked around, looked at her desk, the side table heaped with paper, all the usual places. But nothing that looked like it could be Hersh's file.

As she scanned the room, she was hyperaware of the noises around her, of passing footsteps, someone coughing as he or she walked by. Her nerves were taut.

Then a thought occurred to her. *You a big Trollope fan?*

He'd been showing off when he picked her book safe right off the shelf. But neither one of them had said anything aloud about it being a hiding place. So perhaps . . .

She looked at the bookcase where *Barchester Towers* was shelved.

It was gone.

What the hell? She winced as she thought of her favorite pearl earrings and the pile of cash, almost five hundred dollars. Well, she had bigger things to worry about.

Then she found the book safe on the shelf below. Someone had *moved* it.

Maybe a signal?

She pulled the book off the shelf and opened it. Inside the compartment, in addition to the cash and the earrings, were a couple of folded pages and a small USB stick.

Hersh's file.

Juliana unfolded the papers and realized quickly she was looking at a bank transaction. Multiple transactions. Wire transfers. Between the Russian Commercial Bank of Cyprus, a subsidiary of the VTB bank of Russia, and Mayfair Paragon.

Proof that Yuri Protasov was a Kremlin puppet.

She wondered where Hersh could possibly have found it. She slotted the USB drive into her laptop. That opened a PDF document containing the same information. She downloaded it and e-mailed it to herself.

She wondered how many statutes Hersh had broken in order to secure this damaging information. How many laws he'd broken. All her life, she'd been a rule-follower, she realized. She loved the certainty, the absoluteness of abiding by a set of rules. But the rules were no longer helping. If she was going to survive, and protect her family, she'd have to make up her own rules.

She refolded the pages and put them, along with the USB stick, in her purse. Then she turned off the lights and locked the door, but before she did, she glanced into the hallway to make sure no one was coming.

She left the courthouse the same way, said goodnight to Rodrigo, and walked out into the plaza, into the adjoining Center Plaza building, to the elevator bank. And down into the parking garage. Everything was quiet. The elevator stopped on the floor below and someone got in, a man wearing a hoodie and orange sunglasses and Beats headphones, his head bopping. He pressed his floor button; then he pulled back his hoodie, and she saw the shaved head and the jutting jaw, and her stomach did a flip. The ropy muscles, the powerful build.

The fake janitor. Greaves.

He inserted a small key in the elevator panel, and the elevator shuddered to a stop between floors.

"The good news for you," he said, "is that this is the last you'll be seeing of me."

She froze in place. There was nowhere to run. Her pulse raced. "What do you want?"

"Seems you weren't a good candidate for blackmail," Greaves said. "You got pushed, and you just started digging. Trying to get the goods on us, and maybe getting a little close. So that changes the whole calculation, see. You're clearly not someone who can be intimidated into silence. Not someone who can be humiliated onto the sidelines."

"I'm glad you figured that out."

"Which means there's no point making threats any longer."

"Then what do you call this?"

"Oh, I'm not here to threaten you. I'm here to terminate you." He said it matter-of-factly, as if he were ordering a pizza. In that moment she noticed he was wearing blue nitrile gloves, like a surgeon's.

He lunged at her, shoved her hard into the elevator wall. Her head bounced against the cladding. He was on her now, his big arms around her, his hands clutching her throat, squeezing hard.

She tried to struggle, to kick and swing her arms, but she could barely move them; he was too close, and he was so much bigger. She could smell his meaty breath.

He made unwavering eye contact with her. She could see every capillary in his eyes. What was that thing they say, that if a mammal makes prolonged eye contact with another, it's an assertion of dominance—to be followed by fighting or screwing?

Greaves was going to kill her.

But he was not doing it quickly. If he wanted to, he could surely dispatch her easily and quickly, snapping her neck in an instant. Instead, he seemed to be protracting the process. This was not just a professional task to him. He was enjoying it.

His hands squeezed her throat, and she gagged.

She tried to say "Please," but it came out *blez*.

Finally she wrested a hand loose from his grip. She felt around for her purse, found it on her left side, over her shoulder, just out of reach. She was seeing stars. She could smell the man's aftershave, the gloves, a rancid odor of sweat.

Her fingers scrabbled inside the purse, felt stuff, objects her fingers didn't recognize. Her head was swimming.

Greaves began to talk, in a calm voice. "Somebody with a grudge followed you out of the courthouse," he said. "An aggrieved felon you once sentenced, perhaps."

She screamed soundlessly.

"A criminal you put away when you were an assistant US Attorney, let's say. There will be theories. I see a big front-page story in *The Boston*

Globe. A story about how vulnerable judges are. The governor will say it's shocking."

He squeezed harder now, and her head felt like it was exploding. Her body had gone into panic mode. Her lungs were burning: it felt like they were on fire, like her chest would explode.

"Lots—of people—will show up—at your funeral." He throttled her harder, and her eyes felt like they were going to pop out.

It can't end this way. Her thoughts were like a rusted hinge, shrieking again and again, *Can't end this way can't end this way.*

Can't end this way.

The strength was seeping out of her body, ebbing away, like rice paper dissolving in water.

Then she touched the cold metal of the knife, felt around for the button she'd pressed once before and thumbed it open. The blade jumped in her hand.

She remembered Hersh's instructions: *Upward toward the heart. It's a steeply upward arc through the belly into the pericardial sac.*

She summoned the strength, willed the muscles in her arms to contract, and with a great upward thrust she sliced into the man's body. Not aiming, just driving upward. The blade pulsed and tugged in her hands, like a fishing pole with a hooked fish. Greaves's eyes opened wide. Then wider still. His mouth gaped. His face was contorted. The hands on her throat went slack.

With a sudden surge of strength, he threw her to the floor of the elevator, her arms pinned, grasping her shoulders with talon claws, a big cat pouncing on its prey. She screamed, swung her feet wildly, kicking at him. The man's weight was heavy on her. But then his grip on her let up, and he collapsed, canting to one side, and she was able to wrench herself free. She gasped, deep and hard, choking for air. Her head was swimming.

When she looked at Greaves she saw that something had changed in her attacker's eyes. The fury of his gaze had given way to something more like disbelief. His mouth had gone slack. He looked dazed. At first she wasn't sure if he was dead or alive.

He was still. His blood pooled on the floor.

Maybe he was dead.

She struggled to her feet, and catching sight of the key in the elevator panel, she turned it. The elevator started moving.

It opened on the first garage level. The elevator doors opened. She stumbled out into the darkness, the cool air, the smell of gasoline.

She looked back at Greaves's sprawled body, his staring eyes.

She pressed the elevator's lock button to keep the car from moving.

Then she looked for help. She raced through the garage, low-ceilinged and dark, but saw no one. She saw an exit sign, flung open the door, ran up an echoey stairway, up two flights, came out into a Center Plaza building, dark and deserted, a dingy fluorescent cast.

She ran to the revolving door, then out onto the street. It was drizzling now, the sidewalk gray. No cops in sight. During the day you'd see plenty of police cruisers out here on Cambridge Street, in the vicinity of the courthouses and City Hall.

She crossed the street, no cars coming in either direction, onto City Hall Plaza, a great desolate *campo* paved in brick.

She descended the steps toward City Hall, a hulking concrete monstrosity, looking for a cop.

She had killed a human being.

It was only just sinking in.

She had killed a man. An attacker, yes. But she'd done this.

She was half out of her head. She'd just been almost strangled.

I killed a man.

She wondered what she looked like to other people, her hair matted and damp, her blood-spattered clothes astray. Panic in her eyes. She didn't look like a judge, like an upstanding citizen. She probably looked like a crazy person out here in the middle of the night.

In the lobby of City Hall she found a guard, a black man of around fifty. "I need some help," she said.

"Yes, ma'am?"

"A man is dead," she said.

Before he could even get a word out, she continued, "In the Government Center parking garage." She gestured behind her.

"Let me radio for an officer," he said.

She waited for the response, crackling over his radio. She didn't fully understand it, but it sounded like cops were coming.

About ten minutes later, a weary young cop arrived, presumably a beat cop. A handsome but haggard-looking guy with blue eyes and black hair.

She told him she'd just found a body.

The cop walked with her across the plaza and into the Center Plaza building. In the moonlight, the cool evening, everything had the smeary feeling of a dream sequence.

"He attacked me," she said. "Did I already tell you that?"

"Yes, ma'am," the cop said. His radio was crackling on his hip.

The leftmost elevator's doors were closed. She pressed the button, and it *bing*ed and its doors came open.

The elevator was empty.

Empty.

No blood. No body.

Empty.

She stared in disbelief.

"He was—there," she said.

"Yes, ma'am." She noticed a real change in his expression. Almost an eye roll. "Looks like he left."

"He was dead! I'm quite sure of it."

"Uh-huh."

She was certain it was the leftmost elevator, but what if—being so panicked, so near-hysterical—she was remembering wrong? She tried the other elevator, punching the button. It opened, empty.

"Can I ask—have you been drinking, ma'am?" the cop said.

"No!"

"Or are you on any substances, maybe?"

"That's impossible!" she said. "He was here. If he was moved—"

"Okay, ma'am."

What the hell was going on? She didn't understand it: Greaves was dead. Why was his body gone? Could somebody have moved it? There was no way he'd gotten up and walked away.

There must have been a backup team or something that had come and retrieved Greaves, cleaned up the scene. What else could it have been?

"The man was dead," she said. "This is where he attacked me, in this elevator. I killed him in self-defense. This is the crime scene."

"Okay," the policeman said. "If you want to file a police report—"

"No, he was right here," she said. "Someone moved his body."

"Okay then," the cop said. "I'm at the end of my shift, so let's keep things simple. If you want to file a police report, I'll be glad to pass you on to one of my colleagues."

Something clenched and unclenched in her gut. Because she finally understood. She understood the logic of the loose end. Greaves had failed.

That had turned *him* into a loose end.

The elevator doors closed, and Juliana steadied herself against a pillar. She shook her head. She was finally beginning to think clearly. She had no time to waste. She had to get out of there. She flashed on the prospect of spending hours to no avail in a police station, filing reports and answering questions.

"I'm— I'm sorry to waste your time," she said. Her eyes were out of focus. She saw a trash receptacle and stepped over to it, and her head jerked down and she threw up. Hot acids scalded her throat. It was as if her body were determined to purge itself of some poison. She thought it would bring a sense of relief.

It didn't.

76

She drove home cautiously, uncertain of her driving abilities after so long without sleeping. When she got home, she found the house dark. It was a little after three in the morning. Duncan was asleep upstairs.

But it was too late to go to bed, even though she desperately needed sleep. Instead, she made coffee and sat tensely in the kitchen checking her e-mail and working on exactly how she was going to play the next ten hours. There were just too many unknowns.

Her head kept throbbing.

A couple of hours passed. At five, she decided to wake Duncan, but first she made a fresh pot of coffee. She took her time and fixed it the way he liked it, with half-and-half and Splenda, just the right shade of tan, and brought the mug upstairs. He needed his sleep, but she really needed him to strategize with. Duncan was smart as hell and inevitably thought of an angle she'd forgotten.

She would tell him about what had happened in the elevator, but later.

She nudged him, and he slowly opened his eyes. "It's time," she said.

"I know. Oh, thanks." He took the mug gratefully and took a sip. "Fantastic."

"Will he see you?" she said.

She was talking about Arnold Coren, a professor of Russian history at Columbia who had been Duncan's old mentor when he taught at Harvard.

"Arnie? Of course."

"At his office in Morningside Heights?"

"He's taking me to lunch at the Metropolitan Club," he said. That was a private social club located in a magnificent Stanford White–designed mansion on East Sixtieth Street.

"Drinks first?"

"Many. Whiskey. You know what he's like when he's had a few."

"I do." She laughed grimly.

The doorbell rang, startling her. She looked at her watch. It was five thirty. Yes: the FinCEN guy. Half an hour late.

She went to answer the door, just as Duncan was coming down the stairs.

The man standing on the porch was a tall, stern-looking, black-haired man, wearing a blue windbreaker. He had a heavy brow and looked to be in his late thirties.

"Judge Brody, I'm Alex Venkovsky, from Treasury."

"Right. Come on in."

She saw a large black government-looking vehicle, a Cadillac Escalade, parked in the driveway behind Duncan's car.

"So much for punctuality," Juliana said, glancing at her iPhone.

"Sorry. We spent the last two hours sterilizing the whole neighborhood. Making sure nobody had eyes on the ground."

"Okay. So what's the schedule?"

"Well, ma'am, our plane is leaving earlier than anticipated, so we're going to need to get on the road. Like now. Uh, are we going like this?"

She smiled, glancing down at her sweats and bare feet. "Right, hope you don't mind if I change," she said, opening the door and backing up to let him enter.

"We don't have a lot of time. Mr. McNamer's plane leaves at nine on the dot."

"McNamer, huh? We're talking Giles McNamer?"

"Yes, ma'am. He's a friend of the Treasury Secretary's, and he happens to be going to Nantucket this morning and is very kindly letting us hitch a ride. But he's apparently trying to make a ten A.M. tee time. So he wants us there no later than nine at his FBO at Logan."

Giles McNamer was the co-founder of a huge private equity firm and had been a special adviser on economic policy to President Obama. You couldn't find anyone more Establishment. He sat on the board of the Federal Reserve Bank of Boston; he was a member of the Council on Foreign Relations; he graduated from the Dalton School in Manhattan, and Harvard, and Harvard Business School; was a member of the Steering Committee of the Bilderberg Group; and he went to Davos every year.

"We're flying on his private jet?"

"Yes, ma'am. It's a Gulfstream G650." He said it like that meant something.

"Would you like some coffee?"

"Oh, no, ma'am, I'm good. I can't have coffee when I fly. It gives me a nervous stomach."

"How are we getting downtown? You're driving?"

"Yes, ma'am."

"I'll be back down in a couple of minutes." She went upstairs and changed into the burgundy Armani suit she'd found at Nordstrom Rack, her go-to outfit, the one that always drew raves. It gave her confidence. She needed it. She put on makeup. Because of her exhaustion, everything looked pasty on her. Her lipstick looked too strong against her tired, whitish face.

A car pulled up in front of the house. Duncan's Lyft. It would take him to the Back Bay train station. Duncan was taking the Acela, the express train, to New York.

She put her arms around him and kissed him. Then he said, into her hair, "Please be careful, Jules."

"You know I will."

"I know. But still." And he hugged her, hard.

Venkovsky drove the Escalade into Boston.

"So, Alex Venkovsky," she said.

"Yeah, yeah, it's a Russian name."

"You're Russian?"

"I lived in Moscow until my parents emigrated when I was six. That a problem for you? Are you one of those Russophobes? Think we're all in cahoots with the Kremlin?"

"Seriously?"

"Sorry to be touchy. The circles I move in—I sometimes wonder. German-Americans got the hairy eyeball during the First World War. Japanese-Americans got rounded up in the Second. Now, with all these news stories about Russian mischief, I meet people who think I must keep a nerve agent next to the allspice in my kitchen."

"You ever have reason to use it?"

"The nerve agent?"

"The allspice. Because I'm pretty sure I never have."

Venkovsky let out a laugh. "Okay, apologies. I'm a little hypersensitive on the subject. Moving on."

Half an hour later, they pulled up outside a large, ugly government building on Causeway Street. Venkovsky put a blank parking ticket on his windshield and put on the emergency flashers.

He escorted her into the building, took her up the elevator to the sixth floor. It opened on a bleak expanse of cubicles. He signed her in, took her to a conference room, and introduced her to a man named Glenn Hawkins, a chunky redheaded man in his twenties, wearing jeans and a green polo shirt. In the middle of the conference table was a big box of Dunkin' Donuts coffee and a couple of cartons of doughnuts.

Venkovsky poured them both coffee, and he took a doughnut. "Glenn's going to wire you up," he said.

The redheaded guy lifted a ridged aluminum briefcase and opened it on the table near the doughnuts. It was lined with black foam and held various electronic-looking components. Then he put down a canvas tote bag.

"I understand you've arranged to get into his estate?" Hawkins said.

"That's right." Juliana thought briefly of Nazarov and the favor she'd called in.

"Well, that's the hard part. I'm not going to ask you how you did that." He smiled. "Protasov's spread on Nantucket is more than sixty acres, and it's protected. Fenced in. We can't possibly get close enough to use wireless bugs."

"Okay," she said.

"That leaves us with covert recording devices, which is what we got here. This belt?" He reached into the canvas tote bag and pulled out a skinny black leather belt with a simple silver buckle.

"The recorder's in the buckle. Good quality too. Do you have a Tesla?"

"No."

Hawkins smiled. "Well, now you do." He handed her a small black-and-silver key fob with the Tesla logo on it. He was making a joke, sort of. "This records. Or there's a pen. Which does write. And records." He held up a ceremonial-looking pen with a black lacquer body.

"Do I choose one of these devices, or—"

"How about you take a few of them? As backups."

"Why not?"

"Of course, they might not let you keep your purse with you."

"Who, Protasov's security people?"

"Right. His guys take precautions."

"Okay, and what if they take away my purse?"

"Ma'am, you're a size nine, right? Shoe?"

She nodded.

The door to the conference room burst open and a portly middle-aged man in a white shirt and tie, no suit jacket, barged in, red-faced with anger. He had a bristly mustache and thick glasses and was waving a piece of paper.

"I just read the op report!" he shouted. "This is not happening!"

"Yeah, it is," Venkovsky said quietly.

"You realize this is insane, right? It's totally irresponsible. You're throwing a duckling into a raccoon den!"

"It's what she wants," Alex Venkovsky cut in. "And Brennan said it's happening. So."

The guy in the white shirt kept going. "The idea of sending a civilian on an op with stakes this high, wiring her up—and no backup? Are you out of your freakin' mind? Confidential informants get killed that way! I want you to mark it down in the log that I objected to this op. I want it *on the record*." Red-faced, he said to Juliana, "Do you know about this dude? Do you know what he does to his enemies?"

"I have no choice," Juliana said. She swallowed hard. She didn't want to hear it.

"You think he's just, like, this guy who gives libraries and hospital wings? Yeah, that's the public image. But you wanna know the truth? People who cross him tend to *die*."

She nodded. "Yes, I'm aware."

"If his people suspect you're working for US law enforcement—or God forbid they find out you actually kinda-sorta *are*!—they're not going to hesitate. Anyone can arrange a murder, but it takes a professional to arrange a suicide. Ever hear of a polonium cocktail?"

Alex Venkovsky quietly asked the man in the white shirt to step outside for a minute. She could see, through the window in the door, Venkovsky talking to the guy, gesticulating wildly. Then he pulled out a phone and made a call. After about five minutes, he returned, alone, looking chastened, holding a folder of papers.

Hawkins threw him a look, and Venkovsky returned it by wordlessly shaking his head. She didn't know what they were communicating.

"We're fine," Venkovsky said.

"What does that mean?" Juliana said. "Who was that?"

"No change in plans," Venkovsky said. "The operation proceeds."

"Good." She was glad Duncan wasn't with her. He wouldn't have liked what he heard.

Hawkins reached into the canvas tote bag and took out a couple of shoeboxes. "I'm hoping one of these fits you," he said.

He slid the first shoebox toward her. It was Coach, she noticed. Nothing too high fashion. A sensible shoe.

He said, chuckling nervously, "One's brown, one's black. Both size nine. There's a recording device built into the soles of each shoe. We have an Israeli guy who makes these for us, and he's awesome."

She took out the shoe, a simple brown wedge heel. Then she took off her right pump and slipped on the doctored shoe. It fit perfectly. He saw and said, "Excellent.

"Now, they can detect recording devices with something called a nonlinear junction detector, I have to warn you. They might use one of those. But they're not likely to run it over the bottoms of your shoes. So even if they take away your purse and scan you with a detector, you're probably not going to get caught."

Probably, she thought. "And what if I do?"

He looked at her. "Ma'am, just one thing."

"Yes?"

Venkovsky opened the folder and slid several pieces of paper across the conference table.

She looked at them.

"These are indemnity forms," he said.

"Understood." They wanted to ensure the US Government wasn't legally responsible for whatever might happen to her.

They were bureaucrats, and they were scared.

"We need you to sign these. Holding the US Treasury Department and the US Government blameless in the event of—"

"I know," she said. "I know what they are."

77

Alex Venkovsky drove the Escalade to a terminal at Logan Airport she'd never seen before, a private-aviation terminal. Instead of parking, he drove right across the tarmac and up to the aircraft, a white, swoopy-looking airplane with elliptical portholes.

As they got out they were greeted by a pretty young brown-haired woman who introduced herself as Alison and already knew their names. She was the flight attendant and the "concierge," she called herself. Clearly she worked in some logistical capacity for the plane's owner, Giles McNamer.

Juliana climbed the plane's stairs and staggered inside. The cabin was flooded with sunlight. She was momentarily blinded. She smelled expensive leather and great coffee. Then, once her eyes had adjusted, she took in a beautiful interior. It radiated luxury. There were several big, comfortable-looking white leather chairs next to glass pull-down tables. On the walls, mahogany trim. Cool jazz played on a surprisingly good sound system, given the acoustics of the space.

Alison asked her if she wanted a cappuccino and introduced her to Giles McNamer, a tall, rangy, athletic-looking man in his sixties with graying brown hair and an unironic mustache. His hair was parted like a barkeep in a Western. He was wearing faded Madras shorts and a crisp white Oxford cloth button-down shirt, untucked and rolled up to the elbows. He had the permanent air of someone who'd just changed out of his tennis whites. In one hand he clutched a section of the *Wall Street Journal.*

"All I know is, you're doing something," McNamer said, "and it's government business, and Jordan asked me to give you folks a lift. And I like to oblige my old friends at Treasury." Jordan Kavanaugh was the Secretary of the Treasury.

McNamer parked himself in a chair at the back of the plane, by a TV screen. A girl who looked to be in her late teens, with glossy black hair almost down to her butt, was scrunched up in one of the chairs, wearing short-short cutoffs and a midriff-baring tiny white ACK T-shirt. ACK, Juliana knew, was the airport code for Nantucket. She had earbuds in and was in her own world, her arms wrapped around her legs.

Juliana took the chair next to Venkovsky's. The leather was butter-soft. The chair swiveled.

Venkovsky put his battered leather briefcase on the table and took out some papers, which he handed to her.

She wondered if these were more legal forms to sign. Then she saw the name Yuri Vladimirovich Protasov at the top of the first page, along with a photograph.

"We have just enough time for a quick backgrounder on Protasov," Venkovsky said.

She nodded, skimmed the page. She put on her sunglasses to cut down on the glare.

Alison arrived with her cappuccino. She thanked her and took a sip. She could barely taste it.

Venkovsky was busy sorting through a pile of photographs, eight-by-ten glossies. He slid one across the glass table in front of her. A photograph of an attractive woman—no, more like a *handsome* woman—of around forty, but a hard forty. Blond, cut in an efficient bob, and careful makeup. High cheekbones. A very poised, controlled woman. She looked like a tough broad. Like nobody messed with her.

"Who's she? Protasov's wife?"

Venkovsky chuckled. "Oh, no. She's Protasov's minder. She's FSB."

"Name?"

"Olga Ivanovna Kuznetsova. She's a colonel in the FSB. Lethal woman. Part of Protasov's entourage."

"Security?"

"Partly, sure. But she's also there to make sure Protasov comes when he's called. They own the guy. She's sorta like his nanny. Watch out for her."

"Will do. Olga. But I don't get why the Russian intelligence service has assigned an officer to a private citizen. That seems crazy."

"A private citizen? You don't get it. Yuri Protasov is a multi-billion-dollar Russian-controlled entity. You better believe they're keeping tabs. And no, an SVR officer doesn't tool around with a vanity license plate saying SPY. They've all got covers, bland official jobs, same as our guys. You know there are more KGB agents in Russia today than there were in Soviet days? They just call it by a different name, but same deal."

"I didn't know."

"You know Putin's ex-KGB, right?"

"Sure."

"The KGB basically took over Russia when the Soviet Union collapsed."

She nodded. "I don't actually care, you know. I'm sorry." She felt a strange sort of calm inside. An anger that focused her mind. "I don't care what Russia might be up to, or the KGB or the SVR or the FSB. I care about what happens to my family. My son, my daughter. My husband. That's what I worry about."

"I understand," Venkovsky said. "And I think what you're doing is really brave."

"Brave?" she said. "Or reckless?"

Venkovsky shook his head but didn't reply. She noticed he didn't meet her eyes.

78

The car they gave her to drive was a gleaming black Tesla Model S. As requested. She was surprised they'd agreed. Government bureaucracies were notoriously tight-fisted. She had no idea whether it was borrowed or rented, but it was sleek and beautiful, and it looked and smelled brand-new. Maybe it belonged to Giles McNamer. It had an all-glass panoramic roof.

She familiarized herself with the Tesla for about five minutes and then put it into drive. She was headed toward the part of the island called Siasconset, from time to time consulting the large screen on the dashboard, following the spoken directions.

The entrance to Protasov's property was marked only with a street number. There was a security liftgate across the road. She stopped, and the gate came up and out of the way, and she drove along a narrow unpaved sandy road.

As she drove, she rehearsed what she was going to say. She didn't know how this whole thing was going to play out. She was improvising. She just knew she had to get him aside and have a talk.

Now she was beginning to get nervous, even scared. Her mouth was dry, and her heart raced. This wasn't helpful, she knew. Then she reminded herself about what had happened to her in Chicago and ever since, and it was like tapping into a deep reservoir of anger, and she found it calmed her nerves.

The road twisted one way and then another and then she came to a wooden gatehouse, a small shingled structure with a steep roof. Another liftgate blocked the road. A uniformed guard greeted her unsmilingly.

"Good morning," he said. "A license or some form of picture ID?"

She handed him her driver's license.

He looked at the license, then at a list on a clipboard he was holding. He looked at her, then at the license again.

"Welcome, Ms. Brody," he said, and he waved her through.

The road here was paved with crushed seashells, which crunched under the wheels as she drove. After a while the road widened out into a large, circular drive in front of a sprawling three-story shingle-style house that could have been a hotel. It was certainly large enough to be. In front of the house was a lagoon, glistening in the sunlight. She could see a glimpse of sparkling blue ocean through a breezeway. Blue hydrangeas clustered in front of the house.

A valet took the car, and she got out and stepped into the house, where she was met by a pretty young Asian woman in a pale green linen dress.

"Judge Juliana Brody," Juliana said.

"Welcome. The board members are gathering in the sitting room for some coffee before the meeting."

"Thank you." The young woman assumed Juliana was here for the board meeting, a legal adviser or something. But how long could she keep up the imposture?

She was standing in a broad entry hall with floors of mellow antique pine and a skylight above. She could see that a small crowd, maybe thirty people, was gathering in the next room. She walked into the sitting room. She smelled someone's citrus floral perfume.

She recognized some of the faces. One, shaggy-haired and round bellied, was a former British prime minister. Another was a black woman with lively darting eyes who had once served as Secretary of State. A flame-haired and fiery former United Nations ambassador for the United States. A few people turned and smiled at Juliana, as if they were supposed to know her.

So far no one had called her out, no one had asked her to repeat her name, no one had checked a list to find she wasn't there. Everyone assumed she was there because she was supposed to be there. Look like you belong and you'll fit right in, Rosalind Brody used to say.

A waitress in a short black dress offered her caviar and crème fraîche tartlets on a tray. She shook her head. Didn't seem like breakfast food, and she didn't care for caviar anyway.

Then she saw, across the room, a handsome blond woman with a hard face who had to be Olga Kuznetsova, the FSB colonel. Kuznetsova was wearing a navy blazer over a white blouse, a pantsuit. A heavy gold chain necklace. She was talking with the pretty Asian girl, who seemed to be telling her something. Olga was shaking her head, scowling, clearly the boss.

Olga then turned around and moved shark-like through the crowd until she reached a couple of men talking. Juliana saw it was the man himself, talking to Senator Hugh Comstock of Illinois.

Yuri Protasov was surprisingly short, or maybe he just looked short next to Comstock. He was a virile-looking man in his midfifties, rugged. Graying sandy hair, a closely trimmed salt-and-pepper beard, a heavy brow. He wore an elegant dove-gray suit, a crisp white shirt, a maroon tie. He laughed at something the senator said, displaying very white capped teeth.

She saw Olga sidle up to Protasov and whisper something. She looked angry. Protasov nodded, furrowed his heavy brow, whispered something back. It looked like she was dressing him down.

Then his eyes searched the room and landed on Juliana.

Their eyes locked.

Protasov did not smile politely. His eyes were cold.

Juliana stared back. Her "objection overruled" stare. Then she smiled.

Now he was angling through the crowd, heading toward her, she realized.

When he reached her, he said, "Please come with me," and kept striding. "Certainly," she said, and fell in behind him. She followed him out of the sitting room and across the entry hall into a room with floor-to-ceiling bookshelves, dimly lit. The air in there was cool. She looked around, scanned the shelves, saw books by Tolstoy, Dostoyevsky, Pushkin, Bulgakov, Gogol, Chekhov, Nabokov. Serious Russian literature. These books weren't props brought in to decorate a room. Protasov was obviously some kind of intellectual.

A bulky young guy in a suit that looked too tight entered the library and approached Protasov. They spoke, quickly and quietly, in Russian. Protasov stood back and folded his arms, watching. The young guy came up to her and said, in a thick Russian accent, "Please stand with arms at side."

He gave Juliana a long impassive stare, like a zoologist peering at a specimen that might or might not be a new creature to him. "Mr. Protasov will be with you in minute." Then he produced a metal object somewhat bulkier than a cell phone and proceeded to run it silently over Juliana's clothing, over her shoulders and arms, and down to her legs.

She was frozen in fear. She was wearing a belt, and a pin, and there was a lipstick in her purse that contained no lipstick but recorded. And her shoes. She had multiple recording devices on her person. Any one of them contained microcircuits and were detectable.

The guy was looking for these devices. If he did find one, or several, what would happen then? The not knowing, the very uncertainty, was terrifying.

Her heart thudded, but her face was composed: calm, triumphant, brassy.

Protasov watched, arms folded.

The guard, or whatever he was, finished running his little device over Juliana; then he looked at it closely. He turned and said something quietly to Protasov in Russian.

She waited. Her heart beat so hard she thought it almost might be audible.

But the young guy just nodded and left the room.

Did that mean the recording devices hadn't been detected? She wished she hadn't had so much coffee. On the other hand, she'd needed it to fight the crushing wave of fatigue settling over her from not sleeping.

She could feel her heart dancing in her chest. She had no idea what was about to happen. She didn't know what to expect.

Yuri Protasov walked slowly up to her. "Judge Brody," he said boomingly, "I'm afraid you've caught me at a very busy time. My board is about to meet, and these are not people you keep waiting." He spoke fluent English, his accent British.

"We have a little business to discuss, you and I," Juliana said. "Shouldn't take long at all."

Protasov offered his hand formally, bowing slightly. "Yuri Protasov."

"Juliana Brody."

"So you just show up here uninvited?" He gave a little smile. A flash of white. "And apparently breeze right through my security?"

"If you can't get in the back door, try the front." Another Roz Brody pearl of wisdom.

"Well played. Very clever of you, coming at a time when there are a lot of people around. Protection in numbers, right?"

They understood each other. "Something like that."

"So what do you want?"

"Actually, I'm here to offer you something."

"Well, that's a change. I'm all ears."

"A decision in a case of interest to you. A motion for summary judgment."

"Oh?"

"Your people have made it clear what you want. You want all documents sealed that might reveal that you're the owner of Wheelz. So you want to shut down a sexual discrimination lawsuit against a company you own. I get it."

"I'm not sure what you're referring to." A tight smile. "This sounds like fake news to me."

"You want this whole Wheelz sexual discrimination case thrown out. Well, let me make it clear to you: I think the plaintiff's case is quite strong."

He tipped his head skeptically. "And?"

She said, "And for me to put my beliefs and my morals up for sale, well—that's going to cost something. It's not something I do lightly. That's going to weigh on me for a long time. I'm going to require some serious consideration."

He said nothing, waiting.

"So you will wire ten million dollars to my account. Which I think is cheap, frankly, for a woman's honor."

She opened her purse and located the card that Venkovsky had given her. The business card of an assistant general manager at a Cayman Islands bank. On the other side of the card she'd written out the nine digits of a bank account. She handed it to him.

He looked at it for a few seconds, and then he slipped the card into his front shirt pocket. Did that mean he agreed? She couldn't tell. She was confident that Protasov's people—or maybe the FSB?—had monitored the conversation she and Duncan had had in her lobby.

"After what you put me through—put my family through—I call this compensatory damages."

He blinked a few times, his expression stoic.

"If it comes out that your fund was illegally underwritten by a banned, sanctioned entity, I think it could be ruinous to you. All those fancy board members out there will flee." She waited. Saw his cold hard stare.

Finally he smiled grimly. "Your justice is expensive."

Protasov was no longer pretending to be unaware of what she was talking about. They were past that. And he had just surrendered.

"Well, I hope you're right. I also want it made explicit—and I want to hear you *say* it, right here—that my family will always be protected. That nothing will ever happen to them."

Protasov lifted his chin. "You have nothing to worry about," he said. But his eyes said something different. They were cold and gray and steely. Her stomach turned over.

"You're going to have to be more explicit," she said.

"Your family, your husband and your two lovely children, nothing will ever happen to them; you have my word on that." He spoke gently. "I would never do that."

"Okay, then," she said softly. "So tell me something. Why didn't you try the carrot first, before the stick?"

"You mean why didn't my people offer you a bribe?"

She nodded.

"We didn't attempt a bribe, because your reputation preceded you."

"My reputation?"

"For fierce probity," Protasov said with a tart smile. "But as it turns out, you are full of surprises. So we will do business, you and I. Ten million dollars into your Caymans account. We have an understanding."

She smiled, maybe a little too broadly. She didn't want him to see what she was feeling.

"I think maybe people, maybe they underestimate you, is that right?"

"Occasionally," she said, and shrugged.

She thought of the lipstick in her purse that wasn't really a lipstick, and the belt buckle, and the soles of her shoes. No one had taken anything away from her, patted her down. She was recording him, and if any single device malfunctioned, there were plenty of backups.

Had he been explicit enough? Should she press him harder, try to get him to say more?

She couldn't risk it, she decided. She had enough.

He said, "You know, Catherine the Great was far more ruthless than her husband. First she forced him to abdicate the throne; then she arranged to have one of his guards strangle him to death one night. So then she took over as czarina. She had tens of thousands of her people put to death for daring to rebel against her. Maybe hundreds of thousands. She even executed noblemen. But you know, it's like they say—you can't make an omelet without breaking a few Fabergé eggs."

"Very clever," she said drily.

"I'm actually in negotiations with the Kremlin to buy her crown, the Great Imperial Crown, the crown of all the Romanovs. But a lot of people don't want it leaving the Kremlin. Whereas I say, everything has a price. So we have a deal?"

She nodded.

"Good. Now, have you tried the caviar canapés? They're to die for."

79

She steered the Tesla over to the side of the road about a half mile outside Protasov's estate. A black Suburban pulled in right behind her. The front passenger's-side door opened, and Alex Venkovsky got in. He sat down and opened a Dell laptop.

"How'd it go?" he said.

"No problem." She unbuckled the skinny black belt and handed it to him. "They didn't detect a thing."

"Because we're good," he said with a grin.

"As long as this one worked right, we're all set."

Venkovsky took the belt and began to work the silver buckle, finally taking out a pin from his pocket and using it to pop out what looked like a SIM card. He seated it into a port on the side of the laptop with a click.

A minute later, he'd opened an audio program on his laptop and clicked a green play button.

The sound came through clear and loud. A woman saying, "Welcome. The board members are gathering in the sitting room for some coffee before the meeting."

Then, much louder, her own voice: "Thank you."

"Great," Venkovsky said.

"We got it?"

"Good quality too," he said. "I mean, you can't tell with these tinny laptop speakers, but the sound gradient is excellent."

He clicked some buttons on his laptop, forwarding and clicked play again.

"Please stand with arms at side." The voice of the young guard who had wanded her. The device seemed to have recorded just fine.

"Mr. Protasov will be with—"

All of a sudden the sound became a loud white-noise static roar, like an airplane taking off. She saw the oscillating green sound-wave icon on Venkovsky's laptop twitch and dance on the screen.

And all they could hear was that white-noise roar.

"Shit," Venkovsky said. "When they wanded you, they disabled the recording devices."

"What about the—the key fob?" She pulled the Tesla key fob from her purse. Venkovsky extracted a small black chip-like thing from the back of the Tesla logo and inserted it into his laptop.

He clicked a Play button on his laptop, and a male voice came out. "Mr. Protasov will be with—"

A staticky roar broke in.

"Shit," Venkovsky said again.

"Is it even worth trying the shoes?" she asked.

"Why not."

She took off her left shoe and handed it to him. He located the slot on the side of the wedge heel and pressed a little button, and the black chip popped out. He inserted it into the computer and played, fast-forwarding until they heard "Mr. Protasov will be with you shortly."

There was a long pause and then Protasov's voice. "Judge Brody, I'm afraid you've caught me at a very busy time."

Venkovsky smiled.

"Got it?" she asked.

"So far so good."

They listened for a few seconds longer.

"Good thing they didn't wand your shoes. This is excellent," Venkovsky said. "This is how we get him to play ball with us. This is our pressure point. Because I'd wager that he'd rather spend the next twenty years of his life in some kind of witness protection program in America than face the kind of . . . 'debriefing' process he'd be put through back in Moscow."

She nodded, took out her phone, and texted Duncan. All systems go.

80

She flew home that afternoon on Cape Air, which was a bit of a comedown after Giles McNamer's Gulfstream G650.

Duncan got home from New York much later, looking rumpled and bleary-eyed, and made them both espressos. He had drunk a lot of Scotch at lunch, he said. But he'd accomplished exactly what he'd set out to do, which was the second phase of Juliana's plan.

He had had lunch in New York with his old friend, Professor Arnold Coren, at the Metropolitan Club. What he and Juliana called his "disinformation" lunch.

He and Arnold had been in the Society of Fellows at Harvard, when Duncan was a junior fellow and Arnold a senior. Coren, an old Russia hand, later moved to the Columbia University faculty and had appeared on Russian TV. He wrote a lot for *The Nation*. He'd interviewed Putin, was said to be friendly with him. He defended the Russian invasion of Ukraine, said that Crimea belongs to Russia anyway. He harped on American anti-Russian attitudes, insisting that powerful, greedy, sinister forces wanted, needed Russia to be our enemy. A recent article on him was headlined, "Putin's Favorite Professor."

Arnold Coren made no bones about the fact that he had sources in the Kremlin, what he called his Kremlin drinking buddies.

"We talked a lot about Pale Moth," Duncan said, as they sat at the kitchen table that evening.

"Pale Moth?"

"That's Putin's nickname."

"Putin has a nickname?"

"Apparently. Among Arnie's Kremlin drinking buddies. After our third whiskey, I became indiscreet."

"Sounds about right." She smiled.

"Sure, I told him in the *strictest confidence* about how you'd been brought in to consult with the CIA's new cooperating asset, the oligarch Yuri Protasov. Told him about how Protasov wanted to cut the cord with his Kremlin masters. How he was now spilling all kinds of secrets to the CIA."

"But I'm sure *that's* not leaking to Moscow any time soon."

She remembered seeing at a distance the heated conversation at the board meeting between Protasov and Olga. How she seemed to be berating the oligarch. Juliana's unexpected arrival, which so clearly dismayed Olga, would cause questions about Protasov to be asked in Moscow. Or so Paul Ashmont of the CIA believed. Olga would report back about the meeting between Protasov and an American judge. Then there was the ten million dollars Protasov was about to transfer to an offshore account the Treasury Department had set up, which would look suspiciously like a bribe.

That, in combination with Arnold Coren's well-known ability to circulate rumors that would reach all the way to the Kremlin. Protasov would be summoned back to Moscow, questioned, maybe even arrested. He would no longer be a threat.

It was only a matter of time.

They had no idea how soon.

———

The next morning, as Duncan was watching *Meet the Press Daily* and she was putting away groceries, he suddenly called out, "Jules?"

He pointed, and she looked at the TV. She hadn't been paying attention to the news, but then she heard "philanthropist and investor Yuri Protasov." They were showing video of what looked like a downed helicopter. The chyron on the bottom of the screen read: BREAKING NEWS—BILLIONAIRE PHILANTHROPIST KILLED IN HELICOPTER CRASH.

"—are telling us that Protasov's helicopter experienced a mechanical malfunction of some kind and crashed upon takeoff on the island of Nantucket. We are hearing reports of wind conditions and structural fatigue."

"My God," she said, stunned, sinking into a chair. "My God."

She stared at the television. This she hadn't planned on. The most she'd dared hope for was that Protasov would be summoned back to Moscow and arrested. But not this.

Her phone rang. She wasn't expecting anyone. She saw a 202 area code, meaning the Washington, DC, area. She picked it up.

"Well, you're safe now."

It took her a moment to recognize Alex Venkovsky's voice. The FinCEN guy.

"But the Kremlin—"

"No," Venkovsky said. "The Kremlin has been suspicious of Protasov for a while. They thought maybe he'd gone native. Gone soft. That he'd been so lionized in America and the UK, so deified, that he probably imagined he could slip the Kremlin's strings."

"But why kill the man?"

"Apparently the Kremlin got intelligence that he'd been cooperating with the CIA. And to the Russians, that's betrayal of the Motherland. And turncoats get assassinated."

She thought about Pale Moth and went silent for a beat. Then she said, "Must have been persuasive intelligence."

"And the Russians know that the US Government is moving in on Protasov's empire. Which means that, even if he isn't working for the CIA yet, he could. Meanwhile Olga, Protasov's minder, sees this judge, who may be working with the feds, swan right into this highly secure enclave. That itself was highly suspicious."

"And what about my . . . *kompromat*? The sex tape?" She'd told him about it, of course; she had to. But she hadn't briefed him on Duncan's lunch with Arnold Coren. Her agenda wasn't the same as theirs.

"I wouldn't worry about that," Venkovsky said. "If the video got out, it would focus attention on how Sanchez died. The Kremlin *will* open cans of worms, but only strategically. This would not be strategic. They don't want the details of Protasov's misadventures to become public."

"Understood," she said.

"We've reviewed the interagency briefs. This campaign of his, this operation—they're saying that's all Protasov. That he wasn't acting with Kremlin approval. He went rogue. In Moscow, they're telling each other that the whole disaster was his doing. To finish his work would be to own it, see. So they're washing their hands of the whole thing."

"What does that mean?"

"What does that mean? It means you're safe."

81

Six weeks later

Juliana had put together a feast for Ashley to welcome her back from Namibia: steamer clams, corn, and lobster. The dining table was a mess of lobster shells and clamshells and cleanly shorn corncobs.

Ashley was looking thinner and a little drawn, but at the same time even more vibrantly pretty. She said she'd broken up with Jens, in Namibia, and she was okay with that. Jake seemed genuinely happy to have his sister back. Finally the band was back together. The family was reunited and safe.

They were at the ramshackle old Wellfleet house they rented every summer, just up the dunes off White Crest Beach. The house needed a lot of work, but it was cozy, it was right on the beach, it had an amazing location, and they all loved it. They'd been renting the house for ten years already.

They were sitting around the table finishing off the last of their lobsters. Juliana was feeling relaxed, finally, and not just because of the sauvignon blanc Duncan kept pouring. The Wheelz case had been nicely squared away. The government had seized all of Yuri Protasov's assets, including the complex network of companies he owned through offshore shell companies like Wheelz and including, yes, the ten million dollars he wired to the offshore account that FinCEN had set up.

The government hired a law firm to manage the company, which had immediately fired Devin Allerdyce and replaced him with a well-known female CEO, Cheryl Whitley, who'd run a big tech company.

Her first order of business was to settle the Rachel Meyers lawsuit. She issued a statement: *After a thorough investigation and some soul-searching, the board of the Wheelz Corporation has concluded that mistakes were made and that Rachel Meyers was not treated fairly or appropriately during her time at Wheelz. She deserves to be compensated, and we have made a generous offer to do that. We are looking forward to putting this matter behind us and continuing our efforts to improve the atmosphere in our workplace.*

So Rachel Meyers had gotten what she wanted: acknowledgment of what had happened to her. In addition, she received a five-million-dollar cash settlement.

Juliana found herself thinking, too, about Philip Hersh, about the memorial service she and Martie had organized, how amazing the size of the turnout. People came from all walks of life: taxi drivers, car mechanics, politicians, city bureaucrats, cops, high-priced lawyers, bookies. The guy had touched a lot of people, in his mordant way.

Juliana looked around at her family. Ashley, digging some lobster meat out of a claw, said, "I just saw on Twitter that Kent Yarnell got Me Too'd."

"Yep," Juliana said. *The Boston Globe* had an article that morning on its front page reporting that three women in the Attorney General's office had filed complaints against Yarnell for inappropriate sexual conduct. So he was stepping down. She wasn't surprised.

"Couldn't have happened to a nicer guy," Duncan said.

Jake rolled his eyes. "Oh, come on," he said. "It's all theater. Am I the only one who sees this—?"

Ashley always ignored Jake when he was in verbal diarrhea mode. She cut him off, talking over him: "You always said he was a creep, Mom."

Juliana tried not to smile. "I don't judge. Ash, are you going to help Jake with his college essays?" She worried about how Jake would deal with a process he had so effectively mocked. Probably not so well. Maybe Ashley would be a good influence on him. "What do you think, Jakie—an essay on building a Guatemalan barn?"

Ashley and Jake exchanged a meaningful glance. She got up and located a piece of paper in a pile of mail in front of the TV. Then she handed Juliana a white business envelope. Its return address was Hampshire College, Amherst, Mass.

"What is it?"

"Check out who listens to his blog," Ashley said.

Juliana took out a crisply folded white letter and looked at it. She said, "An old-fashioned letter and everything."

Hope you're considering Hampshire, it read, *where we really value the kind of initiative, creativity, and sparky irreverence you've brought to your podcast.* They were inviting him to visit the town of Amherst.

"They love your podcast!" she marveled. "How did they even *hear* it?"

"Right?"

"'Sparky irreverence'?"

Jake groaned, though he looked secretly pleased. "I can't even," he said.

Her phone rang on the table next to her. She picked it up.

"Is this Judge Brody?" a woman said.

"It is."

"I have the governor."

"Excuse me," she said to the table as she got up. "I have to take this."

Duncan threw her a *who is it?* look, and she got up to take the call in the little bedroom off the kitchen.

Duncan and Juliana walked along the beach very early the next morning, so early that it was still dark. She'd spent most of the night tossing and turning and getting up, and finally Duncan took her by the elbow and out of the house. They walked barefoot along the sand and down to the water's edge. The waves were lapping gently and the moonlight shimmered on the water, and she was momentarily overcome by how beautiful the world could sometimes be.

They walked a mile down the deserted beach. As they set off, Duncan said, "Why are you struggling with this?"

"Because—I mean, who am I to dispense justice, after all I've done?"

The governor had put her on the short list to be named acting Attorney General, with the understanding that whoever he chose would have the party's support in the next election. Juliana just had to tell him whether she was up for it.

"All you've *done*? I'll tell you what you've done. You refused to be a victim. You saved the lives of your family."

They walked in silence for almost a minute before she said, "Yes, but I walked right into their trap. It all started with a decision I made."

"What does that have to do with anything? You need to forgive yourself, Jules." He stopped and picked up an oyster shell. The first pale glimmerings of the morning had begun to appear, blood-orange at the horizon. "Don't be such a hanging judge with yourself. Look, you're a great mom. You take care of people. You make us better than we are."

"Tell that to Calvin."

"Dammit, Juliana. That wasn't your fault. Calvin shouldn't have been driving drunk. And that tractor-trailer shouldn't have been going seventy in a fifty-mile-per-hour zone. Yeah, that's a detail you never remember, because charges were never filed, not when the victim was DWI. You shouldn't *ever* have blamed yourself. Time to dismiss the goddamned case, Your Honor. And let the defendant go free. God knows she deserves it."

"But what I did in Chicago—"

"What you did in Chicago—it's not like in court, when you can strike something from the record. We can't forget what happened. But you move on, right? You live your life forward. You have to."

They walked on some more, and then Duncan said, "Head back?" They turned around and started back the way they had come.

"Anyway," he went on, "it's like Martie says, there's sand in every oyster's shell, but only some of them make pearls. And you, babe, make pearls."

"Oh, please. You've been talking to Martie?"

"Guilty as charged."

"I'm sure she was behind this offer."

"Maybe so, but you're the one they want."

"You really think?"

"Of course. This is your path. You wanted to resign from the bench, here's your chance. You should take it. Martie thinks this is just the first step toward—well, she just thinks you have an amazing future ahead of you."

She nodded.

"Listen, we have a decision to make."

"I know."

"Not what I mean. Another decision."

"Oh yeah?"

"Mrs. Barnet is finally willing to sell."

"She is?" Mrs. Barnet was the elderly widow who owned the house they rented every summer in Wellfleet, except for the summer Jake spent in the hospital. They'd given up asking about buying it from her; the answer was always no.

"And she only wants to sell to us. She likes us, loves our connection to the house, the way we take care of it."

"Can we afford it?"

"It'll be a stretch."

"It does need a lot of work, you know."

"I know. But it's got good bones. And the best thing about it is how it's all on one level."

"So?"

"So in, you know, forty years from now, when we can't deal with stairs any longer, we can live here. We can enjoy it here."

"Forty years, huh?"

"Hey, 'Grow old along with me,' right?" At their wedding, Duncan had read the Robert Browning poem, the one that begins, "Grow old along with me! The best is yet to be."

Her face felt warm.

The house came into view. The kids were asleep, she knew, and would be for hours. In the distance, a pair of seagulls jousted noisily over some scrap of something.

They walked along the edge of the water. She'd fallen silent. "Yes," she said.

"Yes to the house? Yes to the job? Yes to the growing-old part?"

She took his hand and rested her head on his shoulder. She could hear the gulls cawing. She said, simply, "Yes."

Acknowledgments

Five illustrious judges helped me flesh out Juliana's daily and internal life. I want to thank Judge Heidi Brieger, Judge Susan Garsh, Judge Nancy Gertner, Judge Karen Green, and Chief Justice Margaret Marshall for giving me a debt-free legal education and illuminating the customs of the black-robed guild. Their upright and upstanding ways put my own judges to shame. I'm deeply grateful for their help.

Michael Rossi of Conn Kavanaugh in Boston is a terrific lawyer whose contribution to this book was substantial. I couldn't have done it without his legal advice. Thanks as well to Elliot Peters of Keker Van Nest & Peters, for his savvy early guidance on the *Wheelz* defense, as well as Nina Kimball and Justine Brousseau, of Kimball Brousseau, for very helpful advice on the plaintiff's sex-discrimination case. I was assisted too by Joseph Berman, the general counsel of the Massachusetts Board of Bar Overseers, John Markey of Prince Lobel, Paul Dacier of Indigo Agriculture, and Jay Shapiro of White and Williams.

For medical help, I'm grateful to Dr. Mark Morocco of UCLA Medical Center and Dr. Thomas Workman of Winchester (MA) Hospital. My friend and unindicted co-conspirator Giles McNamee lent me his considerable expertise in investment banking and financial engineering. On Russian oligarchs and sanctions, I was assisted by Bill Browder, Anders Åslund of the Atlantic Council, Adam Szubin of Sullivan & Cromwell, and my old friend Mikhail Tsypkin of the Naval Postgraduate School.

For details on technical surveillance countermeasures, many thanks to Ian Sweeney of Mias Consultants International (and thank you, Thomas Slovenski) and, once again, Kevin Murray of Murray Associates. On computer hacking, Kevin Ripa of Computer Evidence Recovery, Inc., was quite helpful, as was Skip Brandon of Smith Brandon, on investigations. On Argentina, I thank Susana Lopez; and on Mallorca, Antonia Ramis Miguel. In Boston, my thanks to Detective Jeremiah Benton of the Boston Police Department, retired Boston Police superintendent Bruce Holloway, and my friend Jay Groob of American Investigative Services. Thanks to Peter Wayner for help on autonomous vehicles and to Jillian Stein for important advice on shoes. Thanks too to Clair Lamb for all sorts of research and editorial assistance.

At Dutton, *Judgment* benefited enormously from some terrific editing by Jessica Renheim and John Parsley. A big thanks to the rest of my wonderful team at Dutton: Christine Ball, Amanda Walker, Carrie Swetonic, Elina Vaysbeyn, and Marya Pasciuto. Thanks to my wife, Michele Souda, for her smart close reading; to my daughter, Emma J. S. Finder; to my awesome agent, Dan Conaway of Writers House; and above all to my brother, Henry Finder.

About the Author

Joseph Finder is the *New York Times* bestselling author of fourteen previous novels, including *The Switch, Guilty Minds, The Fixer, Suspicion, Vanished,* and *Buried Secrets.* Finder's international bestseller *Killer Instinct* won the International Thriller Writers' Thriller Award for Best Novel. *Guilty Minds* and *Company Man* won the Barry Award for Best Thriller, and *Buried Secrets* won the Strand Critics Award for Best Novel. Other bestselling titles include *Paranoia* and *High Crimes,* which both became major motion pictures. He lives in Boston.